PROTECTING PROMISE

"Are you sure you wouldn't be better off if I left? More of your men might get hurt."

"You're not going anywhere," he responded emphatically.

Pushing away from him, she looked up into his eyes. "What if they come back?"

"Then I'll deal with it," he told her.

She couldn't believe he wasn't upset over the trouble she had brought to him. She thanked God for sending a man like Jake McBride to find her. Words couldn't accurately express how she felt.

"Thank you for everything, Mr. McBride. What would have happened to me if not for you?" She leaned up to kiss his cheek, but at the same moment he moved his head and their lips touched. It was accidental, but she didn't move away, and neither did he . . .

Books by Scarlett Dunn

PROMISES KEPT

FINDING PROMISE

Published by Kensington Publishing Corporation

Finding Promise

SCARLETT DUNN

ZEBRA BOOKS
KENSINGTON PUBLISHING CORP.
http://www.kensingtonbooks.com

ZEBRA BOOKS are published by

Kensington Publishing Corp.
119 West 40th Street
New York, NY 10018

All Kensington titles, imprints and distributed lines are available at special quantity discounts for bulk purchases for sales promotion, premiums, fund-raising, educational or institutional use.

Special book excerpts or customized printings can also be created to fit specific needs. For details, write or phone the office of the Kensington Sales Manager. Attn.: Sales Department. Kensington Publishing Corp., 119 West 40th Street, New York, NY 10018. Phone: 1-800-221-2647.

Zebra and the Z logo Reg. U.S. Pat. & TM Off.

First Printing: January 2016
ISBN-13: 978-1-4201-3891-7
ISBN-10: 1-4201-3891-X

eISBN-13: 978-1-4201-3892-4
eISBN-10: 1-4201-3892-8

10 9 8 7 6 5 4 3 2 1

Printed in the United States of America

To Michael—
You are an inspiration.
I am so blessed for your unfailing love and support.
Keep your focus on the future.
Much love to you.

ACKNOWLEDGMENTS

I thank God for my moments of inspiration. When I listen, He has all of the answers to my many questions.

A big thank you to Tory Groshong for all your hard work. I like the way you think, and you are so thorough!

Prologue

Dear Aunt Nettie,

I hope this letter finds you and Uncle John well. Matthew and I were delightfully entertained by the stories of your grandchildren in your last letter. My cousins are certainly procreating at a rapid pace! I am eagerly awaiting our departure for Colorado, heartened to soon be with family again. In all truth, I can barely contain my excitement, but my brother may be somewhat reluctant as he has a sweetheart he is leaving behind. I do not suffer the same hesitation since I have yet to meet a suitor who garners more interest than my painting. Matthew is of the opinion that I would be less willing to leave the familiar behind if I were more conventional like Mother. I remind him that our proper mother married her direct opposite, so she obviously desired some excitement in her life. I daresay I, rather than Matthew, inherited Father's adventurous spirit.

Wouldn't it be grand if Father and Mother were still with us to share in this journey? It was Father's dream to go West, and he always regretted not traveling with you years ago before he became governor. Aside from being with family again, I am absolutely thrilled by the possibility of capturing an actual cowboy on canvas. I am confident the novels over-romanticize these heroes of the West, and they cannot possibly live up to my expectations, but that does not diminish my enthusiasm to see them in person.

We are leaving Mr. Smythe, our barrister, to care for the estate while we are away. He is a capable man whom Father trusted implicitly. I doubt I shall return to Sinclair Hall in the near future, but I will not be surprised if Matthew returns within the year. He is interested in politics, and he would certainly have a future should that be his course.

The families we are traveling with are wonderfully caring people, and thrilled to be joining their families. Uncle John was a dear to provide that piece of land on your ranch so they could start their little community. They are confident God will protect us on our journey, and I truly hope God is listening as they refuse to carry weapons. Mr. Vincent, the leader of the group, told us he will be armed. Because he has made this journey twice, everyone places great confidence in his abilities.

We should arrive in Colorado in mid-August. By the time you receive this post, we will be well on our way. Please pray for our safe journey, and God willing, we will see you before winter. Give my love to Uncle John and my cousins.

Your loving niece,
Promise

Chapter One

If you wrong us, shall we not revenge?
WILLIAM SHAKESPEARE

Dodge City

TELEGRAPH TO COLT MCBRIDE, PROMISE, WYOMING

WE DELIVERED THE JUDGE. MEETING UP WITH THE
CATTLE DRIVE IN THE PANHANDLE. EXPECT US WITH
TWENTY-FIVE HUNDRED LONGHORNS BY END OF
AUGUST. KISS YOUR WIFE FOR ME. JAKE

The telegraph operator peered over his thick wire-rimmed spectacles at the tall, muscular man at the counter. "Is that all?"

"Yep," Jake McBride replied, placing some coins on the counter.

Jake's best friend, Cole Becker, started laughing. "Your big brother is gonna kick your butt all over Wyoming for that last sentence."

"It'll give him more incentive to take good care of that

beautiful woman." Jake wanted to needle his big brother for no other reason than he thought he was the luckiest son-of-a-buck alive. He wasn't jealous of Colt; he was the finest man he knew, and he deserved a woman like Victoria. Plain and simple, he was envious.

Cole slapped Jake on the shoulder. "I don't think Colt needs incentive. I've never seen a man more in love."

That was the truth if Jake had ever heard it. Colt was crazy in love with his new bride. In Jake's estimation, Colt had found the perfect woman, not to mention the most beautiful woman he had ever seen. She was also the reason he needed to get out of Wyoming for a while. Even his brother could see Jake was half in love with Victoria from the moment he saw her. Being recently reunited with Colt, he couldn't allow his feelings to cause any ill will between them. It had taken him ten years to go home to Wyoming, but once he saw Colt, and the ranch where they grew up, he realized it was where he belonged.

Jake had resigned as a U.S. Marshal, as had his partner of ten years, Cole Becker. They'd just escorted the territorial judge to Dodge as a last favor for their boss, and now they were on their way to meet up with the cattle drive headed to Wyoming.

While Colt placed no conditions on his return to the ranch, Jake didn't think it was fair to come back after all this time as an equal partner with no investment of his own. Colt had single-handedly made the ranch more successful than it had been under their father's control, and Jake didn't take that lightly. He couldn't make up for the years Colt had invested in back-breaking ranch work, but he could use his savings to buy cattle to add to the ranch's herd. He also figured the months spent on the drive would give him the time he needed to get his head on straight where his sister-in-law was concerned. Logic told him his infatuation would fade with time, but as he'd learned through the years, logic and emotion didn't often ride double.

Once they exited the telegraph office, Jake looked up at the low-hanging gray clouds. "Storm's brewing, and from the looks of it, it's going to be a good one." The weather hadn't posed a problem until now, but the angry-looking sky foretold that good fortune was coming to an end.

Cole glanced at the sky with a grim face. "Yeah, just as we're headed into Indian Territory."

As they reached their horses, Jake felt the first drop of rain on his Stetson. "Let's ride."

It rained for two solid weeks after Jake and Cole left Dodge, and today was more of the same. Jake was riding point in a torrential downpour well over a mile ahead of the cattle, trying to locate a defendable place to camp for the night. Hearing thunder ahead of him was a sure sign the storm wasn't easing. They were going to be in for a long night with twenty-five hundred head of restive cattle. He'd instructed Cole and the rest of the men to keep the cattle as close together as possible, hoping to forestall problems before nightfall.

An ear-splitting crack of lightning caused him and his horse both to jump. Jake stroked Preacher's neck. "That scared you as much as it did me, huh, boy?" More loud bursts of thunder ahead of him darkened his mood even more. "This storm is getting worse by the minute," he muttered. *Hell's bells! I'm a dang fool for not stopping before now.*

Another round of piercing pops rent the air, but within seconds he realized it wasn't thunder. *Gunfire.* Hearing gunshots out in the middle of nowhere was never a good sign. Nudging Preacher forward with the rain pelting them in the face, he was tempted to set a pace that matched his foreboding sense of urgency, but he wouldn't pose a danger to his horse. They hadn't ridden much farther when the rain started coming down so hard he couldn't see a foot in front of him. Pulling Preacher to a halt, he dismounted and pulled a bandanna from his back pocket to dry Preacher's face as best he could. "I don't think you can see any better than me." It wasn't going to do a bit of good with the rain coming down like it was, but he knew it would soothe his horse all the same. Preacher had also been his partner for ten years, and he knew the horse hated to have water on his face more than anything. Preacher nudged his hand as a thank-you.

When the rain changed to a steady drizzle, he remounted. Pulling his Winchester from the boot, he told himself it might be nothing, but experience warned not to ignore that little voice in his head that told him something was amiss. And right now that little voice was beginning to sound like the seventh angel's trumpet.

He'd covered about a quarter of a mile when he noticed something on the horizon that looked oddly out of place on the usually barren landscape. "Whoa, boy," he murmured, pulling Preacher to a halt again. He squinted, trying to make sense out of what he was seeing. Wiping away the water dripping from his eyelashes, he blinked, trying to focus. What was it? Crazy as it sounded, what he saw reminded him of large white flags whipping around in the storm. Searching the terrain, some movement caught his eye, and he saw riders hightailing it to the trees some distance away. He clicked Preacher forward.

As he drew closer, Preacher laid his ears back and started sidestepping. Jake's senses went on high alert. His horse was as good at detecting danger as any U.S. Marshal he'd ever seen. He stroked Preacher's neck as he assessed the situation. The riders were well out of sight, so he didn't know what had Preacher so worked up. "Settle down, boy. I don't see anyone moving about." He focused again on what he thought were flags, and realization dawned. Covered wagons. They were turned over on their sides and the canvases had been ripped apart, leaving the tattered pieces to flap in the wind like sails on a ship.

"Come on, boy. Let's see what this is about." Preacher snorted at him as though he disagreed with the command, but he moved ahead. Jake counted six wagons overturned as he reined in at the nearest one. Dismounting, he held on to Preacher's reins just in case he needed to make a fast getaway. *What happened here? Indians? Is that who was riding away?* They hadn't encountered any Indians so far, but that only meant one thing; they were due. One thing was certain, if Indians were around, he figured he'd see them soon enough. Not many places to hide out here in the open, but they sure had a way of appearing out of thin air.

The thunder and lightning had lessened considerably, so he figured he could hear trouble if it came calling. Scanning the area, he saw all manner of items from the wagons scattered about. Judging by the destruction, and some costly articles left behind, it occurred to him that whoever did this was looking for something in particular. Spotting a man on the ground near the first wagon, he released Preacher's reins and hurried to him. As he approached, he saw the blood covering the front of his rain-soaked shirt. He didn't need to touch him; his eyes had the vacant stare of a dead man. There was a rifle beside the man and Jake picked it up to see if it had been fired. It hadn't. The man's pistol was still in his holster. He walked to the overturned wagon and peeked inside. There was a woman lying half out of the front of the wagon, so he hustled around to check her. Shot dead. A few feet from her was another man lying dead on the ground. *What in heaven's name happened here?* He ran to the other wagons, praying to God he would find someone alive. He found six more bodies. Everyone shot—no arrows, but Indians had guns, he reminded himself. Questions circled his mind. *Why weren't they traveling with a larger group? Had they been ill and left behind? And why in heaven's name had they stopped out here in the open? Not the best place to stop for the night if they needed to defend themselves from an attack.*

Reaching the last wagon, he saw a woman lying face-down near a large overturned trunk, and a man lying several feet from her. Again, he scanned the horizon to make sure no one was waiting to shoot him in the back. Approaching the woman first, he kneeled down and gently turned her over. Pushing aside her long, wet hair from her face, he saw that her eyes were closed and blood oozed from her temple. He placed his palm on her chest to see if she had a heartbeat. *Alive!* Her heartbeat was faint, but it was there. *Thank God.* Wiping at the blood on her temple, he tried to see how badly she was injured. It looked like a bullet had grazed her, but fortunately it wasn't lodged in her head. He searched her limp form for additional signs of injury, but finding none, he stood and pulled off his slicker to cover her. It didn't make a lick of sense since her clothing was drenched, yet it made him feel better. He walked to the man lying nearby to see if he was as lucky as the woman. He wasn't.

He whistled for Preacher, who came trotting up beside him. He pulled a clean shirt out of his saddlebag and quickly tore it into long strips. Gently, he propped the woman against his thigh and wound the cloth around her head. Two thoughts struck him at once: how fragile she was, and how good she smelled. Odd, under the circumstances, that he'd noticed her fragrance, but he figured it was because since he'd left Texas the only things he'd smelled were cattle and wet earth. While he worked on the bandage, it occurred to him that she was much younger than the other women he'd found. The man lying near her was also younger than the other men. *He must have been her husband. Why would anyone shoot all of these people? What were they searching for? If Indians had attacked, they would have taken some of the items littering the ground, like the tools or sacks of sugar and barrels of flour. They would have taken the young woman too.* He'd seen a lot of evil in his ten years as a U.S. Marshal, but nothing as senseless as this. He took hold of her hand, wishing he could will her to wake. Her hand was so delicate and soft against his calloused skin that he glanced down to look at her palm. This was not the hand of a woman who worked a farm, though he did feel some rough spots on her fingers, which he figured were from holding a horse's reins.

He glanced at the man again. No gun. Realizing that only one man had been armed offered up another set of questions. It was possible that the killers had taken their weapons. Did they also take the horses, or had the horses simply run off when the shooting started? He felt sure the killers didn't take the time to unhitch the teams, so these folks had stopped for some reason.

He could see hoofprints in every direction, but right now he didn't have time to study them other than to make a mental note that they were shod. He knew the rain would wash away the tracks of the men he saw riding away, but his first responsibility was to care for the woman. He'd take her back to meet up with the drive so his cook could tend her. He'd hired Shorty not only for his cooking skills but because he also possessed some doctoring knowledge. Shorty had been on six cattle drives and had tended various injuries, so Jake hoped he would know what to do for her. Once the woman was in Shorty's care, he'd bring some men back to bury the dead. Then he'd have time to try to make sense out of this massacre.

Preacher caught his attention when he snorted and side-stepped closer. "What is it, boy?" Jake looked around and immediately spotted Indians on a knoll less than two hundred yards away. *Damn, if they can't sneak up on a man!* He counted ten braves, and though he wasn't sure, he thought they were Comanche. "Okay, boy, we're leaving." Just as he was about to lift the woman in his arms, he saw a leather-bound book underneath her skirt, and next to it was a Colt .45. He picked up the pistol and smelled the barrel before tucking it in his belt. He grabbed the book and stuffed it inside his shirt to keep it dry. Once he was settled in the saddle with the woman securely in his arms, he pulled his slicker over her head to keep her bandage dry. He turned his gaze on the Indians and breathed a sigh of relief when he saw they were not riding toward him. It was odd how they were just watching, almost like they were afraid to ride closer. He looked around to make sure no one else was lurking about. Before he rode away, he glanced once more at the destruction around him. He was certain of one thing: The Indians hadn't done this. Not one scalp was missing.

Chapter Two

With the woman lying limp against his chest, Jake slowly made his way back to the cattle drive. With the many days of storms they'd had, the plains had turned into a muddy quagmire. Preacher was forced to slog through the muck, which was more difficult with extra weight on his back. As soon as Jake saw Harm, his most experienced trail hand, he rode in his direction. After explaining the situation, Jake told him they were stopping for the night.

"Indians?" Harm asked.

Jake shook his head. "They didn't kill those folks, but there were ten braves watching me the whole time. Tell the men to keep their eyes open."

Jake had two of his men quickly transfer supplies from one of the wagons so he could make a place for the woman. When the wagon was empty, Shorty stacked quilts several inches deep to make a comfortable pallet for her. Once Jake had the woman settled on the quilts, he sent Shorty to find one of his dry shirts. He dropped the canvas opening to have some privacy from the prying eyes of the men riding into camp. He knew as soon as the men heard about the situation, they'd have questions, but right now he had to get her into dry clothes. That meant undressing her, and he didn't need an audience for that. Pulling his slicker from her, all he could think about was how helpless she looked lying there. He wished they had a woman with them who could do what needed doing. But wishing wasn't having, as his father used to say, so he needed to get to it.

Removing his Stetson, he placed it on the floorboard beside the quilts. He pulled the pistol that he'd found under the woman from his belt, and with a quick check of the cylinder, saw it was empty. The gun was in good condition; someone had taken the time to clean and oil it frequently. He placed the gun on the floor by his hat and kneeled beside the woman. He stared at her pale face, noticing that her long, dark lashes resting on her cheeks were a stark contrast to her deathly white skin. Some of her hair was beginning to dry, and he could see the color was a light golden blond. Even wet and covered in mud she was uncommonly beautiful. Her complexion was creamy smooth, her lips full and the palest pink. In his estimation she was nearly as beautiful as his brother's new wife, and that was saying something.

He sat back on his heels, trying to muster the courage to do what needed doing. He wished she'd wake up so she could undress herself. Surprised at how uneasy he was, he told himself that he'd undressed his fair share of women over the years, so it wasn't that he didn't know where to start, but he still hesitated. None of those women had been unconscious, and they'd wanted to be undressed. If she woke up while he was taking her clothes off, she'd probably die of fright. He was as nervous as he was the first time he'd seen a naked woman. *Hell's bells! I was a U.S. Marshal for ten years and chased gunslingers all over this territory. I sure as hell can undress an unconscious woman. Just get on with it!* As he leaned over and started to attack the tiny row of buttons at the neck of her dress, someone tapped on the wagon, causing him to jump up so fast he smacked his head on the wood frame.

"Dang it all!" he muttered, rubbing his head.

"Yo, boss, here's the clothes," Shorty said.

Jake leaned over to open the flap, and there stood Shorty, holding one of his shirts along with a pair of trousers. "Thanks, Shorty."

Shorty pointed to the trousers. "I got these from the smallest man on the crew, but they ain't going to fit without a rope to hold them up." Then he added, "I'm boiling some water, so just whistle when you're ready to get her wound cleaned."

"Will do." Crouching down beside her again, Jake reached for the first button. "I promise, honey, I'm not going to hurt you." He was working as quickly as he could for fear she would wake up, and he kept talking just in case she did. He shivered at that thought. She was such a small woman that he lifted her with ease. He tried to keep his eyes from wandering as he got down to her chemise and bloomers, but the flimsy material was so wet it was transparent, and he dropped back on his heels again and took a deep breath. *Lord, help me*, he pleaded silently, and as much as he tried not to look, he couldn't drag his eyes away. His next thought was he should just leave those things on her, but he decided that wouldn't do. He didn't want her catching a cold, yet if she came to and he had stripped her as naked as the day she was born . . . well, he didn't even want to think about that. He grabbed his slicker to throw over her before he removed her underthings. He had no problem removing her bloomers with his hands under the slicker, but he didn't have the same success with the laces on her chemise. He fumbled around, but he couldn't find the secret of those ties without seeing what he was doing. His frustration mounting, and a few curse words later, he jerked the slicker aside, pulled his knife from its sheath, and slit the laces. Before he even allowed himself a peek—well, almost—his fingers latched on to the slicker and he threw it over her like she was a rattler ready to strike. He glanced at her face and was relieved to see she was still out cold. Only then did he let out a loud breath he wasn't aware he'd been holding. He was drenched to the bone, but he was still sweating like a pig being chased by hungry men preparing for a pig roast. And he still had to get her into dry clothing. He made short work of getting her into his dry shirt, and he quickly buttoned it up to her throat. Grabbing the trousers, he held them up and determined Shorty was right; they were way too large, so he decided to leave them off. His shirt covered her to her knees anyway. Hopefully, he'd find some clothing for her when he returned to the wagon train.

Exhausted, he wiped the sweat from his brow with his wet shirtsleeve. When he went to hang her dress to dry, he was surprised at how heavy it was. He wondered how such a slight woman could stand up in a dress so heavy since the darn thing weighed as much as she did. Dismissing the thought, when he started to hang it from a nail he saw a label inside the neckline with a name stitched on it, which he couldn't read, and beneath the name it said *Paris, France*. They sure made dresses heavy in Paris, France.

He leaned out of the wagon and gave a shrill whistle. Shorty came running with the water and some of his special salve. After cleaning and bandaging her wound, they tried to clean the blood from her thick mass of hair.

"I ain't never seen so much hair in my life," Shorty said.

"I don't know how she holds her head up when it's wet. It's heavier than my holster," Jake said.

"Is she hurt somewhere we can't see?"

"I didn't see anything else, but I have never seen anyone stay unconscious for so long. Have you?"

"Not this long." Shorty absently stroked her silky hair.

"She sure is a pretty little thing. Dang those polecats for hurting a sweet little thing like her."

"I found a man near her who could have been her husband. The two of them were younger than the rest of the folks." He didn't know which would be worse, having her wake up to find everyone she knew was dead, or not waking up at all. "Maybe we'll find something that will tell me where they were headed."

They looked at each other, both at a loss as to what to do next. Jake got to his feet. "I guess I'd best get back to bury those people."

Shorty scrambled up behind him. He was so lacking in stature that he didn't need to crouch down like Jake inside the wagon. "You ain't plannin' on leavin' me alone with her, are you?"

Jake glanced down at the motionless woman. "I don't think she'll give you any trouble."

Shorty let out a loud snort. "You know that ain't what I'm sayin'! What if she . . . well . . . what if she . . . ," he said, his voice quavering. "You know . . . goes to meet her Maker?"

Jake placed a hand on his shoulder. "You're the best hope she has, and I need to get back there before animals get to those folks. They deserve a decent burial, and I'm hoping the trail of those killers won't be totally washed away. You know that in her condition I can't take her all the way back to Dodge right now."

"I've tended plenty of sick cowhands, but hellfire, I ain't never tended a woman," Shorty complained, raking a hand through his thinning white hair.

Jake didn't have the time to reassure his cook, but he tried. "You've stopped the bleeding, and that's about all we can do for her right now. I think it's a good sign she doesn't have a fever."

Shorty nodded, wanting to hold on to that thread of hope. "Yeah, that's good."

Grabbing his slicker, Jake opened the canvas flap and jumped from the wagon, with Shorty right behind him. "Just check on her every few minutes in case she wakes up. After what she went through, she'll likely be scared to death. And stay alert, there are killers afoot, and I doubt they are too far away."

"Will do, boss."

"If you need anything in a hurry, have someone ride to get me. It's doubtful I could hear gunshots."

"You need to eat before you go back there. You ain't had nothin' since breakfast," Shorty reminded him like a worried parent.

"No time. I'll eat when I get back. Keep that coffee hot." With that said, Jake donned his slicker before making his way to the makeshift corral where the two wranglers kept horses saddled at all times. He figured Preacher had earned some rest, and it was going to be a long night getting those people buried, so he had Billy, one of the wranglers, pick out a fresh horse for him.

"I already brushed, fed, and watered Preacher," the young man told him. He knew how his boss valued that horse, and it was the first time Jake hadn't cared for Preacher himself. He always did that first thing when he rode in, even before he saw to his own needs. And every cowboy on the drive knew they'd best follow suit.

"Thanks, Billy. He deserves a good rest. Wipe his face off a few times tonight," Jake said.

"Sure will, boss."

Jake patted Preacher before he took the reins of another animal. The rain was coming down in sheets by the time he gathered Cole and three other men to ride with him. Their progress was slow since they took an extra wagon for any belongings they could salvage for the woman. The other men could have ridden ahead of the wagon, but Jake didn't want to leave one man to his own defenses with killers and Indians in the area.

When they reached the wagon train, despite the pelting rain every man took off his hat in a sign of respect for the deceased.

"What kind of men did something like this?" Ty asked when they dismounted and saw the carnage.

"Just plain mean," Cole answered.

"They must be plumb crazy," Ty added.

"*Diosito*," Rodriguez said softly, reverently.

They turned to the vaquero and watched him make the sign of the cross before he dismounted.

"Keep your eyes peeled for those Indians," Jake told them. The four men he'd chosen to accompany him were capable gun hands. He almost wished the killers would come back. They'd find it'd be a lot more difficult to kill them than it had been to kill those folks on the wagon train. When Jake found an area he determined suitable for burying the dead, the men pulled out their shovels and started digging. After the graves were dug, and the people buried, the men removed their hats again and stood in silence.

Rodriguez was the first to speak. "*Vaya con Dios*."

Jake nodded his agreement, and repeated the sentiment in English. "Godspeed." He felt there was little else to say, so he put his hat on and gave instructions to the men to start collecting all items worth taking back for the woman.

The men set about gathering anything that hadn't been destroyed. Jake walked to the wagon where he'd found the woman, and righted the large trunk he'd seen earlier. He noted the ornate silver initials on the closures. Opening the lid, he looked inside and found an expensive silver-handled mirror and matching brush with the same initials, a box filled with ladies' hats, and a Bible. Moving those items aside, he found a large bundle wrapped in a heavy cloth. He lifted the bundle out and pulled the cloth away. He couldn't believe his eyes. He was looking at a beautiful oil painting of the last man he'd buried. It was the same man who had been lying near the woman he'd found alive. There were more paintings, along with brushes, canvases, and oils. Underneath the paintings he found a leather pouch, and when he glanced inside he saw several charcoal drawings. Though he was curious, he didn't want them to get wet, so he wrapped them back inside the pouch. After returning the items to the trunk, he started picking up the clothing that was strewn about. He gathered so many dresses he lost count, along with a fur cape and a furry thing that women wore to keep their hands warm. He'd never seen so many pieces of delicate silky undergarments, other than the times he'd been at brothels. It sure was a lot of clothing for one woman. While he didn't consider himself an expert on ladies' fashion, he could tell the clothing was of high quality, like the dress he'd removed from her. He'd have Shorty wash some of her dresses so she would have something to wear.

Looking around to see if he'd missed anything, he noticed a pair of ladies' boots a few feet away. When he reached for the boots, something glittering in the mud caught his eye, so he pulled the object out of the wet earth and wiped the dirt off on his chaps. It was a beautiful comb that a woman would wear in her hair. The initials on the comb were encrusted with what he thought were diamonds, and they matched the initials on the trunk. He started to place the comb inside one of the boots, but he felt a piece of cloth tucked inside. Pulling the small bundle out, he found a delicate crystal bottle that was fully intact and filled with perfume. Along with the perfume, he found bars of soap that smelled so good he almost wanted to eat them. After he placed everything in the trunk, he spotted a large bathing tub several yards from the wagon.

Cole and Rodriguez approached as Jake was dragging the tub to the wagon.

"This clothing is very costly," Rodriguez said in his perfect English, eyeing the items Jake had placed in the trunk. "This trunk must have been made for someone of wealth," he added, running his hand over the hand-carved silver embellishments.

"That's what I thought," Jake confirmed. If Rodriguez said the items were expensive, they had to be. Jake had never seen as much silver on a saddle as the vaquero had on his. Rodriguez was the son of a wealthy rancher, having arrived from Spain years ago, and his family owned the largest spread in the New Mexico Territory. Rodriguez was well educated, and was expected to take his father's place running his vast empire, but Rodriguez wanted to see the country before he settled down. He was also the best vaquero Jake had ever seen, more at home on a horse than he was on the ground. Even though the other men didn't understand why Rodriguez would leave such an affluent life, they respected his abilities and work ethic.

"I've never seen a tub that large," Cole added. "What I wouldn't give for a hot bath right now."

"Let's get it loaded," Jake said.

"What do you think the killers were looking for?" Cole lifted one side of the tub.

Jake hoisted the other side of the tub and they loaded it in the wagon. "I don't know, but it was something they decided was worth killing these folks in cold blood."

"I only noticed one man wearing a holster," Cole said.

"The same man wearing that holster had a rifle, but the rest of them weren't armed. I figure the killers could have taken their weapons, but if they did, they also took their holsters."

Cole pointed to the trunk. "I found a smaller trunk similar to that large one, with some men's clothing inside.

We found furniture, some books, and Bibles. Do you think they were religious folks? That might be the reason there were no guns."

Jake questioned the sanity of anyone who would travel into this territory without guns. "Could be." He pointed to where he'd seen the riders leaving the area. "I saw men riding off in that direction. I think there were about eight riders."

"One thing's for certain; there won't be any tracks left now," Cole told him.

"I don't think I scared them off riding in alone, so they probably spotted the Indians."

"Maybe they found what they were looking for and took off. I just can't figure out what these folks would have that was worth all this killing," Cole mused.

"You know as well as I do that some men will kill for no reason." Jake looked around at all of the debris. "Still, it does look like they were looking for something in particular." That was the only explanation he had for the destruction he saw. A loud crack of thunder shook the ground beneath them. "We can't follow them tonight, not with this storm and the cattle to keep calm. We've been lucky so far, and I just hope that our luck holds out tonight. If all goes well, I'll ride that way tomorrow and see what I can find."

Cole picked up one side of the trunk. "What's in here, gold bars?" Cole joked.

Jake picked up the other side. "I've never seen so many dresses in my life," Jake replied. Every article of clothing was wet, which might account for why the trunk was so heavy. Once they positioned the larger trunk, he glanced down at the initials on the smaller trunk. An S was the center initial on both trunks, giving credence to his belief they belonged to a married couple.

Ty walked up with another handful of dresses. "These

arc all of the dresses. You want me to collect more things, boss?"

Jake wished he could take some more items in case they belonged to the woman, but space was limited. "No, we're full. Let's get back to the cattle." What he left unsaid was he wanted to hurry back to camp to see if the woman had awakened, because right now he had more questions than answers.

Chapter Three

"Boss, that little gal hasn't moved an inch," Shorty informed Jake as he shoved a cup of steaming coffee at him. "I guess the Good Lord figures she needs sleep right now."

Jake wrapped his hands around the coffee. "Thanks, Shorty. I don't know how you keep the fire going in this mess, but I sure do appreciate this hot coffee."

"It ain't easy, but I've got a small fire going under the tent. Some men are sleeping under there, so get yourself inside that wagon so you can eat your food out of this blasted rain. It wouldn't hurt you to get some dry clothes on. You've been soaked to the bone since daybreak." He took the horse's reins from Jake and pointed toward the cook wagon. "I'll see to your horse."

Jake threw his saddlebag over his shoulder and accepted Shorty's offer. "Thanks, Ma," he teased. He was grateful to have the hot cup of coffee more than food. It was near midnight, and every muscle in his body told him he'd been in the saddle too long. He plopped some beans and corn bread on a plate and he crawled inside the wagon. *Bless Shorty*, he thought when he saw the second pallet the cook had prepared near the woman. He appreciated the gesture, though he wouldn't have objected to sleeping on the dry wood floor.

Setting his plate and coffee aside, he leaned over to look at the woman. Shorty was right; it didn't look like she'd moved at all. After retrieving some dry clothes from his saddlebag, he tossed it in the corner with his slicker. Removing his holster, he placed it alongside his rifle, within easy reach. As he started unbuttoning his shirt, he felt the book he'd stashed inside earlier. Thankfully, it didn't get wet, so he placed it on the pallet by the woman. Once he changed into dry clothes, he sat down and ate his dinner.

Shorty stuck his head through the opening. "You want me to sit with her?"

"No, I'll stretch out in here for a while. It's nice to be dry for a change."

Shorty held out the coffeepot. "Well, put that cup over here and I'll warm it up."

Jake held his cup while Shorty filled it to the brim. "Tell Cole to wake me when he comes in and I'll take the second watch."

"Will do, boss. She ain't feverish, is she?"

Leaning over, Jake placed the back of his hand on her forehead. "No, but I don't understand why she hasn't come around. That wound shouldn't have caused this."

"I can't figure it out. I checked her wound earlier and it looks fine, no infection." Shorty ran a hand over his white whiskers. "I guess she could have hit her head when she was grazed, and that did the damage."

"She was on the ground, so that's possible."

"Call me if you need anything, boss."

Jake leaned back, drank his coffee, and stared at the woman. He figured she had a right not to wake up; she'd probably been terrified if she'd seen everyone murdered. He wondered if she saw her husband being killed, or whether she had been shot first. He was of the opinion it would have been more merciful if she was shot first so she wouldn't have to witness the atrocities committed by those killers.

Closing his eyes, he listened to the steady rain beating on the canvas. It was a nice, comforting sound if you weren't out in it. He pondered the woman's situation. Maybe he should try to take her to Dodge City tomorrow to see a doctor instead of trailing the killers. Yet, he questioned if he should leave her alone in Dodge with no one to look after her. He worried someone might take advantage of a beautiful woman like her, especially in a place like Dodge City. He figured they could stay where they were for a day or two to see if she came around. Normally, he wasn't an indecisive man, but he didn't like any of the alternatives where she was concerned.

Where were these people from, and where were they going? He opened his eyes and looked down at the leather-bound book beside her. Cole said they'd found several Bibles, but this wasn't a Bible. Opening the book, he realized it was a journal, and the beautiful script told him it most likely belonged to a woman. While he wasn't a man to snoop, he reasoned it might give him some insight to her identity. On the inside cover was one word. *Promise*. Puzzled, he glanced in her direction, wondering if that was her name. He started reading.

> *Sleep is eluding me tonight. After much planning and waiting, we find ourselves on the eve of our grand adventure. As excited as I am, I can't deny there are many things I will miss about home: the gentle breeze coming off the ocean, walking along the shore at dusk, and the sweet fragrance of the magnolias and oleanders. Of course I will miss our good friends, but most of all I will miss my daily visit to Mother and Father's grave site. It has been*

*a comfort to know they are there. I know they
would understand my desire to be with family
for a while, and I will not be gone forever.*

*Everyone says I will miss the social life here,
but Aunt Nettie assures me there are many parties
and social events on the ranch. I dare not divulge
the truth to my friends, but parties have never held
much interest for me. I much prefer painting than
attending socials. Part of my excitement about
going West is the opportunity it affords me to paint
new subjects. I simply cannot wait to paint the
cowboys on Aunt Nettie's ranch!*

*I packed my large trunk days ago, and Matthew
said it is so heavy that the animals may not be able
to pull the wagon. Mr. Vincent told us to find a safe
place for valuables and to keep such information
private. Quite naturally, the ladies discussed their
ideas on the perfect hiding places. Mr. Vincent said
he had no difficulties when he made this trip before,
and I pray we will have the same good fortune on
this journey. God be with us.*

Assuming the book belonged to this woman, Jake was
obviously reading her private thoughts. At least he had
more information than before. She hailed from the coast,
and she had painted the pictures he found in the trunk.
Glancing down at the woman who could have penned
these words, he found it surprising someone so beautiful
would prefer painting to parties. His gaze returned to the
open book and he stared at the one word . . . *Promise. Is
that her name? Wouldn't that be a coincidence!* He heard
his brother's voice in his mind. Colt always said there were
no coincidences in life. He called them God-incidences.
Jake couldn't help himself from turning the page to the
next entry.

*Before we left this morning, Charles Worthington
arrived to plead with us not to leave. I must say,
Matthew surprised me by agreeing with Charles.
After months of preparations, I can hardly
comprehend that he is questioning our decision.
I am regretful that I hurt Charles, but I think this
is the right decision. I told Matthew he could stay
if he wanted, and I would write him upon my
arrival, but he was adamantly opposed to that
idea. Here we are on our way, and Matthew seems
miserable. It is difficult for me to be excited while
he is so unhappy.*

Closing the book, Jake fixed his eyes on her again. She
looked so lovely lying there, reminding him of an angel
with that mass of blond hair surrounding her like a golden
halo. Did she actually think her husband would permit her
to attempt such a journey without him? He'd heard about
independent women, but surely no man would contemplate
allowing his wife to go on such a dangerous journey alone.
It was difficult for him to imagine that a man would even
allow a woman who looked like her out of his sight. He
surely wouldn't. He wondered about Charles Worthington.
Who was he and why had he tried to talk them out of their
journey? Why didn't her husband want to go West? He
shook his head at himself; the U.S. Marshal in him was
coming out. It was a hard habit to break. It frustrated him
that he had no answers, and without them he couldn't
help her.

Before he called it a night, he reached into his saddlebag for the cloth he needed to clean his firearms. It was a
nightly ritual he enjoyed, since it generally calmed him
down enough to do his best thinking. He also cleaned the
pistol he'd found beneath the woman. Once that task was

finished, he turned the woman on her side because she'd been in the same position for such a long time. After he felt her pulse to make sure it was still strong, he turned the lantern down and stretched out on the pallet. He fell asleep staring at her, questions spinning in his brain.

It was still dark outside when a loud crack of thunder woke him. He groaned, dreading another day of thunderstorms. His muscles still ached, but on the positive side, he did smell fresh coffee. He leaned over to check the woman again. Her breathing was steady, but she hadn't moved, so he turned her again. It was time for him to relieve Cole, so he pulled on his boots, grabbed his gear, and jumped from the wagon. He'd taken only a few steps when Shorty met him with a cup of coffee. "Here you go, boss."

"Thanks. What time is it?"

"It's going on five o'clock," Shorty answered.

He didn't feel like he'd slept that long. "Why didn't anyone wake me for my watch?"

"Cole said to let you sleep because you'd only had two hours of sleep in forty-eight. Cole and Rodriguez split your watch."

Jake didn't know how Shorty kept track of everything, but he was thankful for the extra rest. He leaned against the wagon, drank his coffee, and looked at the lightning in the distance. "I sure wish this rain would let up for a few hours."

"I guess that little gal didn't come around?"

"Nope. I moved her a couple of times since she'd been on her back so long. I was thinking about taking her to Dodge and having a doctor look at her. What do you think?"

"I'm not sure she should be moved right now."

"Maybe we should stay here for a day and give her a chance to heal. Jostling around in the wagon might make her worse," Jake mused. "I could take her to Dodge tomorrow and have a doc look after her."

"Boss, you can't leave that poor gal in that town with no family to look after her."

Shorty was voicing all the things Jake had considered. "I don't see how we can take her with us. A drive is no place for a woman."

"That's true enough. Some men think women are downright unlucky on a drive, but I still don't think you should leave her alone in Dodge. That just ain't right."

Jake couldn't disagree, so he changed the subject. "There's some clothes in that large trunk that look like they'll fit her. They'll need washing, but the least we can do is provide something decent for her to wear when she comes around."

Before Shorty could respond, another crack of thunder shook the earth and the downpour began. Jake handed Shorty his cup and took off to saddle his horse. He rode out to relieve Cole, and to tell the men they were going to stay put for the day. Jake instructed them to change watch every couple of hours, which lifted their spirits. Staying on a horse all day in the rain was something no cowboy enjoyed. They'd been pushing hard for weeks, and they deserved the rest.

Before Cole rode back to camp, Jake discussed the situation with the woman. When Cole raised the same objections he'd heard from Shorty, he figured since they were all on the same page, he'd wait another day to see how she was before he made a decision to take her to Dodge.

Chapter Four

Jake stayed with the cattle all day so Cole could get some rest, but he left instructions with Shorty to have someone alert him if the woman awoke. No one on a cattle drive liked to stay in one place too long. It was best for the men and cattle to keep moving. Men got bored, especially in such inclement weather, and the cattle had to keep eating. As it was, they had been lucky to travel ten miles a day in the rain. Jake didn't need more delays, but right now he didn't have a choice.

Once again, when he rode back to camp at dusk, he was drenched to the bone. After unsaddling Preacher, he dried him off, and found a nice dry spot for him under a canopy of trees. When he reached the cook's wagon, Shorty was waiting for him. "Any change?"

Shorty knew he was asking about the girl. "No change, but I moved her like you did. I think that is a good idea." Shorty gave him a cup of coffee. "Boss, I got somethin' to show you." Jake followed Shorty to the wagon where the trunks were located. When Shorty opened the flap, Jake saw dresses hanging everywhere. There were even more than he'd first thought.

Shorty held up a piece of clothing that resembled a pair

of very small trousers with wide legs. "What in the devil is this?'

"That's what you wanted to show me?" Jake knew he sounded short-tempered, but after his day in the saddle in that downpour, he was exhausted. "Hell's bells, I don't know."

"Nope, that's not what I wanted to show you. I was just wondering what it was since I ain't never seen anything like it." He put the unidentified item aside and picked up one of the dresses. "I was washin' some of these dresses and those flimsy underthings women wear. I ain't never seen anything so fine as her . . . you know . . . bloomers and such . . . but there sure ain't much to 'em . . . sort of a waste of good money, if you ask me."

Jake sighed loudly, thinking he didn't need Shorty to tell him how flimsy her undergarments were. He'd seen them on her firsthand, and that was a sight he was unlikely to forget anytime soon.

Hearing Jake's sigh, Shorty stopped rambling. "Anyways, I kept thinkin' those dresses sure were heavy. Now I know there's lots of cloth to the things, with these wide skirts and all, but it still didn't feel right." Shorty held a dress in the air and showed him how full the skirt was.

"They could be heavy because they're wet," Jake said impatiently, wishing Shorty would get to the point so he could get into some dry clothes.

Shorty snorted. "No, it ain't that!" He shoved the hem of the dress at Jake. "Feel this."

Drawing his brows together in confusion, Jake did as Shorty instructed. He took the hem of the dress between his thumb and forefinger. He pulled the entire hem through his fingers, and his eyes widened at Shorty. "What the . . . ?"

"That's what I thought! So I opened the stitches in one of those dresses." He reached inside the wagon and pulled out a can and pushed it into Jake's hands. "This is what I found."

Jake was stunned speechless. The tin can was filled to the brim with gold coins.

"Each coin was stitched in place so they didn't move around." Shorty pointed to all of the dresses hanging in the wagon. "Every one of these dresses has the same thing at the bottom. Boss, this is a whole lot of money," he whispered.

Jake recalled the dress he'd stripped from her earlier. This explained why the darn thing was so heavy. With that added weight, he was surprised she could walk. He picked up a coin off the top. It was a twenty-dollar double eagle. "All of these came out of one dress?"

Shorty nodded his head. "There were seventy-two of those double eagles in that one dress, boss."

"How many dresses?"

"Twenty in that trunk. And those dresses were made in Paris, France. But there are more dresses in the wagon that weren't in the trunk. Those dresses are larger and not as fine a cloth, so I don't think they belonged to that gal. Coins are sewn in them too, but not as many, and not gold eagles."

Jake figured those dresses belonged to the other women they'd buried. If twenty of those dresses held the same amount of gold eagles, that was, as Shorty stated, a whole lot of money. He figured this explained what the killers were looking for. Money was a powerful incentive for those men to slaughter all those people. Nothing else made sense because they'd left all the other items behind. They probably hightailed it out of there when they saw Indians, or they knew the cattle drive was not far behind.

"That's not all." Shorty reached into his pocket and pulled out a leather pouch. He opened the pouch and poured the contents into his palm.

Jake gaped at Shorty's work-worn palm. Several pieces of fine jewelry, sparkling like stars on a clear night, covered Shorty's hand. Many pieces held large stones, and Jake figured they were diamonds, rubies, and emeralds.

"The pouch was sewn into one of her dress pockets. What do you make of this?"

Jake shook his head. "I don't know what to think. But keep this to yourself; we don't need anyone else knowing about this, or the money. If we get to a town, I don't want the men talking out of turn if they get liquored up." Jake trusted Shorty to stay quiet, but when men started drinking they often got loose tongues without meaning any harm. "Leave the money in the other dresses." He figured he'd never seen such a crafty hiding place for valuables, which was confirmed by the fact that the killers hadn't figured it out, if that was what they were after.

"Yessir, this could be too much of a temptation for some men. You said them low-down dirty skunks were looking for something in particular. Well, I reckon somehow they knew those folks was carrying a lot of money."

"Yeah, judging by the destruction, I had a feeling they knew what they wanted." Jake pointed to the can filled with coins. "It makes sense, now that you found this."

"Since those polecats didn't get what they wanted, you know what that means."

Jake knew exactly what that meant. "They'll be back if they know she's not dead. If they came back after we left last night, they probably counted those graves and know one person is missing."

"Boss, knowing what we do now, you just can't take that gal to Dodge and leave her alone."

"No, I can't do that now that I know what they are after. She would never be safe." Jake had fifteen men on this cattle drive, and he needed to make sure they knew what was going on so they couldn't be bushwhacked. He'd tell

Cole to inform the men out on watch, and he'd tell the men at camp before he got some rest.

Once the men were told to be on alert for the killers, Jake decided to go check on the woman. While he was out on the range he'd started thinking of her as Promise. When he climbed inside the wagon the first thing he noticed was how good it smelled. Shorty had put the bars of soap and her perfume in the wagon. Kneeling down beside her, he examined her face closely. She looked less pale than she did last night, but that in itself wasn't encouraging because she was deathly still. Shorty had changed her bandage again, but Jake peeked at the wound anyway. It looked like Shorty had also combed her long, blond hair. "Is your name Promise?" He felt the pulse at her neck and thought it stronger than before. He pulled his pallet closer, and after he took off his holster he stretched out beside her and started talking. "I'm from a town called Promise. It's in Wyoming, and that's where we are taking the cattle. My brothers and I own a ranch there." He turned to face her to see if she reacted in any way while he was talking. "I sure would like to know where you were going so we could help you get there safe and sound. I found your book, and I hope you don't mind me reading what you wrote. I'm not a man to read a person's private thoughts, but I was hoping it might tell me where you were headed. You must be from back East, or maybe the South near the coast somewhere. It's mighty brave of you to come all this way." Mentioning her book gave him an idea. Perhaps if she heard her own words she might come around. He picked up her book and read the third entry aloud.

"'After one week, I would think Matthew's mood would have improved, but he is more irritable than ever. Most of the day I walk, which is really difficult since my dresses are so heavy with the added weight, but it is better than riding in the wagon with him. Tonight I plan to tell him—'"

Jake stopped reading since he didn't think she sounded
particularly happy that day, and if there was trouble between her and her husband it might be best not to read this
aloud. He was curious so he finished reading the entry
silently.

> *Tonight I plan to tell him that once we reach*
> *Aunt Nettie's he should turn around and go back*
> *home. If he is pining for Emily Bouchard, he can*
> *just go back to her! I'm tired of his sulking!*

Jake stared at her. She was going to tell her husband to
leave her alone once they reached wherever they were
going! Maybe her husband should have turned her over his
knee and showed her who was boss. He didn't know why
her husband didn't want to leave their home, but surely he
had a good reason. But what if there was another woman
in the picture . . . this Emily Bouchard? Impossible! How
could any man want another woman when he had a woman
as beautiful as this one? Of course, she could be a shrew,
he told himself. He'd seen beautiful women with quick tempers, and they quickly became less attractive. He moved to
the next entry, but first, he thought prudently, he'd read it
to himself.

> *Since Matthew and I talked, his mood has*
> *greatly improved, and the trip is much more*
> *enjoyable. The ladies and I spend a great deal of*
> *time talking as we walk, and I couldn't ask for more*
> *agreeable traveling companions. While Mr. Vincent*
> *is a competent leader, I am still concerned about*
> *the lack of firearms. I understand their religious*
> *beliefs, but I do think it unwise that we are out*
> *here in this wild country with no means of defense.*
> *Matthew agreed to their stipulations that we would*

*bring no weapons, saying Mr. Vincent's own wife
was on this journey, so it had to be safe. I did not
agree, nor did Mr. Vincent ask my opinion. Why do
men assume a woman cannot shoot? I haven't told
Matthew that my pistol is hidden inside my fur
muff in my trunk. I feel better knowing it is there,
and I'm grateful to Father for teaching me how
to shoot.*

He could hardly believe what he was reading. He looked
over at her again. The gun was hers. Those men had no
guns, not even rifles! That made him angry. If they didn't
care about their own hides, they should have considered
how they would protect the women. Reading that, he almost
understood why she wanted her husband to go back home
if he wasn't the kind of man who would protect her. If she
were his wife he would do everything in his power to keep
her safe from harm. He didn't know where that thought
came from, but it was the truth. As far as he was concerned,
she had more guts, not to mention sense, than all those
men combined. He read this entry aloud as he kept his eye
on her for any indication that she could hear him. When he
said the word *father*, he was sure her eyelids fluttered.

He leaned over her. "Honey, are you awake? If you can
hear me, just know you're safe and no one will hurt you
here," he told her softly. This time he was positive her
eyelids moved, almost like she was too tired to open her
eyes. "If you can, you need to wake up, you need something to eat. If you don't mind my saying so, you don't
have any weight to lose." His eyes roamed over the quilt
covering her. She was delicately built, but he remembered
what she looked like in her wet undergarments. To his way
of thinking she was perfectly formed, with a lot of curves
packed into a small frame, but she could use a few pounds.
He continued talking to her until he fell asleep.

When Jake awoke, his first glance was at Promise. He scrambled to his knees when he saw that she had changed positions. "Honey, are you awake?" She didn't respond, so he checked the pulse at her neck. It was definitely stronger than before, but she was still asleep or unconscious. He wasn't sure what to call her condition. Last night, before he drifted off, he decided he'd ride back to Dodge City, find a doctor, and bring him to her. He also planned to find out if anyone from the small wagon train had stopped in Dodge. There was always a chance they'd stopped for supplies like he had. It wouldn't take him that long to get to town, and that seemed like the best alternative, not to mention he'd rest easier once a doctor checked her out.

When Jake walked through the door of the general store in Dodge, the owner recognized him from his first visit. A man his size was sure to draw attention, plus he had the most uncommon eyes, black as night, and an overall intimidating appearance. "Did you forget something?"

"No, I had some questions for you, if you don't mind."

"Sure thing." The owner stopped stacking cans on the shelf and moved to the counter.

"Do you remember if any men came in here just before my last visit who might have been with a wagon train?"

"Yessir, I do. Three men came in for supplies. They said they were from the Southeast coast and were going to Colorado."

"Did they say where in Colorado?"

"No, they didn't say, but they told me they'd saved up for several years to make that trip. Said they had grown children in Colorado that they hadn't seen in a long time. Grandchildren too. Nice folks, but there was something odd about them."

"How's that?"

"They weren't armed. Well, I didn't notice it myself, but some men who were in here buying some cartridges noticed, and told them they might run into Indians. I expected the travelers to say they left rifles with the other folks on the wagon train. But you know what they said?" He didn't wait for a response, saying, "They said they weren't even carrying guns, it was against their beliefs." He shook his head as if he still couldn't believe what he'd heard. "Can you believe that? They were traveling all that way with no guns."

"Did you know the men who talked to them?"

"No, they were strangers, but they'd been in town a few days. Spent most of their time in the saloon, drinking and playing poker. Looked like troublemakers, if you know what I mean."

Jake knew, all right. He'd seen plenty of men like that. "Did they say anything else that you can remember?"

"Not that I remember. But those drifters talked to them while they were loading their supplies."

"Have you seen those drifters around town lately?" Jake asked.

"Yeah, they're still hanging around. You can probably find them at the saloon."

Jake walked to the saloon, but finding it empty, he headed to the sheriff's office. According to the sheriff, there had been about a dozen strangers hanging around town, but he hadn't seen them for a couple of days. He described them in the same way: no-account drifters. The sheriff didn't know anything about the folks on the wagon train. Once Jake finished talking with the sheriff, he went in search of the doctor. Thirty minutes later he was riding out of Dodge with Doc Parsons.

Chapter Five

"I've seen two cases like this before," Doc Parsons told Jake after his examination of Promise.

"Do you think she's going to come around?" Jake asked.

"Hard to say, but she's young and her heart is strong, all good signs. Still, no one can last long without food and water."

"We've been tryin' to get some soup and water down her, but I don't think much is going down," Shorty said.

"You said she's moved?"

Jake nodded. "Sometime during the night."

"One time today when I checked on her I was certain she was going to open her eyes," Shorty added. "Her eyelashes looked like butterfly wings flutterin' in the wind."

"I saw her do that last night," Jake said.

"That's good. I think this bodes well for her. This is just the third night, so there is time." The doctor turned to Jake, his expression serious. "I'm compelled to tell you, sometimes when people have been unconscious for a while, their memory can be a bit sketchy when they regain consciousness. I treated one man who took a nasty hit on his head and it took him a few days to come around. It was almost a year before he regained his full memory. In some cases I've read about, the people never remember what happened to them."

"But she might remember everything right away?" Jake hoped when she came around she would be able to tell him who was responsible for killing those folks.

"Yes, it's possible. I'm just preparing you for what could happen." The doctor patted Jake on the shoulder. "Let's hope for the best."

"Do you think it would hurt her to travel?" Jake asked.

"I can't see why it would. She doesn't have any broken bones. You might as well be on your way. From what you told me, she would be safer with you than in Dodge."

Jake reached into his pocket and handed the doctor some money. "Doc, keep what I told you to yourself. It'll be morning before long, so you should get dry by the fire and rest for a few hours. I will have two of my men ride back with you." Jake couldn't really spare the men, but the doc had been nice enough to ride all this way in the drizzling rain. It was also too dangerous for one man to ride alone in this territory.

"Thanks, I'll take you up on that. If you happen to stop in Denver for supplies, my brother, Clarke, owns a general store there. You'll want to see him instead of his competition; he'll deal honestly with you. It seems like a rancher by the name of Schott is trying to take over everything in Denver. He's tried to buy my brother out, but Clarke's stubborn. He had the first store in town, and he says he'll go tocs-up before he lets Schott drive him out. The last letter I received, he wrote that Schott has bought out, or forced out, most of the other smaller ranchers."

"That's good to know since we'll be stopping in Denver. Thanks again, Doc." Jake shook the doc's hand. "Shorty will get you something to eat if you're hungry."

"Sounds good."

Jake climbed back inside the wagon with Promise. He

took off his boots and holster before he stretched out on
the pallet without removing his wet clothes. He glanced
at the woman, thinking he no longer had any options. He
wasn't about to leave her in Dodge, since those murdering
skunks were still around. They'd assumed she was dead
like the rest of those folks on the wagon train. If he took
her to Dodge and those killers saw her, they'd make sure
she was dead this time, after they got what they wanted.
All he had were more questions and few answers. He
picked up her journal next to his pallet and started reading
where he last left off.

> *This trip is proving very difficult for the other
> ladies. I know they are considerably older because
> they speak of their children who are my age. I try
> to do the cooking when we stop at night so they
> can get more rest. Mr. Vincent does his best to
> accommodate them as much as possible by
> traveling at a slower pace than he prefers. The
> ladies do not want to relinquish what few items
> they are taking with them in order to make room
> to ride in the wagons. I understand the desire to
> hold on to things dear, but the men are less
> understanding. More than once, Matthew has
> threatened to throw my trunk in the next river, but
> he understands I packed so many dresses out of
> necessity. If he does rifle through my trunk he will
> ruin his own birthday surprise, and it would serve
> him right. I now spend most of my time walking
> in this dreadful rain. I keep myself occupied by
> daydreaming about the cowboys of the West.*

Jake smiled. He wondered if her husband was aware of
her daydreams. If she would wake up, she could have her
wish to meet a cowboy. She'd certainly given him plenty to

think about when he was on horseback for hours at a time.
He wanted to know why she was so anxious to go West,
and he was curious to hear what her voice sounded like. He
imagined she might want to go back home when she awoke
and remembered everything that had happened. Yeah, he
had done his own daydreaming. He finished the final few
lines on the page.

*I do wish I could ride my beloved Hero, but
none of the ladies ride—another thing they cite as
scandalous and against their religious beliefs. So
I walk with Hero's reins in my hand so he doesn't
have to ride behind the wagon all day and have
mud in his face. I fear he thinks I am cross with
him because I am not riding. Still, I am so happy
he is with me, and I simply could not leave him
behind. Sometimes I think Hero is the only one
who understands me.*

*The women are quite rigid in their beliefs.
Today it was so humid that I unbuttoned the top
two buttons of my dress to cool down, and the
ladies went into a dither. It is tiring at times to hear
the many things they view as indecent. It's not like
we are at a social function with the upper crust of
society. Who is here to see us out in the middle of
nowhere? I have not seen a single soul outside our
group. How I wish I could climb on Hero's back
and feel the wind on my face!*

This was some woman! She could ride and shoot, and
she had the face of an angel. Not only had she lost her husband and all those people, but her horse that she obviously
cared a great deal about. It was likely the men that attacked
them took her horse. It saddened him to think about how

much this little gal would have to face when she regained consciousness.

Looking down at the book, he decided to look at some of her later accounts to see if she'd recorded anything prior to the attack, which might give some insight to the location of her family's ranch in Colorado.

> *This land has a rugged beauty that I wish I could capture, but there is no time to stop for painting. My drawings will have to suffice for the time being. When we are settled at the ranch, I shall use them for reference. Mr. Vincent plans to go to Dodge City tomorrow for supplies, but the ladies are not allowed to accompany them since he fears it is a wild town and we would not be safe. I wanted to inform him I have read about the cowboys and they are said to be gentlemen of the first order, but I remained silent. It has been necessary for me to bite my tongue more than once on this trip.*
>
> *I long to see such a place as Dodge, and when I said as much to Mrs. Vincent, I thought she would have the vapors. If Matthew accompanies Mr. Vincent, I shall have him recount every detail upon his return.*

Jake turned to the last page, still smiling over her account of cowboys.

> *Matthew told me all about Dodge, and it sounds fascinating. He even surprised me with some peppermints for Hero, his very favorite treat. I think he is trying to make up for his surly behavior on this trip—Matthew—not Hero!*

Matthew voiced his concern over conversations with men at the mercantile in Dodge. He described them as very rough-looking characters who struck up a conversation with Mr. Vincent and Mr. Colbert. Matthew thought Mr. Colbert divulged too much information about the people on the wagon train, telling them we were transporting all of our worldly goods. Matthew said Mr. Colbert revealed our identity to these men, and hinted we were carrying a large sum of money. I could tell Matthew was extremely upset over this. We have both been taught to be cautious of strangers, and I think that wise, but Mr. Colbert is more trusting. I'm sure he meant no harm discussing our background.

Jake considered what he'd read. Logic told him those strangers were the killers. He could understand her husband not wanting anyone to know the amount of money they were carrying, but why would it concern them for people to know who they were?

He finished reading the remainder of the entry.

Today, as we made camp, some men were watching us from the ridge. Matthew said they were the men they saw in the mercantile, but they did not ride down to greet us. Matthew is quite troubled, and I am fearful these men are bent on doing evil. Mr. Vincent said he will ride to meet them after dinner to find out their intent.

Jake put the journal aside. She must have written this not long before the attack. He figured Mr. Vincent never made that ride.

* * *

Three hours later, Jake told the men that they would be moving on. He planned to go at a slower pace than normal, and stop midday to see how Promise was handling the travel. He picked two men to escort the doctor back to Dodge, instructing them to get back as soon as possible.

Jake and Shorty arranged an extra-thick pallet at the front of the wagon for Promise, so Shorty could keep an eye on her as he drove. Before he saddled Preacher, Jake walked to the supply wagon to search Promise's trunk for the leather folder with her drawings. He pulled it open and hurriedly looked through all of the drawings: landscapes, the women and men on the wagon train, and a drawing that might prove useful. A drawing of her horse. All the drawings were very well done, but this one was magnificent. At the bottom of the page she had written *Hero*. The horse was a beauty, big and dark, and his distinctive markings would set him apart: four white stockings and a star on his forehead. No doubt about it, he would recognize this horse if he ever saw him. He would bet the killers took Hero to sell. Such a fine-looking animal would bring a good price.

"If I never see another thunderstorm, it will be too soon," Cole said, when he rode up beside Jake.

It was a short day in the saddle, but Jake was as tired of the incessant rain as his men. "Amen. As soon as Harm gets back we'll stop for the day."

"You think they're going to come back, don't you?"

Jake knew Cole was talking about the killers. "Yep. Their kind won't give up."

"Yeah. I just can't figure out what they want."

Knowing Cole would keep the information to himself, Jake shared with him what Shorty had found in the dresses.

"No wonder they didn't find what they were looking for. Who would have thought to look in those dresses? That was a smart thing to do."

"It sure was. I've read some of her journal from the trip, and she mentioned that a few men rode into Dodge for supplies. While they were there, some drifters talked to them in the general store. The next day they saw men on horseback watching them, and her husband said they were the men from Dodge. That was the last thing she wrote."

"You're thinking if they went back to that wagon train after we left, they suspect someone is still alive and may have the valuables."

"That's the way I see it. If the killers were watching them before they attacked, then they knew how many people should be in those graves. There's one grave short."

"She's going to have a tough time when she comes around," Cole said.

"I know." Just thinking about what he had to tell her when she woke made Jake sad and angry. Somehow he would find out where her family was located in Colorado and make sure she got to them. He wanted to go back to Dodge and track down those killers, but he knew that right now his priority was to protect the woman. But he made a vow to himself that he would find them if it was the last thing he did on this earth.

Chapter Six

Shorty had good news for Jake when he rode into camp a few hours later. "I just checked on her and she's moving."

"That's the best news I've had all day. I'll watch her for a while," Jake told him. He climbed in the back of the wagon, removed his hat, and sat on the side of her pallet. "Honey, Shorty tells me you moved today. I hope you wake up soon so you can have something to eat. Shorty is a pretty good cook, but don't tell him I said that."

The words had barely left Jake's mouth when Shorty threw back the canvas opening and popped his head inside with a plate of food in his hand. "I'm more than good! I'm the best dang cook you'll ever find on a wagon train."

"You'll get no argument from me there." Jake accepted the plate Shorty shoved at him. "Thanks." Shorty left and Jake turned back to the woman. "Honey, you need to wake up and have something to eat." He shoved a spoonful of food in his mouth. "This is real good." He looked over at her and this time he was certain he saw her eyelids flutter. Placing the plate of food aside, he leaned over her. "Sweetheart, are you awake?" He put his finger to her neck to feel her pulse. "Come on, sweetheart, open your eyes." There was no question her pulse picked up when he spoke to her.

Promise heard someone calling her sweetheart. The voice sounded familiar, but she didn't know why. It was a deep, commanding voice, full of authority. But who was it? It wasn't . . . who? Why couldn't she think of anyone? She tried to open her eyes, but she felt so tired she couldn't seem to manage. Had she been ill? Where was she?

"Come on, honey, I see your eyes moving," Jake coaxed.

Slowly, Promise blinked her eyes open. When she was able to focus, she found herself staring into the black eyes of a stranger calling her sweetheart.

Jake smiled at her. "Well, hello." He'd wondered what color her eyes were, and when he finally got to see them he wasn't disappointed. Just like the rest of her, they were more beautiful than he imagined. They were a warm golden whiskey color and so large they dominated her small face.

Promise stared at his face. She didn't think she knew him, because she couldn't ever imagine forgetting such a formidable man. His darkly tanned face was very masculine with a strong, chiseled jaw, a straight nose, and intense black eyes. His penetrating stare might have been more threatening if not for the unbelievably long, thick lashes. As it was, she couldn't pull her eyes from his.

"Would you like a drink?"

She nodded, and he gently lifted her head with one hand. He didn't have anything else in the wagon to drink, so he put his cup of coffee to her lips. "Go slow."

When she finished, she whispered softly, "Thank you."

"Are you hungry?"

"No." Her voice was raspy, like she hadn't talked in months. She continued to stare at him. "Who are . . . ?" She was so weak she couldn't finish her question.

"I'm Jake McBride. This is my cattle drive, and we're headed to my ranch in Wyoming."

"Where are we?"

"Right now we are in Indian Territory." He watched her as she processed that piece of information.

Her brows knitted together as she tried to remember . . . anything. Why would she be in Indian Territory? "Have I been ill?"

"You don't remember what happened to you?" The doctor's warnings smacked him in the face. He tried to remember how long he said she might not remember things.

"No . . . I don't remember." Her lower lip started to tremble.

Jake hadn't wanted to consider the possibility that she would have no memory, and was at a loss how to respond. Considering her weakened condition, he didn't think it would be wise to mention the wagon train and all the folks that were killed. He'd give her time to regain her strength before he told her about the events of that day. With some luck, her memory might return soon and spare him that decision. "You were injured and I happened to find you. You've been unconscious for a few days. I had a doctor from Dodge examine you, and he said you might have some memory loss for a few days." He made an effort to sound more positive than he actually felt.

"Dodge." She repeated the word, but it didn't sound familiar. "Do you know who I am?"

Her question threw him. The doctor indicated some people might not remember how they were injured, but he hadn't mentioned she might not even remember her own name. He kept his surprise to himself, but decided it best to tell the truth. "No, honey, I don't." He reached over, picked up her journal and handed it to her. "You had this with you. I admit I looked inside. I wasn't prying, I was just trying to find out who you are and where you were going. The inside cover says *Promise*. Does that mean anything to you?"

Tears filled her eyes as she looked at the book. She

shook her head. Nothing was making sense to her. Why couldn't she remember her own name? Who was she? Was Promise her name? Something about that seemed familiar, but she couldn't remember why.

Jake saw tears welling in her eyes. "Now there's no need to get worried. The doctor said this is a common thing when you've suffered a head injury." He might have made it sound a bit more common than the doctor indicated, but he didn't want her getting upset. "I was a U.S. Marshal, and we will figure this out. I know you are from back East and headed to Colorado. I just don't know where in Colorado, and it's a big place, so I planned to take you to Wyoming with us. I figured that would give you time enough to recover. Then we'll know where you were headed, and I'll take you there." He thought of something that might help her. "Hold on a minute, I'll be right back."

He climbed out of the wagon and raced to the supply wagon. He threw open her trunk and pulled out the drawings. He almost pulled out the oil painting of her husband but changed his mind. He took the drawings back to the wagon. "I found these in a trunk that I think belongs to you." He opened the folder for her and handed her the first drawing, the one of her horse. He watched her closely as she looked at the drawing.

She stared at it for a long time, and even ran her fingertips softly over the drawing, almost reverently. Her gaze drifted to him. "Did I do this?"

"I think you did. In that journal you wrote about drawing and painting. From what I read, I think that is your horse."

"He's beautiful. Is he here?"

He should have realized she would ask that question. "No, he wasn't with you." He quickly showed her some of the landscape drawings, but nothing jogged her memory. He avoided showing her the drawings of the people on the wagon train. He didn't know what else to do, so before she could ask more questions, he decided to get some food in her. "I'm going to get you something to eat."

She watched as he moved to the opening, taking in every detail of his muscled frame before he deftly jumped from the wagon. It was hard to judge from her position, but he looked quite tall. On his right hip he wore a pistol; on the left, a large, lethal-looking knife was sheathed. He appeared to be a nice man, and since he said he had been a U.S. Marshal, it seemed he would be a good person to trust. She'd obviously been safe with him, and he'd cared for her since . . . since whatever had happened to her. What was her alternative to staying with him? She didn't know where she would go. Nothing made sense. How could she not know who she was? She tried to keep calm, telling herself it served no purpose to get upset.

She glanced around the interior of the wagon, and her eyes landed on the dress and undergarments hanging in a corner. Lifting the quilt covering her, she saw she was dressed in a man's shirt and nothing else. The clothing must belong to her, but who had undressed her? Maybe they had women with them. Or perhaps the doctor undressed her to examine her. She preferred that option to ease her mind. She looked back down at the drawing of the horse. How she wished she had him with her right now.

As Jake filled a plate of food for her, he made a mental note to tell the men not to mention what had happened to the people on the wagon train, once she was able to leave the wagon. He didn't see that any good could come of her finding out about that too soon. Juggling the plate, coffee, and water, he hoisted himself back inside the wagon, where he helped Promise into a sitting position. "Do you mind if I call you Promise?"

"I don't mind." She reached up to push her hair out of

her face and felt the bandage on her temple. "Did I hit my head?"

Sitting beside her, Jake held the two cups in the air. "Coffee or water?" He was buying time, trying to figure out the best way to answer her.

"Water, please."

Go with the truth, he told himself. "I think a bullet grazed you."

"A bullet?" She looked at him with eyes wide. "Why would someone shoot me?" She dropped her face to her hands. "Nothing makes sense," she whispered. When she lifted her face, tears were streaming over her cheeks.

Jake didn't know what to do, but her tears were breaking his heart. He moved closer and put the plate of food aside so he could pull her into his arms. He couldn't imagine how frightened she must feel. "Honey, we'll figure this thing out. Don't you worry, it will all work out. You'll be safe with us, and I'll find out where your family is located."

She buried her face in his shirt, terrified, but at the same time thankful this man was so kind to her. "Thank you."

He took her chin in his fingers and lifted her face to his. Lord, she was a beauty with those whiskey-colored eyes. "Now you need to eat a little."

She nodded. "I'll try."

The only thing he had to offer her to wipe her tears away was the bandanna in his pocket, but it was clean. He fished it out and handed it to her. "Wipe your tears so you won't ruin Shorty's food. Shorty is the cook, and he's also been tending you."

Giving him a shaky smile, she did as he requested, and Jake handed her the plate. He pointed to the dress hanging in the corner. "Shorty washed some of your clothes, so they are clean. Your trunk is in the supply wagon, and it's filled with dresses." He took a sip of coffee and watched her pick at her food. "When you feel up to it, maybe reading what you wrote might help you remember some things." Considering what she had written in the journal about her husband, he questioned whether he should have told her to read it right now. But he would have to tell her sometime, and he knew if he were in her position, he'd want to know as much as possible to help sort things out.

She ate a few bites and drank some water before she set the plate aside. "I thank you for all you've done for me."

Jake thought her voice was already sounding stronger, and some color was in her cheeks. He realized she probably needed to see to her other needs. "If you need to . . . uh . . . well . . ." *Why couldn't she be a man? This would be a lot easier.* He took a deep breath and started again. "If you need to see to your needs, I'll take you outside."

"Thank you. Is there a place where I could wash?"

He should have realized that would be one of the first things she would want. "I'll have Shorty warm some water and we'll bring the tub in here."

"I think that would make me feel much better." She wanted some time alone to think things through.

Jake left to find Shorty, to tell him to warm the water while he lugged the tub to the wagon. He told Shorty about her lack of memory, and asked him to pass the word among the men that no one should mention the wagon train or the killings.

A short, wiry little man with a frizz of white hair opened the flap to the wagon and handed some pails of hot water to Jake.

After Jake introduced him, Shorty said, "If you need anything, ma'am, you just holler for me."

"Thank you, sir. And thank you for your care."

"Everyone calls me Shorty." He pointed to the corner of the wagon where he'd put the bars of soap with some of her delicate underthings. "I found the soap in your trunk."

Jake and Shorty left the wagon to get the rest of the water. Once they were some distance from the wagon, Shorty turned to Jake. "She's just about the prettiest thing I ever laid eyes on."

"That she is."

"Did you hear how she talked? She must be from the South," Shorty added.

"Uh-huh." Jake thought she did have a Southern lilt to her voice.

"You don't think you should tell her about her husband?"

"Not right now. Besides, I'm not positive it was her husband. I figure when she's had time to get her bearings, and get some of her strength back, I'll tell her then if she hasn't remembered." Silently, he hoped he was making the right decision.

"That makes sense. It's gonna be a lot for her to face, however she finds out."

Chapter Seven

Jake was sitting outside the wagon when Promise stuck her head outside. "Mr. McBride?"

"Right here." He'd been sitting against the wagon wheel, listening to her splashing in the tub for what seemed like an eternity. He hadn't even noticed that the rain had slowed to a drizzle. He did notice the fragrance of her soap drifting from the wagon, reminding him how long it had been since he'd seen a woman bathe. The way he saw it, watching a woman attend to her nightly toilette was one of the most exciting ways a man could spend an evening. He'd been lost in his thoughts and didn't realize she was finished until he heard the flap being tossed open. Jumping up, Jake saw that she was dressed, so he lifted her to the ground.

She was wearing one of the dresses Shorty had washed for her. He wondered if she would be able to walk with the weight of that dress, she was so weak. "Feel better?" he asked, thinking how good she smelled. He reminded himself of his brother's dog, Bandit, the way he was sniffing her.

"Yes, thank you so much. I hate to ask, but would you have a comb? I washed my hair and I'm in need of one."

She pulled her long hair over her shoulder and tried to run her fingers through the wet tangles.

"I found one that I think is yours. It's over in the supply wagon, if you feel up to walking with me." He glanced at her wound and saw how nicely it had healed.

"I'd like to walk, if it's not too far." She lifted her skirt to keep the hem from dragging in the muddy earth.

"Not far at all." He took hold of her elbow and steered her away from the men milling about. He wanted to give her time to get comfortable with her surroundings before she was overloaded with questions and stares from cowboys. They weren't accustomed to seeing a woman on a cattle drive, and as pretty as she was, she was sure to receive a lot of attention.

"How did you happen to find me, Mr. McBride?"

Uh-oh, Jake thought. "I just happened to be riding in that direction," he responded. He pointed to the cattle grazing in the distance. "Do you think you've ever seen a cattle drive?"

She couldn't believe the number of cattle. "Oh my! How many cattle do you have, Mr. McBride?"

"Call me Jake. We're driving twenty-five hundred head to Wyoming."

"Oh mercy, that many?"

He smiled to himself. She did have a very pronounced Southern accent that he found charming. "Yes, ma'am. If we're very lucky we will get there with most of them."

"How long will it take to get to your ranch?"

"We should be there sometime in August."

"August," she repeated. Jake caught the look on her face. It seemed like mentioning the month stirred something in her memory. She frowned. "What month is this?"

That question made him realize the magnitude of her condition. He couldn't imagine how she felt, being unable to remember anything and at the mercy of complete strangers. "June."

Reaching the supply wagon, he opened the flap and pointed to the trunk at the back. "I think that is your trunk."

She looked at the trunk, but like everything else, it didn't seem familiar.

Shorty came around the corner of the wagon and Jake asked, "Shorty, did you find a comb?"

"Yessir, I did." He scrambled into the wagon, opened the trunk and pulled out a brush, comb, and mirror and handed them to Promise.

She looked at the silver design on the back. It bore the engraved initials *PS*. An older man's image flashed before her eyes. He was handing her a wrapped present. Just as quickly as it came, the memory disappeared. It occurred to her she didn't know what she looked like, so she turned the mirror over to see her reflection.

Jake and Shorty exchanged a quizzical glance as she inspected her face.

"Are you as pretty as you remember?" Shorty asked.

A soft blush colored her cheeks. "I couldn't remember what I looked like."

"Well, you're about the prettiest gal I ever saw." Shorty was sincere with his praise. He couldn't imagine ever seeing a prettier gal.

"Thank you." She held the back of the mirror for Jake to see. "My name must be Promise."

Jake glanced at the initials and nodded. "There are other personal items in the trunk if you need them."

"This is all I need right now." Glancing inside the wagon, she saw the many dresses hanging from nails. "Are all of those dresses mine?"

"We think so. They all looked like they fit you."

She lifted the skirt of the dress she was wearing. "I hope all of them are not as heavy as this one."

Shorty looked at Jake to see if he was going to mention the money, but saw he wasn't going to comment. "Boss, are we covering a few more miles today?"

Jake looked down at Promise. "Do you think you're up to traveling? It's a lot of jostling in that wagon."

"She can ride on the seat with me if she doesn't want to stay in the back of the wagon," Shorty offered.

"Please don't let me hold you up, Mr. McBride. I'll be fine."

"Jake, remember." Jake glanced at Shorty. "Tell the men we'll pull out in thirty minutes."

Promise excused herself to see to her personal needs, but Jake remained nearby. He felt like he was walking a fine line, trying to give her some privacy and protect her at the same time. He didn't want her to be alone, and he instructed Shorty to stay by her side every minute when he wasn't around.

Promise listened patiently as Shorty talked nonstop as she rode beside him on the seat of the wagon. It seemed his preferred topic was Mr. McBride, and he had many stories about the tall cowboy. Shorty didn't hide his admiration for the man, spending hour after hour discussing him. She was grateful that he talked so much; it was a pleasant diversion, keeping her mind off of her dire situation. It occurred to her that he was intentionally avoiding any conversation regarding her circumstances for fear of upsetting her.

Shorty revealed that Mr. McBride had stayed with her throughout the night while she was unconscious, and he would hear him talking to her. That must be the reason Jake's voice seemed so familiar when she awoke. Several times today she'd seen him at a distance riding toward the rear of the drive, but he never stopped at the wagons. His size and the way he sat in the saddle made him easy to distinguish from the other men. When she questioned why Jake rode back and forth, Shorty explained that he was checking on the drag rider because, next to the point rider, that man was the most isolated person on the cattle drive. Watching the men with the cattle, she was awed by how hard they worked. They were always in motion, attuned to the movements of the cattle, and dedicated to averting dangerous situations. Several times over the course of the day, Shorty mentioned Jake worked harder than any man, and she'd seen that for herself. The man didn't stop.

When it was time to make camp for the night, Shorty and one of the men constructed a tent so they could keep a fire going, and everyone could have a place to sit to eat their dinner out of the rain. Promise kept busy helping Shorty prepare the evening meal. Every time a rider rode into camp, she found herself looking up to see if it was Mr. McBride. Long after most every man had eaten, Jake finally rode into camp. She noticed him glancing her way as he cared for his horse. Once he walked to the fire, she prepared a hot plate of food and poured a cup of coffee for him.

Jake had thought about hot coffee all afternoon, but seeing the plate of food, he realized how hungry he was. "Thank you. This looks good." *Funny how seeing a beautiful woman in camp made me forget about the long day in the saddle.*

"It's better than good. God sent us an angel who can make a perfect biscuit," Shorty told him. "I think she wants my job." He shoved a plate into Promise's hand. "You need to sit down for a while and eat. You've done too much for your first day on your feet."

"Did you forget we've been sitting all day?" she replied in a teasing tone.

Shorty laughed. "Yes, ma'am, but that wagon will wear you out, and you haven't eaten all day." He overturned a pail next to Jake's saddle, for her to use as a seat. "We rough it out here, missy."

"Thank you, Shorty." She took her seat, and Jake sat on his saddle.

"Boss, we know one thing about her already. Cooking over a campfire seemed natural for her," Shorty said.

"That's good news. Did you remember cooking before?" He was hoping some details of her life were coming back to her. All day he'd worried that she might ask him more questions about how he found her. He wasn't inclined to lie to her, though he didn't relish telling her about her husband.

"I didn't think about it, I just wanted to lend assistance to Shorty."

"She made those biscuits, and they're a whole lot better than mine," Shorty said.

"It's nice to eat them warm and dry. I'm glad I listened to you, Shorty, and brought these tents with us. They've been a big help," Jake said.

"I told you we would need them, boss."

Several men joined them around the fire, each filling his cup with fresh coffee. Since most of them had already eaten, Jake was certain they were there just to get a look at Promise. It was probably a good thing for him that she was such a looker. That alone would keep the men from grumbling about having a woman on the drive.

Cole walked over and took a seat on a nearby stump. Having heard Shorty's comment on the food, he said, "I agree, Shorty, these biscuits are better than yours."

Jake knew Cole would come sniffing around Promise as soon as he could. Cole would always find a way to finagle an introduction to a pretty woman. "Promise, this is Cole Becker. He was a U.S. Marshal too, and we rode together for ten years."

Cole stood again and tipped his hat. "Ma'am." Getting

his first good look at her, Cole couldn't stop staring. Jake had told him she was almost as pretty as his brother's wife, but the way he saw it, this gal wouldn't play second fiddle to any woman.

"You are no longer a marshal?" Promise asked Cole.

"No, I decided I like Wyoming. When Jake told me his plans, I decided it might be time for me to settle down, and Wyoming sounded like as good a place as any. Besides, he would just get into trouble without me," Cole teased.

Jake glared at him. Why did he have the feeling Cole had never thought of settling down until he took one look at Promise? He wouldn't have been surprised if Cole started quoting Shakespeare, like Jake's big brother. Cole told him if quoting Shakespeare helped Colt win a woman like Victoria, he was going to borrow his books.

Jake glanced at Promise to gauge her reaction to his glib-talking friend. To his surprise, Promise had her head bowed in prayer over her meal. Jake removed his hat, and the men followed his lead and waited for her to finish. Jake had never seen his men stop eating or drinking their coffee for anything before. It shamed him that his own manners needed polishing, and he didn't think he'd said a prayer over a meal since he was a boy.

Once she finished praying, Jake introduced her to the rest of the men. When he came to Rodriguez, the vaquero came forward, removed his hat, and bowed before her like she was a queen. "It is my great pleasure to meet such a beautiful lady in such a dreary place." He reached for her hand and brought it to his lips.

Promise barely felt his lips brush over the top of her hand. "Thank you, Mr. Rodriguez." She didn't know what to make of the well-mannered, regal-looking man. There was a vast contrast between Rodriguez and the other cowboys on the drive. She gazed up at him through her dark lashes, taking in his perfect white teeth gleaming under a thick, black mustache.

"Rodriguez Ruiz Dominguez Santoya," he said, bowing again. "It would be an honor if you would call me Rodriguez."

When her eyes slowly met his, she had another surprise. Clear blue eyes were staring back at her. He was smiling at her as if he knew what she was thinking.

"My family is from Spain."

"Of course," she responded shyly.

"I am sorry for your troubles, señorita. If there is anything I can do for you, do not hesitate to ask."

"That is very kind, Rodriguez." All of the men were so kind to her that she found herself becoming emotional. She refused to allow herself to wallow in self-pity, reminding herself that God had sent Mr. McBride and these wonderful men to find her. She should consider herself blessed.

As much as he wanted to stay and talk to her, Rodriguez knew every man was listening. "Good evening." He gave another slight bow before he walked away.

Promise watched him walk into the darkness. She had the feeling he was not the usual kind of man that would be found on a cattle drive. He seemed almost aristocratic in his manner, reminding her of someone she might meet . . . where? There were memories on the edge of her mind that continued to elude her.

Jake noticed Promise watching Rodriguez. He figured she'd been taken by his good manners, and the vaquero had them in abundance.

After a moment, Promise turned her attention to Cole. "Do you also have a ranch in Wyoming, Mr. Becker?"

Cole liked the sound of her soft Southern voice. "Call me Cole. Not yet, but I found a place I like."

That was news to Jake. He listened to them talk until he couldn't take anymore of Cole's flirting. Forcing his mind back on business, Jake pointed to four men. "Take first watch with me. He glanced at Cole, saying, "The rest of you can relieve us in four hours."

Ready to retire for the night, Promise stood and said good night to the men in camp. Shorty offered to walk with her to the wagon, but Jake nixed that idea when he jumped up. "I'll see her to the wagon."

Jake grabbed a lantern and took hold of her elbow as he led her from the fire. Rodriguez wasn't the only man with manners, he told himself. He just had to work a bit harder at dusting his off now and then. He'd noticed her perfect deportment as she interacted with the men. She gave her full attention to each man she spoke with, listening intently to what he was saying, as if she didn't have enough problems of her own. He had to admit, that was difficult for him at times, with the way some of the men droned on and on. He had never met what he thought was the quintessential Southern belle, but it seemed to him that the title suited Promise perfectly.

"How did you enjoy the first day of your cattle drive?" Jake hoped he sounded as though he engaged in polite conversation with ladies every day. That wasn't easy; for weeks on end he'd been around men who were rough as cobs.

"It was quite informative, and Shorty is very entertaining." Promise looked up at the large man beside her. His face was shadowed by the brim of his hat, and his eyes were so dark she couldn't really see them.

Reaching the wagon, Jake tossed back the canvas flap and put the lantern on the floor before he helped her inside. "Do you have everything you need?"

"Yes, thank you." Her gaze swept the surrounding dark terrain, unable to stop thinking of the possibility danger was lurking in every shadow. All day she couldn't stop questioning why someone would shoot her. It was a question with no answers; she didn't even know if she had enemies. It occurred to her that whoever shot her could come back and try again. Surrounded by darkness, her fears increased.

Sensing her anxiety, Jake wondered what was making her so nervous. She seemed fine during dinner. "Is there something on your mind?"

"Hmm . . . yes." She looked up to see him staring intently at her with those midnight eyes. "I was wondering if . . . whoever shot me . . . well, do you think they might try again?"

"You haven't remembered anything about that, have you?"

"No, and that is what concerns me. Not knowing who or why, how am I to know if the person is near me?"

His gaze didn't leave her when he said, "You will be safe with us."

She believed him, yet it did little to set her mind at ease. "Shorty said you slept in here when I was unconscious. Is this where you normally sleep?"

"No, I usually catch a few hours outside before I take another watch. I just wanted to be close if you came around, because sometimes I can sleep pretty soundly if I'm overly tired." He correctly assumed she didn't want to be alone right now. "I can stay for a few minutes if you want."

"Oh, that would be lovely," she replied, obviously relieved.

He gracefully jumped in the wagon.

She gave him a tremulous smile. "Shall we sit?"

"Yes, ma'am. I can't stay bent over this way for long."

He did look uncomfortable, doubled over to keep from hitting his head. She sat on her pallet and watched him remove his hat as he took a seat across from her. When he stretched out his long legs, she realized he took up a lot of space. "I don't mind if you sleep here."

It was one thing to sleep inside with her when she was

unconscious, but now that she was awake, he didn't think that would be such a good idea. He wondered if she would make the same offer if she wasn't afraid. He gave her another grin. "I have my reputation to consider."

Embarrassed that she hadn't considered how inappropriate the offer sounded, she blushed at his response. "I didn't consider how that would appear."

Seeing that she was flustered, he added in a teasing tone, "Not that I would mind spending the night with a beautiful woman." Even in the dim lamplight, he could see her cheeks turning pink. He felt certain many men had told her she was beautiful, and even his own men couldn't take their eyes off of her, yet she didn't seem to realize the effect she had on them. "If it makes you rest easier, I will sleep right beside your wagon when I'm in camp. When I'm on watch, I'll have someone else take my place."

Relief washed over her, knowing he would be close. Though she didn't know him, she trusted him without question. "It helps to know that. The only thing that seems familiar to me is your voice. Shorty said you talked to me when I was unconscious, so that is probably why I find it so familiar."

When she looked at him with those large whiskey-colored eyes, he was tempted to forget she was a recent widow. "I didn't know if you could hear me. It seemed to me it might be a comfort to know you were safe."

"Did the doctor say how long it might take for my memory to come back?"

He tried to think about how he would feel if he didn't know who he was. It had to be frustrating for her, but he had to be honest. "He wasn't sure."

"I read some of my journal, and I wrote about someone named Matthew. He was obviously someone I traveled with. Do you know who he is?" At first, she thought

Matthew might be her husband, but for some reason she was certain she was not married.

Now what was he going to say? Exactly as he feared, she'd asked the very question he didn't want to answer. "I'm not sure who he is," he responded. He was hedging, but in all honesty, he wasn't positive Matthew was her husband. "I do think you were traveling with him." Before she could ask him what happened to Matthew, he said, "Why don't you lie down and try to sleep."

"I can't sleep in my dress. You don't have to stay. I'll be okay now that I know you will be near."

Jake stood and retrieved his hat. "If you need anything, I'll be right outside."

"Thank you, Mr. McBride. Good night."

"Jake," he reminded her. "Good night."

When he approached the fire to retrieve his saddle, he noticed all the men looking his way. He started to ask them why they were staring until he realized they weren't really looking at him; they were looking past him to the wagon. He turned to see what held their attention. Promise was sitting at the back of the wagon and the flap was still open, so they could see her brushing her hair over one shoulder. It was such a simple task, but one that made every man stop and stare. Jake understood how they felt. It had been way too long since any of them had spent time with a woman. Suddenly, she stopped brushing her hair and dropped her face into her hands. It was obvious she was crying. It broke Jake's heart, and the heart of every man watching her. She was frightened, and who could blame her? He couldn't imagine being in her position, and at the mercy of strangers. All in all, she was handling things much better than he would. Finally he saw her lift her skirt to dry her eyes, and he turned to the men. The look on their faces said the scene had affected them much as it did him. "Okay, men, let's get moving." He knew his tone sounded

harsher than he intended. Not a word was spoken as the
men went about their business.

"Why are you angry?" Cole asked.

Jake hadn't noticed him standing there. "She has a lot
to deal with and she doesn't need an audience." Jake bent
over and picked up his saddle and bedroll. "She's going to
be with us a long time, and I don't want the men hanging
around her every minute."

"They are not going to be able to avoid her."

"I wonder how they would feel if they were on the receiving end of their stares?" Jake barked. He wasn't angry
at the men, he was angry at her situation. And he wanted
more than anything to go after those killers. That was what
was truly troubling him.

Cole chuckled. "I'd say they'd like the attention if it was
Promise doing the watching."

Now there was the problem. He'd seen how the men
watched her at dinner, Cole in particular. It was unusual for
the men to hang around after they finished their dinner. If
they weren't on watch, they were getting some much needed
shut-eye. At this rate, every man on this drive would be in
love with her before they reached Wyoming.

Chapter Eight

Jake didn't come back to camp when he was relieved; he stayed with the cattle and let some of the other men get some extra rest. It was almost three o'clock in the morning when he rode to camp. His plan was to rest for an hour or two, and true to his word, he was right below Promise's wagon using his saddle for a pillow. It wasn't the most comfortable place to sleep since it was still raining. He'd covered as much of his large frame as he could with his slicker, but water was still finding a way to his skin. Pelting rain wasn't his only problem. He could hear every move Promise made as she tossed and turned inside the wagon. It was evident she wasn't sleeping any better than he was. In a few short hours he'd be in the saddle again, so he'd just about given up on getting any rest.

When he heard the canvas flap open he almost groaned. *Does she need to do her business now?* But before he could ask, he heard her say, "Mr. McBride, is that you?"

"Yes, ma'am. Do you need something, sweetheart?"

"Would you mind if I came out there to sleep? I haven't been able to fall asleep the whole time you were gone."

Jake scrambled to his feet and moved to the opening and looked at her. "It's pretty wet out here."

She hated to be such a coward, and she was aware how much trouble she had caused him, but she was scared to be alone inside that wagon. Every little sound she heard nearly caused her heart to stop beating. She'd known the minute Jake had taken the place of the man stationed below her wagon. It surprised her that she could tell it was him by the sound of his spurs when he walked.

"Do you think you could go to sleep if I stay in there for a little while?" His better judgment told him it was a bad idea, but on the other hand he was sick and tired of being wet.

"I think so." She silently thanked God for sending a man like Mr. McBride to protect her.

When Jake jumped inside the wagon he hadn't realized she was so close to the flap and he collided with her. She went flying backward, but thanks to his quick reflexes, he caught her by the shoulders before she fell. "Sorry, I didn't know you were so close."

The light in the lantern had been dimmed, but he could see that she was covered from head to toe in the nightgown and robe he had seen in her trunk. It didn't matter that only her toes were visible; his mind immediately conjured up the flimsy underthings she wore. "Okay, I'll just be over here." He pointed to the pallet that was not nearly far enough away since she looked so lovely and smelled so wonderful. "Now try to get some sleep." Fat chance he would. His mind kept going back to the night he'd undressed her.

"Thank you, Mr. McBride," she whispered. "I'm not sure why, I just can't relax when it's dark."

"Call me Jake. I think it's understandable that you would be nervous." He glanced at her pallet and saw the open journal. He figured that was the reason she wasn't able to sleep.

"I read some of the journal, and I have a million questions swirling in my mind."

"That's understandable as well." He didn't know if she wanted to talk about what she'd read, so he waited for her to say more.

When she finally spoke, she said, "I do apologize for keeping you awake. I imagine you are quite tired."

"I'm fine, honey. You need to sleep. We have a long day ahead and you'll need some rest."

Promise awoke feeling so warm and snuggly that she didn't want to open her eyes. She didn't want to remember her situation, she just wanted to stay right where she was, feeling safe and secure. When she finally opened her eyes, she gasped. No wonder she was so warm! She was snuggled on top of Jake, her head resting on his broad chest. It felt like she was lying on top of a stove. She placed her hand on his chest and tried to move away, but his arm was wrapped tightly around her. Slowly, she tried wiggling inch by inch underneath his arm and was making some headway when he opened his eyes and looked directly at her. She froze in place.

"Well, hello," he said, in a deeply masculine morning voice. Jake wasn't sure if he was actually awake or having a great dream. If he was awake and on this side of the daisies with a beautiful woman snuggled up close, well, that was about as near perfect as life could get. If he was dreaming, he figured even that was better than nothing. He gently pulled her closer to his chest, securing her with both arms, pressing her tightly to him. She felt so good, soft and warm . . . but . . . who the devil was she? He couldn't remember where he was, or who she was, but did it really matter? It wasn't the first time he'd fallen asleep in some woman's room. He must be in some saloon . . . somewhere. Then he kissed her. Soundly. She tasted as good as she felt. What a way to wake up! He ran a hand over her back and wondered why she had on so many clothes. He intended to remedy that problem in short order. His lips moved to her neck in search of some skin, but tasted cloth instead. He had to be dreaming because he had his clothes on too.

Promise tried in vain to push away from him, and when his lips finally left hers and she regained her senses. "Mr. McBride!"

Immediately, the fog of sleep cleared and realization dawned at the sound of that Southern voice, answering his questions from one second earlier. He remembered *where* he was, and who *she* was. He wasn't dreaming! *Hell's bells!* He pushed her away like she had the plague, jumped to his feet, banging his head on the beam at the top of the wagon in the process. "Dang it!" he growled, rubbing his head. "I'm sorry, I didn't mean . . . well, I did mean to . . . but, I didn't know who you were." He could tell by the look on her face that he was digging the hole deeper. He closed his eyes and pinched the bridge of his nose, trying to collect his thoughts. He had a pounding headache, and probably a dent in his skull from hitting his head so hard. He just wanted to get out of that wagon pronto, and get on his horse. Opening one eye, he saw that it was already light outside, which meant he had overslept again. Which also meant the cattle weren't moving. Which also meant every man in camp knew where he'd spent the night. The last thing he remembered about last night was thinking how good she smelled in the close confines of that wagon. He looked down at her, feeling guiltier by the second. In an attempt to explain his behavior, he said, "I wasn't fully awake. I told you I'm a sound sleeper." When that sounded inadequate even to his own ears, he added, "I'm sorry." Then it occurred to him that he awoke in the same position he was in when he went to sleep . . . *on his pallet*. She was the one who had moved. He gave her a quizzical look.

"Why were you on top of . . ." He decided he'd better put that another way. "Why were you . . . ah . . . lying here?"

Promise looked around the wagon. He had a point. She was the one who was no longer on her pallet; she was sharing his. Blushing to her toes, she whispered, "I must have gotten cold in the night."

Jake's mind was spinning. Had she mistaken him for her husband in the night? He could see that would be a natural thing for a woman to do if she was cold. He couldn't think of anything he'd like more than a woman like her cozied up to him on a cold night, but the thought of her confusing him with her husband was a different story. She looked so embarrassed that he felt sorry for her. "It was just a mistake, let's not worry about it." Grabbing his hat from the nail, he opened the flap and jumped out of the wagon, only to feel the continuous drizzling rain pelting him. *Perfect.* "You best get something to eat. We'll be leaving soon," he instructed over his shoulder.

Left alone in the wagon, Promise touched her lips with shaking fingers. She didn't even know if she had ever been kissed by a man. As comfortable as he seemed performing the act, there was little doubt he'd done a lot of kissing. If she had been kissed before, she couldn't imagine it felt as good as Jake McBride's kiss. He was such a handsome man it seemed likely that he had a . . . Oh no! He could have a wife! Shorty hadn't mentioned whether Jake was married, and she hadn't asked. Until this very moment, that question had never occurred to her. If he was married, he'd probably assumed she was his wife when he kissed her. That thought brought her up short. To imagine him kissing another woman, even if it was his wife, caused her to have emotions she wasn't sure she'd ever felt. Was it jealousy? Surely not. She hadn't known him long enough to develop such strong feelings that she should be emotionally invested in his marital status. Yet there was no denying her powerful attraction to him. She reasoned that he was a man with many fine qualities most women would find attractive, so it was a normal response on her part. Perhaps time was no factor when the heart was involved. And she feared her heart was definitely in danger of being involved with Jake McBride.

Once Jake gave Shorty a good tongue-lashing for not waking him, he saddled Preacher and headed out to get the men and cattle moving. Shorty tried to tell him nobody had asked where he was, but Jake wouldn't listen.

Shorty and Promise had been in the wagon for over an hour when he finally mentioned Jake's bad mood. "Boss sure was in a fit this morning."

"Was he?" Promise didn't think he was angry when he left the wagon. Embarrassed maybe, but not angry.

"He didn't even have coffee or nothin' to eat. He just tore outta camp like the devil was on his tail."

"Why was he upset?" Promise was genuinely puzzled.

"I guess he was mad 'cause I didn't wake him. But I didn't figure a couple of hours would hurt anything. I asked Cole, and he said I should let him sleep," Shorty grumbled. "I told him most of the men were out with the cattle, and no one asked where he was anyway." *Dang it!* He hadn't meant to say that. Sometimes he should just keep his trap shut, he told himself.

Promise understood the implication of what Shorty said, but she remained quiet. Jake must have thought the men might misunderstand the reason he was in her wagon. And if he was a married man, that compounded the problem, not to mention that kiss was most inappropriate. She wanted to ask Shorty if there was a Mrs. McBride, but she wasn't quite sure how to go about it. She didn't want Shorty to get the impression she had a personal interest in his boss.

If she did find the courage to ask, and Shorty told her Jake had a wife, what then? Oh, she simply couldn't bear the thought! She might not remember her past, but she knew she wasn't the kind of woman who would allow the advances of a married man. Not even if that man was Jake McBride, and no matter how much she wanted more of his kisses.

Every man who tried to talk to Jake found out in short order that he was about as friendly as an old hungry grizzly. He was angry with himself for the situation he'd found himself in earlier that morning, and he was taking it out on everyone. He didn't want the men to get the wrong idea where Promise was concerned. Not only that, but he wasn't happy thinking about how good it felt to kiss her. She was a distraction he didn't need. He couldn't exactly keep his distance from her if he was going to protect her, but he sure wasn't going to step inside that wagon again.

Cole ignored the warnings from the other men to stay away from Jake, and rode up beside him. "Did you wake up on the wrong side of the bed this morning?"

Jake's mind was racing with unanswered questions, and he didn't hear Cole ride up. "That's not funny," he grumbled. "I can't believe Shorty didn't wake me. I fell asleep waiting for her to fall asleep. She was afraid of being in there alone."

Cole gave him a lecherous grin and arched an eyebrow at him.

"Don't go there," Jake warned.

Cole laughed, and in his own best interest decided to stop teasing him. If there was one thing he was certain of, Jake wouldn't take advantage of any woman under any circumstance. "Don't blame Shorty. I told him to let you sleep. I didn't figure an hour or two was any big deal. You haven't had much sleep since we left Texas."

"I don't need sleep that badly. We need to get the cattle to Wyoming, and the sooner the better," Jake growled.

"We've been at this for almost eight hours. Don't you think it's time we took a break? We're all soaked, and it'd be kinda nice to get into some dry duds, not to mention have some hot coffee."

Jake had to agree there. A steaming cup of coffee sounded good. And his stomach was reminding him that his own temper this morning had kept him from eating. "Yeah, we need to stop," he admitted.

"I don't know about you, but I'm beginning to think it's going to rain all the way to Wyoming," Cole said.

"It sure looks that way," Jake agreed miserably. "Go on and tell Shorty we'll be stopping for the night. I'll see you at camp after I make sure the men have all been in to eat. That should give you enough time to catch some rest."

The men were grumbling about the incessant rain, and Jake's mood was about as rank as the longhorns. He'd made sure every man had eaten and had time to rest before he rode back to camp.

He'd been in the saddle nearly ten hours by the time he got to camp. Shorty handed him a cup of coffee. "Sit yourself down and I'll grab you some grub."

Jake had just taken his first bite when the lightning and thunder started. He waited a minute to see if it would stop, but when the ground started rumbling, he knew every man had to get back on his horse. *Will this never end?* Throwing his plate aside, he ran to get a fresh horse. He rode out, facing the worst storm he'd ever seen. He'd heard stories about lightning striking entire herds, but he'd never seen the tips of their horns glow like they were now. It was an eerie sight, and he had a foreboding sense this was just the beginning of another very long night.

"I've never seen anything like that." Cole yelled to be heard above the rumbling thunder.

"Me neither. I don't like the looks of this." No sooner had the words left his mouth when another ear-splitting eruption shook the earth.

"Boss, these cattle are gonna bolt," Harm shouted. "They were restive before this started, and now they're gonna go crazy."

Harm was his most experienced cattleman, and Jake paid attention when he spoke. Another deafening crack of thunder erupted, and just as Harm predicted, the cattle bolted in every direction. They were running like Lucifer himself was chasing them down. The men split up and raced after them in pairs, doing their best to guide them in one direction.

On one hand, the lightning provided the only light they had, and the conditions were dangerous to men and animals in the dark. On the other hand, if this storm didn't stop, some of the cattle might keep running until they dropped dead.

They rode for miles before they were able to get the stampeding cattle under control. Jake knew there would be strays to be found later, and he was bound to have lost some, but as long as he didn't lose any men, he could deal with everything else. In a situation like this, anything could happen. Over the next few hours as the storm calmed, the cattle quieted, too exhausted to run farther. Jake and Cole split up and rode the perimeter to make sure no man or horse was injured.

When Jake saw Ty, the young man who was driving the supply wagon, he realized no one had stayed behind with Shorty and Promise. He cursed himself for not thinking to tell someone to stay. By now, they were several miles from camp, and that troubled him. He spotted Cole and whistled for him to join him. "Let's hurry back to camp. Shorty is there alone with Promise."

Cole saw the concerned look on Jake's face. "You think something's amiss?"

"I just have a bad feeling."

That explanation was good enough for Cole.

Exhausted as they were, they pushed their animals as fast as they could safely go toward camp. Jake figured they were about a quarter of a mile away when they heard gunshots.

"It's coming from the direction of the wagons," Cole shouted.

"That's what I thought." Jake kicked his horse into a gallop.

Riding into camp with guns drawn, Jake spotted Shorty and Promise slumped on the ground with their backs against a wagon wheel. Their clothes were plastered to their bodies from being out in the elements. Both had a pistol in each hand, and there were four rifles leaning against the wagon. With the rain hampering his vision, Jake wasn't sure they were even alive until Shorty called out.

"Boss, you missed the party!" Shorty yelled, sounding energized from the excitement. "They hightailed it out of here a few minutes ago when she winged one of them sons of bit—" He glanced at Promise and stopped. "Pardon, ma'am. Anyways, I think she winged one of those sons of Satan." He smiled at Jake and guffawed, patting Promise on the back. "You should see this little gal shoot. I bet she can give you a run for your money! She's the one who saw them coming when we were packing up."

Kneeling before Promise, Jake saw that her hands were shaking. He took the guns from her and gripped her by the shoulders. Examining her pale face, he feared she was in shock. "Are you okay?"

"Yes, I am now." She was relieved beyond measure to see him.

Jake took a deep breath to calm himself. Thank God she wasn't hurt while he was out chasing cattle. "How many were there?"

"Eight or nine. We've been holding them off for a while. I was sure you would hear the gunfire eventually," Shorty answered.

Cole picked up an empty cartridge box. "How long?"

"Well, we weren't exactly timing it. We were kinda busy shootin', and we are both near deaf right now."

"We couldn't hear anything out there, between the storm and the stampeding cattle," Cole explained.

Jake was still trying to wrap his brain around the fact that the two of them had been holding off eight or nine men. Just like last time, he wanted to ride after the killers, but he couldn't leave her again. He should have been there to protect her in the first place. He'd failed miserably on that score, and the two of them were lucky to be alive. Even if they'd heard the gunfire, he and his men had been too far away to help them.

Cole could see the dilemma Jake was in. "You want me to go after them?"

Jake wasn't going to lose his best friend by doing something stupid like sending him alone to face that many men, and he couldn't spare another man to go with him. "No, they'll be back. Next time I won't make the same mistake. If I'm not in camp, you will be for the rest of the drive. I don't care if the whole damn herd stampedes to hell and back, they won't find them alone again."

Jake helped Promise to her feet. "Did you know you could shoot a pistol?"

"Not really. I just assumed after what I read in my journal I must have learned to shoot. When Shorty handed me the pistols, I seemed to know what to do. I remembered . . ." She paused, trying to explain her vision. "I think I remembered shooting at someone before now."

"Do you know who it was?"

"It didn't really make sense, just like a flash of something in my mind. I don't know why I would shoot at anyone."

Jake turned his attention back to Shorty. "Did they get close enough for you to see their faces?"

"No sir, we kept them pinned down pretty good."

"Let's finish loading the wagons and meet up with the men," Jake instructed. "Cole and I can drive the wagons."

Cole and Shorty walked away to store the provisions in the wagons, but Promise didn't move.

"Mr. McBride, could I have a moment of your time?"

"Sure thing." He turned his attention on her and noticed she was still shivering. "You best get some dry clothes on first. We don't need you getting sick on us."

"I will change in a minute, but there is something important I need to tell you. I found something I think explains the reason those men were attacking us." She reached into her pocket and pulled out a stack of gold coins and held them out to him. "I found these in my dress."

Jake glanced at the money in her palm. "I already know about the money. You have coins in all of your dresses."

Her eyes widened at his revelation. "You knew?"

"Shorty found them when he was washing some of your dresses. I didn't mention it since I hoped if you found them it might help you to remember."

"I didn't remember. I was just trying to find out why my dress was so heavy. Unfortunately, I only have more questions. Do you think this is what those men want?"

"Yes," Jake answered quickly. "You also have some valuable jewelry, and I'll tell Shorty to give it to you. Maybe it will stir a memory." Jake debated on what he should say, but he wanted her to be aware these men could come back. "Honey, you were traveling with quite a bit of money, expensive jewelry, and your clothing is obviously of fine quality, much nicer than the dresses of the folks you were traveling with." He hesitated, but decided to tell her more. "I guess you know from reading your journal that you were on a wagon train with some older folks. The other women had money sewn into the hems of their dresses, but not as much as you had. I was hoping we could find out who those folks were and get the money to their families. I think those men heard about the money and that was the reason for the attack."

"And the man that you thought I was traveling with?"

He hated to tell her the truth, but he saw no way around it now. "He's dead."

Her eyes filled with tears as realization dawned. "You said you wanted to get the money to their families. What happened to the rest of the people?"

Jake took a deep breath, and looked directly into her eyes. He had no choice; she needed to know the reason those men would come back. "We buried nine people."

She stared at him, disbelief in her eyes. "How many were traveling with me?"

"Nine."

She couldn't believe what he was saying. "No one else was alive?"

Jake shook his head.

Her unshed tears started streaming over her cheeks. "Do you think any of these people were my family?"

Jake debated whether she was strong enough to hear the truth, but he knew in her position he'd want to know. "Let's go inside the supply wagon." He took her by the hand and led her to the wagon and lifted her inside. After opening the trunk, he pulled out the painting of the man he assumed was her husband. "Does this man look familiar to you?"

Promise searched the face on the canvas. He was a handsome man, with pale blond hair like hers, and intriguing golden eyes. His face did seem familiar, or was it wishful thinking on her part? She wanted so badly to remember something. "I'm not sure."

Jake placed the painting back inside the trunk and turned to her. "That was the man I found near you." He allowed her a few minutes to digest that piece of information before he added, "We'll find out who you are."

She tried to wipe her tears away, but they continued to flow.

Jake pulled her into his arms. "Shhh . . . We'll figure this out, I swear to you."

She sobbed on his chest as he held her. Several minutes passed before she looked up at him. "You think he was my husband," she stated, not really expecting an answer. "Were our things in the same wagon?"

"The contents of the wagons were emptied onto the ground. We found another trunk very similar to yours, and it's in the other supply wagon. The initials on that trunk were *MS*. Your trunk bears the initials *PS*, so yes, I thought he was your husband. You can go through the other trunk when you feel like it. But right now, you need to change out of these wet clothes."

"I'm sorry for holding you up. I know we need to leave."

Taking her chin in his hand, he lifted her face to his. "There's nothing to be sorry for. You are not holding me up. I just don't want you getting sick."

Her gaze met his and they stared at each other for several long seconds. He didn't know how she could look so beautiful, covered from head to toe in mud, her nose red from crying, but she did. Lowering his eyes to her lips, his heart started pounding in his chest. When he heard her quick intake of breath, he knew that whatever he was feeling, she was feeling it too. His mind drifted back to the kiss he'd given her when he was half asleep, and how good she tasted. He was tempted beyond reason to kiss her again. But he was wide-awake now, and he knew he shouldn't do something he'd regret when he was thinking clearly. He mentally ticked off the reasons he needed to get out of that wagon. First of all, she was vulnerable to any man who could protect her right now. He reminded himself that he might have just buried her husband a few days prior, and he wouldn't be much of a man to take advantage of that situation. He was lured by her beauty, no doubt about it, and female companionship had been a rare thing over the last several months. And the plain fact was, if he kissed her again he wasn't sure he'd have the fortitude to stop. Finally, his inner dialogue was making headway. *Back off, McBride.* Leaning over, he gave her a chaste kiss on her forehead. "You're a beautiful woman, and much too tempting for a man to be alone with in a wagon," he said lightly. "Asleep or awake."

Chapter Nine

The storm continued throughout the night, forcing all of the men to pull nighthawk duty. They rode into camp in pairs for hot coffee and to catch an hour or two of sleep before they went back out. Their only relief from the steady downpour was under the tent Shorty had set up over the small fire, hoping they would have a chance for their clothing to get somewhat dry.

Like the men, Promise had a difficult time keeping her clothing dry as she helped Shorty keep a fresh supply of coffee over the fire.

It hadn't escaped the sharp-eyed cook that the bottom half of Promise's skirt was drenched. "You need to get in that wagon, get some dry clothes on, and try to rest for a few hours, missy," Shorty told her.

"I don't think I can rest right now. I've had too much coffee." She couldn't say for sure her nervousness was due to coffee, or because of the intimate encounter with Jake in the wagon. Replaying that moment in her mind, she'd thought he was going to kiss her again, and God help her, she wanted him to. But he'd left the wagon, rode out, and she hadn't seen him since. She wanted to be awake to make sure he made it to camp safe and sound.

Shorty figured she was probably still tense from the action earlier, so he didn't push the issue. "I might as well get breakfast started since it'll be dawn soon, and no one is getting much rest anyway. Jake didn't even get to eat his dinner last night, so his stomach is probably saying howdy to his spine."

Promise smiled at his choice of words. "I'll make the biscuits."

"I know the men won't complain about that."

The first light of dawn was peeking through the clouds when Jake rode into camp. Shorty and Promise were carrying the pans to the fire when they saw him caring for his horse.

"He has to be worn out, but he keeps going," Shorty commented to Promise.

Shorty often voiced his concern for his boss, and she'd come to realize that the burden Jake carried on his broad shoulders wasn't lost on his men. And she had unwillingly become his biggest burden.

Watching Jake walk to the campfire, she was struck by his rugged appeal, and thought he would be a remarkable subject on canvas. Without thinking, she ran to the supply wagon and pulled out her tablet and charcoals from her trunk. After finding a small space under the tent where her tablet wouldn't get wet, and she had a clear view of Jake sitting with his back to a tree, she started sketching. Her fingers moved swiftly and skillfully over the paper. The flickering light of the fire highlighted the chiseled contours of his face. She worked quickly, capturing the square lines of his jaw, the sharp cheekbones, the strong, straight slash of his nose, and those dark eyes fringed in long, lush lashes.

Her fingers stilled over the drawing. Somewhere in the back of her mind, she knew she was doing something she had always wanted to do. How did she know she'd always wanted to draw a man like Jake? Her gaze drifted from the drawing to Jake's face. Glancing back down at her work with a critical eye, she thought it was good . . . better than good. She'd captured the very character of the man.

Shorty leaned over her shoulder. "Dang, you sure can draw. That looks just like him."

She smiled at him. "He's a very interesting subject."

"I think this is a good sign," Shorty told her. "Doing things you used to do will surely help your memory."

"From your mouth to God's ears," she replied. She glanced back at Jake and saw that he had moved. He was lying under the tent on his bedroll with his head on his saddle, his slicker covering him and his hat pulled over his eyes. Under that rugged exterior, no one would ever guess the gentleness of the man. She'd seen firsthand that side of him when he'd held her while she cried. Her feelings for Jake were confusing. She didn't know if she was attracted to him because he had saved her life and she felt safe with him, or if her feelings ran deeper. But how could she allow herself to feel these things for Jake with all of the unanswered questions haunting her—questions about the handsome man in the painting. Was he her husband? Should she be grieving the loss of a husband, and possibly other family members? Rationally, she knew she needed answers before she would be ready to move on. Rational or not, she couldn't keep her gaze from drifting back to Jake.

Jake wasn't sleeping; he was too tired to sleep. He'd just pulled his hat over his eyes so he could have some privacy to think things over. The situation could have been much worse, in his estimation. He didn't know how many cattle he'd lost, but that was nothing compared to what could have happened. Promise and Shorty were safe, and that was what really mattered. He'd told his men he wanted them in pairs for the remainder of the drive. It was going to be difficult because he didn't have that many men, but it was necessary. It was obvious the killers knew that Promise was the one person who'd survived the wagon train massacre. As he'd suspected all along, they wouldn't forget someone who looked like her, and they were counting on the money being with her. They had demonstrated their cunning by taking advantage of the stampede to get to her. Fortunately, they hadn't succeeded. He really wanted to go after them, but he had to consider all of his options. If he rode alone, it would give the killers the perfect opportunity to ambush him and take him out of the equation. If he took a couple of men to track them, that would leave the camp vulnerable, and not enough men to take care of the cattle. He thought about riding into the next town to see if he could pick up some more men for the drive, but that posed a risk in itself. Hiring strangers without recommendations could prove fatal. He hadn't met every man on this drive before he hired them, but Shorty knew each and every one of them. Shorty's recommendation carried a lot of weight, and he was pleased with every man he'd taken on. Not many were handy with a gun, but he had hired cowpunchers, not gunslingers.

He wished his brother Colt was with him. As good as Colt was with a gun, he would make up for ten men. Thinking of Colt made his mind automatically drift to his brother's new bride, Victoria. He'd never thought he would see another woman nearly as beautiful as Victoria. Her kind and loving nature made her even more so. Odd, but he hadn't thought much about her over the last few days, and he considered that a good thing. Promise's face flashed in his mind, and he guessed she was what kept his mind off of his brother's wife. Whatever the reason, he was happy Victoria was no longer occupying his brain.

His thoughts drifted back to Promise, and how she'd handled herself after the shootout with those killers. Most women would have been hysterical after such an event, and she had every right. Hell, he'd been scared to death when he'd heard those gunshots. He hadn't known what he would find riding into camp.

But it was when he told her the fate of the people on the wagon train that she'd started crying, and her tears were his undoing. He could no more resist pulling her into his arms than he could stop the rain from falling. On hindsight, it was probably a big mistake on his part. He was a man and she was a beautiful woman who needed him at that moment. That was a potent combination for a man, and he'd almost succumbed to the temptation.

Hearing Promise laugh brought his mind back to the present. Cole was talking to her, and he had a way about him that made everyone relax. After seeing her tears earlier, her laughter was a joyous sound. It didn't take long for some of the other men to join in their conversation. At least he knew she was well protected with that many men around, so there was a chance he might actually get some sleep. But that proved difficult when Shorty started relating the gun battle to the men, giving a blow-by-blow account. Hearing Shorty's version of how they traded gunfire with those killers made the hairs on the back of his neck stand up. There was no chance he was going to get any rest thinking about how close she came to death again.

An hour later, Jake was up and ready to face another dismal day. He instructed Shorty not to lag behind; he wanted the wagons within his sight at all times. The cattle traveled three or four wide, and a drive this large often was spread out over a few miles. Jake rode up and down the line on the outside of the cattle to make sure there were no problems along the way, and to check on the drag riders. He wanted the wagons at the midway point so he would pass them each time he rode by. He'd made sure two men were riding drag, and he told Harm not to ride too far ahead today. He wanted to be able to keep up with each and every man.

When they took their noon break, Promise approached Jake. "Mr. McBride, would it be possible for me to ride a horse this afternoon?"

Jake sipped his coffee while he contemplated her request. She would be more exposed, but he would be right beside her the whole time. But he doubted this Southern belle had ever ridden astride. "I don't have a sidesaddle."

"I don't think I need a sidesaddle."

Jake furrowed his brow. "I'm not sure you would want to ride astride in a dress. And this rain is not going to stop. You'll get soaked."

"I don't mind a little water, and I have appropriate apparel," she assured him.

At that comment, Jake wasn't sure what she meant to wear. Was she planning on riding in those thin bloomers of hers? No way, no how. "I saw all of your . . . apparel, and unless you are preparing to ride in your bloom . . ."--he thought better of saying that—"underthings, you would be showing a lot of . . . a lot of . . ." He didn't know how to finish what he'd started. *Lord, why couldn't she be a man? I'll just give her a slicker to wear.* "Shorty couldn't find pants that would fit you."

Without another word she whirled around and headed to the supply wagon. When she exited the wagon, Jake saw she had something in her hand. She held up a wide-legged garment. "These are for horseback riding. That's how I knew I didn't need a sidesaddle. I've obviously ridden astride."

Jake stared slack-jawed at the garment. Shorty had shown him those things, but he had never seen a woman wear them before. His own mother didn't ride, and as far as he knew, neither did Colt's wife, so he wasn't too familiar with women who rode horseback astride. "Oh," was all he said, trying not to imagine how the garment would cling to every curve of her rear end. "If you're sure you're up to it, I see no problem with riding as long as you stay right beside me at all times." And here he was trying to stay away from temptation. *Hell's bells!*

Promise smiled in satisfaction as she climbed into the wagon to change her clothing. It was going to be such a treat to get on a horse and get out of that wagon. It jarred every bone in her body each time they hit a rut or rock, and Shorty hit them all. She didn't know how he stood it for hours on end, particularly considering his age, but she didn't dare voice that to him. She heard the men ribbing him about his age, and he didn't seem to find it amusing.

She changed and left the wagon to find Jake waiting for her with a saddled horse. After he stopped staring at her in that split skirt, he gave her a leg up, her backside nearly touching his nose. *Yep, they definitely show her rear in all its perfection.* Walking to Preacher, he grabbed the extra slicker he got from Shorty. "Put this on. I don't need you coming down with something."

She wasn't sure what precipitated his gruff tone, but she ignored it and asked sweetly, "But what will you wear?"

"That's an extra slicker. Anyway, I've been wet since I left Texas. It's not going to bother me." *Looking at that slicker is better than looking at your backside all day.* He watched as she shoved her hair under a hat Shorty found for her.

"Thank you. I think it will be much more comfortable on horseback than in that wagon." She was so excited to be on a horse, she was almost giddy. A little rain wouldn't deter her.

Settling himself in the saddle, Jake relaxed. He understood her sentiment about the wagon. "I've never been one to enjoy riding in a wagon."

They rode in silence, Promise ignoring the gloomy

weather, enjoying the rhythm of the horse. Jake surveyed his surroundings, on guard for any potential surprise attacks. He didn't figure the killers would confront them head-on; he'd already figured them for cowards who attacked the weak and defenseless.

"I wanted to ask you if you lost a lot of cattle."

"About forty or fifty head," he replied.

She wanted to help in some way. "I'd like to pay you for the cattle you've lost." Seeing he was about to object, she quickly added, "If you hadn't stopped to help me, you might have missed all this bad weather. I've caused you considerable problems."

"Don't you worry about that. I expect to lose some more cattle before we get to Wyoming. That's not unusual on a drive this size, and it has nothing to do with you."

"I would still like to repay you in some way for the trouble you've faced because you helped me. I know you've lost some time at the very least."

Jake lanced her with his dark eyes, wondering what exactly was troubling her. "You haven't caused me any trouble."

Seeing he wasn't going to relent, she let the subject drop for the moment. She would find a way to help him.

Two hours later, they were still riding side by side. Jake found himself admiring how skillful she was on horseback. Why he was surprised he didn't know, particularly after what Shorty had told him that morning about her accuracy with a pistol. Shorty said he hadn't even told her how to use the pistol; she just checked the chamber and started shooting and reloading like she'd done it thousands of times. She was obviously equally good at riding. A woman of many talents.

"You've ridden a lot," he commented.

"I feel very comfortable on horseback." It felt as natural as walking, and she felt it must be something she'd done her whole life. "Your horse is a beautiful animal."

"This is Preacher. He's been my partner for several years."

She pointed to her mount. "What is his name?"

Jake laughed. "I call him Stubborn, since that's what he is most of the time." He'd intentionally picked out that horse for her to see how the horse behaved under a woman's hand. The horse was tame, so he wasn't worried about her being thrown, but the animal just liked to do things in his own time. But he was on his best behavior for her, just like the two-legged animals on the drive. "He seems to work well for you," he told her.

"He's wonderful," Promise replied. "But we must give him another name. Stubborn will not do."

Jake smiled at her. "You think of a name."

"I will, but I will have to think about it." Since she was so comfortable on a horse, she might be useful helping with the cattle. She wanted to be more than a hindrance to him. "I've been watching how you and the men work with the cattle, and I feel I can be of some assistance. If you could teach me the basics, I might be more than a burden to you."

Now, he figured, they were getting to the core of the problem. She kept making comments about causing him problems. And he'd noticed how she was always looking behind them as if she expected the killers to sneak up on them. He admired her all the more for her willingness to help, but he wanted her to know it wasn't necessary. On the other hand, it might be a good idea to keep her busy, and working cattle certainly kept one's mind occupied. She wouldn't have time to fret about the killers. He was already worried enough for the both of them.

"First of all, you're not a burden." There was a part of him that wanted to keep his distance from her, but that had more to do with his basic instincts as a man. Since he couldn't avoid being with her and keep her safe at the same time, he was determined to keep her at arm's length, at least emotionally. He would do everything in his power to get her to where she was going in one piece. If he had to think of her as his sister, then that is exactly what he would do. He just had to keep his eyes off her backside. "I don't see why I can't teach you the basics of handling cattle, since you're an excellent rider."

Rodriguez rode up beside them on his stunning black-and-white, spirited horse. "Señorita, you are a very fine rider!" He had been watching how she handled her horse and was impressed with her skills.

"Thank you. Mr. McBride has been kind enough to allow me to ride one of his horses, and it's a wonderful reprieve from the wagon," she said.

Rodriguez thought her smile was beautiful. "You are welcome to any of my horses in the remuda."

Jake could see her confusion about his comment, so he explained. "Rodriguez is the only man who brought his own horses with him on the cattle drive. He has six in our remuda."

"*Sí*, I train my horses the way I like them to be trained. It is good to know what to expect from your animal at all times, no?" He looked out over the horizon and spread his arms wide. "A man's horse is the most important thing in this country."

She liked his easy manner, and his respect for his animals. "I can see that is true."

"I was going to explain the basics of working the cattle to her," Jake told him.

Rodriguez leaned over in his saddle so his face was closer to hers, and gave her a serious look. "Did you know, señorita, that the cowboy learned everything from the vaquero?" He didn't wait for a response. "Tonight after dinner I will begin your instruction on the use of the lariat to further your education on becoming a cattlewoman. You should learn from the best." He winked at her and rode away.

Jake chuckled. Leave it to Rodriguez to mention the superiority of the vaquero.

"He seems very confident." Promise watched Rodriguez expertly twirl his lariat.

"He's a very good vaquero, and next to my brother, he's has the best-trained horses I've ever seen."

"Your brother trains horses?"

"Colt has a unique bond with animals. Running the ranch takes up most of his time, but he trains horses for the ranch hands. I hope he'll have more time when I'm there to help out."

She could hear the love and respect in his voice when he spoke of his brother. "Not many people have such a special talent with animals."

"Rodriguez is right; a man's horse is his most important property out here, and we depend on them more than they do us. Rodriguez doesn't let anyone else care for his animals, and to my knowledge he has never allowed another person to ride them."

"That was kind of him to offer."

Jake didn't think kindness had anything to do with it, but he kept silent. Instead, he began explaining the reasons for the positions of the men on the drive, and their specific responsibilities. He taught her some of the language cowboys used, at least the words that were proper for a lady's ears. He'd never seen a more eager pupil. She seemed to thoroughly enjoy learning all about cattle, and asked him dozens of questions.

That evening after dinner, Rodriguez approached Promise with lariat in hand. "Are you up to the challenge to learn the lariat?"

Even though she was tired, she was determined to be as helpful to Jake as possible for the remainder of the drive. "Yes, if you have time."

Rodriguez was forfeiting his own rest just to spend some time with a beautiful woman. He offered his hand to her. "Then let us begin."

They walked to an area not too far from the fire so they could see what they were doing. After he showed her the essentials of throwing the rope, it didn't take her too many attempts until she had lassoed the small tree trunk he'd designated as a target.

"Señorita, you are a very excellent student." He was pleased that she was so adept. "Did you learn to ride so quickly?"

When she didn't respond, Rodriguez looked at her and saw her brow furrowed as if she was trying to remember something. He had forgotten about her loss of memory, and he regretted his mistake. "I do apologize, señorita, for my ill manners," he said.

Shaking her head, she said, "Oh no! No apology necessary. I just saw a man teaching me to ride." In her mind, she saw herself as a young child on the back of a pony. The man teaching her must have been her father.

Rodriguez could see the sadness in her eyes, and he reached down and took her hand in his. His voice softened when he said, "All will be well, señorita. God is on your side."

Chapter Ten

Having left Promise in the care of Rodriguez near the wagons, Jake rode with Cole to the front of the drive to talk to Harm. "I still feel like we're being dogged," Jake said.

"I've had the same feeling," Cole chimed in.

"It's been over a week and not one thing out of the ordinary has happened. It stands to reason they are waiting for the right opportunity," Jake replied.

"I doubt they will give up without getting what they want," Cole said.

"They'll play hell going through our men to get her," Harm stated.

Jake smiled. Like every man on the drive, Harm had taken Promise under his wing. When the men first saw her riding on horseback with Jake, there was some grumbling about it being bad luck. They had changed their minds quick enough when they saw how she helped with the cattle. She worked as hard as the men and they respected that.

"They're waiting for us to let our guard down and leave her vulnerable again. They won't come at us head-on," Jake said.

"Maybe the killers can't tell which one she is with that hat and slicker," Harm said.

"That was my intention." Jake didn't say he was trying to hide her rear end.

"It's difficult for the men riding in pairs. Just not enough of us to be everywhere we need to be at all times," Cole said.

Directing his thoughts away from Promise's assets, Jake said, "Yeah, and they're tired, not to mention their nerves are on edge."

"We'll be at the river tomorrow and that's always a dangerous situation. Everyone needs to be ready," Harm reminded them.

"We'll have our hands full," Jake admitted.

Cole knew Jake was troubled over keeping Promise safe. "Promise told me she keeps remembering some things, but she still hasn't put together where she was headed, or if the people on the wagon train were her family."

Jake had noticed when he returned to camp after his night watch that Cole was always talking with Promise instead of resting. The two of them seemed to have a lot to talk about. "You sure seem to spend a lot of time with her every night." He didn't add that Rodriguez also spent time with her every night. And when she slept, one of them was always by her wagon. Before long, the men were going to have to draw straws. It was like they were trying to fill up her dance card.

Cole glanced at Jake, thinking he was joking. "Why wouldn't I? She's a beautiful woman. It sure beats jawing with the men."

Jake pulled Preacher to a halt. "We may have buried her husband."

Cole stopped and chuckled. "I'm not asking her to marry me! And I believe it was you who insisted someone be with her at all times."

Harm reined in and looked from Jake to Cole. While he figured Cole was teasing, one look at the set of Jake's jaw said he wasn't.

Water was flowing over the brim of Jake's hat, so he took it off and slapped it against his thigh. He'd had enough. Enough of the rain, enough of waiting on these killers, and enough of the men sniffing around Promise like she was a tasty morsel of their favorite dessert. He wanted to punch something or someone, and right now Cole was in his sights. "I don't think you should be cozying up to a woman who is in such a vulnerable state."

Cole finally realized Jake was serious. "Maybe she needs a friend right now."

"Is that what you are? A friend?" Skepticism laced Jake's question. He'd never seen his best friend spend so much time with a woman unless he was taking her to bed. In his book, that didn't necessarily count as friendship.

Before Cole answered, Harm rode between them. "Talk about everyone's nerves on edge. I think you both need some rest." He'd seen plenty of friendships end over a woman, and a woman who looked like Promise could certainly come between two lifelong friends. "How about telling Shorty to stop for a while and you two get some shut-eye?"

Before they could agree to Harm's suggestion, a shot rang out behind them.

Harm was the first to speak. "That was some distance away."

"Yeah," Jake said, urging Preacher into a gallop. He'd told Promise to ride close by the wagon with Shorty, and he'd told Rodriguez to keep watch over her. Reaching the wagons midway, he spotted Promise beside Rodriguez. Shorty was gesturing with his arms, so Jake slowed Preacher to hear what he was saying.

"We're fine, boss. Sounded like it came from drag!" Shorty shouted, pointing behind him.

Jake nodded and headed for the rear of the herd, with Harm and Cole close behind. That morning, he'd specifically instructed Wes, one of the more experienced cowboys, to ride drag with Will, the youngest man on the crew.

When Jake reached the rear of the drive he saw Wes crouched over a body on the ground. It was Will. Jumping off his horse, he ran to the young man's side. "What happened?"

"I went after a few strays and I heard the shot," Wes answered. "I shouldn't have left him alone."

Jake put his palm on Will's chest. "He's alive." He pulled off his bandanna and held it to the wound on Will's shoulder. After staunching the bleeding, Jake turned him over so he could see how badly he was injured. Relief washed over him when he saw it wasn't serious. "It went through, he'll be okay." He glanced at Cole and Harm, and instructed, "Get him back to Shorty. Wes, you keep sharp." He grabbed Preacher's reins and jumped on his back. "Wes, what direction?"

Wes pointed to a dense patch of trees.

"You're not going alone," Cole stated.

"You stay at camp with Promise until I get back."

"I'm coming with you. Harm can take care of things," Cole said.

"This is my fault for not going after them before now. I'm going alone. Now get Will out of here, and stay with Promise." He gave Cole a level look. "I'm trusting you to keep her safe." He'd had enough. Promise, Shorty, and Will could have been killed because of his inaction. Well, no more. He rode off fast and reached the trees in minutes. It didn't take him long to find fresh tracks in the mud. There were four men this time. He found the area where they'd waited in the cover of the trees. Dismounting, he studied the hoofprints, committing them to memory. He figured they'd decided to pick them off one at a time as the opportunity presented itself.

Something caught his eye at the base of one of the trees. He leaned over and picked up an empty box. Adorning the cover of the package was a buxom woman in a red dress: Gypsy Queen cigarettes. He'd seen the same brand in a large box sitting on the counter at the general store in Dodge. He shoved the empty container in his pocket, and grabbed Preacher's reins.

"He's fine, nothing vital was hit," Shorty assured the men. "Promise is looking after him while I get supper started."

Cole poured himself some coffee. "That's good news."

Once Shorty placed his stew over the fire, he turned and gave Cole a hard look. "Why did you let that dang fool go after those men alone? There are too many of them!"

"I told him I wanted to go with him, but he said he was going alone. You know how stubborn he can be."

"You should have gone with him anyway. We can protect that gal. He has no business going off by himself, not knowing who he's chasing. On top of that, he's rarely had more than two hours of sleep a night since we left Texas. He's running on coffee and determination, nothing more."

Cole felt guilty enough; he didn't need Shorty pointing it out to him. He'd thought about riding after Jake, but he wasn't sure that was the right thing to do. He understood Jake's thinking; that was one of the benefits of riding by his side for over ten years. Most of the men on the drive could shoot a rattler if necessary, but if real trouble came calling he didn't know if their skills would be enough to protect lives. Few cowboys faced gun battles, and it wasn't as if they signed up for a gunfight, though he knew none of the men on this drive objected to the possibility if it became necessary. Jake had made it clear he wanted him to protect Promise, which was confusing since he jumped all over him for just talking to her. He considered the possibility Jake was taking an interest in her and he was just acting like a jealous fool. But that didn't really make sense because Jake had admitted he was smitten with his brother's wife. Of course, Cole knew he would never act on those feelings. Jake was the most honorable man he knew.

Admittedly, Cole was attracted to Promise, like every red-blooded man on the drive. She was a beautiful woman, and any man in his right mind would be attracted to her, but he didn't intend to jump on her like a buzzard on a dead carcass. He decided Shorty was right; Jake was acting like an unreasonable grizzly because he hadn't had much sleep and he had more problems than he'd ever expected on this drive. And the incessant rain had taken its toll on everyone.

Promise sat beside Will and prayed, asking God for Will's speedy recovery and to keep the other men safe. Even though Shorty assured her the young man would have no lasting damage to his arm, she couldn't help feeling responsible he was shot. She would gladly give those killers what they wanted if they would stop hurting people. It was difficult to understand what would possess those men to kill for money.

By the time she retired to her wagon for the night, Jake still hadn't returned. Turning her lantern down, she decided she wouldn't undress in case he came back soon. She sat on her pallet and leaned against the side wall. She was frightened. Not only was she worried about him, she was always more nervous when he wasn't near. Logically, she knew Cole and the other men would protect her from those killers, but it was Jake, with his quiet confidence, who made her feel nothing could happen as long as he was around.

She regretted being the cause of his problems, and wouldn't blame him if he asked her to leave. It would be better for him if she did. That seemed to be the only way to prevent another shooting. The next time, one of the men might be killed. Jake might be killed. That thought frightened her more than anything. It was high time she stopped acting like a scared rabbit. She'd already proven she could shoot quite accurately, and she was comfortable on a horse. Shorty had mentioned Denver wasn't that far away. It might be best if she purchased a horse from Jake and took her chances alone. It seemed plausible that she could protect herself to a point, and she felt confident if she had a fast horse she could outrun most men with her lighter weight. It was frightening to consider, but it was more terrifying to think of Jake, or anyone else, getting shot. Since the killers would never expect her to leave the safe confines of the cattle drive, she might have a better than average chance of making it to Denver before they found her. Surely, there would be a sheriff there who could handle the killers.

She closed her eyes, but she couldn't stop thinking about Jake. He was out there risking his life because of the trouble she had brought to him. If he was killed, she would never be able to forgive herself for not taking action. She knew what she needed to do. Now, she just needed to muster her courage. Leaving the cattle drive played in her mind until she finally dozed off with the rain pelting the canvas top.

Chapter Eleven

Forced to stop because of the dark, Jake and Preacher found shelter under some trees. *Damn rain. Is this destined to be the wettest cattle drive in history?* he grumbled to himself as he wiped Preacher's face. He lifted the saddle off Preacher and placed it next to a tree trunk so he could have a place to sit that wasn't in five inches of mud. What he wouldn't give for a cup of Shorty's hot coffee right now. He had to make do with rolling a cigarette in hopes that would keep him awake.

He sat on his saddle with the tree at his back and his arms resting on his knees as he thought about the situation. It looked like the killers were headed toward Denver, but he suspected that wasn't their true destination. More than likely they were leading him on a wild-goose chase, and were going to meet up with the rest of their gang at some point. Maybe they were going to Denver, maybe not. There was only one thing he felt confident about at this point: They would keep coming back until they got what they wanted.

Watching the rain increase in intensity, he resigned himself to the fact that tracking them was going to be next to impossible come daylight. The smart thing would be for him to turn around and head back to the cattle drive since he was ill prepared to follow them for several days. He needed to think, but right now, he was too tired to even do that.

Crushing his cigarette into the soggy earth, his mind drifted to Promise and how frightened she must be. Losing her memory was bad enough, but then to know these men could appear at any moment compounded the problem. He'd seen the dark circles under her eyes, and he knew she wasn't sleeping at night. He dropped his head to his forearms and closed his eyes as he reflected on his best course of action. He promptly fell asleep.

He awoke to Preacher nudging him in the shoulder. "Yeah, yeah, I'm awake," he told him, rubbing his muzzle. He didn't know how he'd slept in the torrential downpour, but he managed. When he tried to straighten his legs, he realized he'd been in the same position for a while because he was as stiff as a board and he ached all over. Gaining his feet, water sloshed from his slicker like a waterfall.

He retrieved a dry shirt out of his saddlebag to rub Preacher down before he saddled him. His mind felt clearer after that bit of rest. When the killers attacked Shorty and Promise during the stampede, he thought they were trying to kill Shorty to get to Promise. But now he knew he'd missed the obvious. These killers were not only after the money; Promise had seen their faces and they didn't know she'd lost her memory. They assumed she could identify the men who killed those people. They wanted the money, but they also wanted to silence her. She was the only one between them and a noose. With the knowledge they wouldn't stop until Promise was dead, he couldn't waste another minute. There was only one thing he could do right now.

"Let's go back, Preach," he said, throwing his saddle over the horse's back.

* * *

Cole had the cattle moving before dawn. He'd ridden beside Promise for most of the morning, pleading with her to ride inside one of the wagons to stay dry. As wet as she was, he worried she would catch a cold, or worse. She looked tired and on edge, and he wanted her to get some dry clothes on and get some rest.

"I wish you would ride in the wagon," he said for about the tenth time. "You're going to keep on until you get sick." Were all women this exasperating? Jake would kick his butt all the way to Wyoming if she was sick when he got back.

Promise didn't look at him when she said, "Do you worry about your men getting ill from a little rain?"

Cole blew out a deep breath. "The men have faced weather like this before," he ground out between clenched teeth, clearly on the verge of losing his patience. "And they haven't suffered any injuries lately, either."

She decided she might as well ask Cole what she intended to ask Jake when he returned. "I think I know how you can get me out of your hair."

"I wasn't trying to—" he began, but halted when she held up her hand.

She didn't want to hear his denial. She knew the drive was being compromised because the men were trying to keep her safe. "I wanted to ask if it would be possible for me to buy a horse."

He was puzzled why she thought he wanted her *out of his hair*, as she put it. But her question really threw him. "Why do you want to buy a horse?"

"I've decided I'm going to ride to Denver."

Cole couldn't believe what he was hearing. "Alone?"

"Certainly," she said, trying to sound more confident than she felt.

"Now why do you want to do a fool thing like that?"

Maybe there was something more wrong with her than losing her memory, if this was what she was thinking.

"It seems logical that Denver is as good a place as any to find out if I have family there. It makes little sense for me to remain with the cattle drive with those men following me, waiting for any opportunity to create havoc. That young man was shot because I am traveling with you."

Cole stopped his horse and glared at her. "No."

She reined in beside him. "No, what?"

"Take your choice. No, I will not sell you a horse. No, I will not hear of you taking off to Denver alone." He took a deep breath. "And no to any other harebrained idea you have in that pretty little head of yours."

While Cole was not as intimidating in appearance as Jake McBride, she could tell he was every bit as determined when he made up his mind.

"I will just ask Mr. McBride upon his return." She nudged her horse to a gallop.

"You go right ahead. He'll just say no," he yelled after her. Once he recovered from the shock of her request, he remembered he was responsible for looking after her. He picked up his pace to catch up to her.

After dinner, Promise retired to her wagon, but like the previous night, she was too on edge to rest. She picked up her brush and ran it through her hair, then twisted her hair on top of her head and reached for her comb. After she put the comb in her hair, she reached for the other comb . . . there was a second comb. In her mind's eye she saw a woman handing her a gift. She saw herself opening the beautifully wrapped package that contained two matching combs. The woman she saw in her mind must have been her mother. She desperately wanted to remember everything. These little bits and pieces were frustrating, but she clung to the fact that her memory was returning.

Sitting on her pallet, she picked up her tablet and flipped through the pages. Of the people she had drawn, Jake's portrait was by far the best, in her opinion. She hoped one day she would have the opportunity to paint him. Staring at the drawing, she realized her attraction to him had been growing stronger each day. It wasn't only because he was a stunningly handsome man; his strong character was what made him irresistible. He was everything she'd hoped to see in the West. She stopped . . . *Where did that come from?* How did she know that? Another unanswered question. There were few things she was certain about, but she was certain of one thing: She was definitely not a married woman.

It was the middle of the night when Jake spotted Cole and Harm as he rode to camp. After he talked with them, he rode to the corral to take care of Preacher. While he was rubbing him down, Rodriguez came up beside him. Jake could tell he had something on his mind. "What's bothering you, Rodriguez?"

"The señorita is very sad. She does not rest when you are not here."

Jake hated to hear that. "Has she remembered anything?"

"I do not think so, and there is nothing any of us can do," Rodriguez replied.

Jake understood his feelings of helplessness. "Get some sleep. I'm going to find something to eat, Cole and Harm are on watch and I'll relieve them later." He walked to the fire and tossed his bedroll under the tent where the men were sleeping before grabbing a cup of coffee. Since there

wasn't a light in Promise's wagon, he figured she was
sleeping.

Sitting at the back of the wagon in the dark, Promise
watched as Jake removed his chaps and hung them near
the fire. When he started unbuttoning his shirt, she knew
she should turn away, but she couldn't. The shirt came off
and her eyes were riveted to his bare chest and arms. Every
inch of his bronzed torso was roped in hard muscle. She
couldn't remember if she had ever seen a man's bare chest,
but seeing Jake, it was inconceivable that she would forget
such a sight. He was magnificent. How could any man be
so perfectly made? She had the urge to grab her oils and
paint him exactly as he looked in that moment, with the
fire blazing behind him. For the life of her, she couldn't
move.

Once he sat down to drink his coffee, Promise climbed
from the back of the wagon and walked toward him.
"Would you like something to eat?"

Jake almost went for his gun until it registered who was
speaking to him. "I didn't hear you."

"I'm sorry if I startled you. I thought you might be
hungry," she replied. She kept her gaze lowered so she
wouldn't stare at his bare chest.

"I was going to see if I could find something. How's
Will?"

"He's already up and around." She turned away. "I'll
warm something for you to eat."

Some of the men were sleeping under the makeshift tent
constructed between the fire and the back of the cook's
wagon. "I don't want to wake the men. If there are any
biscuits, I'll eat them cold." She moved quietly to the back
of the wagon and found some cold biscuits and cooked
slabs of bacon. When she returned with the plate of food,
the rain started coming down harder. "If you don't want
soggy biscuits, I think you'd better eat in the wagon."

He was eager to get out of the rain and there wasn't a spare space under the tent. At the same time, he hadn't forgotten his vow that he wasn't going back in that wagon, but at this very moment the thought of being dry was the temptress. Plus, he was just too tired to argue with himself. "I think you're right." He picked up his saddlebag, grabbed a lantern and followed her to the wagon.

Once they were in the dry confines of the wagon, he pulled a dry shirt out of his saddlebag and shoved his arms through the sleeves, but left it unbuttoned. He sat down and looked at her. Rodriguez was right when he said she wasn't resting. She looked tired and pale. "Why aren't you asleep at this late hour?"

She sat on her pallet, covertly watching his every movement. She didn't want to stare at his chest, but she couldn't keep herself from stealing an occasional glimpse. "I couldn't sleep."

"Why?" He didn't notice how her gaze kept drifting to his unbuttoned shirt. He was busy adding the bacon to his biscuits.

"I was worried."

He assumed she'd been worried about the killers attacking them again. "You don't have to worry; we will be ready the next time. If there is a next time. There will always be extra men in camp now."

"I was worried about you going after them alone," she admitted. "There were too many of them."

He looked up at her then. Rodriguez was right, she looked very sad. "You don't have to worry about me. I can take care of myself." He noticed she was wearing the comb he'd found in the mud. "I see you found your comb."

Her finger automatically touched the comb in her hair. "Yes, I think I had two of them."

"You remembered something else?"

"Earlier tonight I had a memory of opening a present

and inside there were two matching combs. I think it was a Christmas gift from my mother."

"It's good you're remembering some more things." He held out a biscuit to her.

"No, thank you."

After polishing off his meal, he leaned back against the wagon and closed his eyes. They were burning like the devil from lack of sleep.

Promise debated if now was the time to discuss Denver with him since he was obviously so tired, but she wanted to get it over with. "I wanted to know if I could buy a horse."

Jake's eyes snapped open. "Why do you want to buy a horse? You can ride Stubborn anytime you want."

"I've decided I will ride to Denver."

The look he gave her clearly said he thought she'd lost her mind. "Are you saying you are planning on riding to Denver alone?" He shook his head. He must be more tired than he figured if he just heard her say she wanted to take off by herself with killers on the loose.

"I do have a gun, and I obviously know how to shoot. I think I can handle any problems. Cole said no, but I think it is a mistake not to consider this."

"You already asked Cole?" It irritated the hell out of him that she would discuss this with Cole first.

"Yes, but he refused," she admitted wearily.

"Well, why are you bothering to ask me?" He sounded cantankerous, but right now he didn't care.

"Will was shot because of me! You are having all of these problems because of me! I would rather take my chances alone so no one else will get hurt. When I find out where I'm supposed to be, you could send my things to me, if you wouldn't mind."

Jake jumped to his feet, smacking his head again in the process. "Damn!" Was he never going to learn the height of that damned wagon! He wanted to pace, but the space was too small, so he hunkered over and glared at her. "Let me get this straight. You're worried about me following those killers, but you think you should ride alone to Denver?"

She was taken aback by his angry outburst.

He jabbed his finger at her. "You can get that notion out of your head right now. That's not happening. If you're determined to go to Denver right now, I will take you." Once the words were out of his mouth, he regretted his offer. He wouldn't leave her alone in Denver, and he couldn't stay with her and wait for her memory to return, which might not happen anytime soon. The cattle had to eat, which meant he had to keep moving and get them to Wyoming. "I don't think that is the best thing, since your memory hasn't returned. It wouldn't be safe for you to be there alone."

"Do you think Cole could take me?"

Cole again. He ground his molars. "No, I can't spare my men."

"Of course," she said. She briefly considered leaving some money for a horse and riding out when she got an opportunity, but what would that solve? She knew he would come after her and that would waste more of his time. She wanted him to understand how she felt. "I don't want anything to happen to you, or your men. If I left, those men would stop causing you trouble."

Once he understood her altruistic motives, some of his anger abated. It humbled him that she was so worried about him and his men that she would risk her own life. He had to allow she was so exhausted her thoughts were probably as muddled as his. He winked at her and grinned. "Didn't I mention that trouble was my middle name?"

The man was unnerving. That wink of his and that irreverent grin gave her a tingling sensation all over, and she couldn't stop the blush moving over her cheeks. She didn't know whether to scream or laugh. "Wyoming, then."

Rubbing his eyes, trying to keep them open, he said wearily, "Wyoming, then." He stared at her a minute longer. "I best get out of here and get some sleep."

"Stay," she said softly. "I sleep better when you're here."

He wondered if she'd already asked Cole. Whether she knew it or not, it was his cattle drive and his responsibility to make sure everyone on it was safe. *Not Cole.* He was too tired to care if the men gossiped. And he couldn't figure out a better way to keep her safe than to stay close to her. Besides, he could be dry for more than an hour, and that was very appealing. "You promise to sleep if I stay?"

She smiled at him. "Yes, I'm sure I will."

"It's a deal." He stretched out on the pallet. He wanted to pull on some dry pants, but he didn't have the energy to leave the wagon to change. The lantern was next to him and he started to turn it off when he saw she was reaching for her hairbrush.

When she removed the comb, she pulled her hair over one shoulder and started brushing.

As tired as he was, he still felt a surge of desire watching her perform that simple feminine task. It reminded him of the night he and the men had watched her brush her hair, but this was different. Sitting just a few feet from her made it seem much more intimate. His gaze lingered on her soft, delectable neck. He could almost feel his lips moving over her skin. *God, give me strength!*

Promise turned to face him, trying to avoid looking at the dark hair peeking through the opening of his unbuttoned shirt. "I don't think I am, or was, married."

Jake pulled his eyes from her neck and searched her face. He wondered why she made that comment. *Where is this conversation headed? Is she trying to tell me she has an interest in someone else?* He thought about her connection with Cole. She was comfortable enough with Cole to discuss leaving before he knew anything about her plans. Had something happened between them while he was gone? He knew Cole was attracted to her, but he didn't know if she was ready to move on.

"I know you thought the man I mentioned in my journal, Matthew, might be my husband . . . but I don't think he was."

He wondered if she had a direct line to his thoughts. "Why?"

"It's just something I feel. I don't feel like a married woman." She couldn't tell him that she found him wildly attractive and just being near him left her breathless. He was the one who occupied her thoughts, not some man she didn't remember. Definitely not the feelings of a married woman who loved her husband.

Jake was quiet for a long time, unsure how to respond. He decided it was best to be honest. "It seems logical that you were married because the two of you were traveling together."

"It may seem logical, but I just don't think so," she stated emphatically. Another thought struck her. If she was married, perhaps she didn't love her husband. For some reason the possibility of being in a loveless marriage saddened her even more.

Jake didn't want to disagree with her about her marital status, but he wasn't as confident. Every man on that wagon train had been lying near a woman that fateful day. It followed that the men were making some effort to protect their women, just like he would have done. There was one big difference between him and the men on the wagon train. He would have had a gun to even the odds. "Try to sleep. It will be dawn soon."

* * *

Jake jerked awake from a deep sleep at the sound of Promise screaming, "Get your hands off me!"

He looked over at her and saw her thrashing about. Moving to her pallet, he gently touched her shoulder. "Honey, wake up. You're having a bad dream."

She struggled as if she were fighting off demons. "Let me go!"

"Sweetheart, wake up!" he said louder.

She opened her eyes, and Jake said quickly, "Honey, you were having a bad dream."

She threw her arms around his neck, burying her face in his chest, and started sobbing.

Jake sat down with her in his lap. "Shhh, it's okay now. Just a bad dream," he whispered. She felt so delicate and fragile in his arms, and he wished he could take all of her fears away.

Her face moved to his neck and he could feel her tears. "Those men . . . one was holding me down . . . he said . . . he said he was going to . . ." Her words trailed off as she recalled what the man had said to her.

Jake had to lower his head to hear her since she was speaking just barely above a whisper. The pain in her voice was palpable. He gritted his teeth, imagining what that coward holding her down had said to her.

"They were shooting . . . everyone." She paused and struggled to breathe between sobs.

He couldn't bear the agony in her voice. Those men were going to pay for what they put her through, he would damn sure see to that.

"Everyone was shot! They were throwing everything out of the wagons. I pulled away from the man holding me and ran to my trunk. All of my things were scattered. I was looking for . . ." She stopped, trying to remember what she was looking for. After a moment, she uttered in a soft voice, "I don't know what I was looking for." She looked up at Jake through wet lashes. "Why would anyone do such a thing?"

There was no explaining the kind of men who killed like that. "Do you remember their faces clearly?"

Replaying the scene in her mind, she began to shiver. "I saw some of them very clearly. The man who held me down and . . ." Her words drifted off. She couldn't continue. She didn't want to remember that evil face, but she had seen him very clearly. "I know what he looks like. He was big . . . very big."

Jake wasn't merely angry, he was enraged. Just thinking of a big man holding down a small woman like her made him want to tear the man's heart out. He wanted to go after those killers and not stop until they were in jail or dead. He promised himself he would find each and every one of them, and they'd better pray they didn't give him a reason to kill them. What was important right now was for him to remain calm and listen as the events unfolded in her mind.

"Were these people my family? Why can't I remember?"

"You will remember, you're just not ready right now."

Suddenly she said, "Indians! There were Indians on the ridge." She grew quiet, and Jake knew she was trying hard to remember everything.

"I can't remember what happened after . . . until I awoke and saw you." Suddenly, the import of what Jake asked dawned on her. "They aren't only coming back for the money, are they? I can recognize them. They don't know I lost my memory."

"I've considered that. So don't even think you are going off to Denver by yourself," he said firmly.

"I wish I could remember more," she said sadly.

Tightening his arms around her, he felt a shiver run down her spine. Feeling her soft cheek on his bare chest, he involuntarily took a sharp breath.

"Are you sure you wouldn't be better off if I left? More of your men might get hurt."

"You're not going anywhere," he responded emphatically.

Pushing away from him, she looked up into his eyes. "What if they come back?"

"Then I'll deal with it."

It was difficult for her to believe he wasn't upset over the trouble she'd brought to him. She wasn't sure why God blessed her with a man like Jake McBride, but words couldn't accurately express how she felt. "Thank you for everything, Mr. McBride. What would have happened to me if not for you?" She leaned up to kiss his cheek, but at the same moment he moved his head and their lips touched. It was accidental, but she didn't move away, and neither did he. Very lightly, he brushed his lips over hers, and still she didn't move. He didn't think, he responded. At first he was gentle, and when she responded by pressing closer to his chest, he cupped her head in his hand and kissed her in earnest. She wrapped her arms around his neck and curled her fingers in his hair. Within seconds he was breathing heavily, his skin felt like it was on fire, and he wanted more, much more. Thankfully, sanity returned before his desire got the best of him. Dragging his lips away, he rested his forehead on hers and closed his eyes, trying desperately to rein in his runaway emotions. He must be crazy to do a fool thing like that. He reminded himself of his vow to keep his distance, and not be the worst kind of man and take advantage of her situation. Any woman would naturally feel beholden to a man who saved her life. When he finally opened his eyes, his gaze drifted to her hand resting on his chest, and he was nearly lost again. It'd been a long time since he'd been touched by a woman, and her touch was unlike anything he'd ever felt. He wouldn't have been surprised if his heart actually beat out of his chest. It took every ounce of effort he had to gather his control. He took her hand in his and brought it to his lips. He kissed the back of her hand. "Honey, I won't let anything happen to you. And you don't owe me anything." Before she could respond, he shifted her to the pallet and jumped from the wagon. As he walked away, he wondered if she'd thought about Cole while he was kissing her.

Chapter Twelve

Four days passed in relative quiet. To the relief of the men, there was even a blessed pause in the rain. Cole was riding beside Promise, as had been the case since the night Jake kissed her. Jake was determined he wasn't going to make the same mistake twice, so he avoided temptation. His willpower eluded him every time he was around her, and he knew he was asking for trouble anytime he went near that wagon. Since she was on very friendly terms with Cole, he'd assigned him the task of staying with her at all times. Cole was the one sleeping under her wagon and Jake stayed away from camp as much as possible. When he needed a fresh horse, he would ride into camp, change horses, slap some meat on a biscuit and take it with him as he rode. He even slept in his saddle. But no matter how he tried, she remained on his mind.

Today was the first day he wouldn't be able to avoid her. They would be crossing the river, and it was his responsibility to make sure every person knew what to expect, and how to respond if there were problems. He'd just ridden back to tell Shorty they would be making camp after they crossed the river, but once he reached the wagon, he heard shots from behind him. He yelled for Cole to get Promise inside the wagon with Shorty and to stay with them.

Jake rode fast to the front of the herd, which was difficult since the cattle were bolting in every direction. He breathed a sigh of relief when he saw Harm riding toward him. He'd feared that he might have been the target.

"They shot the Judas steer," Harm yelled above the noise.

"Were they taking shots at you?" Jake asked.

"I'm not sure, but I was faster than the steer. I almost went after them, but I figured that was what they wanted."

Jake figured they planned to stampede the cattle, hoping his men would give chase and leave Promise vulnerable. He felt like his men were sitting ducks, and there was little he could do about it. If he gave chase, the killers would see him coming and move on. On the positive side, the killers had to stay a good distance away, hidden so they didn't become targets. "Let's get these cattle under control. This close to the river, we could have some real problems if they don't settle down," Jake told him.

"Yeah, and the river is high and moving fast," Harm replied.

They neared the river and Jake left three men at the front of the herd so he could ride back to the wagons. "Shorty, we're ready to start crossing, so get the wagons to the bank and stay close to Promise."

Promise stuck her head through the opening. "Mr. McBride, was someone shot?"

He'd noticed she still called him Mr. McBride. She was on a first-name basis with all the other men, including Cole, and that rankled him. "Just a steer."

He directed his attention back to Shorty. "Shorty, see that she gets a man's shirt and holster. When we get to the river, I want her on a horse so she can cross with the remuda." He knew the river would be the best place for the killers to get to Promise if they had decided to forget the money and kill her, because his men would be focused on getting the cattle across.

"Sure will, boss."

His eyes slid back to Promise. "Put you hair up under the hat and wear the holster." He rode closer to her and handed her his bandanna. "Put this around your neck like some of the men wear theirs. Can you swim?"

"I'm not sure." The set of his square jaw told her he had too much on his mind right now to trouble him with questions she wanted to ask. Questions about why he had ignored her since that night in the wagon when he'd kissed her. He hadn't so much as spoken to her in days, and she'd lost sleep trying to figure out why. She'd enjoyed his kiss . . . more than enjoyed it, but he'd obviously decided it was a mistake. His actions told her he didn't want to be around her, so she certainly wasn't going to throw herself at him. She told herself to face the fact that his feelings didn't run as deep as her own.

Jake pulled Cole aside and spoke quietly with him for a few minutes before he rode away to talk to the other men. River crossings were always dangerous; it wasn't uncommon for men and cattle to drown, and he didn't need the added pressure of killers lurking about, trying to pick them off one at a time. He wanted every man to get across that river in one piece. When they'd crossed the river in the Panhandle, he'd discovered four of his men couldn't swim. Two almost drowned, but he'd managed to pull one to shore, and Cole saved the other man. Since this was going to be a more dangerous crossing, considering the fast current, he wanted to keep the cattle in a tight line, no more than ten across. It would take longer to cross, but it'd be safer for men and animals. Cattle could be swept away, or if they spooked, a multitude of things could go awry. The men needed to be alert and stay calm. He wanted to be everywhere at the same time, but he knew his attention would be on Promise, no matter what.

There were eighty horses in the remuda, and he planned to have several men riding with them, along with Promise. It would be necessary for some of the men to make several trips across the river. He wasn't happy about that, but he didn't have a choice. When he spoke to the men, he asked for volunteers, and to a man, each one volunteered, including the ones who couldn't swim. There wasn't a man on this drive lacking in guts and determination. He'd make sure they received a nice bonus when they made it to Wyoming.

Spotting Rodriguez, he reined in to talk to him. "I'm going to have Promise cross with the remuda. I know you will be with your horses, so stay close to her. I figure the three of us can keep her safe."

"*Si*. Can the señorita swim?"

"I don't think she knows for sure, but I want men around her that can."

"I will stay close," Rodriguez promised.

Before they could take the wagons across they had to distribute the weight evenly between them. Hearing Jake's discussion with Shorty about the weight of the wagons, Promise said, "If you need to leave the trunks behind, please do so. I know they are very heavy, and I don't want to put the animals in danger."

"We won't need to do that, we're just moving some things to the other wagons," Jake replied. He gazed at her outfit. Just as he'd instructed, she was wearing the gear he'd requested. Even in that getup, she looked beautiful. Hopefully, at a distance she would pass for a young man, because up close, she for darn sure wouldn't fool anyone. "I want you to get your paintings and drawings out so I can strap them on top of the wagon. They have a better chance of staying dry up there."

She couldn't believe he'd even thought of her drawings at a time like this. He had many more important things to think about. "You don't need to go to the trouble."

"No trouble, just pull them out."

Promise hurriedly scrambled into the wagon to retrieve her work. Jake carefully wrapped them in the canvas that Shorty used for the tent, and tied the bundle on top of the wagon.

"Thank you for taking the time to do this, Mr. McBride." She was grateful her work might be spared from the water, particularly the drawings of him.

Jake kept his eyes fixed on his task. "This is probably the only thing that might stay dry." Once the bundle was secured, he explained the plans for crossing. "I want you in the middle of the horses. Cole, Rodriguez, and I will be right beside you at all times."

She wasn't fearful for herself, she was worried about him—about the men, the animals, everything. "Is crossing this river very dangerous?" she asked. She was near tears, but not out of fear. She hated the tension between them and his cool attitude. If there was one thing she'd learned about Jake McBride, it was that he was a passionate man.

"It's always dangerous for the cattle when the water is moving this fast. But the remuda will cross after the cattle, so you don't have to worry." He turned and mounted Preacher. "Ride Stubborn, since you're used to him, and he's dependable in water."

"Prince."

Jake looked at her and arched his brow. "Prince?"

She smiled. "You told me I could name him, so his name is Prince. He's a wonderful animal, and Stubborn just doesn't fit."

In spite of the seriousness of the situation, Jake chuckled. "Prince it is," he said before he rode away.

Riding back to point position, Jake slowly led the way

into the river. Longhorns were unpredictable creatures, so it didn't come as a surprise when one cow panicked in the fast current and was in danger of drowning. Jake pulled his rope from his saddle and tossed it around its horns. With the rope secured to the pommel, Jake felt Preacher struggling with the panicked animal. Slipping out of the saddle to lighten the load for his horse, Jake held on tight to Preacher's reins. He swam beside his horse with his knife between his teeth in case he had to cut the rope and let the cow go. He wasn't going to lose Preacher, no matter what. Exhausting minutes passed before they were able to gain purchase on the river bottom. Once ashore, they pulled the cow to the bank, leaving it and his horse winded from the exertion. After catching his breath, he jumped back into the saddle and rode back into the river.

The crossing proved to be as difficult as Jake feared. Billy was one of the young men who couldn't swim, and he was swept from his panicked horse. The fast-moving current pushed him into a longhorn, causing a nasty deep gash in his side. Jake reached him before he went under, pulled him across his saddle, and got him to shore. After leaving Billy in the care of one of his men, Jake rode back into the river. It took a long time to get the cattle across, and he'd lost some, but not as many as he could have.

The wagons crossed without incident, and Shorty started tending Billy. The three men who couldn't swim stayed with Shorty and Billy while the rest of the men started back to help with the horses.

Cole and Rodriguez were waiting to cross with Promise in the midst of the remuda. Jake and the rest of the men were halfway across the river when he turned to make sure his men were not having problems, and he saw Indians out of the corner of his eye. He counted eight warriors, and they were just several yards from where he'd left Shorty with Billy. There were three other men with Shorty, but they were not the best shots. He told the men beside him to continue on to the other side, and he turned Preacher back toward the Indians. The men wanted to go back with him, but Jake was adamant they get to the other side. He told them no matter what happened they were to protect Promise. He had a feeling the Indians weren't the only unwanted visitors watching. "Tell Cole to stay where he is." Jake knew Cole well enough to know he would be inclined to cross the river to help him out.

Just as he reached the shore, Shorty yelled, "Boss, you go ahead and protect that gal. We can handle these braves!"

"I'll see what's on their mind, and maybe we can get out of this without a fight." The warriors were slowly moving closer, and Jake instructed Shorty and the men to pull their rifles out, but not to take a shot unless he pulled his weapon.

"Boss, what if they don't understand English?"

"They'll understand enough." Jake rode toward the Indians.

"What is that crazy fool doing?" Cole asked when the men reached the other side of the river.

"He said for you to stay put," Ty replied.

"Is there anyone in this godforsaken territory that isn't dogging us?" Harm asked.

Cole was torn. He didn't know if he could sit there and watch as his friend rode alone toward the Indians.

Promise's heart was pounding as she watched Jake's progress toward the impressive warriors. The artist in her was mesmerized by their fearsome appearance, from the feathers hanging from their long, dark hair, to their bare chests, down to their knee-high moccasins. When her gaze drifted back to the imposing man facing the warriors, she found him equally magnificent. His bronze skin was nearly as dark as the braves', but that was where the similarities ended. Next to Jake's large muscled frame, the warriors looked more like boys.

All afternoon she'd watched him save men and cattle in the fast-moving river. He had to be exhausted, but he showed no signs of slowing down. She knew the moment he'd spotted the Indians. Without hesitation, he'd turned Preacher around and headed back to shore. She'd never expected him to confront the Indians alone. His courage didn't surprise her, but she quickly asked God to stay by his side. Still, she didn't think she could sit there and do nothing to help him. There was no doubt in her mind that the men were staying with her because of Jake's instructions. "Shouldn't we go help him?" she whispered.

"He told us to wait," Rodriguez answered. "He has a plan. The men across the river are ready."

Though Rodriguez sounded confident, his words didn't calm her pounding heart. Her eyes darted to Shorty and the men on the opposite bank as they trained their rifles on the Indians, and Jake's back.

Everyone watched in silence as Jake stopped a few feet from the eight braves. When one brave moved forward from the group, Promise could hear her own heart thumping. The expression on the faces of the men beside her indicated they were as frightened for Jake as she was. "Please don't stay here for me. Go help him."

"If we cross the river now, they might see it as a threatening move." Cole hoped that explanation calmed her because it wasn't helping him at all.

As the minutes passed, everyone remained motionless, waiting . . . waiting. Surprisingly, even the cattle across the river seemed silent for the first time in weeks. In the quiet, they could easily hear Jake's deep voice reverberating across the water. While they couldn't make out his words, it was clear he was communicating with the brave. His tone indicated the interaction was not a friendly one. After a lengthy exchange of words, the lead brave appeared clearly aggrieved about something, if the motion of his lance was any indication. As he spoke, he jabbed his weapon in the air with every word. Jake's tone was brusque as he shook his head from side to side, obviously saying no. The brave was not receptive. Even from across the river they could hear his angry, clipped response. Jake's hand moved to the butt of his pistol. Everyone held their breath as the men behind Jake lowered their heads to their rifles and took aim. Jake spoke again, and this time the braves turned to confer with each other. Within seconds, heads started nodding in agreement.

Jake turned his horse around, and amazingly, two of the warriors rode peacefully beside him, back toward the men with their rifles pointed directly at them. Separating three steers from the herd, Jake said a few more words to the warriors before they rode away with the steers in tow. The men kept their eyes on the departing Indians, but Promise's eyes were on Jake as he made his way back across the river.

When he stopped in front of them, she searched his face for any sign of fear, but saw nothing other than his familiar determined expression.

"Comanche?" Cole asked.

"Yeah."

"What was all that jabbering about?"

"Their people are starving. We made a trade," Jake answered calmly.

"Free passage for three steers?" Cole asked.

"Something like that. Let's get these horses across. The current is getting worse." What he left unsaid was what the braves had really wanted, and they weren't happy they did not get their way.

Cole knew Jake didn't want to discuss the situation with the Comanche braves. He also noticed Jake scanning the area behind them.

Jake tried to keep his concern from showing. The braves had told him they saw the white men following them, and they were the same men who attacked the wagon train and killed everyone but Promise. They said Promise shot two of the killers, but she hadn't killed them. When the killers spotted the Indians, they rode away. The Indians were going to make sure no one was left alive that day, but they saw Jake and feared he wasn't alone. When they saw Jake ride away with Promise, they knew she was still alive. Jake figured the only reason they hadn't attacked them was they were outnumbered. What he couldn't tell Cole in front of Promise was that the leader demanded he turn the woman with the "sun hair" over to him. When Jake refused, the brave became angry, and Jake fully anticipated a challenge. Jake wasn't a man to tell a lie, but he'd told the brave that he'd made Promise his woman, and he didn't share. He offered three steers in lieu of Promise, and demanded their word they wouldn't attack or steal more cattle. They were appeased for the moment, but Jake had a feeling the lead brave wasn't going to take no for an answer when it came to Promise.

Chapter Thirteen

It looked like they were going to get the horses across the river without incident, but then one horse started losing the battle against the rapid current. The horse slammed into Promise's horse, causing Prince to panic. Struggling to stay in the saddle, Promise gripped the saddle horn, trying desperately to keep her seat until Prince calmed. Jake was closest to her, and quickly moved Preacher against the panicked horse and easily plucked her from the saddle. After settling her in front of him, he said, "Hold on to the reins." When she had control of his horse, Jake slipped out of the saddle and swam to Prince. Once he managed to get in the saddle, he was able to get the frightened horse under control before he could be swept downstream. Within minutes, they all made it across the river without injury or loss.

After the incident with the Comanche, Jake was tempted to continue a few more miles, but everyone was so exhausted he decided it was best to camp where they were. He figured this was as good a place as any to confront the braves if they came back for Promise.

* * *

While everyone was making preparations for the night, Jake walked to the cook's wagon and told Shorty to give him a bottle of whiskey. When Shorty handed him a bottle, he added, "Grab a few bottles so every man can have a full cup with their dinner tonight. They've earned it." A little whiskey could also go a long way to keep the men happy after such a harrowing day. He grabbed three cups before leading Preacher and Prince to the makeshift corral Ty was constructing. Cole and Rodriguez were unsaddling their horses, and Jake poured a good portion of whiskey for them.

After Cole took a long swig, he asked Jake, "What was all the head shaking about when you were talking to those Comanche?"

"They wanted Promise."

"I sort of figured that's what they had in mind, with all that blond hair of hers. That's why you kept insisting she wear a hat?"

"One of the reasons," Jake admitted.

"They got a raw deal accepting three steers instead of holding out for her," Cole mused.

"*Sí*, I'm surprised they gave up so easily," Rodriguez added.

"I'm not so sure they have. I tried to convince them that she belonged to me." Jake's eyes automatically shifted to Promise leaning over to stir something in a pot. She was still wearing the hat and holster.

Cole followed the direction of Jake's gaze. "Your woman, huh?"

Jake glanced at Cole and saw his eyes were on Promise. "Yeah, it seemed like the thing to say at the time. But I don't think it makes much of a difference to them. The lead warrior wanted her for himself. I have a feeling we'll see them again."

"You speak Comanche?" Rodriguez asked.

"Very little, but they spoke some English, some Spanish. We managed to muddle through. They've seen the killers on our tail."

"Not surprising," Cole stated.

"Why do you think they are waiting?" Rodriguez asked.

"They're like most cowards, they'll wait until everything is in their favor." Thinking about what Promise told him about a big man holding her down, Jake added, "They won't confront men with guns who can fight back."

"They want to catch us spread out, like the last time, or maybe they'll do something to distract us," Cole added.

"That's the way I see it," Jake confirmed. "We need to keep alert and our minds on business."

Cole wondered if he was really saying *he* should keep his mind off Promise. If that wasn't the pot calling the kettle black, he didn't know what was. Using his better judgment, he left what was on his mind unsaid. He was having a difficult time understanding his friend. Jake said he wasn't interested in Promise, and he'd even assigned Cole to watch after her. But half the time Jake looked like he wanted to strangle him when he was near her.

"Too bad the Indians didn't go after the killers and save us the trouble," Rodriguez said.

Jake nodded. "Yeah."

After dinner, Jake took another bottle of whiskey and before he questioned what he was about to do, he walked directly to Promise's wagon. Shorty had told him she was in a dither about something and indicated she would feel more comfortable talking to Jake. He hadn't planned on going inside that wagon again. Though he'd almost come to accept the fact that he had little self-control when it came to her. As he tapped on the wagon, he reminded himself he was stronger than his desires. "Can I come in?"

Stunned to hear Jake's voice, Promise opened the flap and smiled. "Certainly."

He held up the whiskey bottle and two cups as he stepped into the wagon. "I thought you might like a night-cap to help you sleep tonight. It's been a long day, and sometimes it's difficult to settle down after such an experience."

He eyed her as he sat on the pallet and poured her a cupful. When he held it out to her he noticed she'd changed and was wearing a nightgown and robe. And she sure smelled good. He'd already had more whiskey than he'd had in months, but he filled himself another cup. "Have you ever had whiskey?"

"I couldn't say, but I would doubt it," she replied, taking a seat across from him. She wondered if he meant it was difficult to settle down after crossing a river, or watching him face down eight braves.

"Go slow. I wouldn't want a drunken woman on my hands." He clinked her cup with his and said, "A safe trip the rest of the way."

"A safe trip," she repeated as she stared into his black eyes. As soon as she took a small sip she started coughing. "That's awful!"

Laughing, Jake said, "You have to develop a taste."

His eyes looked bloodshot and she wondered if he'd already had too much of the liquid fire. "How many cups have you had?"

He chuckled, thinking that might be the reason he was sitting here against his better judgment since he was already feeling the effects of the alcohol. Whiskey brave. "I'm not drunk, if that's what you're thinking."

He might not be drunk, but she wondered why he was in her wagon when he had avoided her for days. She swirled the contents in the cup, trying to find something to say other than what she was thinking. Each time she looked at him all she could think about was the kiss they'd shared, and his bare chest, and how it felt when she touched his muscles.

"Something on your mind?"

"Shorty said that your lead steer was shot." That question was one of the many things troubling her. "He said that it was the most valuable one."

"Yeah, he was."

"Why is it called the Judas steer?"

"Because he will lead the cattle to slaughter."

She nodded, and raised the cup to her lips again. This time she didn't cough. Jake might be right, it didn't taste too bad this time. "I know you won't understand, but I want to replace that steer."

Jake looked at her a long moment before he spoke. No wonder she looked so tired; she was carrying a lot of weight on those small shoulders. She was feeling guilty about everything that had happened. "There's no need. We'll lose more cattle before we get to where we're going."

"What will you do for a lead steer?"

"Another one will take the lead," he said simply. "Now finish your whiskey so you can get some rest tonight. No arguments."

Slowly she continued to sip her whiskey and was amazed at how quickly she felt the effects. A feeling of warmth came over her, and her mind started to relax. She stared at Jake, thinking he was so handsome he took her breath away.

Jake watched as the whiskey worked its magic. Just as he expected, a good stiff drink would keep her from thinking of her troubles for a while.

Once she finished the whiskey, she set the cup aside and stretched out on her pallet. She looked at him with those large amber eyes. "Are you married, Mr. McBride?"

No question, she was feeling the effects of the alcohol.

Her cheeks had a nice rosy glow, and she looked more relaxed than he'd ever seen her. "No, ma'am."

His deep warm voice soothed her more than the whiskey. "Have you ever been married?"

"No, ma'am."

She leaned up on her elbow and gave him a quizzical look. "Haven't you ever wanted to marry?"

Her question made him think of his brother and his new wife. He couldn't say he'd ever thought of settling down before he'd seen the kind of relationship Colt and Victoria shared. The love between them was palpable, and it stirred something inside of him. He knew he wanted to feel that kind of love for a woman. Hopefully, with a woman like Victoria. And the thought of his new nephews made him smile. He'd never seen two more active boys in his life, and so full of questions. In the short time he'd spent with them, they'd given him grief every time he said *hell's bells,* as was his habit. They told him their ma would wash his mouth out with soap. "Being a U.S. Marshal isn't a life for a married man. I didn't spend too much time in one place."

"And now you plan to stay in Wyoming?"

He watched her struggle to keep her eyes open. "That's my plan."

"And you're not a marshal now," she whispered.

"No, I'm not a marshal." He thought he might have some regrets when he gave up his job, but he didn't. In all truth, he couldn't wait to get home to Wyoming and start ranching with his brother. Before he left Wyoming he picked out the spot where he would build his home. Colt had told him he could share his home, but he figured his brother needed privacy with his wife and adopted sons. Someday, if he was as lucky as his brother, he'd fill his new home with sons and daughters, but that day was a long way off. It'd be a while before he was ready to settle down. He glanced at Promise to see why she had quit asking questions. She'd drifted off to sleep with a smile on her face, looking like an angel.

The days were long, and the men were getting testy waiting for something to happen. Jake was more wary than ever. There were too many reasons for those killers to want to get to Promise, and he knew they weren't finished. Every day he reminded the men not to be complacent even though there was no visible threat. After two weeks of calm, it came as a surprise when Shorty spotted three men riding into camp.

Cole had just returned to camp for his dinner when Shorty handed him a plate and asked, "You see them hombres riding in?"

"Yep, I see them. Tell Promise to stay in the wagon. I'm sure Jake will be coming in soon."

"I don't know about that. That dang fool is working himself into an early grave," Shorty groused.

Rodriguez walked up behind them. Overhearing their conversation, he said, "The señor is aware of those men." He'd seen Jake at the corral and when they'd spotted the men riding in, Jake told Rodriguez to stay near the camp.

Cole didn't know if Rodriguez was expressing an opinion, or if he knew for sure Jake was on his way, but he didn't have time to ask. "Let them do the talking. Shorty, stay close to Promise's wagon, and post Will at the back." Will wasn't the best with a pistol, but not many men were in camp, so he had to use what was available. He noticed Rodriguez positioned himself nearby with his rifle next to him.

The three men stopped several yards short of the fire. "Mind if we come in for some coffee?" one of the men asked.

"Come ahead," Cole responded easily. He noted their

appearance: dusty, and their boots were caked with mud as though they'd been out in the elements for a while.

The men dismounted, tied their horses to some brush, and walked into camp. "That coffee sure smells good," one of them said.

"Pour yourselves some," Cole told them, pointing to the cups Shorty had placed on the rocks around the fire.

Rodriguez noticed the men didn't care for their horses before they helped themselves to the coffee. Out of the corner of his eye he saw Jake approach their mounts and examine each one.

"We ran out of coffee a few days back," one of the men said.

"We make sure we always have plenty," Cole replied. "Been on the trail long?"

"Yeah, we're headed to Denver."

"From?" Cole asked pointedly.

"Wherever we could find work," one man responded evasively.

The men tried to disguise their interest in their surroundings, but Cole watched them surveying the camp. It seemed to him their eyes lingered overlong on the wagons. He glanced at Promise's wagon and saw that the light was very low and he couldn't see her inside, so he breathed a bit easier.

"Planning on working in Denver?" Cole asked in a conversational tone.

"Yeah, we're going to work for Schott's outfit," the man answered. "You headed to Denver?"

"No," Cole answered.

"Well, where are you headed? If you're going in that general direction, maybe we could sign on for a while," the man suggested.

Jake heard the question when he walked up behind the

strangers. "We're headed to Wyoming, and I don't take on men once the drive starts."

"Now that don't seem too friendly," the man stated.

Moving to the fire, Jake poured himself a cup of coffee and squatted down with one long leg stretched out in front of him. After he took a drink of his coffee, his dark eyes pierced the man. "Who said I was friendly?"

The man doing the talking eyed Jake. "We're experienced cattle punchers."

Cole noticed the muscle in Jake's cheek flexing and knew something about these men had set him off.

"You sure as hell don't know much about horses," Jake stated bluntly.

The man threw his coffee cup to the ground. "What the hell is that supposed to mean?"

Jake stood and faced him. "It means your horses have been run to death, and you come in my camp to help yourselves to my coffee without taking the time to loosen their girths, much less take their saddles off and water them. And you think I'd trust you with my animals?"

Seeing the deadly glint in Jake's eyes, the man backed up a step. "We were waiting to see if this was going to be a friendly camp before we asked to stay and rest them."

The man's excuse rang hollow in Jake's estimation, but he didn't want to see any horse run to death. "You can rest your horses for the night, but you best be gone from here at first light, or I'll kick your ass to Denver for abusing your animals."

Cole could see in the man's eyes that he was about to go for his gun. "That would be the last mistake you ever make," he said, his revolver pointed at the man's companions.

The man looked from Jake to Cole and threw his hands in the air. "We don't want no trouble. We appreciate the hot

coffee, and we'll rest our animals and take off in the morn."
The three hurried off to unsaddle their horses.

"Did they see Promise?" Jake asked.

"No. Shorty is over there in front of her wagon and Will
is at the back. The light is low, and I expect Shorty told her
to stay down."

"I sure would like to know if she recognizes these
hombres," Jake said.

"But if she came out here, they'd see for sure she's a
woman even if she's wearing that holster and hat," Cole
replied.

"It would be a pleasure for me to take care of them,"
Rodriguez said, making a slicing gesture with his thumb
across his throat. "For mistreating their animals," he added
with a wicked smile.

Jake grinned at him. "Tempting as that is, I think we'll
pass on that option." He glanced over at their horses.
"Those horses are in bad shape. I never could figure out
how a man would mistreat the only thing that is between
him and disaster in this country." He found himself re-
thinking Rodriguez's offer. "I got a look at their hoofprints.
They're not the horses I was tracking when Will was shot.
In Dodge I learned there were about twelve to fifteen men
who rode together. They could be part of that group, and
they may be taking turns dogging us."

"Makes sense," Cole said. "We could follow them when
they leave in the morning."

"I plan to be right behind them," Jake replied. "They'll
make better time, but we'll make sure they are headed to
Denver. After we are a few miles east of Denver, a couple
of us can ride in for supplies. If by then Promise remembers where she was headed, we can take her with us."

Once the three strangers settled around the fire for the
night, Jake walked to Promise's wagon and spoke to Will

and Shorty. "You two get some rest. I'll stay by Promise's wagon."

"Will do, boss. Just holler if you need us."

"Shorty, those three will be staying the night to rest their horses. I told them to take off at first light," Jake said.

"I don't like the looks of them," Shorty replied.

"If their animals didn't need some rest, I would have run them out of here tonight. Sleep with your gun at the ready."

When Shorty walked away, Jake tapped on the wagon. "Do you have everything you need for the night?" he asked quietly.

"Yes," she whispered.

"Those men will be leaving at dawn," he explained. "I want you to stay in the wagon until they leave." Just then, he realized she might need to take care of her personal needs. "Ah . . . if you need to . . . take a walk . . . I can lift you out the back of the wagon so you'll be out of sight," he offered.

She wasn't about to leave the wagon until those men were out of camp. "I will be fine until those men are gone."

"I'll be right outside your wagon."

In the middle of the night the canvas flap was tossed open, and Promise scooted to the rear of the wagon, scared to death. Fortunately, with the light from the moon she was able to make out Jake's large form climbing inside before she could scream.

He leaned over and whispered in her ear. "Shhh, stay down behind me, darlin'."

Silently, she moved behind him as he positioned himself behind the flap. He pulled his revolver and cocked the hammer. She could barely hear the footsteps nearing the wagon over the rapid beating of her own heart. When the canvas moved a few scant inches, the barrel of Jake's .45 was pointing directly at a man's forehead.

"You looking to get killed?" Jake asked in a deadly calm voice.

The man took a step back from the wagon with his hands in the air. "I was lookin' for the chuck wagon . . . for some water," he responded nervously.

Jake stepped from the wagon, his pistol still aimed at the man. "Does this look like the chuck wagon to you?"

"It's dark. I can't see too good in the dark." The man gulped. "We just wanted some water before we left."

Jake motioned with his pistol for the man to keep walking. "Before my finger gets tired, I suggest you three get out of my camp."

The man kept backing up until he was abruptly halted by the solid barrel of Shorty's shotgun.

Jake saw the other two men waiting by their horses. He debated whether to take them to Denver himself, but he didn't want to be away from Promise that long. There was also the off chance these men could be just who they said they were, and not involved with killing those people on the wagon train. His gut told him that they were involved, but that could have more to do with the way they treated their horses. Experience told him that men who didn't value their animals were generally no-accounts. "Now get on your horses and ride out of here before I change my mind."

Chapter Fourteen

"I'm glad those skunks are gone," Shorty said, watching the three men ride off.

Jake agreed with Shorty, but it crossed his mind that he might see them again. At least they were headed in the right direction if Denver was their destination. Skeptical as he was, he figured they'd live a lot longer if they were telling the truth about jobs awaiting them in Denver.

"You think they're part of that group of killers?" Shorty asked.

"I couldn't prove it, but my short hairs tell me they are. I sure didn't think that cowboy was looking for water, and they could have been thinking about robbing us."

"If they were cowpunchers, I'll eat my hat," Shorty added. "They're saddle bums, and I'd bet they ain't never seen an honest day's work."

Jake couldn't argue with Shorty's assessment. "I wouldn't take that wager." He glanced back at the wagon, wondering why Promise hadn't come out now that the strangers were gone. Sensing something was wrong, he headed toward the wagon.

He tapped lightly on the wagon. "You can come out if

you want, honey." Not hearing a response, he threw the flap back and looked inside. "Promise?"

Promise was sitting in the corner of the wagon with a strange look on her pale face.

Moving inside, Jake kneeled in front of her. What he saw frightened him. Her skin was damp with perspiration and her eyes were expressionless. "Sweetheart, are you okay?"

She blinked several times, trying to bring Jake's face into focus. "My name is Parker Promise Sinclair. My brother and I were headed to Denver from Charleston, South Carolina. He's the man . . . in the painting . . . the young man that you . . . buried. His name is Matthew." By this time, tears were falling faster than she could wipe them away, but she continued as though she had to say it all at once or she might forget. "My aunt and uncle, John and Nettie Hollister, have a ranch in Denver, and we were going to stay with them for a while. Matthew and I were traveling with families from Charleston. All of those people have family living on land my uncle John gave them." She stopped abruptly. Her thoughts were on all of the people in Denver waiting on their loved ones who would never arrive. She dropped her face in her hands. Through her sobs, she said, "Mr. Vincent said God would protect us from evil."

"Aw, honey. I'm sorry." He moved beside her and lifted her to his lap, just as he did the last time she cried. He wasn't sure how long he sat there, but the front of his shirt was wet before he felt her muscles go limp. He pulled his bandanna from his pocket and dried her face, much the same way he did Preacher's. "Do you want to tell me about it?" he asked cautiously.

"Earlier, when you cocked your pistol, I started remembering things. It seemed like the whole journey came back to me at one time. I remembered"—her voice cracked, but she continued—"the men we saw watching us were the ones who attacked. Then . . . well, you know what happened." She halted, and stared off into space for a few moments.

While he was happy she'd regained her memory, it was tearing his guts out to see what it was doing to her. It had to be overwhelming for her. "Sweetheart, I'm sorry about your brother." He didn't know which was worse, to lose a husband or a brother. Either way, she was in a lot of pain.

"Matthew and I were very close." She clutched his shirt in her fingers. "Matthew had a sweetheart in Charleston that he didn't want to leave. My parents were killed in a carriage accident a little over a year ago, and I wanted to visit my aunt and uncle."

Jake didn't know what to say, so he kissed the top of her head, wanting so badly to take the pain from her.

"I remember I told Aunt Nettie in a letter that Matthew would probably turn right around and go back to Charleston after we arrived in Denver. I think he only agreed to go because he knew that was what I wanted. I missed my mother and father so much, and I wanted to see our family. Now I know why I wrote in the journal that I was going to tell him to go back home. It was because he couldn't hide his misery from me."

Jake remembered reading what she wrote in her journal. At the time, he was surprised she planned to tell her husband to go back home after they arrived in Colorado. But the man wasn't her husband. Promise told him she didn't think she was married and she was right.

"I shouldn't have insisted we leave Charleston. He would be alive right now."

Jake wouldn't allow her to think along those lines. "Your brother made his own decision. Of course he wanted you to be happy. Any man worth his salt would have taken you to Denver to be with your family."

"But he would be with his sweetheart if I—"

Jake put his finger to her lips, stopping what she was

about to say. Her dull and lifeless eyes alarmed him. "Stop that right now. You are not responsible for anything that happened. Those men are responsible. Sometimes there are just no answers for things that happen, and this is one of those times."

She stared into his black eyes, wanting badly to believe he was right. But she knew her brother hadn't wanted to leave South Carolina, and she felt his death was her fault. What was she going to do without him? He was her best friend, and they had weathered everything together. Ten minutes earlier she hadn't even remembered she had a brother, and now she felt lost without him. "But why didn't God protect us, like Mr. Vincent said?"

He wished he had an answer for her. The leader of that wagon train should have had more sense than to travel without protection. It amazed him that the man had made that trip before with no guns and lived to do it again. "Darlin', sometimes there are no answers to those questions. But I think God wants men to protect their loved ones. That's where I would have parted company with Mr. Vincent. He should have made sure every man was armed."

"They didn't believe in carrying weapons of any kind. Matthew and I argued over this. I told him to tell Mr. Vincent we would bring a rifle, but my brother wouldn't go against his conditions. I hid my pistol . . . I didn't even tell Matthew I had it with me. He would have been angry with me. But Father taught me to shoot, and I knew he would have wanted me to have a weapon on such a journey. Matthew would not listen to reason." Now she wondered if Matthew had perhaps accepted Mr. Vincent's terms in the hopes that she would change her mind about leaving.

Jake wondered how her father had been able to teach her the importance of self-protection, but not her brother.

"You did the right thing. I don't mean to criticize your brother, but he should have been armed too. This is wild country and everyone should be prepared to protect themselves."

"I can't remember Matthew getting shot. I do remember I shot my pistol when I got away from that big man." After a moment she added, "God help me, but I hope I shot whoever it was that killed Matthew."

Jake squeezed her to him. "I hope so too. If you didn't, I promise you I will find them once I get these cattle to Wyoming."

She looked up at him. "Will you?"

He could tell she wanted to believe him. "I give you my word. I'll find them."

Her eyes filled with unshed tears again. "Thank you," she whispered. She was thinking about her brother, buried out in the middle of nowhere, and she knew what her parents would want. "I will have to take Matthew back to Sinclair Hall for a proper burial. You'll have to draw a map for my uncle so we will know where to find his grave."

"Where is Sinclair Hall?" Jake asked.

"It's our home in Charleston."

He was curious if her uncle would want to make a trip across country to bury her brother in South Carolina.

"I guess we know where I belong now," she said. "I'm sure it will be a relief to get me off your hands."

He didn't feel relief, but he was glad to know where she belonged. "We will be near Denver in a couple of days. I'll ride ahead and find your aunt and uncle and come back to get you." He wanted to make sure it was safe to take her to her uncle's ranch.

"Thank you." She scooted off his lap and picked up her hat. "I know you need to get the cattle moving."

"I'm in no hurry if you'd like for me to stay for a while."

"I'll be fine," she replied, determined that she would no longer be a burden.

He didn't want to leave her alone, but he wasn't sure what she really wanted. She might need some private time to handle her grief in her own way. "Do you want to ride in the wagon today?"

"If you don't mind, I would rather ride Prince." Watching the cattle gave her something to do, and she hoped it would help to keep her mind off of her brother. "I wonder what happened to Hero. I remember giving him some peppermints that morning." Her eyes widened with alarm. "You really didn't find any animals that day? They didn't kill him, did they?"

Jake gripped her shoulders and lowered his face to hers so he could look her in the eyes. "I wouldn't lie to you. I didn't find any animals. If they didn't take him, he might have run off."

She shook her head. "He wouldn't have run off. I watched Hero foal, and we were inseparable. My father used to say he had to keep watch so I didn't let him sleep with me because he followed me around like a puppy."

Jake smiled at that. She sounded so sure that he didn't argue with her, even though he'd seen many horses take off at the sound of gunfire. But he'd also seen firsthand she had a way with horses, and he figured she would know how her horse would respond under the circumstances. It was difficult to believe any man would kill a fine animal like that, yet there was one thing he knew for certain: Killers were unpredictable.

Jake left her to make preparations to get back on the trail. She watched him walk away from the wagon. Her time with Jake McBride would soon be coming to an end, and that saddened her even more. She reminded herself she should not be sad, she should be grateful that he had found her. She was alive because of him.

Chapter Fifteen

Sheriff Gilbert used his pipe to point to the coffee warming on the stove. "Help yourself, if you like it strong."

"Thanks." Jake poured himself a cup and walked across the sheriff's office to look out the window in the direction of the saloon.

"Denver's growing, and we have a lot of strangers coming and going every day. It's hard to keep track of them all," Gilbert said.

"I heard in Dodge these men travel in a group as large as twelve, maybe fifteen men," Jake told him. He hadn't divulged the reason he was in Denver until he figured out if the sheriff was a man he could trust.

"Sorry. Unless they are men we've arrested, I couldn't tell you about most of the people passing through." He took a puff on his pipe and let it rest in the corner of his mouth. "You're welcome to ask my deputies when they get back, but they'll probably tell you the same thing."

"Three men rode into my camp a few days ago saying they were going to work for the Schott Ranch. Is he hiring?" Jake asked.

"He has a huge spread, and he's always looking for men, so I wouldn't be surprised."

Jake turned to face the older, graying man. "Is Schott as tough as I've heard?"

"You've heard right. Old man Schott is hard as nails, and he's not a man to mess with. He runs almost everything around here. Not many can compete with him. If you're needing supplies, you can buy everything you need at Schott's Mercantile."

Interesting the sheriff hadn't mentioned Parsons' Mercantile, and he wondered if the doc's brother was still in business. "Where's the Hollister ranch?"

The sheriff arched a bushy eyebrow at him. "You're asking about a lot of people in my town."

"Yep."

When Jake had introduced himself, the sheriff hadn't let on that he'd heard of him before. As a U.S. Marshal, Jake McBride's reputation was well-known. He wondered about his interest in the people he was asking about. When Jake didn't offer an explanation, he said, "Hollister's ranch is about eight miles east of town. Schott's spread shares a boundary with Hollister's on the west side."

Jake finished his coffee. "Thanks."

Shoving back his chair, the sheriff pushed to his feet and walked around his desk to look out the window. "I don't know what your business is here, but I've heard your name, and I know you were a U.S. Marshal, not a trail boss."

"Yep."

The sheriff chewed on the pipe for a minute before he said, "Well, whatever your business, keep it legal. I'm getting ready to retire at the end of the month, and I don't want any headaches before then. You'd best be careful if you have dealings with Schott. He has a lot of people on his payroll."

"What about the law?" Jake asked bluntly.

Gilbert gave him a hard look. "He's never owned me.

But to tell you the truth, I think a couple of my deputies are a mite too friendly with him and his men, if you know what I mean. They'll deny it, of course, but there it is. Schott knows how to grease the palms that need greasing." He turned and opened a tobacco tin on his desk and started to refill his pipe. "I can't prove anything, of course. I'm inclined to retire while I'm still breathing. Maybe I'll regret that decision to ignore what's going on, maybe not."

Jake felt a decent man would regret that decision, but it wasn't up to him to save the sheriff's soul. "Thanks for the information."

The sheriff watched as Jake walked out the door and across the street to the telegraph office.

After sending his telegram to Colt, Jake rented a room at the hotel before heading to the saloon. Since it was Saturday, he figured it would be the perfect time to pick up information at the saloon, as it was sure to be filled with drinking cowboys. He wanted to make sure the killers weren't lurking around in Denver so he could feel confident Promise would be safe once he left her on her uncle's ranch. The killers were aware the wagon train was going to Denver, but he didn't know if they knew she was headed to the Hollister ranch.

On his way to the saloon he spotted Parsons' Mercantile and made a detour. In Dodge City, Doc Parsons had told him he could trust his brother to be a good source of information. After introducing himself to the doc's brother, Clarke, he asked about the drifters in town.

"They haven't been in here, but I've seen them before. If they are the same men you are looking for, then I should tell you they are a rough-looking gang."

"Your brother mentioned that Schott is trying to buy you out."

"Yeah, but that's not going to happen. A lot of folks

around here are loyal to me, and they don't like the way he does business."

"What about the sheriff? Is he honest?"

"Honest enough, I reckon. At least he used to be. Since he decided to retire, he turns a blind eye to most of what's going on around here." Clarke leaned over the counter and lowered his voice so the other customers couldn't hear what he was saying. "But don't trust those deputies further than you can throw them, particularly Potter."

Jake nodded. "How about John Hollister?"

"A good man. I guess you could say he's my best customer. If it wasn't for his business, I might not be able to make it against Schott."

"I have two men who will be coming in soon for supplies," Jake said, handing him a list of the items he needed. He'd told Ty and Wes to make sure they went to Parsons' Mercantile.

"I'll have everything ready for them, and thank you for your business, Mr. McBride."

"Your brother did me a favor in Dodge. He's a good man."

Clarke's expression turned serious. "There's no way you could know, of course, but I got a telegram from a friend of his in Dodge a few weeks ago. Some men beat him up pretty bad. It's going to take some time for him to get back on his feet."

Jake was sorry to hear this news. "Do they know who did it?"

"No, they don't. It doesn't make sense to me that someone would have a grudge against him. He's a man who's done nothing but help people all his life."

Jake agreed with that assessment. "Give him my best when you write to him."

"I surely will. You take care, and watch your back."

As Jake left the store he saw Ty and Wes coming down the street. He waited to greet them and let them know he

would be spending the night in Denver. As Jake walked
to the saloon, his mind was on Doc Parsons. Why would
anyone attack a town doctor? He wondered if his beating
had something to do with Promise. It seemed like a strange
coincidence that this happened right after the doc saw her.
Once again, his brother's words came to mind. *There are
no coincidences.* If the killers had been dogging him since
he was in Dodge, they more than likely saw the doc with
him. They probably figured out the doc had tended the
woman they'd left for dead.

Entering the saloon, Jake posted himself at the bar and
listened to conversations going on around him. Generally,
his size alone kept people at arm's length. He took full
advantage of his intimidating demeanor tonight. He
wanted to listen and not engage in meaningless conversation. It didn't take him long to learn that most of the men
at the poker tables worked for Schott. He'd seen several
men coming and going, but not the three men who had
ridden into his camp.

He intentionally kept his business in Denver to himself.
While Sheriff Gilbert was a likable man, he'd confessed
that he basically didn't trust his own deputies, so it seemed
wise to keep quiet. He watched as a man with a star on
his chest came through the doors and took a seat at one of
the tables. He was on real friendly terms with the men from
Schott's ranch. After several beers, Jake hadn't heard or
seen anything suspicious, so he returned to the hotel.

Placing his holster on the bedpost, he kicked off his
boots and stretched out on the bed. He felt guilty about the
luxury of sleeping in a bed when Promise was sleeping on
a pallet in a wagon. He'd told Shorty and Cole to keep a
close eye on her, but not to ply her with questions. She had

a lot to work out, and she needed time to grieve for her brother.

He planned to leave early in the morning and arrive at Hollister's ranch by dawn. He hated to be the one to tell them about the death of their nephew, but it would be easier on Promise if they knew the details before they saw her. Promise told him the other families lived on Hollister's ranch, so he planned to see them too. Knowing the next day was going to bring a lot of sorrow to so many people made it difficult for him to find sleep that night.

By dawn Jake was already on the Hollister ranch, and was pleased to see that it was a sizable spread. The home was almost as large as his brother's, and it eased his mind some to know that Hollister appeared to have the means and the men to protect Promise.

Reining in at the porch, he hadn't dismounted when the front door opened and five children came barreling out and started peppering him with questions. Their rapid-fire inquisition reminded him of his brother's boys. Close on their heels was an older woman, waving a dishcloth in the air and clucking like a mother hen. "Children, remember your manners, and get yourselves back inside to get ready for church."

The children stared at Jake, wanting badly to know who he was, but the woman pulled the oldest boy by the ear to emphasize her instructions. "Inside, and wake your parents. Tell them it's time for church."

"Yes, ma'am," the boy said, turning around to march the unruly group back into the house.

"Ben, that's my son, and his wife, stay here as much as they stay at their own home. They tell me it's because they like to visit with me. But they are not fooling me with that nonsense. I know it's because they need a break from those kids. I apologize, but my grandchildren forget their manners at times," she said.

Jake chuckled. "I'm sure my mother said the same thing about me a time or two." He heard a hint of a Southern accent that sounded a bit like Promise.

"I'm here to see John Hollister. My name is Jake McBride."

"Come in, come in." Preceding him through the door, she pointed down the long hall. "My husband's in the kitchen having his last cup of coffee. Can I get you some?"

"That sounds good. I haven't had a cup this morning."

"Would you like to go into the kitchen with me, or would you prefer to wait in John's study?"

"I'd prefer the kitchen," he said, thinking it might be easier for them to be together to hear what he had to say.

Jake followed her through the house to the kitchen, located at the end of the hallway. John Hollister stood when he spotted Jake behind his wife. After she introduced them, the men shook hands and Hollister asked, "How can I help you, Mr. McBride?"

"Honey, give the man time to have his coffee before you start acting like the children and chew his ears off," his wife said.

"You must be Nettie," Jake said.

She smiled at him. "I certainly am. Have we met before?"

"No, ma'am, Promise told me about you."

Her smile grew wider. "You know my niece? What good fortune! You can see her soon since she is due to arrive any day now."

"I know," Jake said. "I need to talk to both of you about Promise."

John heard the seriousness in Jake's voice. "Have a seat, Mr. McBride."

"Jake, please," he replied, taking a seat at the table as Nettie pushed a cup of coffee in front of him.

Sensing Jake wasn't there to deliver good news, John thought he might want to hear what he had to say without his wife present. "Honey, would you tell Ben to go ahead to church with the kids? We'll stay behind today."

When Nettie left the room, John asked, "Is Promise okay?"

"Yes," Jake said, "but I'm afraid I have sad news for you. Her brother is dead." He quickly told John about the murders before Nettie returned.

John told Nettie the news when she came back to the kitchen, and by the time Jake had answered all of their questions, Nettie was in her husband's arms, crying.

"I'm sorry I had to deliver such bad news, but I wanted to make sure those killers weren't in Denver before I bring Promise to your ranch."

John cleared his throat before he spoke. "I appreciate what you've done for our niece, Jake, and for taking care of Matthew and those folks."

Nettie wiped her tears and looked at Jake. "Are you sure my niece is okay now?"

"Her memory came back slowly, but she remembers everything but Matthew getting killed. I don't think she is ready to remember that right now."

Nettie nodded her head in agreement. "You are probably right. They were the closest siblings I have ever seen."

"I need to go see the families of the other people on the wagon train. Promise said they farmed on your land."

"No one would sell land to them when they came here," John said.

"Why is that?"

"Two reasons. They're farmers, not ranchers, and everyone was too afraid of Schott to sell to them. I don't particularly care for the way Schott tries to muscle people around, and I have enough land that a few acres wasn't going to hurt me."

"They don't associate with folks outside their own community, and that makes some around here uncomfortable," Nettie added. "They have turned that plot of land into their own little town, so it's not necessary for them to buy many of their goods from the merchants in Denver. That's another point of contention with Schott."

Jake liked the way Nettie Hollister spoke her mind. She made it clear she was no fan of Schott's.

"Jake, I'll ride out there with you to see those folks, if you don't mind," John offered.

"I don't mind. It might make it easier since they know you. I want them to know their families had a decent burial," Jake said. "We found some personal items that belonged to those folks, which I'll bring back with me." Jake told him how the women had sewn money in their dresses. "Of course, I don't know what family owned what, so their children will have to sort that out."

"That won't be a problem. Those families share everything," Nettie said tearfully.

After visiting the families, John and Jake were on the way back to the ranch, and John took that opportunity to ask Jake more questions. "Jake, from what you've said, Promise could still be in danger. If you have no objections I would like to take some of my men and go with you to get her."

Without Mrs. Hollister around, Jake was more comfortable speaking freely. He didn't want her to worry about Promise's safety. "You're right, I think she is still in danger, and I have no problem with you coming along. Actually, I was going to bring some of my men along when we return to your ranch. If you have men to spare to ride with us, my men can keep the cattle moving."

"I expect those men still want the money," John said.

"Yes, you can count on it, and they know one person lived and can identify them. I also have reason to believe the killers have been in Denver recently." Jake told him about the conversation with Clarke Parsons.

"Did you know Promise's father was the governor of South Carolina? I'm certain that was the reason Matthew was upset if someone revealed their identity to those men. Matthew was naturally wary of strangers, with good reason. They are a very wealthy family."

Jake had heard of Governor Sinclair, but he hadn't linked the name when Promise said her parents were killed. "She didn't mention it, and I didn't make the connection."

"Sinclair was a very wealthy man before he became governor. They have a sizable estate in South Carolina, as well as an estate in New Orleans."

Jake was stunned. Even though Promise was traveling with a good sum of money, she didn't act like a woman of means.

"You're surprised?" Hollister asked, seeing the look on Jake's face.

"I never expected she came from that kind of background."

"Promise has always surprised everyone in that way. She's an adventurous young woman, never conforming like most well-bred young women. Her father taught her how to ride and shoot, and she was much better than her brother at both. God rest his soul. Being the only male, Matthew was groomed to manage the estates, and Promise was sent to boarding school." Hollister paused and smiled as though a pleasant memory had just skipped across his mind. He gave a little shake of his head, trying to keep control of his emotions. "That little gal spent more of her time trying to find a way to get back home than she did learning. Her father decided to allow her to try things her way with painting, but her mother wanted her to find a husband and settle down. Promise would have none of that. She started painting portraits for their friends, and in no time she was receiving a sizable sum for her work. Her father was so proud of her, proud of both of them. Promise and Matthew were as different as night and day, but like Nettie told you, they were very close, and she has to be devastated."

Jake gleaned much about Promise's character listening to her uncle. She was even more amazing than he'd realized. "She told me she would have to take her brother home for burial."

"I'm sure she'll want him buried at Sinclair Hall with her mother and father," Hollister said.

It wasn't that Jake didn't understand their desire to have the family buried together, but it would be a dangerous undertaking. Then he thought about his own brothers, and he knew he would do the same thing. "That'll be a long, hard trip. I didn't want to say anything in front of Mrs. Hollister, but we encountered Comanche on the way."

"I was worried about the wagon train running into Indians on their way to Denver, but I certainly never expected anything like what happened," Hollister admitted.

"One of the Comanche braves wanted Promise, and to be honest, I'm surprised they haven't been back."

Hollister was beginning to see how much Jake had done for his niece. He thanked God a man like Jake McBride had found her. "How did you deal with them?"

"I gave them three steers, but I have to admit I expected them to come back with a war party."

"We'll take plenty of men with us in the morning and a wagon. If you prefer to stay with your drive, I'm sure we will be fine," Hollister said.

Jake shook his head. "I saw what those killers did to the folks on that wagon train. I'll be riding back with you to get Promise and on our way back, I'll ride to Denver. I'm planning on staying there a day or two to see if those men show up again. If they aren't around, I'll head to Wyoming, and once the cattle are delivered to the ranch, I plan to come back to find them."

Hollister heard the conviction in his voice. He liked Jake. Too bad his niece didn't want to marry. If she ever changed her mind, she'd be lucky to find a man with half the character of Jake McBride. "Tell me about your ranch and your family."

They discussed the ranch and his brothers for the remainder of the ride back to Hollister's ranch.

Chapter Sixteen

McBride Cattle Ranch
Promise, Wyoming

Victoria moved up behind her husband and slipped her arms around his waist. He'd been on the porch, leaning against a column for the longest time, puffing on his cigar. It wasn't like Colt to be idle for long, so she knew he was troubled. Ever since the telegram from Jake arrived, he'd been unusually quiet. Jake said he'd run into some problems in Denver, but he hadn't explained what kind of trouble, a clear indication he figured he could handle the situation. That didn't prevent his older brother from worrying about him.

"Honey, why don't you go to Denver and see about Jake?"

Colt threw his cigar to the ground and turned around to take his wife in his arms. "I don't want to leave you, especially now." If his beautiful new wife weren't pregnant with their first child, he would already be halfway to Denver.

"Stop being an overprotective husband. I won't have

this baby for months, and I'm in good health, so there's nothing to worry about. Besides, you know Mrs. Wellington and Bartholomew would be happy to stay with me while you are gone." Mrs. Wellington was like a mother to Victoria, and Bartholomew worked an adjacent farm that Victoria had inherited.

Colt hugged her close to his chest. He couldn't help but worry about her. She was the most precious thing in his life. "The doc told you to take it easy because he said you can expect a large babe since I was the largest baby he ever delivered."

"I'll be fine. You don't have to worry," she assured him.

He kissed the top of her head. "Have I told you today how much I love you?"

"I don't think you have," she said, smiling. "And don't change the subject."

"If Jake needs me, he will let me know." He wished he felt as confident as he tried to sound, but uncertainty was nagging at him. "Cole is with him, so I'm sure they can handle any problems." Jake and Cole had shared many dangerous situations—at least that is what he kept telling himself.

"I hate to see you worry."

"I think another piece of your cherry pie would take my mind off my problems."

She didn't think she was going to change his mind. "Let me call the boys and all three of you can have some pie." Before she pulled away, she stood on her tiptoes and kissed him.

"Maybe I'll forget about the pie." He leaned over and picked her up and carried her inside. "Are you sure you're eating enough? You don't feel any heavier." He worried about her carrying this baby because she was such a small woman.

She ran her fingers through the black curls on his neck. "Honey, I'm only three to four months along, so give me time. Before long you'll be teasing about not being able to lift me. The boys told me they want a sister. What do you want?" Thanks to Jake's pull with the judge, they had officially adopted the twins, Cade and Cody, immediately after they were married. Victoria had taken the twins from a burning saloon when they were young, and while she'd never adopted them, they had been a family ever since. When Colt met Victoria, he not only fell in love with her, he'd lost his heart to those boys. They were his boys, and he saw no difference from the love he felt for them and the babe his wife now carried.

His dark eyes bore into hers. "I want a healthy baby and wife. That's why I think you should let me hire someone to help you out around here. You do all the cooking and cleaning, not to mention taking care of the boys. Then you make those bag things for the ladies."

She yanked on a lock of his hair and laughed. "They are called reticules. And I'll have you know I just received some orders from Paris, France."

"That makes my point. Helen can't be of much help to you now." Helen was the woman who had been with him since he was a boy, and she was getting too old to handle the work in such a large house.

"We are doing fine. I have Mrs. Wagner to help with the sewing," she replied. She would never complain, because she enjoyed cooking, cleaning, and taking care of the boys and her new husband. She'd never dreamed that her life would be so fulfilling and happy. She considered herself very blessed.

"When the baby comes, we'll need the help anyway, so we might as well find someone now," he went on, just as if he hadn't heard her objections.

"Maybe Jake will bring home a wife," she teased.

He gave her a horrified look. "On a cattle drive? I think not. Most men think women are the kiss of death on a cattle drive." At the mention of the cattle drive, he started worrying about his brother again.

He wasn't quick enough to hide his concern from Victoria. She took his face between her hands and looked into his eyes. "Honey, go to Denver. You can come back with the drive. It won't take that long, and I will be fine. If you don't go you are going to worry until you see Jake."

He didn't want to miss one day of Victoria's pregnancy, but she was right, he would worry until he saw Jake rein in at the ranch. Still he hesitated. "I don't want to be away from you. This is our first baby—"

"You'll have many more months left to watch me waddle around when you get back." She didn't want him to leave; she hated the thought of him being away for any length of time. But if something happened to his brother because she tried to keep him with her, she would never forgive herself. "Now why don't you get everything ready so you can leave in the morning?"

Victoria awoke in the middle of the night to find Colt standing at the window. "What is it?" she whispered.

He turned and walked back to bed. "I'm sorry I woke you." He crawled under the covers and pulled her to him. "Go back to sleep."

"Colt, tell me what's wrong," she urged.

"I can't explain it. I just have a feeling that Jake . . . that something is wrong with him."

She'd never met a man like her husband. He was strong, courageous, and he never expressed fear of anything. It was troublesome to see him so worried. "You are going to Denver in the morning, no arguments. If you don't, then I'm going," she threatened.

Colt chuckled at her threat. "I can't have you traveling to Denver in your condition."

"Then you'll go?" she asked tentatively.

"Honey, it would take me several days to get there."

"The sooner you leave, the sooner you'll get home."

Colt was silent for so long that Victoria nudged him. "I'll go if you promise me that you will not go anywhere alone and Mrs. Wellington will stay here while I'm gone. I'll have T. J. fetch her and Bartholomew in the morning."

She kissed his cheek. "Do you think Mrs. Wellington would let me go anywhere alone? Just like you, she'll watch my every move."

He couldn't disagree. Mrs. Wellington was more protective than he was, and Bartholomew was almost as bad. "Is it so terrible to have a husband who loves you so much?"

She snuggled into his muscled chest. She felt so blessed to have this man love her. She could never thank God enough for giving her so much. "I love my husband as much. So promise me you will be careful. Why don't you take T. J. with you?"

He would do anything to keep her from worrying about him while he was away. "I need T. J. to stay here and run the ranch. But if it keeps you from worrying, I'll take Strait with me."

"I'd worry less if you took more men."

"There's no need for you to worry about me. Besides, Strait is a better shot that any two of the other men," he said. "Now give your husband some kisses, since they are going to have to last me for some time."

Once T. J. brought Mrs. Wellington and Bartholomew to the ranch the next morning, Colt was ready to leave.

He lifted Cade and Cody into his arms. "Boys, I expect

you to look after your mother. Help her out and take care of Bandit."

Hearing his name, Bandit jumped up on Colt's leg. He knew his master was leaving and he was already whining. Victoria had the urge to whine like the dog but kept a smile pasted on her face.

Colt lowered the boys to the ground and rubbed Bandit's ears. "You have to stay here and look after the family, boy." He knew the dog would follow him, so he looked at the twins and said, "Take Bandit inside so he doesn't run after me."

Cade and Cody hugged him again. "Good-bye, Pa," they said in unison.

"You will come back, won't you?" Cody asked.

His question stunned Colt. He bent down on one knee and looked Cody in the eye. "Why would you ask such a thing?"

Cody gazed at the ground, avoiding Colt's eyes. His brother spoke for him. "Well, our other pa left us, but we was just babies and didn't know him."

Colt pulled them into his arms. His voice was thick with emotion when he spoke. "I'm your pa now. Don't you two know that nothing is more important to me than you and your mother? There are times when I will have to leave, but don't you ever doubt that I will always come back. Nothing on earth could keep me from you."

"Ain't Bandit 'portant to you?" Cade asked.

Colt smiled and ruffled his blond hair. "Of course Bandit is included."

"What about Razor?" Cody asked.

"Razor too." Leave it up to them to ask about his horse. He knew they were just trying to delay his departure, but he didn't mind. He wanted them to know how important they were to him. "Your new little brother or sister too," he said before they could ask.

Knowing the boys were likely to complete the list of names of everyone on the ranch, Victoria said, "Your pa has to leave, so take Bandit inside."

"Okay," they said together, and hugged Colt's neck one more time.

"They are going to miss you," Victoria said. She tried in vain to blink away her unshed tears. "I will too."

Colt lifted her off the ground and hugged her to him. "Not as much as I will miss you."

He kissed her passionately, and she clung to him when his lips left hers. He whispered in her ear, "And you better stop kissing me like that or I will never leave."

"Take care, husband, and come back in one piece."

"I plan to," he said, chuckling. "I know how you like all of my parts."

Strait rode up to the porch holding Razor by the reins, along with two spare horses. Colt had told him they would be riding hard to Denver. "You ready to go, boss?"

"Yep, if my wife will let go of me," Colt teased, gazing into Victoria's watery sky-blue eyes. "I'll send a telegram when I arrive."

She could barely speak for the huge lump in her throat. "Okay," she finally uttered. They hadn't been apart since they had married, and she didn't want him to know how much she would worry until she heard from him.

Colt understood how she felt because he felt the same way. He leaned down to kiss her one more time. "Don't worry about me, honey. I'll be back before you miss me."

"Impossible."

"I won't ride back with the cattle drive. That would take too long," he said, winking at her.

They stared at each other for a minute without saying a word, but in that moment they said everything.

Chapter Seventeen

"Uncle John!" Promise ran from her wagon into her uncle's outstretched arms.

"Oh, honey, it's so good to see you!" he exclaimed.

"Matthew . . ." She started crying as soon as she said her brother's name.

Her uncle patted her back and said softly, "I know, I know. Jake told me everything."

At the mention of Jake's name she turned to him. "Thank you, Mr. McBride, for bringing my uncle."

Jake thought she looked even thinner than before he left. "No thanks necessary."

She glanced from him to the men surrounding her uncle.

Seeing her puzzled expression, Jake said, "Your uncle wanted to have some extra men for the ride back to the ranch. Nothing to worry about."

"He's right, honey," her uncle said. "No need to worry. I didn't want Jake to take his men from the cattle drive since they need to get to Wyoming. Now let me introduce you to my men."

Jake watched as Hollister's men stared wide-eyed at Promise. It'd probably been a long time since they'd seen a woman as beautiful as Promise. If ever. Still, he didn't care for the way they were gawking. If they were his men, he would have told them in no uncertain terms to keep their bug eyes in their heads, but Hollister seemed oblivious. As much as he wanted to say something, it wasn't his place. He decided it was in their best interest if he just walked away.

As Hollister's men transferred Promise's belongings to the wagon they'd brought with them, Jake had a chance to talk to Cole and Shorty.

"I'm going back with Hollister, so I'll catch up to you as soon as I can. We're making good time, so just keep moving," Jake told them.

"It helps that the rain finally stopped," Cole said.

"I'll be sorry to see that little gal go," Shorty said, surprising both Jake and Cole.

Seeing their stunned expressions, Shorty added, "I got used to the help, that's all. And she's a darn sight better to look at than your ugly faces all the time!"

"The way Hollister's men are hovering around, she won't lack for suitors in Denver," Jake said. Every time he glanced in her direction, two or three of Hollister's men were on her heels.

"Sounds like that 'green-eyed monster jealousy' to me. What do you think, Shorty?" Cole teased.

Jake wasn't sure, but it sounded like Cole actually quoted Shakespeare.

Shorty eyed Jake. "Sure does," he agreed, smacking Jake on the back. "He'll be beatin' them off with a stick before he gets back to Denver."

That rankled Jake. He had no interest in Promise in that way; he only wanted to see her safe. "All I care about is making sure they can be trusted."

"Have they worked for Hollister long?" Cole asked, serious again.

"Yeah. I just hope no one can offer them enough money to do something stupid," Jake replied.

"Let's just hope they can handle trouble," Shorty pointed out.

Shorty was right. Problem was, he couldn't get out of his mind what he'd seen that day when he found Promise. He wasn't sure a good man like Hollister would be prepared for the kind of men who'd killed all of those people.

"Are you leaving in the morning?" Shorty asked.

"Yeah, I plan to spend some more time in Denver. I didn't find those three men who rode into camp, and I'd like to see if they are working for Schott. I'll catch up with you in a few days."

As Jake rode out to talk to the men guarding the cattle, Promise and her uncle were sitting alone, talking quietly. He was glad her uncle had decided to accompany him, since talking to family would probably do her a world of good. Jake thought about what Hollister told him about the kind of life she'd led in South Carolina. Who would ever expect a lady of privilege to be out on the Great Plains, working cattle and trading bullets with killers? Now, that was a woman full of contradictions.

When it was time to depart, Promise became very emotional saying good-bye to Shorty. She'd grown very fond of him over the weeks on the trail.

"I'll be staying for a time in Wyoming on the McBride place, so you know where to find me if you ever need anything," Shorty told her.

Promise tried to hold back her tears as she hugged him again. "I'll write to you, and if you are ever in Denver, please come to visit."

Shorty held her by her shoulders. "Here now, no crying. You're going to be just fine with your family."

"Thank you for everything," she said. She handed him the hat and holster he'd given her to wear.

"Now you keep those. I know Jake would want you to wear them until you get to where you are going."

Cole and Rodriguez rode to camp so they could say their good-byes.

She looked at both of them and tears started flowing again. These men who had risked their lives to protect her had become her friends. "Thank you so much." She hugged them both.

"It was a pleasure meeting you. If you ever want to see Wyoming, you know where to reach me," Cole said.

"I'd like that," she answered. "And you both have a place to stay if you come back to Denver."

"I am sorry to see you go. You added much beauty to our dreary surroundings. Keep practicing with the rope, señorita. You will soon be an expert vaquero," Rodriguez told her.

"Thank you for teaching me. I will continue to practice."

She felt a light grip on her elbow and turned to see Jake standing beside her holding Prince's reins.

Jake heard her tell Cole she would like to see him again, and he knew Cole would like nothing better. "We better get going."

Outside of Denver, Jake told Hollister he was going to make a detour into town while the rest of them rode on to the ranch.

"Nettie will have my hide if you don't come to dinner. I'm sure she will have a feast now that Promise is here," Hollister said.

"I'm just going to talk to the sheriff again. I won't be long." Jake didn't want to say he planned to see if the killers were in Denver.

"We will wait dinner for you, Mr. McBride." She wasn't ready to say good-bye to Jake. It had been difficult enough for her to say good-bye to his men. She'd become very attached to him, and it made her sad to think she might never see him again.

Jake gazed at her a moment, trying to read the expression on her face. "I'll be there."

"We'll have apple pie." Shorty had told her Jake loved apple pie so much that he'd had a lady in Texas bake six pies before they left on the drive.

Jake lifted his hat, resettled it on his head, and gave her a wink. "Then nothing could keep me away."

Chapter Eighteen

Instead of wasting his time talking to the sheriff again, Jake went straight to see Clarke Parsons.

"I didn't expect to see you back so soon," Clarke said, shaking Jake's hand.

Jake asked him again about the drifters that had been in town earlier. And to Jake's surprise, it was his lucky day. Clarke told him the same men rode in earlier, and they'd purchased some things that they couldn't find in Schott's store.

"How many?" Jake asked.

"I'd say about a dozen," Clarke replied.

Jake glanced down and saw some peppermints alongside boxes of Gypsy Queen cigarettes. He pointed to the cigarettes. "Anyone purchase these today?"

Clarke looked at him like he was a soothsayer. "Why, yes, one of those drifters bought a box."

"Describe him."

"A tall man, almost as tall as you, but heavy, and ugly, real ugly, with a huge honker and scraggly blond hair hanging down his back," Clarke answered. "Is he one of the men you are looking for?"

"Might be."

"They are in the saloon right now. If you need help, remember what I told you. Don't look to the sheriff or his deputies, especially Potter," Clarke whispered.

Jake nodded. "Understood." He picked up two boxes of the peppermints, remembering that Promise mentioned she liked to give them to her horse. She might like to give some to Stubborn . . . Prince, he reminded himself. He knew Prince could not take the place of her horse, but he'd planned to give him to her since she'd grown so fond of the animal. He figured she'd lost enough. Picking up another box of peppermints for Preacher, Jake paid Clarke and headed to the saloon.

After tying Preacher's reins to the rail in front of the saloon, Jake reached into his shirt pocket and pulled out one box of peppermints. He put a few pieces of candy in his palm and held them to Preacher's mouth. He chuckled at his horse's reaction as he made quick work of the peppermints. "Don't take my fingers with them." An unusual noise from one of the horses tied to the rail caught his attention. It sounded like the horse was in pain, so Jake walked around to see which horse was raising such a ruckus. He found the horse tied to the rail four horses down from Preacher. Talk about his lucky day. He couldn't believe his eyes; four white stockings and a white star on his forehead. This was the horse in Promise's drawing. It was Hero, or his identical twin. He checked him out to see if something was wrong with him. After looking him over, he could tell he'd been ridden hard, and he looked thin and worn out, but otherwise okay. Jake moved to his head to get another look at the white star on his forehead. No doubt about it, this was Promise's horse. "Is your name Hero?" he asked. The horse nibbled at Jake's pocket. "So you smell the peppermints, huh?" He pulled the peppermints out and the horse nearly took the box from him. After giving him a handful, Jake decided to take the horse to the livery to be fed and to get a good brushing. He grabbed his reins along with Preacher's and headed to the livery. He guessed he could be accused of being a horse thief, but since it was a stolen horse, he couldn't see anyone turning him in.

Twenty minutes later Jake was at the bar in the saloon, ordering a beer. He didn't have much time before he had to get back to Hollister's for dinner, but he wanted to get a good look at the men Clarke told him about. Several of the tables were filled, but he immediately spotted the man Clarke had described. Clarke's description was apt; the man was as big as his brother Colt, but where Colt was all muscle, this man was just slovenly and soft. And ugly— real ugly. He decided he'd bless him with the moniker Big Ugly. Yep, that suited him. Was this the man who'd held Promise down? He couldn't allow himself to dwell on that thought, or he would take him outside and beat the daylights out of him.

Looking into the mirror behind the bar, Jake watched everyone in the room. It was easy to spot the drifters from the hardworking cowboys. The man to Big Ugly's right was the deputy he'd seen the last time he was in the saloon. It looked like Big Ugly and the deputy were well acquainted. Every time he glanced at Big Ugly, he found him looking his way.

Forced to order another beer that he didn't really want just to watch the patrons a little longer, Jake put coins on the bar, never taking his eyes off the swinging doors as men came and went. He kept waiting for one of them to turn around and walk back in to say he didn't have a horse. Whoever was riding Hero obviously hadn't left yet. Since he had to get back to the ranch, he decided before he left he'd let Big Ugly know he was on to him. Nearing the table, he saw Big Ugly reach for a cigarette from a Gypsy Queen box.

Jake leaned over and tapped the box of cigarettes with his finger. "I found a box just like that where someone waited to take a shot at one of my men."

All movement stopped at the table, every set of eyes moved to Jake. Big Ugly looked up at Jake and smirked. "You got a reason for telling us this sad tale?"

"Yeah, I got a reason. I expect you might know who shot my man," Jake retorted, picking up the box of cigarettes. His black eyes bore into Big Ugly's beady ones, as he twirled the cigarette package in one hand. "Only a coward lies in wait to shoot a man."

"Mister, I don't know you, and a lot of men smoke those cigarettes," Big Ugly said.

Jake tossed the cigarette box in the air, and it landed with a thud on the table directly in front of Big Ugly. "You'll be seeing me around."

The deputy stood and faced Jake. "Mister, you need to get on about your business." Jake gave the deputy a look that had him backing up and second-guessing his interference. "I got to get to work," he said to no one in particular before hightailing it out the door.

Jake waited a heartbeat to see if Big Ugly was going to get up, but when he didn't, he turned to walk out the door.

The deputy was standing outside the saloon looking in both directions as if he'd lost something. He glanced at Jake before he walked back into the saloon.

Through the window, Jake watched the deputy walk directly to Big Ugly and whisper something in his ear.

"I didn't take him," Big Ugly responded to the deputy, loud enough for Jake to hear outside the saloon.

"Well who the hell took him?" the deputy asked, looking around the table.

No one at the table said a word. They all shrugged their shoulders.

Definitely my lucky day. He turned from the window and waited for the deputy. "I have the horse," Jake said once the deputy walked back through the swinging doors. "He belongs to a friend of mine, so I took him to the livery. Are you the one abusing that animal?"

The deputy glanced at Jake, trying to decide the best way to handle him. He figured this was the U.S. Marshal the sheriff had mentioned, so he decided to be cordial. "I bought that horse a few weeks back," he responded in a friendly tone.

Jake pointed to the saloon. "Did you buy it from your big ugly friend in there?"

"Nope, I bought him from a stranger in town," the deputy replied.

"You have a bill of sale?"

"Yeah, I got one, but I don't have it on me."

"Leave it at the sheriff's office. I'll be in to look at it tomorrow."

"Why don't you have your friend who you think owns the horse come in and have a look?" the deputy asked.

Jake smiled, but it wasn't a friendly smile. "Because I'm doing it for him."

"It'll be in the sheriff's office."

Jake knew he was lying, and as badly as he wanted to, he couldn't just take the horse. Horse thieving was a hanging offense. There was the remote possibility the deputy was telling the truth. "Make sure it is."

The deputy watched Jake walk across the street to the sheriff's office before he walked back into the saloon.

"Sheriff, what do you know about that big black horse that your deputy says he purchased a few weeks ago from a stranger?" Jake asked.

"Not much. He told me the same thing. I didn't see the

man he bought it from; he just came in with the horse one day. Why do you ask?"

"The horse is stolen. He said he had a bill of sale and I want to see it. I'll be back tomorrow and he'd better have it, or all hell is going to rain down on that deputy," Jake promised.

"Can you prove it was stolen?"

"I sure can, and if he was in on the theft, he's in one hell of a lot of trouble. More than horse stealing," Jake responded, and stalked out of his office.

When he got to the livery, Hero was gone and the livery owner told him the deputy came to get him. Jake saddled Preacher and left for Hollister's ranch. He decided he wouldn't mention the horse to Promise right now. It would just upset her more, and he hoped he could get him back. He just hoped the deputy didn't take off with Hero now that he knew someone was questioning his rightful ownership.

Deep in thought on the way to Hollister's, Jake almost missed Preacher twitching his ears, alerting him that something was amiss. Jake looked around for what might be bothering Preacher and saw a man on horseback behind him. Thinking quickly, Jake rode to a copse of trees, waiting for the rider to get closer. He recognized the deputy and rode out to meet him.

"I've been trying to catch up with you," the deputy said.

Jake saw he was riding a different horse. "Why?"

"I have that bill of sale I wanted to show you." The deputy reined in and put his hand in his vest pocket.

It occurred to Jake that the deputy's horse wasn't winded or lathered, like he'd been riding to catch up to him. That wasn't a good sign. He'd been careless. His hand went to his gun. Too late. A blast came from the trees. *It might not be my lucky day after all*, was his last conscious thought.

A bullet slammed him in the chest, knocking him off Preacher, facedown into the dirt.

Big Ugly rode from the trees and holstered his gun. "You want to take his horse?"

The deputy dismounted, walked to Jake, and kicked him hard in the ribs to make sure he was dead. Preacher darted between Jake and the deputy and reared on his hind legs, barely missing the deputy's head. The deputy scrambled backward away from his dangerous hooves. "That's one crazy animal! Leave him here with the dead man. I don't want anyone else asking about another stolen horse."

Chapter Nineteen

Promise was peeling apples for the pie she was baking for Jake, and talking with her aunt, trying to keep her mind off saying good-bye to him. "I thought my cousins would be here with your grandchildren."

"I told them to give you the night to rest before they came to the house. Those grandchildren are a handful, and they're sure to ply you with a million questions." Nettie also wanted time alone with Promise, to give her time to talk privately if she wanted.

"I can't wait to see them," Promise replied.

"You will be seeing a lot of them since they spend more time here than they do at their own homes." Nettie noticed Promise made several trips to the window to look out. "Honey, what are you looking for?" she finally asked.

"Mr. McBride should have been here by now. He's been gone for hours," Promise replied.

Nettie walked over and put her arm around her niece. "Honey, now don't get yourself worked up. Something probably kept him in town longer than he expected. There's a man who can take care of himself if I've ever seen one."

"Something's wrong. I know it. I think Uncle John should have someone go look for him."

Her uncle walked into the kitchen in time to hear the last part of their conversation. "Who do you want to look for?"

"Mr. McBride. He should be here by now," Promise told him.

"It's not that late. We can delay dinner," he replied.

Promise shook her head. "I know Mr. McBride. He would be here by now if something wasn't wrong."

John glanced at his wife. He didn't want his niece to worry needlessly. She'd been through enough. "I guess I can ride to town and see what's keeping him, if that will put your mind at ease."

Promise grabbed her uncle's arm. "Please don't go alone." She was terrified she was going to lose the rest of her family.

John smiled down at her. "I'll take some men, honey, don't you worry."

Within minutes of leaving Promise and Nettie in the kitchen, Hollister and two of his men were riding toward Denver. Less than three miles from the ranch, they saw Jake's horse standing in the middle of the road. When they got closer they saw the horse nudging a body on the ground.

They jumped off their horses, and Hollister reached Jake as one of his men grabbed Preacher's reins to pull him away. Hollister knelt beside Jake and turned him over and saw the gunshot wound in his chest. Blood was still oozing out of the wound, leading Hollister to think Jake hadn't been lying there long. He felt for a pulse in his neck, not really expecting one. "He's alive . . . barely." Hollister took his bandanna out and stuffed it inside Jake's shirt over the wound.

"The ranch is closer than town," one of his men said.

Hollister hesitated, fearing Jake might not make it. Promise couldn't handle it if Jake died. Yet Jake deserved the best chance he could give him. "Let's get him across his horse."

It took the three of them to lift Jake across Preacher's saddle.

"Jeb, you go on to town, get the doctor and tell him to come quick," Hollister instructed.

Promise and Nettie were waiting on the front porch when the men rode in slowly. Promise jumped from her chair as soon as she recognized Jake's horse. Seeing Jake over Preacher's saddle, her hand flew to her mouth. "Oh no!"

Hollister jumped off his horse, yelling for another man to come help them lift Jake and carry him inside the house.

"Dear Lord, what happened, John?" Nettie asked, pulling the door open for them.

"We found him on the road," John explained. The three men struggled under Jake's weight, but they managed to get him inside. "Take him to the room at the back of the house. We'll never get him upstairs." John glanced at Promise. "One of my men has gone for the doctor, he'll be here soon, honey."

"Promise, help me heat water and get some bandages ready." When Promise didn't move, Nettie feared she was in shock. She touched her niece gently on the shoulder. "Honey, he needs us now. Let's do what we can." Taking her by the hand, she led Promise to the kitchen.

Once in the kitchen, Promise managed to get control of her fear. She tore a large sheet into strips while Nettie set some water to boil. "Shouldn't the doctor be here?" she asked her aunt.

"I'm sure he will be here soon," Nettie replied calmly. "Go ahead and take the bandages. I'll be there as soon as the water is hot."

Promise hurried to the back room, praying to God that

Jake would survive. As soon as she walked through the door, she saw him lying motionless. His shirt had been removed, and her uncle was holding a pillowcase against the wound. He looked up when she neared the bed, and the anguish on her face was unmistakable. "He's alive, honey."

Nettie entered the room with the water and placed it on the table by the bed. "Promise, do you want me to clean his wound, or would you prefer to?"

Looking at her aunt through her tears, Promise was grateful she had asked. She remembered the way Jake had cared for her. "Let me."

"John, why don't you remove his boots while I cover him so we can get those pants off him," Nettie said.

John gently tugged off Jake's boots. "He's going to be uncomfortable on this bed since he's at least a foot longer."

Nettie knew her husband was just trying to make conversation so Promise wouldn't think he was worried. "We'll pull a trunk in here and put it at the foot of the bed. I can add some quilts on top to make it more comfortable for him."

"That's why I married you, honey. You're the brains of this outfit." He glanced at Promise as she gently cleaned Jake's chest. The tears streaming down her cheeks broke his heart.

Nettie settled the sheet over Jake from the waist down, and then moved to the opposite side of the bed. "John, I've unbuckled his holster. Can you lift him a bit and I will pull it off?"

John gently lifted Jake's hip on one side, trying hard not to jostle him. Once Nettie slid the holster off, John removed his pants.

"I hear the door," Nettie said, hanging Jake's holster on the bedpost.

John walked to the hall and yelled, "Doc, we're in the back."

Doc Rawlings hurried into the room, acknowledging John and Nettie.

"This is my niece, Promise," John said.

Promise moved out of the way so he could tend to Jake.

The doc smiled at her. "I've heard all about you from your aunt and uncle." He leaned over and poked around the gaping hole in Jake's chest. "You've done a fine job of cleaning him up."

"Will he be okay?"

"That bullet has to come out." As he felt Jake's pulse, he looked him over, taking note of his muscled body. "But he looks as strong as an ox, and that's a good thing." He looked at the wound again before he started pulling the contents from his black bag. "That bullet is lodged very close to his heart. It could prove tricky getting it out."

Nettie glanced at Promise and saw she was clenching Jake's hand. "What can we do to help?"

"You've been doing it. You might get some whiskey while I go wash my hands."

"I'll get the whiskey," John said. When they reached the kitchen, John asked in a low voice, "Can you get that bullet out without killing him?"

"I didn't know how much I should say in front of Nettie and your niece, but it's going to be tough. It looks like it's just a hair's width from his heart. I can't say I hold out much hope."

Bracing his hands on the table, John hung his head. "Doc, do your best to save him. This man saved my niece's life, and I don't think she could handle it if he didn't make it."

"Is he her betrothed?"

"No, it's nothing like that. I'll tell you all about it when this is over."

The doctor patted John's shoulder. "I'll do my best. Now get that whiskey and let's get to it."

Returning to the room with the doctor, John inclined his head at his wife, hoping she understood he wanted Promise out of the room. "Honey, why don't you and Promise make some coffee for the doc? If we need you, I'll come get you."

Nettie could tell from her husband's grim expression that the doc was not confident Jake would survive. She placed her arm around Promise, urging her toward the door. "Come on, honey. Let the doc do his job. We have our own work to do."

Promise leaned over and kissed Jake's forehead. She silently asked God to watch over him before her aunt led her from the room.

After they made coffee and sandwiches, Nettie and Promise sat at the kitchen table drinking their third cup of coffee. Nettie tried to engage her in conversation, but Promise didn't seem to hear her. "Doc Rawlings is a good doctor. I'm sure he's seen difficult wounds before."

Finally, Promise turned her attention to her aunt. "Mr. McBride has done so much for me, and now he could die because of me."

"This is not your fault, honey, so don't you go thinking it is," her aunt said.

Promise's eyes filled with unshed tears. "Mr. McBride said the same thing to me when I wanted to leave the drive because he'd had nothing but trouble since he found me."

"And he was right," her aunt replied.

* * *

"Can you hold that light a little closer?" the doc asked John.

John moved the lamp an inch closer. "Any closer and I will singe your eyebrows."

"John, this bullet is about as close to his heart as it could get without making things worse. And I'm not as steady as I once was."

John was close enough to see the beads of perspiration on the doc's forehead. He didn't want him making a mistake on Jake. "You need a shot to steady yourself before you try to pull it out?"

The doc glanced at him over his glasses. "I think I do." He swiped his forehead with his shirtsleeve.

Setting the lamp aside, John poured two healthy glasses of whiskey and handed one to the doc. "Here's to steady hands," he said.

Nodding his agreement to the toast, the doc downed his whiskey in one gulp, took a deep breath, and pushed his sleeves above his elbows. He looked at John and said, "Grab the lamp." He pulled a bottle of chloroform out of his bag and handed it to John. "If he so much as twitches, put a small amount of this on a cloth and hold it over his mouth and nose. I don't want this big buck moving while I'm working."

Long minutes later, they had another shot of whiskey before John yelled to the women to bring them some coffee.

The women entered the bedroom, and Promise held out a cup of coffee to the doctor. "How is he?"

"I removed the bullet without hitting his heart, but it's too soon to tell. He's lost a lot of blood." He paused, noticing the terrified look on the young woman's face. He softened his abrupt bedside manner. "He's a strong man, and from the looks of him he's in good health, and that's in his favor."

John picked up the bottle of whiskey and poured some in the doc's coffee. "I think you need this after what you've been through."

"Enough of that now," Nettie scolded. "You two need to get something to eat."

"I'll stay with him," Promise said.

"He's likely to be out for a while. But if he should come around, don't let him move an inch," the doc said.

Promise sat in a chair next to Jake and held his hand while she watched his chest move up and down, fearful that he might stop breathing at any moment. Thinking of the many days they'd spent on the trail, she'd rarely seen him when he wasn't in motion. It was terrifying to see this larger-than-life man so still. What she wouldn't give right now just to see him open his eyes. She leaned over and gently stroked his cheek, thinking of the first time she saw him. At the time, she thought he was extremely handsome, albeit quite formidable. Before long, she realized there was much more to Jake McBride than his intimidating countenance. She recalled the many stories Shorty had told her about Jake, and she'd learned that Shorty had never exaggerated; they were all true. Jake was a man of integrity, admired by many, feared by some. In her mind no other man could ever measure up to him. She couldn't pinpoint the exact time when it happened, but somewhere on the trail she'd lost her heart to this man. He was one of a kind, and her life would never be the same if he died, whether he felt the same way about her or not. *Please take care of him, God. I couldn't bear to lose him too.* She leaned over and pressed her lips to his.

Chapter Twenty

Riding slowly at dusk, Colt and Strait heard the cattle before they saw them. Within minutes, a large herd of grazing cattle came into view. Colt felt certain that this was Jake's drive, and he caught sight of two men riding the perimeter. Colt could tell even at a distance that neither man was Jake, but one of them looked like Cole Becker. Colt's attention was diverted by a group of eight men riding toward Cole and the other cowboy.

Colt didn't like the looks of this face-off. "Strait, let's go join this party." When they reined in, every head turned to them. Colt gave an imperceptible nod in Cole's direction.

"Mister, I suggest you and your friend keep on riding," the leader of the group of eight said.

Colt gave him a hard look. "I didn't ask for your suggestions."

The man glared at Colt before turning his attention back to Cole. "I warned you drovers once. Mr. Schott doesn't want free grazers on his land."

"Like I told you before, we're on open range and we will be moving on in the morning. Not before," Cole responded with a hard edge to his voice.

"You work for Schott?" Colt asked. Colt had met Schott before.

"Yeah, we do. Mr. Schott owns the largest ranch in Colorado," the man replied. "What's it to you? You riding with this outfit?"

As a rancher, Colt understood how cattle grazing on open range could leave an area bare, but he also understood cattle had to eat. "Schott knows this is open range."

"Mr. Schott was here long before anyone else, and his cattle graze on this land, so that makes it Schott land. He don't tolerate free grazers."

"As the man told you, they are moving on in the morning," Colt said.

"You're wrong. They're moving on now," Schott's man replied.

"Maybe you lost some of your hearing. We'll be moving on in the morning," Cole said.

Colt watched intently to see if any of Schott's men were thinking about going for their guns. Seeing a few hands inch toward their holsters, Colt warned, "I wouldn't." He moved to Cole's side, with Strait following his lead.

The leader of the group wasn't sure he wanted to do battle with Colt. It was more than his size that intimidated him; he had a hard edge, indicating he was a tough hombre who could back up his words. "You heard what we said. We'll be back with more men," he said without looking directly at Colt.

Colt moved his horse forward until he was side by side with the man doing the talking. He leaned over in the saddle until his face was inches away. "I'm Colt McBride, and these cattle are headed to my ranch. If one man on this drive gets so much as a hangnail, or one steer trips and hurts himself before they leave Colorado, I will hold you personally responsible."

"A lot of men work for Mr. Schott. You can't take us all on," the man boasted.

"I'm not worried about how many men Schott has. I will find you."

Schott's man looked into the darkest, most foreboding eyes he'd ever seen. An involuntary shiver ran down his spine. He glanced at the men next to him. "Let's go."

Once the men were out of sight, Colt turned to Cole. "Sorry for butting into your argument, but something about that cowboy just rubbed me the wrong way."

"No problem. They didn't hear what I had to say. I have a feeling you made the point better than I could have," Cole responded. Colt's threat would have made him nervous if he were on the receiving end. "What are you doing out here?"

"I received a telegram from Jake. He mentioned he had some trouble, and I wanted to see if he needed any help," Colt explained. "Where is he?"

"Denver. Let's get to camp and we'll fill you in on what's happened."

"Why is he still in Denver?" Colt asked as soon as he got off his horse. He allowed the wrangler to see to the animals so he could talk to Cole.

Shorty poured Colt and Strait some coffee. "Sit and have something to eat while we tell you."

The men explained about the wagon-train killings and about Jake finding Promise. They filled him in on the events since that day, omitting no detail.

"We expected Jake to catch up with us by now," Cole said, obviously worried. "I told Shorty if we don't see him by tomorrow, I'm going back to Denver. That's the reason we are staying in the area again tonight."

Listening to Shorty and Cole, Colt felt a keen sense of

urgency. Something had happened to his brother, he just knew it. "I can make it to Denver by tomorrow," he told them.

"Not unless you're planning on riding all night," Shorty responded.

Colt jumped up. "That's exactly what I'm going to do." He glanced at Strait and said, "You deserve a rest after the ride we've had. Stay the night, get some rest."

Strait stood and reached for his gear. "No way. I'm coming with you."

"Colt, be careful. There's at least a dozen men involved in that attack," Cole warned.

"If they've done anything to my brother, they'll need more than that to stop me."

Cole had seen Colt in action with a gun, and he had no doubt he could take on all of those killers at one time and be the one to walk away. "I'd really like to come with you, but I promised Jake I'd get the cattle to the ranch," Cole said.

"Then that's what you should do," Colt agreed. "If those men come back with more guns, you'll be needed here."

"Wait a darn second before you go riding off. Let me put some food together to take with you," Shorty said, scurrying off to the cook's wagon.

After Colt and Strait left, Shorty looked at Cole. "Now there's a man I wouldn't want to tangle with. He's the biggest man I ever saw, and I bet he's a mean one if need be. Those black eyes of his told me he was Jake's brother straightaway."

"Believe me, it's not only his size that intimidates. I've seen him in action, and he's so fast you can't even see his gun leave his holster," Cole told him.

* * *

Night had fallen by the time Colt and Strait rode into Denver the next day to see if Jake was there. Cole had told Colt that Jake didn't necessarily trust the sheriff and his deputies, so Colt planned to steer clear of them. He figured the saloon would be as good a place as any to see if Jake was in town. If he wasn't there, his next stop would be Hollister's. If he got lucky he might even see the eight men who'd visited the cattle drive.

"Let's take the horses to the livery before we go to the saloon. We can see if Preacher is there," Colt told Strait.

"Sounds good."

In the livery, Colt looked around for Jake's horse, but Preacher wasn't there. He figured Jake must be at Hollister's. They cared for their horses, paid the owner to give them some grain, and walked toward the saloon. Colt spotted the telegraph office and stopped to send his wife a telegram like he'd promised. He didn't want her fretting about him.

Before entering the saloon, Colt glanced at every horse tied to the rails, thinking he might recognize the animals ridden by the eight men who'd threatened the drive. But they didn't look familiar, so he and Strait walked inside and headed to the bar, where they ordered whiskey. They casually looked around the room as they sipped their drinks. Colt's gaze landed on a big man at a poker table who seemed particularly interested in him.

"Looks like someone has seen a ghost," Strait said in a low voice.

"Yeah."

A man with a star pinned to his chest sat next to the big man. The big man leaned over and whispered something to him. The lawman's head snapped up and he looked across the room, directly at Colt.

This was getting interesting, Colt thought. Out of the

corner of his eye he saw the bartender. "Can we get a couple of steaks?"

"Yessir, I'll see to it," the barkeep replied.

Colt and Strait grabbed the bottle of whiskey and walked to a table at the back of the room that gave them a clear view of the saloon.

"They seemed real interested in you," Strait said.

"I had the same feeling."

The bartender arrived with their steaks and Colt asked, "Can you tell me where the Hollister ranch is located?"

The bartender gave him directions, but before he walked away he said, "I saw a man in here a few days ago that looked a lot like you."

"Is that right?"

"Well now, he wasn't as big as you, but if not for that, he was near your double."

"Did he leave town?" Colt asked.

"Yeah, I saw him ride out and I ain't seen him again. Are you relations?"

"Might be."

Seeing Colt wasn't going to offer more information, the bartender walked away.

Colt and Strait finished their steaks and left the saloon to head back to the livery. A man exiting the livery stared slack-jawed at Colt. "I apologize for staring, but you look just like a fellow who was in my store a few days ago. Your name wouldn't be McBride, would it?"

"It is," Colt acknowledged.

The man stuck his hand out. "My name is Clarke Parsons. Your brother came in for supplies. He'd met my brother in Dodge—he's the doctor there. Jake had him take care of a woman he'd found injured."

Colt shook his hand and introduced Strait. He'd heard about the doctor from Cole and Shorty. "Do you know if my brother is at the Hollister ranch?"

"Then you don't know?" Clarke asked.

"Know what?"

"I hate to have to tell you this, but your brother was shot. Doc Rawlings told me that John Hollister found him on the road, shot in the chest and left for dead."

Colt felt a stabbing pain in his own heart. "Is he . . ." His words faltered and he couldn't finish the question. *Dear God, please don't let him be dead.*

Clarke put his hand on Colt's shoulder. "No, no, I'm sorry, I didn't make it clear. He's still alive, but Doc says he's in a real bad way."

Colt was so choked up he couldn't speak, so Strait asked the question he knew Colt would ask. "Is he at the doc's office?"

"No, Hollister's place was closer, and the doc said if they'd ridden to town with him in his condition, he wouldn't have made it."

Colt calmed down enough to ask, "Who shot him?"

"The doc didn't know. Your brother was asking some questions about strangers in town who might have had something to do with those people who were killed on that wagon train. I told him about the strangers hanging around at the saloon."

"Are they still here?"

"Yes." Clarke gave him the descriptions he'd given Jake.

One description fit the big man Colt had seen at the saloon. "We saw one of the deputies with the big man."

"That was Potter. I'll tell you the same thing I told your brother. Don't trust the deputies in this town," Clarke replied.

"What about the sheriff?" Strait asked.

"He's just trying to make it to retirement, so he's not taking much of an interest in anything." Clarke glanced around nervously to see if anyone was watching them. "I was thankful Hollister found your brother, because I have a feeling some of the deputies are involved in whatever is going on. When I last saw your brother he was walking to the saloon. I noticed he stopped to look at the horse one of the deputies has been riding."

"Potter?" Colt asked.

"Yep, and the horse is right over there," he said, pointing toward the saloon. "It's that big black with the white stockings and star on his forehead."

Colt glanced at the horse tied at the rail, curious why his brother was interested in that particular animal. "I'll be right back." When he reached the horse, he noticed he was a fine-looking animal, but much too thin. Jake was as much of a stickler for the care of horses as he was, and he didn't abide any man abusing them. He figured that was the reason for his brother's interest. He pulled the horse's reins from the rail and led him back across the street.

"How long has that deputy been riding this animal?" Colt asked Clarke.

"Several weeks," Clarke said.

"Thanks for the information."

Clarke knew Colt was asking for trouble taking Potter's horse. "You better watch your back. I don't want to see you ambushed like your brother."

"I'm taking him to the livery to have the man there feed him and give him a good brushing. If anyone has a problem with that, tell them where they can find me."

Before Clarke walked away, he said, "Mr. McBride, my brother was nearly beaten to death in Dodge. I just received a letter from him yesterday. He said a friend there overheard strangers in the saloon asking about my brother tending that gal your brother found on that wagon train."

Colt digested that piece of information. "Did Jake know?"

"He knew my brother was beaten, but I didn't know at the time that there was a connection with the woman he'd found until I received his letter. My brother said he didn't give the men any information."

Colt pulled some coins out of his pocket. "Send your brother a telegram. Tell him I appreciate what he did, and if he needs anything to let me know."

The livery owner was surprised when Colt walked in with the horse. "This horse was left with me a few nights ago by a man who looked a lot like you," he said.

"What did he have to say?" Colt asked.

"Just said he saw the horse wasn't being fed and wanted me to care for him. Same as you. Paid me before he left."

Colt handed him some coins. "If you see him in front of that saloon again in the same condition, I'd consider it a favor if you'd bring him down here and care for him until I have a chance to talk to the deputy about how he treats this fine animal."

The man smiled wide. He'd like to see this big man knock Potter's teeth down his throat. "I'd be happy to. I don't have any use for Deputy Potter. Never have."

"If the deputy asks what you're doing, tell him my name is Colt McBride and I paid you to care for him. I'll be around if he wants to see me."

"Will do."

Chapter Twenty-One

John Hollister saw the two riders before they reached the house. When they got closer, one look at Colt told him he was Jake's brother, so he set aside the rifle he'd been holding.

After the introductions, Strait said, "I'll see to the horses. Colt, you go on in and see Jake."

Colt handed him Razor's reins. "Thanks, Strait."

"When you're done, come on to the house and Nettie will get you two something to eat," Hollister told Strait.

John led Colt back to Jake's room. "As I said, he hasn't awakened yet. Because the wound is so close to his heart, we stay with him at all times to make sure he doesn't thrash about. He developed a fever earlier today, and the doc said he would be back tonight."

As soon as he entered the room, Colt saw a beautiful young woman standing over Jake holding a cloth to his forehead. She didn't notice them.

"Honey, this is Jake's brother," John said.

Promise glanced up and stared at the big man next to her uncle. "Oh, I didn't hear you!" she said as she walked toward him. There was no question it was Jake's older brother. He looked exactly like Jake, except a larger version.

"You must be Colt," she said, extending her hand. "I've heard so much about you. I'm Promise Sinclair."

"Nice to meet you," Colt replied, surprised by her Southern accent. Cole and Shorty had told him how beautiful and brave she was, but they'd failed to mention she was a Southerner.

"Your brother saved my life," she told him. "I'm afraid all of this is my fault. He was shot because those men are after me."

If the sadness in her voice wasn't enough to tell him how guilty she felt over Jake's condition, the look on her face certainly did. She'd lost her own brother, and she didn't need this guilt added to her heartbreak. "This is not your fault. The responsibility lies with those men who ambushed my brother."

No matter how many people reassured her, she didn't believe it herself. "How did you know Jake was shot?"

"I didn't. The last telegram I received from him just said he was having problems. I felt something was wrong, so I came to see if he needed my help."

"Maybe he will awaken when he hears your voice." Promise moved out of the way so he could be next to Jake.

"I'm going to tell Nettie we have guests," John said.

"Would you like to be alone with him?" Promise asked Colt.

"That's not necessary." Colt leaned over his immobile brother. He felt better seeing his breathing was steady. He was going to make it, of that he had no doubt. *Thank you, God.*

Promise moved to the chair on the opposite side of the bed. She couldn't take her eyes off Colt. It was uncanny how similar in appearance they were, their features almost identical. Jake was an unusually large man, but his brother was taller and even more muscular.

Before Colt took a seat, he saw a tablet on the chair.

When he picked it up he noticed the drawing that was a perfect likeness of Jake.

"Oh, I'm sorry," Promise said, jumping up to take the tablet.

"Did you draw this?" Colt asked.

"Yes. It's difficult to capture Jake, since he doesn't sit still for more than a few minutes at a time. Until now."

Colt handed her the tablet. "It's a true likeness."

"Thank you."

Colt reached over and gently put his hand on Jake's shoulder, careful not to shake him. "Jake, can you hear me?"

"I've been changing the cloths every few minutes, trying to lower his temperature," Promise said.

Removing the cloth from his brother's forehead, Colt dipped it into the bowl of water on the table and wiped Jake's face. "Jake, are you awake? I've left my beautiful wife to see what is going on with you. If you don't wake up she's going to want to come after both of us, and she'll chew your butt out for getting shot."

"Did his lips move?" Promise asked hopefully.

"I think so." Colt lightly touched Jake's shoulder again. "I have some good news for you, but I want you to be awake when I tell you."

Promise took hold of Jake's hand. When she saw that Colt was watching her, she said, "Your brother talked to me when I was unconscious and I remembered his voice. Your voice sounds so much like his."

It was evident she thought highly of Jake. "He's tough, and he's going to be okay."

Promise smiled at him as tears filled her eyes. "I know. I've never met anyone like him. He hardly had any rest from the moment he found me, and I keep praying that he'll awaken when he's had enough rest."

Colt thought she needed to get her mind off of Jake for a moment. "Cole told me that you helped with the cattle."

"Oh, you saw the men?"

"Yes, they told me everything that happened on the drive. They also told me you're a pretty good shot."

"My father taught me how to shoot."

"Have you regained all of your memory?"

"For the most part. I recently remembered shooting two men."

Colt hated to cause her pain by talking about the murders, but he needed to know who was trying to kill his brother. "You shot two of them?"

"I hit one of them in the shoulder, but I don't think I killed him. I'm not sure about the other one."

"Can you describe them?"

"He was a big man, maybe as tall as you, but not as wide in the shoulders, and he had long, dark blond hair. I think he was the leader of the group. The other man looked a bit like him, but not as tall."

Colt wondered if it could be the man he saw in the saloon. "Did you see his face?"

As much as she didn't want to, she knew she would never forget that face. The big man had pulled her to him, holding her in front of him as he started shooting. She'd struggled to get away, and when she bit down hard on his hand, he released her. Once she was free she ran for the fur muff they'd thrown on the ground. She grabbed it, pulled her pistol out, and pointed it at the big man. He laughed at her. As he advanced on her, she pulled the trigger and shot him. A second man came after her with his gun pulled and she pulled the trigger again and again. She kept shooting until her gun was empty, and she felt something hit her. Then everything went black. She saw the big man's face in her mind. "His face looked like evil."

"Could you draw him?"

Her eyes widened when she looked at him. She hadn't

even thought of that. "Yes!" Releasing Jake's hand, she pulled a piece of charcoal from her pocket.

As Promise worked on the drawing, Colt changed the cloths on Jake's forehead and continued to talk to him. At times, some of Colt's words filtered through her concentration, and his calm manner reminded her so much of Jake. Both men were not what they appeared on the surface. They made intimidating foes, but they also possessed an unexpected gentler side. She heard that softness in Colt's voice when he mentioned his wife and boys.

They were interrupted when the doctor walked in and introduced himself to Colt before he checked his patient. After he examined Jake, he turned to Colt. "You look like you can hold him if he starts to move about."

"He won't be moving." Colt moved to the other side of the bed while the doc removed the bandage.

"Your brother is a tough one. That bullet would have killed most men. I wouldn't have said he was going to make it the first night I saw him."

Once the bandage was removed, he examined the wound. "This is looking good," he said, more to himself than aloud. He cleaned the wound and grabbed the clean bandages. "I'm not saying he's out of danger, but I give him a much better chance now. I don't think his fever is high enough to worry about right now. Just keep a close watch."

The doc glanced at Promise. "You've done a real good job taking care of him."

"He's been so still that it isn't difficult. I feel better now that his brother is here," Promise admitted.

"Just make sure when he comes around that he stays put, no moving about." The doc eyed Colt again. "I'm sure you can handle that task."

After the doc left, Nettie came into the room carrying a tray and placed it on a table by Colt. "Mr. McBride, I brought you some sandwiches and coffee. I didn't think you would want to leave your brother right now."

"Thank you, but you didn't need to go to the trouble."

"No trouble at all. I have rooms ready for you and Strait when you are ready to rest. If you need anything else, please don't hesitate to ask," she said.

"We don't want to be a bother. We can go to the bunkhouse."

"Out of the question! And I'll brook no arguments."

You shouldn't argue with her, Mr. McBride. You won't win," Promise told him.

"Okay, no arguments. I appreciate your hospitality," Colt said.

Nettie smiled at him and left the room. Colt had just reached for his coffee when a sound came from his brother. Colt leaned toward him, trying to hear what Jake was saying.

"He . . ." Jake murmured.

"What are you trying to say, Jake?" Colt placed his large palm over Jake's hand. "Jake, can you hear me?"

"Hero," Jake whispered hoarsely.

Colt frowned, trying to figure out what his brother was saying.

Promise quickly moved closer to Jake. "Hero is my horse. He was with me on the wagon train. I don't know if he ran away, or if those men took him, but he wasn't with me when Jake found me." She smoothed Jake's black, curly hair from his face. "He saw my drawing of him, so maybe he's dreaming about him."

Colt reached for the water. "Jake, can you drink?"

Jake didn't respond, but Colt held his head up and tried to give him a drink. Jake took a small sip without opening his eyes before his head sagged over Colt's arm. "I think he's out again," Colt said.

"That's probably a good thing. I'm sure he will be in a lot of pain," Promise replied.

Colt placed Jake's head gently on the bed, and he looked over at Promise. "Can I see the drawing of your horse?"

Promise reached for her tablet and pulled out her drawing of Hero. "Jake said you have an unusual bond with animals."

"I train horses when I have time." Colt eyes were on her drawing. He instantly recognized the horse as the one he took to the stable; the very horse that the deputy was claiming as his own. He knew from the livery owner that Jake had seen the horse and must have concluded the deputy was involved with the murders. Promise's horse led directly to the killers.

Colt didn't want to say anything to Promise right now about seeing her horse. She'd been through enough heartache and he wasn't going to be the one to disappoint her, particularly if he was wrong. He handed back the drawing. "He's a beautiful animal."

"Yes, he is. I hope I see him again." She looked up at Colt. "Do you think it's possible for an animal to find its owner?"

Seeing the hope in her eyes, Colt understood how she felt. If he lost his horse, he would feel the same way. He gave her a reassuring smile. "It's been my experience that animals are a lot smarter than humans, so I wouldn't be surprised."

"I will hold on to that thought. Hero is very smart." She liked Colt; just like Jake, he was a man of strong character. She knew if Jake could hear his brother, he would rest easier knowing Colt was with him and would take care of any problems. "Your brother was excited about going home to ranch with you." After meeting Colt, she knew she would always envision Jake riding on the ranch with his brother. She would miss Jake desperately, but knowing he would be happy would make the parting easier.

"I'm glad to have him back home." Colt watched as she toyed with a curl on Jake's forehead. It reminded him of how Victoria would yank at a lock of his hair in a playful manner. He had a feeling she cared a great deal about his brother.

"He also spoke highly of your new wife." She didn't say she believed Jake was in love with his brother's wife. It hadn't escaped her notice that every time Jake spoke of his new sister-in-law, his eyes lit up like a child looking at a jar of candy.

Colt chuckled. "He's like every man on the ranch. They are all half in love with her."

Promise glanced at him, surprised that he knew what his brother was feeling. "That doesn't bother you?"

Colt shrugged. "I take it as a compliment. She's a beautiful woman, and the men all notice. Can't blame them for that. Jake's no different." He leaned over and braced his elbows on the bed and looked directly into her eyes. "Trust me, Jake's not in love with Victoria. He's just infatuated. He wants the same thing I've found, but not with the same woman."

"I couldn't really say what he feels." She was embarrassed that he seemed to read her mind. "We never really talked about that."

Colt had a feeling that she really wanted to know how Jake felt about her. He thought his brother might be a fool if he walked out of this woman's life. He shook his head, wondering what in the hell was wrong with him. Before he knew it, he would be matchmaking just like Victoria and Mrs. Wellington.

Chapter Twenty-Two

Jake awoke in the middle of the night to a dimly lit room. It took a few minutes for him to remember where he was and what had happened to him. Every inch of him hurt; he felt like he'd been hit by a cannon. Slowly his wits returned and he remembered what happened to him. He figured he was at Hollister's ranch. He heard someone snoring softly beside his bed. Gingerly turning his head to the side, he saw his brother slumped in the chair with his long legs stretched out. His unshaven face and disheveled appearance told him Colt had ridden hard for days to get here. He didn't know how long he'd been out, but on some level he'd known that Colt was beside him. He must be in bad shape if his brother left Victoria to come to Denver.

It didn't surprise him to see Promise curled up in a chair on the other side of the bed. Like Colt, she looked exhausted. Her skin was so fair that the dark circles under her eyes were especially prominent. But to him, she was still incredibly beautiful with her pale blond hair piled high, held in place with the diamond-encrusted comb. Looking at that comb in her hair made him think of the night he'd spent in her wagon when she'd removed the comb and her hair fell in long waves around her body. In that moment he couldn't ever recall seeing anyone so beautiful. It was one of those moments in life that remained with you, a moment he knew he would remember on his deathbed. But today wasn't that day, thanks to the Good Lord.

"She's some woman," Colt whispered.

Jake shifted his eyes to see his brother watching him with a grin on his face. "Yes, she is." His voice was low and raspy.

"Would you like some water?"

"That sounds good. I'm as dry as Shorty's biscuits." As Colt poured the water, Jake said, "You look like hell. Why don't you go get in a bed?"

"I'm fine." Colt held Jake's head while he took a long drink. "I thought I was the only McBride dumb enough to get shot."

"Yeah, well I always had to do everything you did, big brother. How did you know?"

"I didn't. I just had a feeling you might need my help."

Jake gave him a quizzical look, digesting Colt's response. "Can you help me sit?"

"Nope, Doc says you can't move around for a while. The bullet just missed your heart."

Hearing Promise move in her chair, both men glanced her way. They remained quiet for a minute until they could tell they hadn't disturbed her sleep.

"She won't leave," Colt said. "She blames herself for this."

Jake was still staring at her when he said, "She thinks everything that's happened on this drive is her fault. It's hard to believe she's still going with everything she's been through."

Colt studied the expression on his brother's face as he watched Promise. He wondered if he had developed feelings for her. "I saw Cole and the men, and they told me everything that happened on the drive. Cole wanted to come back with me, but he promised you he'd get the cattle home." Not wanting to add to Jake's worries, he decided not to mention the trouble they'd had with Schott's men.

"Good. I feel better knowing he's with the men," Jake responded. "Unfortunately, I didn't hire gunslingers for this drive. If I had, I would have tracked down those killers from the start."

Colt glanced at Promise again. "Your men are crazy about her. They told me she was a beauty, but that doesn't say it by half. I certainly didn't expect a real Southern belle."

Jake smiled at him, remembering how surprised he was when he first heard her accent. "She's a woman full of surprises." After a moment, he said, "Speaking of beautiful women, how's Victoria and the boys?"

Colt noticed how Jake's expression changed when he asked about Victoria. He guessed that answered his question about his brother's feelings for Promise. It wasn't likely he could develop feelings for Promise if he was still harboring a crush on Victoria. "She's good, but I need to send her another telegram to let her know I will be here longer than I expected. If she doesn't hear from me, she might come looking for both of us. And the boys are fine, still full of mischief."

"I think I'm going to live, so you don't have to stay."

Colt leaned forward and whispered, "I saw something in town that I think will interest you, but we need to discuss it when we're alone."

Jake nodded. "Is that your coffee?" he asked, referring to the full cup of coffee on the tray by the bed.

"Yeah, you want some? It's probably cold by now."

"Cold is fine."

Colt held his head again while he drank the cold coffee. When Jake finished, he said, "That's better than water, but a little whiskey in there wouldn't hurt." A few minutes later, he was fast asleep.

Colt watched him for a long time, so thankful that he had awakened. He couldn't wait for Jake to be back on the ranch where he could look after him. Colt would never say that to his younger brothers, but he'd always felt it was his job to look out for them. He'd wanted Jake and their younger brother, Lucas, to come home, get married, and find the happiness he'd found with Victoria. After meeting Promise, he couldn't figure out why Jake hadn't already swept her off her feet. She was a woman any man would be proud to call his own. When Promise wasn't within earshot, he'd ask Jake what he was waiting for on that score. On that thought, he sat back in his chair and drifted back to sleep.

Promise had awakened while the two brothers talked, and though she was excited Jake was awake, she didn't want to intrude on their moment together. She felt it was important for them to have time to themselves. Colt didn't strike her as the kind of man who revealed his feelings easily, but anyone could see his love for his brother. When they'd been quiet for a long time, she opened her eyes and saw they were both sleeping. Knowing that Colt could protect his brother if those killers made another attempt on his life eased her mind. Her eyes remained on Jake's handsome face, watching him breathe peacefully until she finally fell back to sleep.

The next morning when they were alone, Jake filled his brother in on what happened the day he was shot, including the details of the ambush. Putting together the pieces of the puzzle, Colt told Jake that he saw Promise's horse in Denver, and about the big man he saw at the saloon. Jake told him it was the same man he'd encountered at the saloon, and most likely the one who pulled the trigger in an effort to get Jake out of the picture.

After breakfast, when the doc was with Jake, Promise took Colt to the study and gave him a drawing of the two men she'd shot. One of them was the big man he saw in the saloon, and the same man Jake described. Now they had the proof they needed, but they didn't trust the law in this town, at least not enough to convince them the killers would be brought to justice.

Colt left the Hollister ranch to ride to Denver to send Victoria another telegram to tell her about Jake. Jake asked him to send a telegram to the U.S. Marshal's office requesting they send some men to Denver. Colt was going to send the telegram, but he wasn't going to wait around for the marshal to find out what was going on. He intended to find out if the sheriff was aware of his deputy's involvement with the gang of criminals.

On his way to town, Colt had time to consider what the killers' next move might be. If they had been watching Jake, it stood to reason they knew that he'd taken Promise to Hollister's ranch. The killers probably thought that if they took Jake out of the equation, it would be easier to get to Promise. Unless the doctor talked to the sheriff, the deputy might think Jake was dead. Jake said that they wanted Promise because of the money, and to make sure she wasn't around to identify them. It had been his experience that money made men do some pretty crazy things. Knowing Promise was still alive was a threat to their existence as free men. Promise had become their obsession. And that obsession was going to get them killed. They might have momentarily accomplished their goal with Jake, but they hadn't planned on one important factor: Jake had a brother who wasn't going to allow anyone to get away with trying to kill him.

After sending the telegrams, Colt walked to the livery.

Hero wasn't there, so Colt walked to the sheriff's office to introduce himself.

"Doc told me your brother had been shot," Gilbert said after shaking Colt's hand. "Said he was still unconscious."

Colt refused the chair Gilbert pointed to, choosing to stand. He wasn't in the mood to be cordial. He wanted answers. He didn't divulge any information about Jake's condition. "What have you done to investigate my brother's ambush?" he asked pointedly.

The sheriff bristled at the unspoken accusation. "The way I see it, there's not much to investigate since your brother can't tell me who shot him. Doc said he didn't think he was going to make it."

Colt ground his teeth at his callous remark. "Did you even go to the area where he was shot to see if the ambushers left anything behind that could identify them?"

"I sent one of my deputies out there, but he didn't come up with anything," Gilbert grudgingly replied.

"Which deputy?" Colt snapped.

"What difference does that make?"

"I've heard your deputies can't be trusted," Colt growled.

"Where did you hear that?"

"Word gets around. Which deputy did you send?" Colt repeated. When the sheriff hesitated, Colt asked, "Potter?" Colt could tell by the look on Gilbert's face that he had hit the nail on the head. "Where is he?"

"I haven't seen him this morning."

Colt turned to leave, and said over his shoulder, "Tell Potter I'm looking for him."

"What do you want to see my deputy about?"

"He's riding a stolen horse, but I think you already knew that. Last I heard, that's a hanging offense." Colt turned back and gave him a level look. "I'll hang him myself if I don't think you are up to the job."

Walking toward the saloon, Colt didn't see Promise's horse anywhere. He decided to stop in the saloon for a cup of coffee in the hopes that the bartender might be free with information when no one was around.

As he hoped, the bartender was alone, and he was in a talkative mood. Colt asked him about the strangers in town.

"Those men rode out yesterday. I heard them talking about Mexico before they headed out." He poured himself a cup of coffee and sat down next to Colt.

"I hear Potter is on real friendly terms with them," Colt said.

"As thick as thieves, if you ask me."

Interesting choice of words, Colt thought. "Did you hear if the deputy was going with them to Mexico?"

"I didn't hear that, but he was with them before they headed out."

"Have you seen Potter this morning?"

"No, but it's too early for him to be about. I don't know why the sheriff keeps that no-account."

"Did you happen to see the horse Potter has been riding?"

"Sure did, it's a fine-looking animal," the bartender replied. "Said he bought him off a man a few weeks back."

Colt thought the bartender was a good source of information, particularly when it came to who he could trust in this town. Schott wasn't on the list.

"I'd bet Potter is on Schott's payroll. If I were you, I'd steer clear of Schott as long as you are in Denver. He don't take to strangers."

Colt left the saloon and walked back to the livery to get his horse. The last thing he expected to see was Hero in the stall next to his horse.

The livery owner walked up behind him. "The deputy brought him in right after you left."

"Did he say when he would be back?"

"Nope. Said he was leaving town, headed to Mexico. He told me if anyone was interested in the horse I should sell him and keep the money for his board."

"What do you want for him?" Colt asked, stroking Hero's neck.

The livery owner gave Colt a long look. "Mister, Potter never took care of this animal or any other. I think he would be better off with you. You can take him with you since you paid me more than Potter ever did for his care."

Colt pulled out some bills that more than covered a fair price for the horse. "I'll be at Hollister's, and I'd appreciate it if you'd let me know if Potter comes back."

"I'll do that."

Colt pulled some peppermints out of his pocket that Jake had suggested he take with him. And just like Jake said, Hero was jumping around like a little puppy at the mere smell of the peppermints.

The two men chuckled as they watched the horse's reaction.

"If that don't beat all," the livery owner said.

"I expect he's going to be even happier since I'm taking him to his real owner," Colt said. He rode out of the livery with Hero beside him.

Chapter Twenty-Three

Jake was talking with Strait and Promise when Colt walked in. Colt noticed the ranch seemed fairly deserted when he rode in, a sure indication that something out of the ordinary was going on.

"Would you like something to eat, Mr. McBride?" Promise asked Colt.

"Yes, ma'am, that would be nice. And you can call me Colt."

Jake smiled. "Save your breath. She still won't call me Jake."

Promise returned his smile. "I will try."

When she was out of earshot, Colt looked at Strait. "What's going on?"

"Mr. Hollister and his men had to ride to the north range. Someone cut the wire fence and cattle were scattering on Schott's land. It's near where those farmers are homesteading, and I think he figured trouble was certain. I thought I would hang around here until you got back in case someone was looking to get at the gal."

"Good thinking." Colt looked over at Jake. "You think it could be a ruse?"

"It wouldn't surprise me. That's the way these men operate."

"The horse is in the stable," Colt said.

"You sure it's hers?"

Colt grinned at him. "Well, if another horse with a star on his forehead and likes peppermints as much as that big baby, then he might not be hers. It's the funniest thing I ever saw."

Jake chuckled at the memory of the horse nearly taking his fingers off when he gave him peppermints. "I know what you mean."

"I didn't know if you wanted me to tell Promise."

"I think you should take her out to the stable and surprise her. She could use some good news." After everything that had happened to her, Jake knew if one thing would give her true joy, it would be that horse. He'd like to be the one to see the look on her face when she saw her beloved Hero, but he didn't want her to have to wait until he was able to move around.

"I thought she might be worried about the killers being around Denver," Colt said.

"You're right about that. Maybe you should just tell her you saw him for sale in Denver. She doesn't need to be worrying about those men," Jake replied.

"We might be in luck on that score. According to the bartender, they rode out yesterday. He said he heard them planning to head to Mexico. The deputy left this morning, and he told the livery owner to sell the horse." Colt pulled out Promise's drawing of the killers. "Here's the two she shot."

"Yep, that's Big Ugly," Jake said.

"Do you think they've given up and decided to head out while they could?" Strait asked.

"Knowing she is on the ranch with so many men around,

maybe they realized they couldn't get to her here," Jake said. He looked at his brother. "What do you think?"

"It wouldn't be the first time killers took off to Mexico to hide out until they think their misdeeds are forgotten," Colt mused. "One thing is sure, we can't trust that sheriff to do anything."

Promise returned with a tray of food, and once they finished eating, Jake said, "Promise, Colt has something to show you."

She gave Colt a questioning glance. "What is it?"

"You need to go outside with me." Colt stood and settled his hat on his head.

She glanced at Jake and he smiled. "Go with him."

Promise walked with Colt from the house, but when he headed for the stable, she couldn't remain quiet. "Why do you want me to go to the stable?"

"You'll see."

As soon as they walked in the stable, her horse was responding to the sound of her voice with loud snorts. Once her eyes adjusted to the light, she saw Hero in a stall. She looked at Colt with wide eyes. "Where . . . how . . . ?" Without waiting for a response, she ran to the stall and opened the latch. The horse came out so quickly he almost knocked her to the ground.

Colt grabbed a handful of the horse's mane, trying to control his movements lest he injure Promise in his excitement. "Whoa, boy, mind your manners," he told him. "You're stronger than you realize."

The horse lowered his head and nuzzled Promise's neck. She wrapped her arms around him and cried. "Oh, Hero, I've missed you so much."

Colt thought if that horse could have hugged her back, he would have. He'd never seen an animal behave so much like a human.

"He's so thin," Promise said, running her hands over his back. "Where did you find him?"

"I saw him for sale in Denver," Colt answered smoothly.

"Thank you so much for bringing him home, but how did you know he was my horse?"

"Your drawing. I looked him over and I think he's okay. He's not been eating properly, but after some rest and some extra grain, he should be back to normal before you know it." He reached in his pocket and pulled out the remaining peppermints and handed them to her. "Of course, he'll need plenty of these."

She smiled at Colt as she held them to Hero's mouth, and the horse gently accepted the offering. "They've always been his favorite."

Colt patted Hero's neck respectfully. "He's a fine animal." He looked at Promise, and the love on her face for this animal made her even more beautiful. "Jake can spare you for a few hours. Spend some time with your horse," he told her. Knowing she was bound to ask him more questions, he said, "We can answer all of your questions when you come in."

"Are you saying you saw Hero in Denver before you were shot?" Promise asked Jake.

"I saw him when I was in Denver, and told Colt about him. He purchased him when he went to town."

"That means you know who was responsible for stealing him," she reasoned.

Jake looked at Colt and nodded. "We think we know, but they've left for Mexico," Colt answered quickly.

Nettie and the doctor walked into the room. "The doctor came to see the patient, and he has a telegram for Colt."

"Actually the patient is doing great, I just came back hoping Nettie would invite me to dinner."

"You know you are always welcome," Nettie said.

The doc handed Colt his telegram.

"Thank you." Colt opened the paper and started reading.

Jake saw the concerned look that passed over Colt's face as he read. "What is it?"

Colt stuffed the telegram in his pocket. "Nothing that can't wait until later."

Before Jake could question Colt further, the doctor redirected his attention when he started poking at him. "When will I be able to ride, Doc?"

"Not anytime soon. Your wound is healing nicely, but you don't need to be using your arms right now. I don't want you doing anything as strenuous as being on a horse. If you need to go somewhere, you can go in a wagon."

"It's a long way to Wyoming in a wagon," Jake complained.

"No arguing with the doc," Colt said. He was relieved Jake was on the road to recovery, yet he still hated to leave him in Denver. But after receiving that telegram, he knew he had to leave soon. "You don't need to be worrying about getting to Wyoming right now. Cole is capable of handling everything."

"Yeah, but with that many cattle we're going to need every hand we can get on the ranch." He grinned at Colt. "And I know you don't want to be away from your bride too long."

When Colt didn't respond, Jake knew something was definitely wrong. He didn't say anything, but he would find out when they were alone. "So, Doc, a wagon is the only way I can go to Wyoming?"

"I don't see why you couldn't, if you're that anxious to go, but I'd give it a couple of days. That is, if you take it easy and don't try to get there in a week," the doctor qualified.

As soon as the doctor was out the door, Jake looked at

Colt. "What's in the telegram? And don't tell me nothing. I can see by the look on your face that something is wrong."

Promise stood and walked to the door. "I'll give you two some privacy."

"No need." Colt motioned for her to take a seat. "This is nothing you can't hear." He took a deep breath to calm himself down. "Victoria's pregnant." He looked over at Jake to gauge his reaction.

Jake gave him a wide grin. "Well, congratulations, big brother." But when Colt didn't smile in return, he knew there was more. "Why look so down in the mouth? I thought you would be happy to hear this news."

"I knew she was pregnant before I came here. The telegram was from Mrs. Wellington. Victoria told her I wasn't going to be back as soon as I initially planned. Mrs. Wellington wanted me to know what was going on since she knew Victoria wouldn't wire me."

"Know what?" Jake and Promise asked at the same time.

"Victoria's had some problems, and the doctor has confined her to bed until the baby is born. He told her the baby is going to be especially large, and he's worried since she is so small."

"But she is okay?" Jake asked.

"Mrs. Wellington assured me she is fine. She just wanted me to know."

"Thank God," Jake said, sounding relieved. "It stands to reason Victoria will have a big baby since you were the biggest baby the doc ever delivered."

"When I get back, I need to find some more help for her. She's doing too much. The boys keep her busy enough, and she does all the cooking on the ranch now. Not to mention all the time it takes to make those bag things," Colt lamented.

"Bag things?" Promise asked.

"She makes those purses you women carry," Jake explained.

Colt continued with his list of things that kept Victoria busy. "I don't know why I built that house so big; she's always cleaning. Mrs. Wellington is trying to help out, but she's no spring chicken, and she already helps Bartholomew with the chores at the farm."

"Stop worrying. We will find someone to help when we get there," Jake said when Colt took a breath.

Promise listened as Jake and Colt discussed the limited possibilities of finding someone to help Victoria, and considered her options. It had occurred to her that the killers could come back at any time, and with Jake gone it might embolden them to come to the ranch. They had already tried to eliminate Jake, so they wouldn't hesitate to kill her aunt and uncle. If she left Denver for a period of time, the killers might think she'd returned to South Carolina, and they would eventually give up looking for her. Wyoming seemed like the answer to both of their problems. The answer to everyone's dilemma seemed obvious. "I could go with you and help Victoria."

The men didn't hear her offer because their discussions had turned to a bet on whether Victoria would have a girl or boy.

Finally, she said more loudly, "I'll go to Wyoming with you and help. I can do all of the cooking and cleaning until Victoria is on her feet. I'm also fairly good with a needle."

The men stopped talking and stared at her.

"I thought you came here to be with your family," Colt said.

Jake simply stared at her. He didn't know what to say.

"I wouldn't be here if not for your brother, and—"

She was interrupted by Jake. "You're not beholden to me."

"It's not that I feel beholden, Jake. I want to help. I'm also thinking about my family. Until those killers are caught, my aunt and uncle are in danger." She saw he wasn't persuaded, so she added, "Besides, Cole told me I needed to see Wyoming. He said he would come for me if I ever wanted to visit, and I'm sure he would bring me back in the spring." She tried to ignore the fact that she was also delaying the day she would be forced to say good-bye to Jake forever. She knew that day would come, but she wasn't prepared just yet.

I should have known Cole would be involved, Jake thought.

Colt thought about the situation before he responded. If the killers came back from Mexico, if that was really their destination, Promise and her family would be left to their own defenses. Of course, Hollister had some men on the ranch, but they couldn't wait around indefinitely for the killers. If she went to Wyoming with them and the killers returned, they would certainly find out she was no longer here, and maybe they would stop looking for her.

"I don't think that is such a good idea," Jake said. "It's a long way to Wyoming and you've never seen what the winters are like there. You couldn't come back to Denver until next spring." Jake wasn't sure the winters were worse in Wyoming than Denver, but he wasn't going to mention that.

"Hang on, Jake," Colt said. "It might be best if she did leave Denver." Seeing the obstinate look on Jake's face, he added, "If only for a short time. If those men come back from Mexico and see she is no longer here, they might think she's returned home. They wouldn't go clear across country to look for her in South Carolina."

"That is precisely what I thought," Promise admitted. "It would help both of us." As far as she was concerned, the decision was made. "I would need to go to town to see the sheriff before we leave, and I will mention I am returning to South Carolina."

Colt admired her thought process. "I like that plan. The sheriff would certainly tell Deputy Potter if he came back to Denver."

"Well, I don't like the plan," Jake said abruptly. "We can find someone to hire when we get to Wyoming."

Jake's words were spoken with such finality that Promise assumed he was anxious to be rid of her. It hurt to know how he really felt, but she tried not to let it show. "I just wanted to help." With that said, she left the room.

Colt saw Promise was near tears, but he waited until she was out of earshot to give his brother hell. "Don't you think you were a bit harsh? You've hurt her feelings." Colt was puzzled by Jake's behavior; it wasn't like him to have such little regard for a woman's tender feelings. "What's the real reason you don't want her to come with us? You have to admit it is sound reasoning to get her away from Denver right now. Not to mention that it is quite nice of her to offer to help a complete stranger."

Jake looked properly put down. He hadn't intended to hurt her feelings. "I'm going to be busy when we get home."

"She is not going to take care of you," Colt reminded him. "But now that you mention it, it would probably be good to have her along while you are recovering."

"I'm fine."

Colt groaned, his temper getting the best of him. "No, you are not! We won't leave for a few days so you can gain some strength back, but you are definitely not okay."

When Jake started to object, Colt held up his hand to silence him. "If you give me any grief, you can stay right here. I'll not have two people to worry about." Colt jumped to his feet and paced the room. Then he stopped and looked at Jake. "Do you care about that gal?" He had a feeling his brother cared more than he wanted to admit. In his estimation, Promise was perfect for his brother. Why Jake was too hardheaded to recognize that fact, he didn't know.

Jake shook his head. "I like her fine. But if you're asking if I'm ready to settle down right now, the answer is no. I don't want her getting in the way at the ranch."

"Getting in the way?"

"Yeah," Jake mumbled.

Colt wasn't sure what he meant. "Can't you see it might solve some problems for everyone if she left Denver?"

"Yeah, I can. You don't really think those killers went to Mexico any more than I do."

Colt couldn't argue with his assessment. "It's possible, but I think it's more likely they are hiding out."

"That's what I thought."

"If I leave Denver alone, and those men come back, you're in no condition to defend anyone," Colt said reasonably, taking his seat by the bed again. He put his elbows on his thighs and leaned forward, leveling his gaze on his obstinate brother. "Are there any other reasons for your objections, other than the fact that she might not be able to resist your charming self?"

"She drives the men to distraction," Jake admitted gloomily.

Colt laughed. "Are you jealous?"

Jake frowned. "No, I'm not jealous, just practical. They don't work as hard when she's around. You should have seen Cole and Rodriguez on the drive, not to mention Shorty. She had every one of them wrapped around her little finger."

"Sounds like the green-eyed monster to me."

Definitely Shakespeare, Jake thought. "Well, it's not!

I'm not interested in her that way. I want someone more like . . ." He paused, catching himself before he said *Victoria*.

Arching a brow at his brother, Colt finished his sentence. "Victoria?"

"You have to admit, your wife is as nearly perfect as any woman could be."

"I do admit it, but Promise is much like Victoria," Colt told him. When Jake didn't respond, he said, "I think Victoria would like her. Not to mention she would probably like having a woman near her age to visit with for a while." He thought that would sway the argument in his favor.

Jake wasn't sure why he was arguing against this, since he had been planning to take Promise to the ranch before she regained her memory. Something had changed, but he didn't know what it was. He couldn't deny that she would be a big help to Victoria, and Victoria would enjoy her company. That would ease Colt's mind, and his brother deserved that. "You're right. It was nice of her to offer."

Colt cocked his head at him as if to say *no kidding*. "How do you think the men acted when Victoria first came to the ranch? Every one of them was smitten. They thought of more reasons to come to the house than you could imagine." He wasn't exaggerating, all of the men were at her beck and call.

"Okay, okay, you win. She can go with us," Jake agreed. "I imagine she went to the stable to see Hero. When she comes back I'll tell her."

Colt chuckled. "You mean, *if* she comes back?"

Chapter Twenty-Four

The next day, Colt escorted Promise to the sheriff's office in Denver, where she informed him of the murders on the wagon train, and casually mentioned she was going back home to South Carolina. Colt didn't figure the entire gang had left the area, but he didn't mention his concerns to Promise. They left the sheriff's office and made a trip to the bank so Promise could deposit the bulk of her money. Colt sent Victoria another telegram to tell her he would be coming home soon.

When the time came for Promise to say good-bye to her aunt and uncle, she was filled with mixed emotions. To keep from changing her mind, she focused on the reasons she was leaving. She'd seen what these men were capable of doing, and she couldn't stay in Denver and risk her family being harmed. It was even more difficult since her aunt and uncle didn't want her to leave, but Jake assured them he would bring her back in the spring. And she was sure he meant to keep his word. She didn't know what made him change his mind about her going to Wyoming, but she had the feeling it had more to do with his concern over Victoria than actually wanting her there. She figured she would eventually learn to deal with his rebuff, but she couldn't deal with her family being harmed.

"You've done nothing but complain for four days," Strait said to Jake. Strait had been driving the wagon with Jake propped up in the back atop a mattress and a mountain of quilts, thanks to the generosity of Nettie.

"If you didn't hit every dang hole in the ground it might not be so bad," Jake snapped.

"Believe me, I'm all for letting you ride. I'll do anything to shut you up!" Strait shouted, pulling the team to a halt. He bounded off the wagon seat, walked around to the back of the wagon where his horse was tied, freed the reins, and jumped on his back. He rode away fast before he did something stupid, like slug the boss's brother.

Colt helped Jake out of the wagon. "You might take it easy on Strait. He's one of the best cowboys on the ranch, and I don't want you running him off."

"I'm sorry," Jake replied sheepishly. "I can't take that wagon one more minute."

Colt got a fire going a few feet from where Jake was sitting, and then he checked his bandage to make sure he hadn't opened any stitches. Satisfied with the way his brother was healing, he could give him hell and not feel guilty. It wasn't that he didn't have sympathy for Jake's situation; he'd been in the same position not too long ago when he'd been shot. It was difficult, not to mention demoralizing, for a man to feel like a helpless pup. He had a feeling there was something else on Jake's mind. Still, he wasn't going to allow him to take his temper out on the very people trying to help him. "You agreed to this. The doc said you shouldn't ride for at least another week, and you agreed, dammit. And you're damn sure going to live up to your end of the bargain." He started to walk away, but stopped and turned back to him. "You even made me say bad words, after I've worked so hard to clean up my language for Victoria and the boys! Dammit! If you weren't my brother, I'd leave your sorry hide out here in the middle of nowhere. And don't even think you're going to get away with this when we get to the ranch, or I'll kick your ass." He kicked dirt in the air as he walked away, angry at himself for his language. He jumped on Razor to ride after Strait and try to smooth his ruffled feathers.

If he'd been in a lighthearted mood, Jake might have laughed at his big burly brother using the term *bad words*. His nephews had them all watching their *bad words*. But his own foul temper kept him from seeing the humor in the situation. He figured dinner was going to be a quiet affair, now that he'd ticked off Strait and Colt. He'd already made Promise so mad she'd stopped talking to him two days ago. He couldn't really blame her, since he'd done nothing but complain when she'd been driving the wagon. He'd said the same thing to her that he said to Strait about hitting ruts. He'd even complained about her cooking, saying things he didn't really mean. Even though he knew he was in the wrong, he was so ill-tempered that he still hadn't apologized. Now, Strait and Colt probably wouldn't be talking to him for the next week. *Hell's bells!* It was that dang wagon, he told himself. He didn't know how people rode in those things, particularly clear across the country. He glanced over at Promise, who was pulling out supplies from the wagon to cook dinner. She'd ridden a long way in a wagon, he reminded himself. It shamed him all the more when he remembered what she'd been through, and he'd never heard her once complain.

He leaned back and pulled his hat over his eyes, not covering them all the way so he could keep an eye on her. Just to make sure she was safe, he told himself. Knowing he'd been acting like a jackass, he needed to figure out a way to apologize to her without actually admitting he was wrong. As much as he tried not to look, every time she bent over, his eyes traveled down to her rear end. She was back to wearing those split skirts, and that was driving him to distraction. If he wasn't mistaken, they weren't the same ones she'd worn before. She must have gotten them from her aunt. He was positive she only had one pair, and he hoped she'd worn them out. His thoughts went back to that morning in the wagon when he woke up with her on top of him and he'd kissed her. Lord help him, he didn't need to go there.

Promise prepared the food at the wagon and carried the pot to the fire, giving Jake a wide berth. He'd been in such ill humor that she was thankful she had Hero to ride so she could keep some distance between them. Unfortunately for Strait, he had to put up with Jake. She tried to be understanding of Jake's dark mood, but she couldn't help comparing it to the change in his attitude toward her. It was night and day from the way he'd treated her before they'd reached Denver. Once the stew started bubbling, she walked back to the wagon to prepare the corn bread.

Jake and Promise didn't exchange a word the entire time Colt and Strait were gone. They were gone longer than Jake expected, so he figured they were scouting the area before they came back to camp. Once they finally rode into camp and cared for their horses, they walked over to the wagon to talk with Promise. Jake could hear them laughing, but he couldn't quite make out what they were saying.

"Something sure smells good," he said, loud enough for everyone to hear.

His comment was met with silence.

The three walked to the fire, but no one glanced Jake's

way. Colt took the pan of corn bread from Promise and placed it over the flame.

"Promise, do you know how to play poker?" Strait asked, carrying the coffeepot to the fire.

"Yes, my father taught me when I was young," she replied. "My mother was furious when she caught us." She smiled at the memory of her mother giving her father a proper dressing-down, saying a young girl shouldn't be taught such things. She remembered how her father had responded, as if he'd spoken the words only yesterday. *It might come in handy one day for my only daughter to know how to play a hand of poker.*

"We can play after dinner if you'd like," Colt said.

Anything that brought back memories of her father gave her comfort. "That would be lovely."

"That will be a nice change," Jake agreed. When no one acknowledged him, he added, "She's probably as good at poker as she is with everything else. She can shoot and ride as good as any man." As magnanimous as he was, no one spared a glance in his direction, so he asked, "Is that stew about ready? It sure smells good."

Colt, taking pity on his brother, leaned over and looked at the stew. "Looks good."

"About the time the corn bread is ready, the stew will be done," Promise commented without looking Jake's way.

When Promise walked back to the wagon for their plates, Jake found himself gazing at her rear end again.

Colt turned to his brother. "Have you apologized to her yet?"

"Not yet. I can't get a word in edgewise with you two hanging all over her." He caught Strait staring at Promise's backside too.

"Don't start," Colt warned, seeing the direction of his brother's eyes. "Why didn't you say something to her while we were gone? We took it slow coming back because I thought you would use the time wisely."

Seeing Promise was walking toward them, Jake didn't respond.

"Someone has a pile of matchsticks. I think you were holding out on us about how well you played," Colt teased.

Promise was more surprised than anyone by her winning hands. Secretly, she wondered if they were letting her win in an effort to make amends for Jake's rude behavior. "Truly, I haven't played since I was a child."

"She does everything well," Jake said in another clumsy attempt to apologize without actually saying the words.

"I didn't think I could cook to suit," Promise retorted, refusing to accept his compliment.

Jake looked contrite, and was sorry for his cantankerous attitude over the last few days, but he was at a loss how to ask for forgiveness. "You can cook fine," he mumbled.

"High praise," she responded tartly. "That's certainly not what you said a few days ago."

She wasn't going to make this easy, Jake thought.

Colt, recognizing the signs of a woman in high dudgeon, stood and said, "I guess we'd best turn in. Strait, you want first watch?"

"I'll take it," Jake said. "I've had so much coffee I won't sleep anyway."

Colt nodded. "That'll work." He figured his brother wanted to make another attempt to speak privately with Promise, so he glanced at Strait and inclined his head toward their horses. "We'll see to the horses before we turn in."

Promise got to her feet. "I'll see to Hero."

"I'll take care of him," Colt replied.

Once they were out of earshot, Jake thought he'd set things straight. "I like your cooking fine."

Promise started gathering the plates, but she turned to look at him. "I know you blame me for what happened."

Jake held up his hand. "Stop right there. I don't blame you for a darn thing. I just can't stand being in that wagon all day. It's driving me crazy."

Promise could appreciate how he felt, yet she was sure there was more going on than sheer frustration from riding in the wagon. The whole time on the trail he had made her feel safe and secure, but since he'd been shot, his attitude had been nothing but cool. She was distraught over the change in their relationship. Tears were welling up in her eyes, and she absolutely refused to let him see her cry. She turned away, saying, "I need to get some blankets."

Jake sat alone, staring into the dying embers and wondering how everything could have gone so wrong.

"Did you apologize?" Colt asked when he returned with their bedrolls.

Jake wasn't really sure if she understood he was apologizing. "I tried."

Colt plopped down on his bedroll and gave Jake an exasperated look. "Either you said you're sorry or you didn't. It's not that difficult."

"I said that her cooking was fine," Jake replied, as if that was a grand apology.

Strait snorted. "Colt, I didn't know your brother was such a dumb son-of-a-buck," he said, shaking his head

Colt looked at Jake in disbelief. "Neither did I."

"Well, it was a dumb idea taking her to Wyoming anyway!" Jake said, trying to redirect the blame.

Colt and Strait stared at him, confused by his outburst.

Glaring back at them defiantly, Jake expounded on his reasoning. "She's led a pampered life. Hell, she's never had to help anyone out, and she had servants! Her clothes come from Paris, France."

"Tell me how that pampered gal managed to get in the back of a wagon and travel two thousand miles if she's so fragile?" Colt ground out. He felt like knocking some sense into his brother's hard head.

"Yeah, and I bet she didn't whine like a little girl every five minutes," Strait added.

Jake shut his mouth.

Promise returned with some blankets and gave one to each man. She spread her blanket near Colt, as far away from Jake as possible. "Good night," she said.

Colt and Strait said good night and Jake, not one to give up, said, "That stew was real good."

Colt gave Jake a look that said *stop digging that hole.* "Wake me in two hours, Jake."

Chapter Twenty-Five

Jake had minded his manners for several days, trying not to complain every time Strait hit a rut. Promise still wasn't talking to him, other than when it was absolutely necessary, and that aggravated him even more. Now, he was sitting with his back to the side board so he could see what was going on in front of the wagon. He sat in silence, watching Colt ride beside Promise for miles. It looked like they had a lot to talk about.

Colt and Promise slowed their mounts so the wagon could catch up to them. "Two riders," Colt said to Jake and Strait.

"We saw them," Jake answered. "They're riding at a pretty fast clip."

"Yeah. Is your rifle beside you?" Colt asked Jake.

"Yep, and my pistol's in my lap."

"Promise, get behind me," Colt instructed as he maneuvered his horse closer to the wagon. "Do you have your pistol on you?"

"Yes," she replied, moving Hero behind Colt's horse and pulling her pistol from her saddlebag. She stared at the riders in the distance. "I think that is Rodriguez."

"How do you know that?" Jake thought she had to be

guessing because the men were still too far away for him to identify.

"By the way he sits his horse. And the other man . . . well, he sits a horse like you, Jake."

"The only man who looks like Jake on a horse is—" Colt stopped midsentence and stared hard at the riders. "I can't believe it!" Giving his horse rein, Colt headed toward the two men.

Watching as his brother reached the riders, Jake saw Colt lean over in his saddle to embrace one of the men, darn near pulling him off the horse. "It can't be!" Jake exclaimed.

"What?" Strait asked. "Who is it?"

Jake laughed. "That's our younger brother with Rodriguez. Get this wagon moving!"

Promise and Strait caught up to the riders, and Lucas jumped from his horse and ran to the wagon. "Brother, I've been worried about you," he said, not knowing whether to hug Jake or not. He settled for putting his arm around his shoulder. "But I should have known you're too damn mean to die!"

"I couldn't let that happen," Jake replied, choked up at seeing his baby brother.

Rodriguez rode his horse next to Promise. "Señorita, this is a pleasant surprise. I hadn't expected to see you with this party. You are looking lovelier than ever."

"What are you two doing here?" Jake asked.

"You mean you weren't expecting me?" Lucas asked in mock surprise. "Hell, you had every lawman in the country looking for me. I've been expecting to see my mug on a wanted poster before long."

"I expected to see you in Wyoming," Jake told him. He glanced at Rodriguez and said, "If you will stop flirting, I can introduce my baby brother to Promise."

"I feel like I already know her," Lucas said, giving

Promise a wide smile. "I've heard all about her from Cole and Rodriguez."

Promise returned his smile. "They were kind enough to put up with me on the way to Denver." She couldn't stop staring at Lucas. At a distance, he looked very much like Jake. All three brothers were tall and they all had black, wavy hair, but where Colt and Jake had black eyes, Lucas had the most striking blue eyes she'd ever seen. The color of turquoise.

"We didn't think she would be with you," Rodriguez commented to Colt.

"She's coming to help Victoria out for a few months," Colt said. "What are you two doing out here?"

"I was at the ranch when your last telegram came, so I figured I would ride this way," Lucas responded. "I met up with the drive just a few days from the ranch."

Rodriguez took up the story. "Since we were so close to the ranch, Cole figured I should ride along with Luke."

"Cole wanted to come, but he's bound and determined to see the cattle arrive at the ranch," Lucas added. "I imagine the cattle are already grazing on McBride land by now."

Colt smacked his youngest brother on the back. "I'm glad you're here. Let's get going. I'll fill you in on the way. We don't want to waste daylight."

Sitting around the fire that night, Promise was quiet as she listened to Jake and Colt pepper Lucas with questions. While it was joyful to hear them laugh together, it brought back memories of the many times she'd laughed with her brother. Choosing not to allow her melancholy mood to dampen their high spirits, she walked to the wagon to collect the blankets, allowing them some private time.

After a few minutes, Rodriguez excused himself to check on the horses, and Colt used that moment alone with his brothers to ask the question he'd been longing to ask since he first laid eyes on Lucas.

"You ready to come home and settle down at the ranch like Jake?"

Jake chuckled. "Well, you managed to wait about six hours to start badgering him."

"I'm not badgering him, I just wanted to tell him we'd like to have him home," Colt said.

"I've thought about it," Lucas admitted. Coming home had been on his mind for a long time, even before he'd heard that his brothers were looking for him. The only thing that had held him back was his concern that Colt might not welcome him since he'd worked the ranch with no help from his brothers. After he arrived and saw for himself what Colt had accomplished, Luke was even more fearful his brother might resent his coming back now. "Is that the reason you had lawmen looking for me?"

"Yeah. We haven't heard from you in a long time. Since Jake was coming back, well, we agreed it would be nice if you did too. I've wanted you both to come home for a long time."

"I don't have twenty-five hundred head of cattle, but I do have some money. I'm half owner of the Lucky Sunday silver mine," Lucas said.

"You don't need anything to come home. It's your home. Jake didn't need anything either," Colt assured him.

Colt's words brought a lump to Luke's throat. He collected himself and glanced at Jake. "You're really finished being a lawman?"

"I am. I want to go home and stay there," Jake answered without hesitation. "And Colt didn't ask me for any investment. I had saved some money and decided we needed more cattle."

"More cattle?" Luke grinned. "Hell, big brother here"— he jabbed a finger at Colt—"has built an empire."

"You can never have too many cattle," Jake retorted. "Cole turned in his resignation at the same time I did, saying he wanted to experience a real cattle drive."

Colt laughed. "I'm sure this particular cattle drive has been an experience he will never forget."

They were quiet for a moment before Luke looked at Colt and said, "Well, the house you built is large enough for all of us, unless you plan on filling it up with young ones with that beautiful wife of yours."

"I'm doing my best." Colt shoved more wood on the fire, his thoughts centered on Victoria. "How does she look?"

His brothers heard the concern in his voice.

"She looks beautiful," Lucas told him. "I've never seen two more beautiful women," he added, glancing at Promise.

Oh, hell's bells, not Lucas too, Jake thought.

"Is she minding the doc?" Colt asked.

"That Mrs. Wellington wouldn't let her do otherwise," Luke said. "That woman is a tough ol' bird."

"She is that," Jake offered, but his attention drifted to Rodriguez and Promise. They were standing beside Hero, and it looked like they were having a serious conversation.

Following Jake's gaze, Luke said, "I think Rodriguez is in love. He talked about her the whole time."

"Every man on the drive is in love with her," Jake grumbled.

"You mean everyone but you," Colt added.

"Yeah," Jake replied. "I told you what it would be like when we get to the ranch."

"You jealous?" Luke noticed how his brother watched Promise. It seemed to him he had more than a passing fancy where she was concerned.

Colt laughed and Jake frowned. "Hell no! I just want the men to concentrate on work when we get to the ranch."

"I've told you, Promise will be busy in the house. You're

wasting your time worrying about something that will not be a problem," Colt told him.

Jake decided to change the subject. "Luke, you and Rodriguez stay alert. We don't really think those killers are headed to Mexico, but we didn't want to worry Promise."

"Have you been dogged so far?" Luke asked.

"We haven't seen anything out of the ordinary," Colt said. "But these are bad hombres, and they are not opposed to hiding in the trees to waylay us, like they did Jake."

"Cole told me Rodriguez is good with a gun," Luke said.

Jake nodded. "Cole's better, but Rodriguez is pretty good. I'm sure that's why Cole sent him with you."

"How many men attacked that wagon train?" Luke asked.

It angered Jake each time he recalled that scene. "Best I could figure, there were about a dozen."

"That's a lot of meanness in one gang," Luke mused.

Three days passed peacefully. Even Jake's mood improved because Lucas drove the wagon, and listening to his stories kept Jake occupied.

Colt pointed to the Rockies so Promise could see the magnificent sight. It was a perfect day; the clear blue sky was the perfect backdrop for the glorious mountains stretching over the landscape. "Oh my, I don't think I ever expected anything so lovely. How fortunate you are to have that view every day." She planned to paint the mountains while she was at the McBride ranch. "This is beautiful country."

"They are a sight to behold," Colt agreed. He knew the artist in her would appreciate the beauty of the land.

Rodriguez had been riding alone, sometimes well in front of the group, sometimes behind. It almost came as a surprise a few days later when he found signs they were being followed.

It was past midnight when Colt whispered in his brother's ear, "Jake, wake up."

Quickly coming alert at the urgency in his brother's voice, Jake reached for his pistol. "What's going on?" It was so light under the full moon that Jake thought it was morning and he'd overslept.

"Shhh . . . they're coming in, and we need to get to those rocks." Colt lifted his chin, indicating the direction.

Colt assisted Jake from the wagon, and Lucas grabbed his rifle. "I counted ten horses," he told them.

They moved quickly and quietly, positioning themselves behind some rocks fifteen feet from the fire.

Promise was waiting for them with her pistol gripped tightly in her hands. Colt and Jake wedged her between them.

"Where's Strait and Rodriguez?" Jake asked.

Indicating their location with his drawn pistol, Colt responded, "About ten yards away."

Jake noticed someone had stuffed the bedrolls with blankets to make it look like they were sleeping. Colt's trick, most likely. He wasn't surprised to see Colt with a pistol in each hand, indicating he meant business. If the killers had any inkling how deadly Colt was with a gun in each hand, they would have been riding in the other direction.

Out of habit, Jake checked the cylinder of his pistol. Glancing at Promise, he thought she looked frightened, but one look at the pistol she held steady told him she was handling her nerves. The memory of the day on the trail when she and Shorty fought off the killers alone was still fresh in his mind. Like before, she might fall apart after the shooting was over, but right now, she was displaying her grit. He leaned close to her ear and whispered, "Ready?"

In all truth, she was so nervous she couldn't have responded if she wanted to, but she turned her large eyes on him and managed to nod. She wished she could be as calm and collected as the McBride brothers.

Lucas took his position next to Jake. "Can you shoot?"

"These bast—" Jake remembered Promise on his other side and tempered his words. "I'll manage." Oh yeah, he would gladly send all of these killers to Hell.

Strait signaled with a bird whistle, and everyone cocked their guns.

The killers didn't seem concerned about coming in silent; they came in with guns blasting, their bullets pelting the empty bedrolls. When Colt shot the lead man out of the saddle, the men behind him were so stunned they stopped firing to see where the shot came from.

Colt yelled out, "Throw your guns to the ground and you'll still be breathing five minutes from now."

Jake said, "I thought there were supposed to be ten. There's only six."

"Stay sharp, they are probably holed up waiting for their compadres, but we can't be sure," Colt said.

The riders glanced at each other, realizing they hadn't shot anyone. Instead of throwing their guns to the ground, they started firing toward the rocks. It was only a matter of seconds before the remaining five riders were in the dirt.

Promise hung back while the men walked to the bodies with guns still cocked. Two of the outlaws were still alive. Rodriguez and Strait rounded up all of the weapons and fetched the scattering horses.

Colt leaned over one man who was still breathing and examined the wound in his shoulder. "You'll live," he said.

Joining Colt, Jake pointed his pistol at the man's head while his brother relieved him of his pistol.

One look at Jake's ominous expression, and the man pleaded, "Don't kill me!"

Jake and Colt exchanged a brief glance, and Jake knew his brother was thinking the same thing he was. While he wasn't in the habit of killing men in cold blood, Jake let the man think that he would when he placed the muzzle of his .45 under his chin. "Where's Big Ugly?"

The man didn't even question who Jake was talking about. "He's on his way back to Denver," the man responded quickly.

His injured friend heard the man talking and yelled, "Shut your trap, Ritter."

Jake narrowed his eyes at the man. "Thought he was headed to Mexico."

"No, I swear, he's going back to Denver. Please, don't kill me. I didn't even want to do this. I wasn't there that day when they killed those people on that wagon train. I told them we should leave it alone and go on to Mexico."

"Ritter, shut the hell up! This will get back to Schott!" the other man warned.

Jake saw Lucas standing near the man doing the yelling. "Luke, if that back-shooter says one more word, give him an invite to a dance."

"Hell, he's shot in the leg, so he can't dance. I'd rather plug him than shoot at his toes," Luke countered.

It was Colt who turned the full force of his intimidating glare toward Ritter. "Why are you still dogging us?"

"The woman. He wants her. And he wants her dead 'cause she saw him, and she shot his brother dead," he said, his voice ragged from pain.

"What's Schott got to do with this?" Colt questioned.

Ritter hesitated. Jake poked the muzzle deeper into his

skin as encouragement. "It won't take much for me to make you two into cottonwood blossoms."

"You can't hang us!" Ritter shouted.

Colt arched a brow at him. "No?"

Ritter decided the massive man glaring at him was more dangerous than Schott and Big Ugly combined. "Okay, okay. He hired us to keep them folks from coming to the Hollister ranch. He was trying to run those people off that land."

"Why?" Jake couldn't figure out why Schott would have a problem with the people who are farming on Hollister's land.

"Schott offered to buy that piece of land from that rancher, and he got turned down flat. That don't set well with Schott. Nobody turns him down," Ritter answered. "He wasn't about to let anyone else settle on that land."

"What's Big Ugly's given name?" Jake asked.

"Hart Newcombe."

"That's almost funny. He was probably born without a heart." A man like Big Ugly had to have a reputation; he didn't just turn up working for Schott one day, so Jake asked, "Where else is he wanted?"

"Kansas, for murder."

Jake and Colt walked a few feet away from the campfire to discuss their options while Luke and Strait tied up the men. "I say we give them a horse and tell them to ride on out and give Big Ugly a message where we'll be," Jake said.

"Our minds are on the same track," Colt said. "We'll be home in another two days, and they won't reach Denver for several days, if they make it at all. Who knows, they might have a disagreement and kill each other before then. Hell, they might even bleed to death. We can wire Hollister from the next town and tell him what's going on."

"If they don't come to the ranch, then I'll head back to Denver when I'm able," Jake added. He was confident he'd be able to make the trip after he had a week to recuperate.

Strait and Luke joined in the conversation after they bound the men. "We sure as hell don't want to haul their sorry butts home with us, but, Colt, are you sure you want that trouble at the ranch?" Strait asked.

"It's always better to face trouble on your own land, on your own terms," Colt answered.

"Well, if they don't come to the ranch, I'll go to Denver with you when you're ready, Jake," Luke told him.

"You won't need to go to Denver," Colt said with conviction. "They've dogged you this far, and they won't give up now."

Chapter Twenty-Six

Taking the steps four at a time, Colt raced to the bedroom to see his wife.

"Colt!" Victoria's smile was wide when her husband bounded into the room.

Lifting her off the bed, Colt sat in the chair with her in his lap and kissed her like he'd been away for years. Forcing his lips from hers, he said, "I've missed you and those kisses."

Victoria hugged his neck. "I'm so glad you are back. How's Jake? Were you surprised to see Lucas?"

She was asking so many questions, she reminded him of the boys. "On the road to recovery. You will see everyone shortly. I told them I would carry you down for dinner. And yes, I was surprised to see Lucas." He kissed her again. "How are you, honey?"

"I'm fine. I told the doctor that he was being too cautious." She yanked a lock of hair at the back of his neck. "I think he's so afraid of you that he's being overprotective."

Colt grinned. "The man shows good judgment."

"You're impossible," she teased, but secretly she was thankful her husband wasn't embarrassed to show his love for her. Actually, he was exactly the opposite. It didn't

bother him to show affection, or to tell anyone how much
he loved her.

"By the way, we brought you some help." Colt was explaining what had happened on Jake's cattle drive when the
boys ran into the room.

"Pa!" Cade and Cody exclaimed, bounding into the
room with Bandit on their heels.

Colt positioned Victoria on one thigh as the boys jumped
on his other thigh, and Bandit wedged himself between
his legs.

Colt found himself near tears at the greeting. He feared
his new family was going to turn him into a blubbering
fool.

By the time Colt carried Victoria to the dining room,
he'd gotten control of his emotions. But once he saw everyone he loved in the world seated at the table, he had to fight
for control again. After the many years of being alone, he
thanked God for his good fortune to have his brothers back
on the ranch, and to have found his wife and sons. He
would never have guessed that his brothers were equally
emotional just to be with him again.

After Colt introduced Victoria to Promise, the women
soon started chatting like old friends. Victoria liked her
very much, and she hoped Colt was right in his assumption
that Jake cared for this lovely woman. In her mind, she
was already thinking Promise would make a wonderful
sister-in-law.

Promise fell in love with Victoria and the boys, as well
as the woman Colt introduced as Victoria's surrogate
mother, Mrs. Wellington. She understood why Jake thought
so much of Victoria; she was a lovely woman, inside and
out. Throughout dinner, she found herself watching Jake
stare at Victoria. She suspected his feelings for his brother's
wife ran deeper than a mere crush. As much as she wished
she could find something about Colt's lovely wife to dislike,

she couldn't. And she didn't think Jake would ever look at another woman the way he looked at Victoria.

"Thank you so much for coming to help us," Victoria said to her. "I hope my husband and Jake didn't twist your arm too badly."

"Not at all. Actually it was my idea."

"I told her she needed to see Wyoming," Cole said. "But it never occurred to me I would see her here this soon."

Victoria could see that Promise wouldn't lack in suitors now that there were so many single men at the ranch, thanks to the cattle drive. "I am so happy to have you here," she said sincerely.

"The least I can do is help, after all Jake's done for me."

Jake slammed his fork to his plate. "I've told you before that you aren't beholden to me! And I don't need anyone looking after me!"

"I'm sorry, I didn't mean to . . ." Promise couldn't finish because she was so stunned at his outburst. Her lips started to quiver, and she turned her attention to her plate so no one could see she was about to cry. Jake had never been so rude to her, and she was heartbroken.

Victoria wanted to throttle Jake for hurting Promise, but she'd leave it up to Colt to box his ears for his behavior. She tried to make amends for Jake's rude behavior. "It's a blessing that Jake doesn't need help, but *I* can certainly use your help."

Mrs. Wellington caught the ominous look on Colt's face, so she thought it prudent to change the subject. "Jake, it was so exciting to see all of those cattle."

As soon as the words left his mouth, Jake wanted to say he was sorry to Promise, but he didn't. He turned his attention to Mrs. Wellington instead. "I bet the men were glad to get here."

"You can say that again. After that cattle drive, I hope I

don't see rain for six months," Cole said. "And Shorty is so happy here, I think he might just stay."

Colt didn't want to upset his wife, so he didn't light into Jake, though he was about to bite through his tongue. He'd wait until later to set him straight. "That's fine with me," he said. "We added on to the bunkhouse just in case they all wanted to stay."

"Jake, why don't you take the bedroom downstairs until you're feeling better? You won't be forced to negotiate that stairway," Victoria said.

"Luke and I are staying in the bunkhouse," Jake answered testily.

"Surely you would be more comfortable in the house," Victoria countered.

Jake didn't respond, and Victoria looked at her husband, clearly confused by Jake's attitude.

"You are both welcome in the house," Colt commented, knowing that was what his wife wanted.

Luke looked from Jake to Colt, trying to figure out what was going on. "Jake thought we would be in the way."

"You most certainly will not be in the way," Victoria said.

"We've already stored our gear," Jake said with finality.

Colt could tell by the set of Jake's jaw that he wasn't changing his mind. If his dumb brother wanted to exchange the comforts of home, with a beautiful woman looking after him, for a bunkhouse full of smelly men, who was he to argue? He smiled at his wife. "I think that is very thoughtful of my brothers." He wasn't sure if Jake was trying to avoid Promise or Victoria, and he didn't care, just as long as he treated them civilly. He gave Jake a look that telegraphed *you'd better not do anything to upset my wife*. He reached over and squeezed his wife's hand. "Don't worry, honey. You'll see them every night at dinner." Another glare at Jake dared him to disagree.

Knowing her husband would take care of the matter with

Jake, Victoria turned her attention on Promise. "Promise, tomorrow when you have time, I will show you the reticules. Mrs. Wagner, the lady who helps me, will be coming by so we can discuss the new designs. Mrs. Wellington will be joining us, so we can all have a nice visit and lunch together."

Promise had collected herself, and was grateful to Victoria for redirecting the conversation. "I can't wait to see them."

The next day Promise, Mrs. Wellington, and Mrs. Wagner sat in Victoria's bedroom looking at the new patterns Victoria had drawn for her reticules.

"Victoria, these are beautiful," Promise said.

"Thank you. I'm glad I have this to keep me busy in my confinement."

"I'm thankful for the opportunity to earn money doing something I enjoy," Mrs. Wagner added. "I don't know how I would have fed my children if not for Victoria."

Victoria patted Mrs. Wagner's hand. "I'm the one who is fortunate. Your work is beautiful." She glanced at Promise. "Colt told me that you are an excellent artist. I would be honored if you would show us your work."

"I would be delighted to show you whenever you like," Promise replied.

"Why not right now, so we can all see?" Victoria suggested, with Mrs. Wellington and Mrs. Wagner nodding their agreement. "Colt said you did an absolutely lovely drawing of Jake."

It was difficult to imagine that Colt would use the word *lovely*, but Promise kept that thought to herself. "I'll get them."

When Promise left the room, Mrs. Wellington said, "If that young man knows what's what, he'll latch on to that gal."

Victoria knew Mrs. Wellington was referring to Jake, but Mrs. Wagner said, "Which young man?"

"Jake, of course. I can't believe he's been with her all these months and hasn't noticed she is crazy about him," Mrs. Wellington replied.

"Jake doesn't think he is ready to settle down," Victoria offered.

"As I recall, his older brother was of the same opinion until he met you," Mrs. Wellington reminded her.

Victoria hadn't had the chance to discuss Jake's behavior with Colt, but she certainly planned to later today. She had a feeling Jake was fighting his feelings for Promise. "I think he may need a gentle nudge. I have a feeling my husband could provide that."

The women were smiling when Promise came into the room carrying her leather pouch filled with drawings.

Colt made a point of riding in from the range early, so he could have a talk with Jake. Fortunately, he found Jake alone in the bunkhouse. Pulling a chair up next to his bunk, Colt turned it around, straddled the seat, and got right to the point. "I thought one of the reasons we agreed Promise would come here was so she could help look after you."

"I told you last night, I'm fine, and I sure as hell don't need anyone looking after me. She needs to take care of the chores in the house and help Victoria."

"Can you change your own bandage?" Colt asked.

"Shorty can handle what I need," Jake countered. "I'm sure he's changed more bandages than Promise."

Colt shook his head. "Why are you insisting on acting like a jackass? You'd rather have Shorty fussing over you than a beautiful woman? Not to mention, Mrs. Wellington would probably make you some fine pies if you stirred enough sympathy."

For the first time in days, Jake cracked a smile.

Colt noticed. "Damn, I thought you forgot how to do that."

"Do what?"

"Smile."

"Guess I haven't had much to smile about."

"I think you should come at it from another angle. God gave you another chance at life. If not for Promise insisting her uncle look for you that day, you would have probably died on that road alone. I'd say you have one whole heck of a lot to smile about. You could be on the root side of the daisies. You keep saying Promise isn't beholding to you for saving her life, but I'm for damn sure beholding to her for saving yours. You should appreciate how she feels."

Deep down, Jake knew his brother was right. He was acting like a dang fool, but he couldn't seem to stop. "You're right about that."

"Is being laid up all that's troubling you?"

Jake gave his brother a serious look. "I know you mean well, Colt, but I just don't want to stay in the house right now."

"Is it because of Promise or Victoria?"

Stunned that his brother seemed to read his mind, Jake wasn't sure how to respond.

"Jake, you're not the only cowboy infatuated with Victoria. As a matter of fact, half of them on this ranch are. It's only natural that you want what I've been lucky enough to find. If you're not attracted to Promise in that way, then there will be someone else. Just don't go thinking your feelings run deeper than they do for Victoria, and ruin something else right before your eyes that could make you happier than you can even imagine." Jake didn't respond, and Colt said, "'How bitter a thing it is to look into happiness through another man's eyes.'"

Jake wanted to roll his eyes, but he arched a brow at him instead. "Shakespeare?" He thought Colt saved that Shakespeare stuff to impress his wife.

"Yeah, Shakespeare. You should read him sometime. He was a very insightful man."

Jake looked away, thinking about what his brother said. Finally, he asked, "What if I'm not as noble as you?"

Standing, Colt picked up his chair and returned it to the table. "Don't sell yourself short, brother, or I will have to kick your ass . . . rear end." He had to remember to keep the language clean. He reached the door, then turned around. "Do I need to come and carry you to dinner, or are you going to make it on your own two feet?"

There was no question in Jake's mind that his brother was mean enough to carry him into that house like a baby. He might tangle with a lot of men, but Colt wasn't one of them. "I'll be there."

Chapter Twenty-Seven

Over the next few days Jake had a lot of free time to reflect on Colt's words, since he was alone in the bunkhouse during the day. Even Shorty abandoned him to work on the range with the other men. By the third day of his self-inflicted solitary confinement, he thought he might actually go mad, but Cade and Cody paid him a visit.

"Uncle Jake, Ma said we should come out here and see how you are doing," Cody said.

"I'm doing good," Jake replied. He was happy to see his nephews. It looked like they'd grown a foot since he'd left for Texas months ago. They were so cute, and Jake wished they would stay seven forever. "How are you boys doing?"

"Good," they both chimed in.

"Ma said you should come in the house for lunch," Cade told him.

He wondered if his sister-in-law was trying to push him on Promise. "Hell's bells," he said without thinking.

"Uncle Jake!" the boys exclaimed before they started giggling. "Ma told us to 'mind you what was gonna happen if you said bad words," Cade said.

"And *hell's bells* is a bad word," Cody added.

Cade elbowed his brother in his side. "Ma said she would do the same thing to us if we repeated the bad words."

Jake looked at the two pairs of silver-blue eyes staring up at him and winked at them. "I won't tell if you don't."

"Deal!" the boys said.

"You can say *church bells* instead of hel—" Cody stopped before he got another elbow in the ribs. "Instead of that bad word, and we'll know what you mean."

"That sounds good," Jake told them. He just had to remember to break that habit. "Why did your ma want me to come to lunch?"

"I dunno, she just said you should, and we wasn't to take no for an answer," Cade said, imitating Victoria's voice.

"She says if you needed help, we should go get Pa. Do you need me to go get Pa?" Cody asked.

"I reckon I can make it." He sure didn't want to have his big brother carrying him like he'd already threatened.

"Ma says when you're better you can go riding with us and Miss Promise," Cade told him. "Did you know she can ride real good?"

"Yeah, she rode with Cole and T. J. this morning, and she rides as good as they do. T. J. says she's a good cowboy," Cody added.

This was news to Jake. Ranch work must be slowing down if Cole and Colt's foreman could take the morning to go pleasure riding. Maybe he should have brought back five thousand head of cattle. He guessed T. J. was going to be following her around, too. "I thought she had a lot of work to do in the house."

"Ma told her to take a break 'cause she works so hard,

and her horse was sure to be lonesome. Anyways, Mrs. Wagner was there to see to Ma."

These youngsters knew more about what was going on than he did. Leaving his bunk, Jake thought he should at least wash his face and put on a clean shirt if he was going to the house.

"Ma says she's going to have Promise teach her more about riding. Pa didn't get to teach her much since she got in the family way." Cody looked puzzled and asked, "Does *family way* mean we're having a brother or sister?"

Jake chuckled. "Something like that." It was easy to see the love these boys had for Victoria and Colt. Every other word out of their mouths was *ma says,* or *pa says*.

"I'm thinking maybe we need a boy 'cause there's so many women in the house now," Cade said. "Only Promise talks about horses and stuff boys like."

"Yeah, we showed her a frog today and she touched it and didn't think it was icky," Cody added. "She said her brother would bring her frogs all the time."

Jake thought Promise was probably missing her brother.

"Frogs and bugs make Mrs. Wellington scream," Cody went on.

"Pa says Promise is real special, and Ma will find her a husband so she'll always stay here," Cade said.

Jake listened to their conversation while he brushed his hair. So Victoria was going to try to find Promise a husband. He couldn't say he was surprised. Women were always trying to find husbands for single women. But it sure as shooting was not going to be him. If that was her plan, she could get that notion right out of her pretty little head.

"You got a wife, Uncle Jake?"

Jake didn't know which boy had asked. "No."

"Do you want one?" Cade asked.

"No."

"Don't you got to have a wife to have boys?" Cody questioned.

"If you want to have children, it comes in handy to have a wife."

"Don't you want some boys?" Cade asked.

"They could play with us," Cody told him.

"You boys will be grown before I get married," Jake said, hoping to put an end to this conversation. He couldn't believe Victoria would use the boys to try and soften him up. He finished buttoning his fresh shirt. "Okay, let's get to the house."

Each boy grabbed a hand, and Jake noticed they were careful not to pull on him as they led him from the bunkhouse. Victoria must have told them he wasn't well enough to have them jumping on him.

Jake expected he was lunching with all women, but to his surprise the boys led him to the parlor, where he found Colt sitting in a chair with Victoria in his lap. Promise was sitting on a settee between T. J. and Cole. Jake thought there wasn't an inch of space between them.

"What's going on? Are we out of work on the ranch?" he asked, his eyes slicing to T. J. and Cole.

The boys dropped Jake's hands and ran to Colt. "There's plenty of work, no need to worry about that," Colt replied, putting an arm around the boys. "We just thought we would surprise the ladies today, didn't we, boys?"

"Yep," the twins replied in unison.

Colt didn't divulge that it was his wife's idea to get Jake out of the bunkhouse. He'd told Victoria about his brother's infatuation with her, but they both agreed that he was just envious of their happiness. They both thought Jake had deeper feelings for Promise than he wanted to admit. Colt recognized jealousy when he saw it, and he'd seen plenty of that from Jake anytime another man so much as spoke to Promise. He remembered how he'd felt when another man was courting Victoria: He was so jealous he couldn't think straight. He wasn't surprised when Victoria said she had a plan to see if Jake really did care for Promise. What better way to have Jake admit his feelings than to see other men vying for Promise's attention.

"What's the occasion? It's not like you to take time from ranch work," Jake asked.

"I just missed my family, so I'm making up for lost time," Colt replied, hugging the boys to him.

"We missed you too, Pa," Cade told him.

"Yeah, but Ma was really missing you. She was always crying," Cody said.

Colt tightened his arm around his wife. "She was?"

"Well, not always," Victoria said.

"Were too," Cody countered.

"Lunchtime," Victoria said to end the conversation. "Mrs. Wellington worked hard on a very nice lunch, so you boys be sure to compliment her."

"I thought Promise was here to do the cooking," Jake commented.

Victoria glared at her brother-in-law, and Colt said only one word, but it was delivered in a tone that made everyone go silent. "Jake."

Jake looked at everyone's stunned expression and he couldn't figure out what he had done this time. Realizing they thought he was being rude, he quickly added, "I just meant I like her cooking. She makes really good apple pies."

Promise did her best to ignore him. She reminded herself that once spring came, her obligation to the McBride family would be fulfilled. Cole had promised to take her back to Denver, where she planned to stay with her family for a few weeks before returning to Sinclair Hall. Now that

Matthew was gone, her plans had changed. Managing the family holdings was now in her hands, so her dream of staying in the West would come to an end before another year passed. Now, she just needed to concern herself with avoiding Jake McBride until spring.

Colt stood with Victoria in his arms, determined to abide by doctor's orders that she stay off her feet. "Now you can tell me about this picnic over lunch," he said to her.

"Picnic?" Jake asked.

"Victoria wants to have a picnic for all the hands in a couple of weeks, before cold weather sets in. We might invite some of the other ranchers too," Colt responded.

"It's already September, and before you know it we will have snow to our knees. I'd like to introduce Promise to some of the single ranchers," Victoria informed him.

Jake rolled his eyes. Like Promise didn't have enough men drooling over her. He was looking at two of them escorting her to the dining room, looking like a pair of bookends.

Lying in his bunk that night, Jake's mind was on Colt and his new family. It surprised him that his brother would take off in the middle of the workday to have lunch with his wife. He couldn't begrudge his brother for wanting to enjoy his new family; he was due some fun in his life. Other than the time Colt was shot, he'd probably never taken a day off. He figured Colt was right when he'd told him he was envious of the happiness he'd found. It wasn't much of a stretch to see himself in that scenario, with a wife and boys plying him with love and attention.

During lunch he hadn't been able to get a word in edgewise with Cole and T. J. jabbering to Promise the whole time. Come to think of it, everyone but the boys and Mrs. Wellington pretty much ignored him. He knew he'd been surly since he left Denver, but he had tried to apologize. Once they arrived in Wyoming, Promise hadn't said more than a few words to him. Why should he care? He could ignore her, too. He'd be dam . . . darned if he'd say another word about her cooking, good or bad. In a few days he'd be out on the range, and that suited him just fine.

What he couldn't figure out was why Victoria wanted to introduce Promise to more men. He thought the plan was to take Promise back to Denver in the spring, so Victoria was wasting her time. As far as he was concerned, spring couldn't get here fast enough.

"How's it feel to be in the saddle?" Colt asked his brother. They'd been home ten days, and Colt had the doc examine Jake to make sure he was ready to ride.

"Real good. Like that wagon, I couldn't take another day of that blasted bunkhouse," Jake said.

"Why don't you show me where you want to build your home?" Colt wanted to remind Jake of the life he would have on the ranch, and help him imagine what could be if he stopped fighting his feelings.

"Sounds good. Let's go." Jake knew what was on his brother's mind. He wondered if he should tell him he had gained a whole new perspective about his feelings for Victoria. Colt was right, he'd been infatuated, like every man that met her.

They reined in at the spot Jake had picked out for his home before he'd left for Texas.

"I think you picked the perfect spot, Jake." Colt wasn't surprised at the location Jake chose to build; it was the exact place he would have selected if he hadn't built his home where the original home had been located. It wasn't far from the main house, and the mountains as a background made for a stunning setting. "I call this place God's acre."

"Why's that?"

"Sometimes when I'm riding this way back to the house, if the sun is setting just right, the light creates a cross formation on those mountains. It's a sight to see."

A lump formed in Jake's throat as he sat beside his brother, looking at the place his home would be. He was only sorry that it had taken him so long to come home. When he could speak, he said, "I think this is a good place to raise a family."

"Yep, there's not a better place on earth." It was a special moment between two brothers who had been apart too long.

Chapter Twenty-Eight

Two weeks later, the ranch was preparing for the big picnic. Before Jake rode out at dawn, he saw Mrs. Wellington outside, directing men where to set the tables for the picnic. She scurried around behind them, placing the tablecloths. He noticed she'd picked out the shadiest area on the north side of the house, where a nice clump of trees would provide some shade in the afternoon. The aroma of chicken frying in the kitchen was already filling the air, making his stomach growl.

By noon, Jake had bathed and arrived at the picnic after most of the guests were already milling about in the yard. It took him less than a minute to spot several men talking with Promise. At least, he thought it was Promise under that large wide-brimmed Southern-belle hat. He figured she needed the hat because her pale skin would easily burn in the hot afternoon sun. It looked like every man on the ranch, plus some men he didn't know, were maneuvering for attention. When he got a better view, he recognized the blue dress she wore as one of the many he'd found that fateful day. It occurred to him that she'd put on a few pounds since she'd been at the ranch, and they went to all the right places. She looked so beautiful he could hardly take his eyes off her.

Promise hadn't seen Jake when he arrived at the picnic, and she'd only seen him a couple of times over the few weeks before the picnic. Most nights she ate with Victoria in her room so the men could discuss business at dinner. When Colt and the boys joined Victoria, Promise would go downstairs and clean the kitchen, and Jake would already be gone. Her time at the ranch had kept her busy, but she was happy here. She didn't regret her decision to come to Wyoming, particularly if it kept her family safe. It'd taken her some time to stop crying each time she thought of her brother, but she now made an effort to remember the many happy years they had together. She'd even written a letter to Matthew's sweetheart to tell her that Matthew had planned on returning to South Carolina. It wasn't clear if that was Matthew's plan, but Promise wanted to think it was the truth if he'd loved the girl.

Seeing there was no chance he could even get near Promise, Jake glanced up to see Colt at the food table filling two plates. He strolled over, piled a plate high with fried chicken, and followed Colt to where his wife was sitting under a shady tree. When Colt handed a plate with very little food on it to Victoria, Jake almost commented that he was going to starve his wife, but one glance at Victoria's pale face made him hold his tongue. For the first time, he noticed the toll the pregnancy was having on her. It alarmed him how fragile she appeared.

"Did you leave some for the guests?" Colt asked, interrupting his thoughts.

"You're one to talk," he replied, pointing at Colt's plate. After he took a bite of the chicken, he added, "They'd better hurry if they want some. It's so good I plan to go back for more."

"It is delicious. Promise cooked the chicken," Victoria told them.

Jake glanced Promise's way and saw her laughing with Cole. Normally it might have troubled him, but right now he was worried about Victoria. "When's this baby due?"

"We may have a nice Christmas gift," Colt said.

Jake caught the look Colt gave Victoria. His eyes so full of love that he looked like he might explode. "That would be perfect timing," Jake told them. "The boys said they thought they might want a boy."

"We'll be happy with a boy or girl," Colt said.

"I've never been around a baby before," Jake admitted.

"You were around me," Lucas chimed in, hearing the last part of the conversation as he joined them with what looked to be the rest of the chicken on his plate.

"That's true," Jake replied. "Problem is, you never grew up."

"And why would I want to spoil all my fun?" Lucas retorted. He pointed to Victoria's stomach. "What are we going to call this little tyke?"

"Tate if we have a boy, Samantha if it is a girl," Colt said.

Jake heard the sadness in Colt's voice at the mention of Tate. Tate was the young man who'd worked for Colt. He'd been killed and Colt had taken his death hard. "Tate's a fine name."

After they finished eating, Colt stood. "If I can get those ranchers away from Promise long enough, I want to introduce them to Jake and Luke." He leaned over and looked into his wife's eyes. "Do you feel better?"

"Yes, go introduce your brothers. I'll be fine."

"I think I've already met every woman here, but I've decided I'm gonna ask Promise to marry me if everything she cooks is as good as her chicken," Luke said.

"That'll be the day," Jake said. "I don't think you have it in you to settle down."

Luke put his arm around Jake's shoulders. "You're not right about much, brother, but you're right about that!"

As Colt introduced his brothers to some of the men talking with Promise, she saw her opportunity to escape. She'd been forced to listen to ranch business for what seemed like hours, and hadn't found a way to politely extricate herself. Seeing Victoria was sitting alone, she made her way toward her.

"Have the men worn you out?" Victoria asked when Promise took the seat beside her.

"My word, yes. I declare, I didn't know how difficult cattle ranching could be. How do you listen to all this ranch business?"

Victoria laughed. She liked Promise, particularly her honesty. "I don't get a chance to hear much because I'm always busy." She placed a hand on her stomach. "Well, I was busy until the doctor confined me to bed."

"If you don't mind my saying so, you look a little pale today," Promise said.

"I am a little tired today," Victoria admitted. "But, heavens, don't say anything to Colt. He'd have the doc staying all night!"

"Then it's our secret," she whispered.

Victoria saw Promise's gaze move across the lawn. Jake was standing there talking to a very pretty brunette that Victoria recognized instantly. She was one of the women who had been interested in Colt at one time. "Jake seems to be on the mend."

"Hmm." Promise was trying to recall if she'd met the woman speaking with Jake. She assumed the woman knew him well because she was touching his arm every few minutes in an intimate gesture.

"That's Mavis Connelly. She's a widow with three children," Victoria informed her.

Promise turned to look at her. "Who?" she asked innocently.

"The woman talking with Jake."

"Oh." Promise couldn't say she wasn't staring at Jake— she was—but she didn't know Victoria was watching her.

"She's looking for a husband," Victoria said.

Promise averted her eyes from the couple, telling herself she wouldn't look that way again. "Well, she should keep looking, since Jake is in love with someone else."

"Yes, I daresay he is, but not the person you think."

Promise opened her mouth to say something, but she couldn't reveal her suspicions.

"You never told me how you and Jake got along on the trail," Victoria said.

"He was wonderful." Promise noticed Victoria's surprised expression, and amended her response. "He was very kind to me. All of the men were kind to me. He's changed since he was shot. I think he might hold me responsible, as well he should. If not for me, none of the trouble would have visited his cattle drive."

"I don't know Jake very well, but I don't think he would feel that way," Victoria assured her.

"Then I must have done something to offend him, because he has definitely changed."

Victoria thought she had some insight on Jake's behavior. "I think Jake is much like Colt. When Colt was shot and confined to bed, he was like a wounded bear. They are both men who don't like to be idle or feel they can't protect what's important to them."

"I can appreciate not wanting to be confined to a bed or a wagon."

"After being in bed for a few weeks, I can sympathize as well," Victoria agreed.

The women sat in the shade and talked for a long time, sharing stories of their past, and their dreams for the future. They both knew they were forming a bond that would last a long time. Before the day ended, Victoria was positive of one thing: Promise was definitely in love with Jake.

The next weekend, the men planned a trip to town on Saturday night. Like the rest of the men, Jake was looking forward to a night of whiskey and poker at L. B. Ditty's Saloon. "Colt, are you going to town with us tonight?" he asked, when they were brushing their horses down in the stable. "Cole's going with us."

"No, I'm spending time with my wife and boys."

Luke laughed and punched Jake in the arm. "See, I told you he was whipped."

"That's right, and I love it," Colt replied. "When you two wise up, then you will find out what I'm talking about."

"I'm too young to get hitched," Luke retorted.

"Not to mention too stupid," Jake teased.

"Stupid, huh? I'm the only one the women are chasing. I've been invited to Sunday dinner," Luke countered.

"I don't know about that. I just accepted an invitation from Mavis Connelly for dinner tomorrow," Jake bragged.

"I wouldn't take that as much of a compliment, Jake. She's invited every single man—from eighteen to eighty, within a hundred-mile radius—to dinner. She's looking for a father for those kids," Colt said. "And believe me, they are a bunch of hellcats."

Luke couldn't stop laughing. "Have a good dinner. Should I start calling you pa?"

"Very funny," Jake said. He didn't know anything about the kids when he'd accepted the dinner invitation from a pretty woman. "Why didn't you tell me, Colt?"

"I didn't know you were interested in Mavis."

"I'm not interested, I just accepted a dinner invitation," Jake stated resolutely.

"Brother, why would you want to go somewhere else for dinner when you can eat Promise's cooking?" Luke asked.

Jake didn't have an answer to that question. Maybe he was just tired of being ignored. He hadn't seen Promise since the picnic, and they didn't even speak that day.

"Little brother, you might not laugh so hard when I tell you that Detrick has been looking for a husband for his daughter for a few years now. So while your feet are under his table, you might want to keep that in mind. He's not what I'd call an affable man, particularly if he thinks some cowboy is just playing sport with his girl," Colt said. He needed to fill his brothers in on the lay of the land since he'd walked this particular minefield before he met Victoria. Every rancher with a single daughter had tried to wrangle him into the fold. On the other hand, it might prove amusing to see how his brothers got themselves out of such sticky situations.

"She's a pretty gal, so what's the problem?" Luke asked.

"Not pretty enough to put up with her daddy," Colt commented.

"Colt, do you think it's safe for all three of us to be gone tonight?" Cole asked.

There had been no sign of the killers, but that didn't mean they had given up. "I think it might be good to see if there have been any strangers in town. Hollister's last telegram said no one had showed up in Denver," Colt replied. "I'll tell the men to stay sharp while you're gone tonight."

* * *

"How are you boys doing?" L. B. Ditty, the proprietress of the saloon, asked when Jake, Luke, and Cole took a seat at her poker table.

"We're feeling lucky tonight," Luke said, smiling at the buxom woman with a head full of red curls.

"You will have to be lucky to beat me this week. I've already cleaned out my share of cowboys the last few days," L. B. said.

"I think your luck is going to end. I'm due for some good luck." One of the saloon girls passed, and Luke snaked out an arm and pulled her to his lap. "How are you doing, beautiful?"

L. B. asked the gal to bring her a bottle. "First round is on the house, boys."

The woman wiggled out of Luke's lap and hurried to the bar. When she returned to the table, she poured the drinks.

L. B.'s fingers might be pudgy, but that didn't hinder how deftly she shuffled the cards and whipped them around the table, landing directly in front of each man. "How's that brother of yours and his pretty wife?"

"Doing well. It looks like we might be having a niece or nephew by Christmas," Jake answered, picking up his cards.

"I heard she is feeling poorly."

"She's confined to bed, and Colt is making sure she follows the doctor's orders," Luke replied.

L. B. chuckled. "I've never seen a man more in love. That's a marriage that will last forever."

"Yep, it sure will," Cole said.

While they played poker, all three kept an eye on the men coming and going from the saloon. Jake asked L. B., "Have you seen many strangers in town lately?"

"Not many in here tonight, but we've had more than our share lately," L. B. responded. "None of them could play poker worth a darn, but that's always good news for me."

Jake's ears perked up. "You haven't happened to see a big man that's about as big as Colt, but real ugly, have you?"

"How did you know? Please don't tell me that he's a friend of yours." L. B. didn't like the man he was asking about. He was a sore loser, not to mention he tried to cheat. Her bartender, Sam, wanted to show him the door with the business end of a shotgun, but it wasn't necessary when she'd finally cleaned him out on high card.

"No friend of mine. We were just expecting him," Jake told her.

His tone sounded serious to her. "Good, 'cause I caught him trying to cheat." She reached up and pulled something from the back of her hair. "He ran out of money and asked if I would take this as his bet, to try to get some of his money back." The comb she placed on the table twinkled under the flickering flame of the chandelier. "Since they looked like real diamonds to me, I agreed. As you can see, I won the hand. I wonder where a drifter like him got such a pretty thing."

Jake picked up the comb and saw the initials *PS*, an exact match to the other one Promise wore. He remembered her saying there had been two combs. "This is real, and I know the lady it belongs to." Jake proceeded to tell L. B. about the wagon train, and the events that happened on the trail. Once he finished, he said, "I would like to buy this from you."

"I'll not have that. You can have the comb. I'd get no enjoyment wearing it since I know how he came by it. Sounds like that little gal has had enough grief. If that no-account sets foot in here again, I'll take it outta his hide."

Jake put the comb in his pocket. "I thank you. Do you happen to know if they are still in town?"

"No, they said they was headed to Denver, but the big one said they would be coming back."

"I'd appreciate it if you would let me know when they do," Jake said. "And leave his hide to me. I promise you he will get what he's got coming."

Chapter Twenty-Nine

"They're here," Jake told Colt the next morning at breakfast. He pulled the comb from his pocket and showed it to his brother. "This belongs to Promise."

"Did you see them?" Colt asked.

"No, L. B. won this off Big Ugly," Jake replied.

"Do you know how many?"

"She said there were ten riding together."

Colt thought about the news for a minute. "Are you going to tell her?"

"What do you think?" Jake had debated that question all night, and was still no closer to a decision.

"I wouldn't right now. No sense worrying the women until there's a reason." If they could take care of this problem without Victoria's or Promise's knowledge, so much the better. He didn't want Victoria to be worried about anything but having a healthy baby. And he sure didn't see any point in worrying Promise.

"Cole is telling the men, and we have enough hands right now so no one will be on the range alone until this is finished," Jake said. Tucking the comb back into his pocket, he hoped it was possible to keep the women in the dark until the killers were in jail, or better yet, dead.

"Instead of waiting on them, why don't we take the lead in this dance?" Luke asked his brothers.

Jake and Colt stared at him. Finally, Colt said, "You might have something there, little brother. Since we don't even have a sheriff right now, we can't depend on the law."

"I knew you couldn't be as dumb as you look, Luke," Jake added.

Luke grinned at his brother. "Look who's talking. For a U.S. Marshal, you can't seem to find a solution to this problem. I wonder why that is?" Luke had already figured out that Jake's brain was all wrapped up in thoughts of Promise. He didn't wait for an answer. "The way I see it, we already know one of the most important things about them. Every move they've made is an ambush."

"The attack on the wagon train wasn't really an ambush," Jake countered.

"Yeah, that's true, but they were already aware they wouldn't meet with anyone willing to fight back. They knew those folks weren't armed," Colt reminded him.

Luke glanced from one brother to the other. "We need to have a talk with L. B."

Jake and Colt listened intently as Luke outlined his plan, and when he finished, the three were in agreement on how to proceed.

"We'll need to keep some men around the house, but let's not make it obvious to the women," Colt suggested.

"We could keep Cole and Rodriguez around, since they follow Promise around anytime they have a free minute," Jake said.

Luke arched a brow at Jake. "Maybe we should leave you here if you're so worried."

"Not a chance. I want those killers," Jake stated firmly. "Let Cole and Rodriguez fight over her."

The men left the house, and Jake made a plan with Luke to go see L. B. on their way to their respective dinners.

* * *

After an exhausting day on the range, Jake, Colt, and
Luke had just reined in at the stable when they saw a buggy
coming down the lane. "Jake, it looks like the doctor. Can
you take Razor?" Colt asked, dismounting and handing his
horse's reins off to his brother.

"Sure thing," Jake replied.

Colt walked toward the house, keeping an eye on the
visitor. When the buggy drew closer, he realized that it
wasn't the doctor's horse. Turning back to his brothers, he
said, "It's not Doc."

Instead of taking the horses to the stable, Jake and Luke
stayed where they were until they figured out who was
visiting.

Colt was waiting on the porch when the buggy came to
a halt. A tall, well-dressed gentleman stepped out.

"Sir, would Mr. McBride happen to be available?"

Colt noted the Southern accent. "I'm Colt McBride."

The gentleman walked to the porch, removed his gloves,
and stuck out his hand. "Sir, I am forever in your debt."

Colt took the man's hand in his, but he had no idea what
he was talking about. "Why would you be in my debt?"

"I'm Charles Worthington, and I've been told you are
the man who saved my fiancée's life."

Now Colt was truly puzzled. "Who is your fiancée?"

"Miss Sinclair, the woman you saved on the wagon
train."

Odd that Promise had never mentioned she had a fiancé.
This was sure to be news to Jake. "Mr. Worthington, I'm
afraid you are referring to my brother, Jake McBride.
He was the one who found your . . . ah . . . Promise."

"I do apologize. I have traveled a long way, and Mr.

Hollister told me that Promise was at your ranch. Is she still here?"

"She is." Just as the words left Colt's mouth, the door behind him opened and Promise walked out.

"Charles!" Promise couldn't believe her brother's best friend was standing right in front of her. She ran into his outstretched arms.

"I'm so sorry about Matthew," Charles said, his voice breaking at the mention of his childhood friend. He hugged her tightly to his chest, and neither could say more.

As hard as she tried, Promise couldn't keep the tears from flowing when Charles mentioned Matthew. Charles and Matthew were as close as brothers, and the three of them shared everything as children. All of the memories of their carefree younger days flooded her mind, and the heartbreak seemed all the greater because Charles understood her pain. It was a comfort to have someone who knew Matthew well to share in her grief.

Colt felt helpless watching the two of them. He turned away to see if his brothers were watching this scene. They had to be as surprised as he was seeing a stranger cradling Promise. Jake and Luke had tied off the horses to the railing and were walking toward the house.

Regaining her composure, Promise pulled away from Charles and swiped at the tears on her cheeks. "Charles, what are you doing here?"

"I came for you, of course. I traveled to Denver, and your uncle told me you were here. It has taken me some time to catch up to you." He hugged her again. "How are you, darling?"

Jake and Luke reached the porch in time to hear the endearment.

"I'm well," she replied.

"Mr. Worthington, these are my brothers, Jake and Luke," Colt said politely.

"So you are the man who saved my Promise," Charles said, shaking Jake's hand first. "I'm more grateful than you know."

Taking measure of the man, the first thing Jake noticed was Worthington wasn't heeled. Maybe he was like the folks she was traveling with on the wagon train and didn't believe in carrying a firearm. He remembered reading in Promise's journal that Charles Worthington didn't want her to leave Charleston, but for the life of him, he couldn't remember anything else. Since Worthington just called her *my Promise*, there had to be more to this relationship than he'd gleaned from her journal. And Promise certainly hadn't discussed Charles Worthington with him.

After Charles shook hands with Luke, he pulled Promise to him again and kissed her on the forehead. "I don't know what I would have done if anything happened to you." He kept his arm planted firmly around her waist.

"Charles is an old family friend," she said by way of explanation of his forward behavior. "We've known each other since we were children."

"Actually, our families betrothed us when we were very young," Charles added.

Jake's eyes were on Worthington, but when he made that comment, his eyes shifted to Promise.

Noticing everyone's surprised expression, Promise made an attempt to explain Charles's statement. "Charles was my brother's best friend, and my parents naturally thought we would share our future." She didn't want the McBride brothers to think she had a fiancé she'd been hiding. She'd always thought their parents were teasing about the betrothal, but Charles took it for granted she would be his wife. She'd told him a million times that she had no intention of marrying him, but nothing she said discouraged him. Before she left Charleston, he'd presented her with a ring, but her rejection had fallen on deaf ears. She'd made it clear she didn't intend to return to Charleston for a long time, suggesting that he should move on, but he simply refused to listen. She suspected Matthew had assured Charles he would make sure she came back earlier than she intended. Matthew was forever pushing Charles on her, saying he would make the perfect husband. She simply never looked at Charles in that light; she loved him like a brother, nothing more.

She had written Mr. Smythe, the barrister overseeing the estate in her absence, and explained her current circumstances. She told him to expect her in Charleston by August of next year, but she wasn't sure he'd even received her missive, so she had no idea how Charles found out about Matthew. "Charles, how did you know?"

"I telegraphed your uncle to make sure you had arrived safely, and he telegraphed me. I came as soon as I heard."

She hadn't telegraphed or written to Charles for fear he would do exactly what he did . . . come look for her.

"We will be having dinner soon, Mr. Worthington. Please join us," Colt offered. He glanced at Jake, who looked as though he wanted to strangle him for his suggestion.

"Thank you. That is most kind of you, and I do apologize for appearing on your doorstep unannounced."

"As you have probably already figured out, we are less formal out here," Colt told him.

"Yes, it does seem so, but I find it charming." Charles looked out over the landscape of the ranch. "This is a beautiful place, Mr. McBride." Looking at the mountains in the background, he added, "You picked the perfect spot for your home."

"I can't take credit for that. My father built the first house in this exact spot," Colt replied. "Are you staying in Wyoming long, Mr. Worthington?"

"Please call me Charles. I plan to stay for a few days, just long enough to arrange for our departure."

"Our departure?" Promise asked. "Is someone with you?"

Charles smiled at her. "No, dear, I plan to escort you back to Charleston. I'm sure you must be anxious to return now, considering your responsibilities awaiting."

"I am not returning to Charleston right now, Charles," Promise told him. "I've written Mr. Smythe of my plans."

"Surely you understand the scope of your obligations. I had planned to winter in New Orleans, but when I heard about Matthew, I changed my plans so I could assist you."

"I plan to stay here through the winter, then go back to Denver for a visit before returning to Charleston," she told him emphatically.

"My dear, there are many things that need your attention since Matthew's—" He broke off, not wanting to upset her again.

"Charles, this is not the time for this discussion." Promise was embarrassed that he showed no reluctance to discuss her personal decisions in front of everyone.

"Of course, you are right, my dear. I'm staying at the hotel, so we have time to discuss this. Perhaps you can come to town for dinner tomorrow night."

Jake didn't like the sound of that, but fortunately Colt intervened before he could blurt out something he shouldn't. No way were they going to allow Promise to go into town now that they knew the killers were nearby. "You should stay with us, and that way you will have ample time to discuss your plans."

Charles liked the opportunity to spend as much time with Promise as possible. "That is most kind of you. Are you sure it would not be an imposition on you and your wife?"

"I'm sure, and we have plenty of room."

"I've been assisting Mrs. McBride during her confinement," Promise explained to Charles.

"My brothers are going into town tonight, so they can pick your things up at the hotel and save you a trip," Colt offered.

Jake wasn't pleased that he was going to town tonight while this interloper was moving in. He didn't know what to think of this man with his perfect Southern manners, completely at ease taking liberties with his endearments, just like a husband. No, he wasn't pleased at all with this turn of events, but he remembered that old adage, *keep your enemies close*. He didn't consider the fact that he'd already labeled Charles Worthington an enemy.

"You aren't having dinner with us?" Promise asked Jake.

Before Jake answered, Luke spoke up. "Some lovely ladies are cooking us dinner. Jake is going to Mavis Connelly's house, and I'm going to the Detrick ranch to have dinner with Sally."

Jake rolled his eyes at Luke. He wasn't planning on advertising his plans.

"Oh." Promise tried to hide her surprise. Mavis did move fast. But Jake must be attracted to her to accept the dinner invitation. She was disappointed, but she'd already come to accept Jake had no interest in her. "Have a nice time."

Jake and Luke walked off, but Promise overheard Luke tell Jake he would meet him at the saloon after dinner. Not only was he having dinner with a woman looking for a husband, he was also spending a lot of time in the saloon. She'd read many things about the saloons in the West, and the women who worked in them. They were not places well-bred young ladies entered. Well, it was no business of hers where he went or what he did. It couldn't be any plainer than the nose on her face that he'd forgotten what they'd shared on the trail, and she was the biggest kind of fool to be hurt by his actions.

Victoria watched the interaction between Promise and Charles during dinner, finding the situation quite interesting. Charles was definitely head over heels in love with Promise, but Promise was more difficult to read. Though Victoria could see Promise loved this man, she didn't think she was *in love* with him. Listening to Charles's stories of their childhood, it was easy to understand and respect the bond between the two. On the surface, they seemed like the perfect pair. But life had a way of throwing curves, as Victoria well knew. Charles was a very attractive man, as tall as Jake, with dark sandy hair and patrician features. With his impeccable manners, many women would find him more than suitable husband material. Victoria smiled to herself, thinking Charles could certainly give any man some competition.

Colt viewed Charles as another complication in an already difficult situation. While he found him likable enough, and his company quite pleasant, he didn't relish having another person to protect at the ranch right now. If Charles was going to stay around for a few days, Colt would be forced to fill him in on the situation with the killers. He hoped Charles Worthington was a man who could take care of himself, and if necessary, defend the person he loved.

Chapter Thirty

Colt left the house early, giving Promise and Charles time alone over their breakfast. He wanted to talk to his brothers about their visit with L. B. Ditty last night. He reached the bunkhouse just as the brothers were leaving. The three of them walked to the stable while they talked.

"How'd it go with L. B.?" Colt asked.

"Plans in motion. L. B. will be ready for them."

"So what do you make of Charles Worthington?" Luke asked.

He didn't want to appear too interested, so Jake was glad Luke asked the question. But he was interested, all right. He'd thought of nothing else all night.

"Nice man. As a matter of fact, he's going to join us on the range today," Colt said. He glanced at Jake to gauge his reaction. "Did you know about him?"

"She mentioned him in her journal, but she never spoke of him."

"Well, is he her fiancé or not?" Luke asked.

Jake had been wondering the same thing. Her memory had returned, at least everything but seeing her brother killed, so it seemed she would have remembered if she had a fiancé waiting for her. He'd been thinking she had an interest in Cole, but it seemed she'd been holding the truth from everyone.

"I guess we will see soon enough," Colt said, leading the way inside the stable to saddle their horses.

Charles Worthington walked into the stables and strolled directly to Hero's stall.

When he led Hero out to saddle him, Jake walked over. "This is Promise's horse."

Charles smiled and rubbed Hero's muzzle. "Of course it is. I watched him foal." Jake didn't comment, and Charles looked at him. "I assure you that Promise told me to ride him."

"I see," Jake said, but he didn't see at all. He didn't know what in the hell was going on, and he wasn't happy about it, not one little bit.

When Charles was having breakfast with Promise, she'd told him about Jake McBride. Charles had a feeling she was smitten with the big cowboy. While her feelings were understandable—the man did save her life—Charles was confident that it was just a passing fancy. He wasn't about to allow some cowboy to interfere with the woman he'd wanted all of his life. Admittedly, Jake McBride, like his brothers, was a fearsome-looking man with his six-gun hanging on his hips, but that would not deter him. He moved closer to Jake until they were eye to eye. "I'm not sure you do see the way of it. I understand your protective feelings toward Promise. She told me this morning about traveling with you, and everything you've done for her. Don't get me wrong, I am most appreciative of all you've done for her, and I'm indebted to you. But I'm here now, and I will protect her from now on."

Right now, Jake wasn't sure if this man, with his re-fined manners, was up to the task of protecting Promise. And it galled him that Promise had discussed him with this Southern-fried *gentleman*. "Let's get one thing straight right now. You don't owe me anything. I would have done the same thing for anyone I found in that situation. And you need to realize that as long as Promise is on this ranch, we will all be looking after her." He wondered if Promise mentioned the kisses they had shared.

The men glared at each other until Colt walked over to intervene. "I think we need to fill Charles in on what's going on, so he will understand our concern."

They saddled their horses and rode off. Jake and Luke rode ahead, leaving Colt to explain to Charles the situation with the killers.

"This changes my situation," Charles said. "We can't possibly leave until this is resolved."

Colt noticed he said *we*. He wondered if Promise had changed her mind and was planning on leaving with Charles.

"You're welcome to stay at the ranch as long as you like," Colt said. "But we haven't told Promise the killers are here."

"Thank you. I would feel much better staying close," Charles responded. "How will you know when these men are back in town?"

"A friend of ours will let us know."

"Please tell me about Charles," Victoria said when Promise brought her lunch upstairs.

Promise took a seat beside Victoria's bed. "The Worthingtons were friends of my parents, so I've known Charles all my life. He and Matthew were best friends." Promise found herself getting choked up at the mention of her brother.

"Charles seems like a wonderful man," Victoria said.

Promise gave her a wistful smile. "He is wonderful. Actually, Charles is the perfect man for me. He knows me so well, and we've shared so much. I should have listened to him and never left Charleston. Matthew didn't really want to leave."

Victoria heard the regret in her voice, and the guilt. "Your brother wouldn't have left if he didn't really want to, no matter how much he loved you."

"I know what you are trying to do, but he really did leave Charleston for me. That is something I will regret the rest of my life."

"Okay, maybe he did do it for you. But do you honestly think he would want you to live with that guilt the rest of your days?"

Promise was quiet for a long time, then said, "No, no he wouldn't."

"Is Charles your fiancé?"

"He's asked me to marry him a million times, but I've always said no. Before we left Charleston he tried to give me a ring. I told him to find someone else to love, but he refuses. Maybe he's right and I should marry him. Matthew thought I should. I know he's right about my responsibilities now that Matthew is gone."

Victoria noticed she said all the right things except the most important thing. "But you don't love him."

"No, I don't love him, at least not in the way you love Colt. I respect him and I love him as a friend," Promise answered softly.

"Then it wouldn't be fair to marry him. He deserves a woman who will be in love with him."

"Perhaps love grows over time with a shared life."

"Promise, I'm not saying that's not possible. But you want to be fair to Charles, and it wouldn't be fair to marry him if you love another man."

"But I don't love another . . ." She didn't finish because she didn't want to lie to Victoria. "You're right, it wouldn't be fair if I don't love him." She thought Victoria was so lucky that the man she loved was crazy about her. "Did you know you loved Colt from the start?"

Looking back, Victoria remembered the moment she first saw her husband. "The first time I saw Colt was in St. Louis. I thought he was intimidating, fearless, mesmerizing, the most handsome man I had ever seen. But I will save that story for another day."

When Victoria spoke of her husband, the love she felt was written all over her face.

"You are so lucky to have found that kind of love," Promise told her.

"Yes, I am. I think you will be too."

Promise wasn't so sure. "I never expected I would find a man I thought more interesting than painting. I will go back to Charleston next year and then see what happens." She couldn't forget how she'd felt when Jake said he was having dinner with another woman. She didn't want to feel that way again.

The men were on the range all day, and they had time to see what Charles Worthington was all about. They had to give him credit for lasting in the saddle so long. Grudgingly, even Jake had to admit Charles was an excellent rider, and he wasn't afraid of hard work. But he didn't carry a gun, and Jake would bet he couldn't even shoot.

When they rode back to the ranch that evening, Jake had a moment alone with his brothers. "Colt, I think Luke and I should move into the house until this is finished."

Colt and Luke both looked at him. Colt wondered if Jake was suggesting this because he was worried the plan wouldn't work, or because Charles Worthington was staying in the house. "That's a good idea. I expect our plan to work, but I'd feel more comfortable with you two there."

Luke wasn't as generous as Colt. "Are you sure this isn't about Charles Worthington?"

"What's he got to do with it?" Jake snapped.

"I don't know, maybe because we don't know if he is Promise's fiancé or not. And then there's the fact that he seems to think he is her fiancé," Luke teased.

"Why should that bother me?"

Colt chuckled at his brothers. Jake was bound and determined not to admit his feelings for Promise, and Luke was just as determined to goad him into it. "You have to admit, Charles has a good head on his shoulders. He's certainly knowledgeable about the land."

"He should be knowledgeable since he has two estates to manage," Luke agreed.

"This is one of the reasons Promise needs to go back to Charleston. Her brother took care of business, and now that he's gone, it will be up to her," Jake said.

Colt felt guilty he hadn't thought of that. "You're right, Jake. When this is over, we should tell her we will find someone else to help out."

Dinner was an interesting affair that evening. Promise didn't say two words, and Jake spent most of his time glaring at Charles. If not for the boys talking a mile a minute, it would have been a total disaster. The twins asked Charles so many questions that Jake was sick of hearing him talk. It wasn't that he didn't think Charles was a good man—he actually would have liked him under different circumstances. To his credit, Charles was even patient answering the many questions from the twins, and that only aggravated Jake more.

When Victoria saw that Charles was unable to take a bite before answering another question, she told the boys to give him time to enjoy his dinner. That brief reprieve gave her time to ask questions of her own.

"How was your dinner date, Luke?" she asked sweetly.

"Long. The fried chicken was great, but just like Colt said, it wasn't worth putting up with old man Detrick for a couple of hours."

Colt chuckled. "I did try to warn you. But their cook makes really good fried chicken."

"Really?" Victoria didn't realize her husband was so familiar with the dinner fare at Detrick's.

Hearing the tone in his wife's voice, Colt added, "Of course, I haven't eaten there in a long time. I just assume they still have the same cook."

Jake smirked watching his brother squirm.

Colt saw Jake grinning like a Cheshire cat, so he asked, "How about your dinner date, Jake? Was it enjoyable?"

Promise didn't look at Jake, but she listened intently for his response.

Jake knew that question was coming, but he was expecting it to come from Victoria. "I wouldn't call it a date, but the dinner was very good," he answered politely.

"Of course it was a date. When a woman cooks for you, that's a date," Luke said, adding fuel to the fire.

"Mavis always was a good cook," Colt said before he realized the consequences.

Victoria glared at her husband. "I didn't realize you ate that often at her house."

Oh no, Colt thought.

"At least you were alone with Mavis. Old man Detrick didn't give me one minute alone with Sally," Luke lamented.

Thank God for Luke, Colt thought. He ignored his wife's question. "Where were the hellions?" he asked Jake, referring to Mavis's children.

"They were spending the night at her parents' house."

"I can't believe you were all alone with Mavis. I bet you

even got a good-night kiss. Detrick was between us the whole time," Luke complained. "Colt, didn't you tell me Mavis was a good kisser?" Luke was having a grand old time, and grinning from ear to ear.

"Oh really?" Victoria said, arching a brow at her husband.

"Luke," Colt enunciated in a low, warning tone. His little brother didn't know much about women if he was talking about how good another woman kissed with a man's wife within earshot.

Luke was having too much fun with this particular conversation, and Colt didn't scare him. He looked at Jake. "Well, did she kiss good or not?"

No doubt about it, Jake was going to kill Luke as soon as dinner was over and he got him outside.

"Uncle Jake, did you get a kiss?" Cody asked, and punched his brother in the arm. They both puckered their lips and made smacking sounds before they said "phew" at the same time.

"Pa, did you kiss Jake's lady too?" Cody asked, shocked that his pa had kissed someone other than his ma.

Colt didn't know how to answer that question. He didn't want to lie to the boys, but with Victoria looking at him like he was never again going to set foot in their bedroom, he was sorely tempted. He formed a diplomatic reply, but another rapid-fire question came in time to save him.

"Uncle Jake, are you gonna get in the family way?" Cade asked.

Jake looked at Colt, hoping he would put a stop to the questions, but it looked like his brother was about to burst out laughing.

Cody rolled his eyes at his brother. "Girls get that way. He means, are you gonna have kids now that you were kissing?"

"No." Jake felt his face turning red. He couldn't exactly

say that he kissed Mavis. She more or less threw herself at him and kissed him. He didn't think it would be polite to push her away.

"But Pa said that lady you was kissing had lots of kids," Cody added.

"I think she has to move into his room and then do a lot of kissing, like Ma and Pa," Cade said earnestly.

Cody looked confused. "Uncle Luke said a lady has to swallow a watermelon seed, like Ma did, to get in the family way, and do a lot of kissing."

"Is the kissing lady going to move into your room, Uncle Jake?" Cade asked.

Charles and Luke were the only people at the table laughing out loud. Hearing about Colt kissing Mavis upset Victoria, Colt was contemplating murdering Luke, Promise was angry with Jake, and Jake was angry with everyone at the table. Charles was just trying to keep up with the dynamics going on around him.

"Your ma and pa are going to give you a little brother or sister soon," Jake replied, hoping to redirect the conversation.

"But it takes a long time before they are big enough to play," Cody told him, sounding crestfallen that it didn't sound like there would be more kids on the ranch anytime soon.

Luke winked at the boys. "Maybe Uncle Jake will change his mind and have some watermelon with Mavis when he's kissing."

Jake decided he might just shoot Luke and be done with it. Too bad he left his gun in his room. "Don't count on it," he ground out. "And Mavis may not be a widow. She's a California woman."

"You mean she's from California?" Victoria asked.

"No, it means her husband took off for California and

never came back," Luke answered. "So Mavis may still have a husband."

This was news to Colt. Mavis told him years ago she was a widow, but he was smart enough not to comment.

Promise noticed Jake didn't say he didn't get a good-night kiss, widow or not. The one thing she knew about Jake McBride was that he didn't lie. That meant he didn't respond because he didn't want to lie. Not wanting anyone to see she was upset, she left the room to fetch the dessert. When she returned with a cake she baked especially for the boys, Cade said, "I bet that kissing lady didn't cook as good as Promise, Uncle Jake."

"Yeah," Cody agreed.

Promise could have kissed them for their compliments. "Thank you, boys. I'm glad you two like my cooking," she responded, with a not-so-subtle hint about the last time Jake discussed her cooking on the trail and found it lacking. She failed to remember he'd tried to make amends by complimenting her skills anytime he got the chance.

Colt was happy that someone was enjoying this evening. He'd be lucky if he ever got the chance to father more children. "Enough talking for tonight, boys. Eat your cake."

Chapter Thirty-One

Promise learned that ranch work was exhausting and nonstop, but she loved every minute. She was in the kitchen preparing dinner when Shorty came through the door. It was always a joy to see the older man, since she rarely had an opportunity to spend much time with him. Like most of the men, Shorty had decided to spend the winter at the ranch, if not stay permanently. Shorty was the cook for the men now, and he also picked up supplies from town when needed.

"Your painting supplies are here, and so is Mrs. McBride's cloth." He placed her materials on the long wooden table in the kitchen before accepting the cup of coffee she held out to him.

"I'm so glad they came this fast. I have a surprise planned for Victoria for Christmas," Promise replied, ripping into the brown paper package.

Seeing the assortment of brushes and oils she pulled out of the package, Shorty said, "I guess that means you're going to be painting something."

"I sure am, but keep it a secret."

Sitting at the table, Shorty noticed how healthy Promise

looked since they'd arrived in Wyoming. Ranch life seemed
to agree with her. "How are you doing?"

Promise sat beside him so they could drink their
coffee and have a chat. She'd missed listening to his
stories like she'd done for miles on end during the cattle
drive. It moved her that he was interested in her well-being.
"I'm doing well."

"I like that Charles fellow. He's a real gentleman."

Promise knew Charles was spending time on the range
with the men, but it still surprised her to hear Shorty talk
about him. "Charles and my brother were best friends."

"He must think highly of you to come all this way to
take you back."

Promise didn't hesitate to talk about her private feelings
with Shorty. She'd learned he was a wise man. "Yes, he
does."

"I haven't had the chance to talk much to Jake lately.
He's been really busy."

On hearing Jake's name, Promise tensed. Since that dis-
astrous dinner, she hadn't seen much of him, and she'd
made an effort to avoid thinking about him. "I haven't seen
him much, either."

"Cole says you are going back to Denver in the spring,
and that Charles is staying until then too."

"That's the plan. We will visit my aunt and uncle before
we head back to Charleston." No one had been more surprised than she was when Charles changed his plans. Once
she told him she wasn't leaving until spring, she'd expected
him to head to New Orleans for the winter. Instead, he told
her he liked Wyoming and wanted to see for himself if the
winters were as harsh as he'd heard from the cowboys. He
planned to travel with her to Denver next spring and then
on to Charleston. She enjoyed Charles's companionship,
and her only reservation about his staying was his single-
minded determination to make her his wife. Perhaps he

was weakening her resolve. Lately, she'd been thinking more about her future, and she'd come to realize that once she returned to Charleston, her life would change. Charles was right when he told her she couldn't ignore her responsibilities, no matter how much she wished she could. It saddened her to think about leaving everyone come spring. Even though she didn't see much of Shorty right now, she knew she would miss him.

"Will you ever come back to Wyoming?" Everyone on the ranch knew Charles was saying he was her fiancé. In his roundabout way, Shorty was trying to find out if she was planning to marry him.

She shook her head. "That's not likely. Now that Matthew is gone, it is up to me to manage everything."

He guessed he would just have to ask outright. "I guess you'll be marrying Charles."

"Well, that's what Charles wants."

Shorty already knew what Charles wanted. "Is that what you want?"

"I know it makes sense," she said with a hint of resignation.

Shorty stood and patted her on the shoulder. "Well, it's a long time till spring. We'll see what happens."

Promise didn't understand what he meant, but she had to finish dinner, so she walked with him to the porch. "Thank you for picking up our supplies."

Shorty winked at her. "Anything for a gal as pretty as you." He walked to the bunkhouse with his mind on Promise, and wasn't paying attention when someone reined in beside him.

"What's for supper?"

Shorty looked up to see Jake, and he frowned at him. "You're so dang stupid, you don't deserve any supper."

Jake just stared at him. He didn't know what he'd done

to Shorty to make him angry. "What's wrong with you, old man?"

"I just can't believe you're gonna let that little gal go back home without so much as a fight." Shorty shook his head as if he was plain disgusted. "You're just about the stupidest son-of-a-buck I've ever clapped eyes on."

"If you're talking about Promise, why should I stop her from going home?"

Reaching the bunkhouse door, Shorty glared at Jake and rolled his eyes. As he slammed the door, he added, "Yep, you're a dang fool."

Jake sat there on his horse, totally bewildered. He didn't know what had brought that on, but it seemed like everyone had an opinion lately about his intelligence, or lack thereof. Everyone with half a brain could tell there was something between Promise and Charles. If he did happen to catch a glimpse of Promise in the evenings, she was sitting on the porch swing with Charles. Hell, even Cole had mentioned that fact to him. He didn't need Promise to paint a picture; a blind cowboy could see there was something going on between the two of them. In an effort to stay out of the way, he waited until everyone had retired for the night before he went into the house. Sometimes he raided the kitchen before he went to bed, and he liked that quiet time alone to think. He'd decided it made sense for Promise to return to Charleston with Charles.

Well, he was through wasting his time thinking about that situation. Since it was a Friday night, he briefly considered calling on Mavis. It might be nice to have a woman who wanted to pay attention to him for a change. It was a bonus that Mavis did kiss pretty good. Not to mention the fact that she'd made it very clear she was interested in doing a lot more than kissing. Problem was, he couldn't forget the kisses he'd shared with Promise. No matter what Mavis offered, he knew he wasn't really interested in her.

"What are you sitting there thinking about, brother?" Luke asked, reining in beside him.

"Not a damn thing I want to discuss with you." Jake still hadn't forgiven his brother for causing that ruckus at dinner.

Luke laughed. "I see you're still mad at me." Everyone was still mad at him. He actually thought Colt was going to knock his teeth out because Victoria didn't talk to him for two days. Colt forced him to go tell Victoria that he hadn't really said Mavis was a good kisser. It was the truth, Luke had been joking, but no one in this family had a sense of humor.

"Yeah, I guess you could say I'm still mad. And you can thank your lucky stars I haven't shot your sorry ass," Jake responded.

Luke wiggled his finger at him. "Bad words." He laughed at his own sense of humor. "Can't anyone in this family take a joke?"

"Oh, I don't know. Why don't you ask Colt?" Jake knew Colt was even more upset with Luke than he was, and that was saying something. He had a feeling Victoria had never so much as said a cross word to Colt, but Luke had managed to have everyone spatting that night. And his baby brother thought it was funny. In a way, Jake had to admit it was funny. Maybe not at the time, but once he had time to think about it, he did see the humor in the situation. But he wasn't about to admit that to his brother. One thing about Luke, he could take as much as he dished out. He always did like to have a good time, and when he was around, people were generally laughing. Life being the way it was, who could fault him for that? Still, he wasn't ready to concede that point to him just yet.

"Hell, no one in the family is talking to me except the boys," Luke lamented.

"Good!" Jake rode off toward the stable, grinning.

"That's what happens when men fall into that marriage

trap! You can't have fun anymore!" Luke yelled after his brother. He rode off in search of the twins.

L. B. spotted the big man across the room, so she reached for a bottle off the bar and made her way to the table.

"Gents," she said as she took the seat across from the big man. It was the same man who'd lost the diamond comb in a bet.

"My luck is better tonight, so I'm planning on winning my money back," the big man said.

"We'll see." L. B. refilled their glasses. "This bottle's on the house." It was her plan to ply them with whiskey and get them talking.

She wasn't sure how many men in the saloon were part of the big man's gang, but she was sure the men at the table were together. As she played poker, she tried to keep track of the interactions among men at the various tables. Sam, L. B.'s partner and bartender, kept the bottles of whiskey flowing to the table. The men could hold their whiskey, but by their second bottle their tongues were starting to loosen.

"It looks like you boys like our little town," L. B. stated in a conversational tone.

"We heard there's no law here," one man said.

"Not right now. Our last sheriff is in the territorial jail, and no one has accepted the job yet. You interested?" L. B. asked.

"We might be looking for ranch work around here," the big man replied.

"There's a couple of large ranches that are always needing men."

"Maybe you could steer us to the best one," the big man said, laying down the winning hand.

L. B. noticed when the big man won he was friendlier,

so she'd folded a couple of times when she knew she had the winning hand. She shuffled the deck, trying to appear nonchalant about her response. "The cowboys say the McBride ranch is always looking for good men. Men say the big man, Colt, is a tough boss, and don't tolerate any foolishness."

"Is that a fact?"

"But if you are interested in talking to him, you might see him in town tomorrow. I heard one of the brother's taking the noon stage to Denver tomorrow. It might save you a trip to the ranch."

"What's in Denver?" One of the other men asked this question. But L. B. saw him shoot a glance at the big man.

L. B. wanted to appear disinterested in the whole conversation, so she continued to deal as she talked. She finished dealing and placed the deck on the table and picked up her cards. Waving a hand in the air as if she were dismissing the whole subject, she said, "I don't pay much mind to gossip, but I think I heard they were taking some woman back to Denver, and they didn't want her traveling alone. Now enough blabbering, let's play poker."

Sam was listening intently to everything being said at the table. He thought L. B. missed her calling; she should have been on stage in a traveling show.

"Where's this McBride ranch?" Big Ugly asked.

After L. B. gave him the general directions to the McBride ranch, she said, "You could always try Detrick's outfit. He's a tough old bird too, but fair enough." She gave him the directions to that ranch as well, then quickly placed her bid.

L. B. looked over at Sam and gave him a nod. Sam walked to the kitchen and whispered instructions to a boy who ran errands for him.

Thirty minutes later, Bob, the owner of the livery, was riding out of town heading toward the McBride ranch.

* * *

Colt walked to the bunkhouse, looking for Jake and Lucas. Finding no one there, he walked to the stables, where they were brushing down their horses.

"Bob just came out to tell us that they're in town, and L. B. set the bait."

"Good, let's settle this once and for all," Jake said.

"Get everyone together after dinner and we'll meet out here to lay out everything for tomorrow," Colt said. "T. J., Strait, Charles, and Bartholomew will stay in the house while we are gone."

Once dinner was over, the men gathered in the stable. "Luke came up with this plan, and we think it will work. L. B. did her part, so now we have to determine where these killers will try to ambush us," Colt explained to the men.

They discussed the route to the ranch that L. B. had given the killers. Colt drew the map in the dirt floor, and Jake pointed to the place he thought would be the most likely for the killers to strike. "This is where I would attack," he told the group.

Colt nodded his agreement. "Ambush Pass, that's the place I would pick."

"Appropriate place," Luke added.

The plan called for Jake to drive the wagon with Shorty sitting beside him, with Cole and Rodriguez inside the wagon, out of sight. Luke and Colt would ride beside them for a few miles before taking a trail that would place them above where they thought the killers would be waiting. Besides the men inside the house, additional men were going to be posted around the house in the event the killers didn't take the bait.

"Can you handle a rifle, Charles?" Jake asked, convinced the answer would be no.

"Yes, and I assure you no one will get to the ladies unless it's through me," Charles responded.

Colt knew Jake was skeptical of Charles's abilities. "Charles practiced with one of my rifles, and he's an excellent shot."

Jake didn't comment on Colt's revelation.

"What time do we leave?" Luke asked.

"We're supposed to be taking the noon stage, and it'll take over an hour by buckboard, so about ten thirty." Colt replied. He turned and handed Shorty the bundle he had under his arm. "Here you go, Shorty, Mrs. Wellington got this ready for you."

Chapter Thirty-Two

"Would someone like to tell me what is going on?" Promise asked the men sitting around the table the next morning. They'd had breakfast earlier, then they rode in about ten o'clock and told her they just wanted some coffee. Something was definitely wrong.

Jake, Colt, and Luke exchanged looks that silently questioned *who told her?*

"What are you talking about?" Charles asked. It seemed he was the only one able to formulate a question.

Promise had suspected something was amiss when Mrs. Wellington and Bartholomew stayed the night, but she thought Victoria wasn't well. "Is it something about Victoria?" she asked, staring straight at Colt.

"No, Victoria is fine."

"Then what is it?" This time her eyes met Jake's.

"We're just tired. We played poker too late." Jake told himself it wasn't a lie—he was tired.

She knew he was keeping something from her, but she didn't think she should say that, since she didn't want to make matters worse between them. As soon as they walked out that door to get to work, she planned to ask Mrs. Wellington. If anyone knew what was going on, she would.

She didn't have to wait long. After the men had a second cup of coffee, they all got up to leave. To her surprise, Luke was the only one who actually left. Colt ran upstairs to see Victoria before he left, and Charles left the room saying he had to get something from his bedroom. Jake lingered by the door, and Promise assumed he was waiting for Colt. She busied herself cleaning the kitchen in an effort to avoid talking to him.

"I forgot to tell you this morning that breakfast was real good," Jake said. Of all the lame things to say, he thought. He wanted to tell her to keep her gun on her today, but he couldn't without causing her to worry. He wanted to tell her that she looked beautiful in her pink dress. He wanted to say . . . hell, there were so many things he wanted to say, but he didn't.

Promise turned to look at him. "Thank you."

"You know I think your cooking is about the best I've ever eaten, don't you?"

There was no doubt in her mind something was going on. She wondered if it had anything to do with the killers. "What is it, Jake? Why are you being so nice to me?"

That question threw him. "Haven't I always been nice to you?"

She gave him a sad smile. "You were until we arrived in Denver."

Jake leaned against the door and stared down at his boots as he formulated his words. "I never intended to be hurtful."

"Jake, I know something is going on. Does it have to do with the killers?"

Pushing away from the door, he walked over to her and took her by the shoulders. "Promise, I want you to know . . ."

He didn't finish because he heard footsteps coming toward the kitchen. He dropped his hands and moved back to the door.

Charles walked in with a rifle in his hands and placed it against the wall. He looked from Promise to Jake. "Did I interrupt?"

Before either one responded, Colt walked into the room. "I'm ready to go."

Colt preceded Jake through the door, and Jake hesitated. He turned back to see Promise staring at him. "Are we having apple pie tonight?"

His question made her think of the night in Denver when she made him an apple pie and he never got to eat it. He'd been shot on the road on the way back to her uncle's ranch. She wanted to make him tell her what was going on, but she knew he wouldn't. "If you would like apple pie."

Jake grinned at her. "Guess I'll have to be here for dinner then." He shut the door behind him.

She stood there staring at the closed door with unanswered questions swirling in her head. His response was more like the Jake before they'd arrived in Denver. A few seconds passed before she realized Charles was still in the room. "Aren't you going with them, Charles?"

"Not today. I thought I would stay around the house," he replied, almost too nonchalantly.

Bolting for the door, Promise pulled it open and ran onto the back porch. "Jake!"

Jake and Colt stopped and turned toward her. "Yeah?" Jake said.

She hadn't thought of what she would say when she ran out the door. She'd just reacted. Now she didn't know what to say without making a fool of herself. She noticed how quiet it was; no cowboys milling about, no cattle bawling, no horses whinnying. Nothing. Then a gust of wind caught her skirt and the sound of it whipping around her legs was almost deafening.

Jake took two long strides closer. "What's wrong?"

They were just a few feet apart, but it seemed like miles because of the rift between them. Their eyes met and she held his gaze. "Be careful today." Her voice was soft and full of concern.

"Yes, ma'am," Jake said in that supremely confident way of his.

She watched as he turned and walked away with Colt by his side.

Charles was sitting at the table with another cup of coffee in front of him when she returned to the kitchen. "Charles, were they supposed to take this rifle?"

"No." Charles was troubled when Promise ran out the door after Jake. He'd listened, but all she did was tell him to be careful. Her feelings for Jake concerned him, but he was confident once they returned to Charleston she would forget the tall cowboy.

"You might as well tell me what is going on. I know something is not right." She could see the stable from where she stood, so she watched, waiting for the men to leave.

"Nothing is going on, I just wanted to spend some time with you."

"You've never been a very good liar, Charles. Why do you need the rifle?"

"I told Colt I would like to do some shooting, and he was kind enough to lend me his rifle."

"Hmm." Promise was distracted when she saw the wagon coming from the stable with Jake and some woman sitting beside him on the seat. The woman was wearing a large hat so she couldn't see if it was Mavis, *the good kisser*. Why would that woman be at the ranch so early? She didn't hear anyone riding in this morning and she'd been up before dawn, preparing breakfast. Colt and Luke came out of the stable and rode their horses beside the wagon. There was something about the woman's hat . . . why, it was just like the one she owned. It was her hat! Had Jake given her hat to another woman? "Charles, who is that woman in the wagon with Jake?"

Charles jumped up and looked out the window. "I have no idea." Charles was as surprised as Promise to see a woman beside Jake. He didn't realize a woman was in on the scheme. He wondered if she was the owner of the saloon the men told him about.

Promise could tell Charles was telling the truth. Perhaps they'd all been hiding something else this morning, and it had nothing to do with the killers. She felt like a fool, worrying that Jake was going to do something dangerous, and here he was riding away with some woman wearing her hat.

"Shorty, you make a real pretty woman," Jake teased.

Snorting, Shorty grumbled, "I don't know how women wear this gear! I'm all trussed up. That Mrs. Wellington could have made this dang thing a little bigger," he said, tugging at the bodice of the dress that had been altered to fit him. "And I can't see nothing wearing this war bonnet! How in blue blazes do women see where they're going wearing these things on their heads?"

Hearing the exchange from the back of the wagon, Cole said, "What I want to know is where you're hiding your shotgun."

"It's atwixt my legs, and don't go laughing. I reckon I can get to it fast enough and give them dirty skunks a little lead plum when I need to," Shorty told him.

"You wearing bloomers too?" Jake asked.

Lifting the flopping brim of the hat, Shorty gave him a frown. "You ain't that gol-darn funny."

"Hopefully, they can't see your big feet."

Cole and Rodriguez could be heard laughing from the back of the wagon. Even Colt grinned at the banter between them. He understood it was their way of releasing tension before they faced whatever was about to happen.

"Colt, do you think they took the bait L. B. hung out there for them?" Luke asked.

"Yeah, I do. They'll think it's the perfect time to bushwhack us."

"We couldn't have picked a better place for them than Ambush Pass," Jake said. "Sounds like it was named for them."

Promise was washing the dishes when T. J. and Strait walked in the back door.

"What are you two doing here? All the men have left already," she told them.

"We know," T. J. said.

"Could we have some coffee?" Strait asked.

"Of course. Did Shorty run out of coffee?" When no one responded, she turned to look at them.

"Ah, no, we just like yours better," Strait stammered.

Everyone knew the men loved Shorty's strong coffee. Why was everyone acting so weird today? Maybe she could get some information out of them. "Who was the woman in the wagon with Jake?"

T. J. and Strait exchanged glances.

"I didn't see a woman with Jake," T. J. said.

"Me neither," Strait added. He figured it wasn't really a lie since Shorty wasn't a woman.

Promise stared at them, trying to figure out if someone had told them to lie to her. "Well, she was wearing my hat."

"Your hat?" T. J. repeated, sounding like he had just swallowed a frog.

"Yes, my hat. I thought it looked familiar, so I went upstairs to check, and my hat is missing."

"Maybe it was Mrs. Wagner," Strait offered.

Promise had met the woman who helped Victoria sew her reticules, and she couldn't imagine her taking the hat without permission. "No, it wasn't Mrs. Wagner."

T. J. thought it would be wiser to change the subject. "Where's Charles?"

"He's in the parlor playing games with the boys."

Colt had told them to keep the boys inside today, and Charles was trying to keep them occupied.

"Where's Mrs. Wellington and Bartholomew?" T. J. asked.

Promise gave him a puzzled look. "Upstairs with Victoria." She looked from T. J. to Strait. "Okay, why don't you two tell me what is going on?"

Charles picked that moment to walk into the kitchen. He quickly appraised the situation and asked, "Are you two going shooting with me today?"

"Ah . . . yeah," T. J. answered, silently thanking Charles for his quick thinking.

Promise felt insulted that the three of them thought she was so ignorant she would believe their lies. "Enough of this! If you don't tell me what's going on, I'll go ask Victoria."

The three men looked at each other. They didn't know how to respond, but Charles knew Promise would do as she threatened.

Thankfully, Mrs. Wellington walked into the room before they could tell another lie. "I heard your conversation, and I didn't think it was right of Jake to keep this from you."

Promise did not think she was going to like what Mrs. Wellington had to say. "Keep what from me?"

"Victoria doesn't know what is going on, and we are

going to keep it that way. She doesn't need to be worrying about her husband."

"Why would she have to worry about Colt today?" Promise asked, but deep down, she knew the answer.

"They set a trap for those killers," Mrs. Wellington told her.

Promise sank into a chair. She'd suspected that very thing until she saw the woman sitting beside Jake in the wagon. "But why would they have a woman with them?"

"That was no woman, that was Shorty dressed up as one," Mrs. Wellington responded. "I made his dress, and I borrowed your hat for him to wear. The large brim was needed so no one could tell he wasn't a woman."

Promise could hardly believe what Mrs. Wellington was saying. "That was Shorty? But why would he dress as a woman?"

"So the killers would think it was you."

Promise dropped her face into her hands. "Oh no. Why would he do that? Why would Jake allow him to do that? Haven't enough people been killed?"

Mrs. Wellington walked to her and placed her arm around her shoulders. "My dear, you must have more faith in the McBride brothers. I've learned much about these men since I've been here, and I can assure you they know how to win a battle."

Charles sat in the chair beside her. "They have a good plan."

"But what if their plan doesn't work?" Promise moaned through her tears.

"It will work," T. J. said emphatically.

Promise looked up at Charles, her eyes so sad it broke his heart. "Oh, Charles, how could you allow this?"

"As Mrs. Wellington said, I think you are underestimating the brothers. It seems to me two former U.S. Marshals should know what they are doing. And I daresay Colt has seen his share of skirmishes. Have you seen him shoot?"

Promise wasn't comforted; she wanted details. "Since everyone knows but me, you must tell me everything."

After they explained the plan to Promise, she had one last question. "If they were so positive the plan would work, why didn't all of you go with them?"

Chapter Thirty-Three

"Jake, this is where Luke and I take the other trail," Colt said, coming to a halt. "A couple of days ago I timed both trails to the bend where they'll most likely be waiting. The higher trail takes longer, and due to the terrain we will have to leave the horses some distance away and walk in. So stay here fifteen minutes before you leave, and then keep a steady pace. It should take about thirty minutes to reach the bend. By the time you get there, we'll be in position above them."

Everyone checked their guns as they ran through the plan one more time.

"I expect them to split up and come at us from both sides of the pass; you and Luke take the ones on the west side, and we'll take the ones on the east ridge with rifles," Jake said.

Colt looked inside the wagon, and said to Cole and Rodriguez, "You can untie the canvas on the west side and slip out when the firing starts so you can use the wagon for cover."

"You're saying that it'll take twice as many of them to do what you and I can do alone?" Luke joked.

"Hell, Colt's wearing both guns, so I figure that'll make it even," Jake replied.

Colt looked at Jake, and when he spoke, his tone was serious. "Keep the wagon to the west side of the trail. You will be the most vulnerable, so stop this thing in a hurry and haul ass off the right side of the wagon. Have your rifles at the ready in case we haven't picked them off the ridge."

Cole shoved two rifles through the opening in the canvas to Jake. "Here you go."

Jake looked at Shorty. "I know you like that shotgun underneath your skirt, but now might be the right time to get it ready."

As Colt and Luke rode away they heard Shorty's response. "I might just let them low-down dirty skunks shoot your sorry keister."

Colt and Luke rode at a quicker pace and tied their horses off so they could walk the last quarter of a mile. Just as they expected, the killers were at the very place they hoped they would be. The two of them descended slowly, trying to remain out of sight from the men on the opposite ridge. They found an area behind some large boulders that was the perfect position to see everything on both sides of the trail. Colt held up five fingers and pointed to the position of the killers below. Luke nodded, and held up four fingers pointing to the ridge on the other side of the trail. There was a slight breeze, and Colt grabbed a handful of grass and threw it in the air to see how it would affect his shots. Just then, he heard the sound of the wagon coming down the trail.

The killers below Luke and Colt also heard the wagon. They pulled their guns and peeked around the rocks, waiting for the right moment to start shooting. One of the men on the west side signaled the men on the east ridge.

Colt and Luke braced their rifles on the rocks. They watched as the killers braced their arms on the rocks, pistols pointed at the road. Seconds later the horses came around the bend. Colt could only see the far side of the wagon, so he knew Jake was keeping it as close as he could to the west side of the trail. Colt and Luke knew the moment the killers saw Jake and the person they thought was Promise because all hell broke loose. The killers started firing. He hoped Jake and Shorty had jumped out at the right moment, because the horses took off at a full gallop down the trail, the wagon bouncing around behind them.

Once the killers realized they were being shot at from behind, they turned and scattered, trying to find cover. Colt and Luke could hear the rifles firing below, and were stunned to hear pistols returning fire. The killers obviously didn't plan ahead. They hadn't thought to take their rifles as they prepared their ambush. In short order, Colt and Luke dispatched the five men, and moved down the ridge to make sure they were no longer a threat. "How many left?" he yelled to his brother.

"Two still firing," Jake responded. He fired off another round, and yelled, "Make that one."

Colt grinned as he pulled his rifle to his shoulder and scanned the area to find the one remaining man. Once he spotted him, he took aim and fired one time. The man fell from the rocks to the road.

"Make that zero," Luke said. "Good shot, big brother. I'm heartened to know you haven't lost your touch."

"Everyone all right down there?" Colt asked.

"Not so much as a scratch," Jake answered. "At least not if you don't count Shorty getting caught up in his skirt and falling out of the wagon. He probably skinned his fair knees."

"At least I saved Promise's hat," Shorty countered.

"Looks like these varmints can't shoot worth a damn if someone else is shooting back," Luke said.

Next came the task of checking every man to see how many were breathing. They found three alive. One gut shot, so he wasn't going to make it, but the other two would live. Jake recognized Deputy Potter; he would survive his arm injury. "It looks like you're in luck today," he said.

"Yeah, I feel real lucky," Potter whined.

"Well, I can sure put your sorry ass out of your misery," Shorty offered, poking him with his shotgun.

Potter looked at the little man dressed in women's clothing. "So this was a setup," he stated.

"Looks that way, don't it, stupid," Shorty said.

Colt was checking the last man and Jake called out, "Is it him?"

"No."

"Where is he?" Jake asked Potter.

"Who?"

"Hart Newcombe," Jake ground out.

"He didn't come with us."

This came as a surprise to Jake. "Why not?"

"This morning he just told us he'd meet up with us on the way back to Denver," Potter said.

"Why Denver? Is Schott in on this?"

When Potter didn't immediately respond, Shorty urged him on by poking his wounded arm with this shotgun.

"No!" Potter shouted. "Schott just wanted those people off the land. He wanted Newcombe to get it done and he didn't care how."

"Jake, do you believe this sorry jackass?" Shorty asked.

"I'm not sure."

"Let me plug him in his other arm and see if his story changes," Shorty offered.

Jake grinned. "Sounds good to me. I'm tired of his caterwauling."

Shorty raised his shotgun and Potter shrieked, "I'm telling the truth! We wasn't gonna stay in Denver 'cause Newcombe has a woman at the border he's itching to get back to."

"Why would he want to miss this party, since he's gone to all this trouble to find us?" Jake asked.

"I don't know. I know he wanted that gal dead more than anything, even more than the money. He told us if she didn't have the money with her, just kill her anyway."

"What's this woman's name, and what town at the border?"

"Her name's Juanita Torres, and she lives down past El Paso."

Jake figured that was the truth. "How many are left?"

"No one. We had two that said they'd had enough and took off to Mexico a week ago. Did that gal really have a lot of money like Newcombe said?"

Jake glared at him. "It don't matter none one way or the other, 'cause you're going to hang and you'll never know." Holstering his gun, he walked over to where Colt was standing with Luke and Cole. "I'm going after him."

"I'm going with you," Cole said, his tone indicating it wasn't open for discussion.

"Me too," Luke added.

Jake looked at Luke. "Luke, I thank you for wanting to help, but I would consider it a favor if you would stay and help Colt. He's going to have his hands full with all these cattle, and I hate leaving him right now and putting all the work on him again. I'd say he's done enough over the last ten years."

Colt understood Jake's need to finish this, so he didn't

argue about him tracking Newcombe. He didn't want either of his brothers to leave, but he knew he would do the same thing. "Don't worry about me. Let's get back to the ranch and you and Cole can get your provisions."

As much as he hated to let Jake go alone, Luke couldn't argue that Colt would have too much work with winter coming on. "If you two need any help, then wire us and I'll be on my way," Luke told them.

As they walked to their horses, Jake said, "Colt, we're taking Potter's word that Newcombe was meeting up with them on their way to Denver, so if he's lying to us, that bushwhacker could be anywhere. If he comes to the ranch, I know you'll take care of him."

"We'll be ready if he shows up there. Since Newcombe is without his gang now, I don't think even he's stupid enough to try that," Colt assured him.

Jake glanced at Luke. "Can you and Rodriguez take these vermin to jail, then wire the U.S. Marshal and tell him where to find them?"

"Sure thing," Luke said.

"There's not a sheriff in town, but there's a deputy. He's not much in the way of enforcing the law, but I guess he can keep them in jail until the marshal gets here," Colt told them.

It didn't ease Promise's mind to hear about the plans already in motion, and her nerves were at a breaking point. Fortunately, they were able to keep the secret from Victoria and the boys.

Promise and Mrs. Wellington were in the kitchen baking pies when they saw the wagon pull up to the stable. On seeing Jake leap from the wagon, Promise breathed a sigh of relief. She kept her eyes on him as he walked hurriedly to the stable, and she spotted Cole walking toward the bunkhouse.

"Charles, keep everyone inside until I find out what's going on," T. J. said as he and Strait walked out the door. They intercepted Colt walking to the house and spoke briefly.

When Colt walked into the kitchen, all eyes were on him. T. J. had told him that Promise was aware of their plans, so there was no reason for him to hide anything. "Everyone is fine."

"Did it go as expected?" Charles asked.

"Yes. Luke and Rodriguez are taking two of them to jail." He didn't say the ringleader was missing and the rest were dead. He didn't wait for more questions; he walked through the kitchen and headed upstairs to see Victoria. Realizing Colt had spared the details from the women, Charles left the house to go to the stable to hear the specifics from the men.

Every few minutes Promise glanced out the window, hoping to catch a glimpse of Jake. When she did see him, he was riding out with Cole at his side. Though she was disappointed she hadn't had a chance to talk to him, she consoled herself knowing she would see him at dinner.

Luke and Rodriguez returned from delivering the killers to jail just as Promise and Mrs. Wellington were putting dinner on the table. Once everyone was seated, Colt said a prayer, and his last request was asking God to look after Jake and Cole and bring them back safely.

As soon as he said amen, Promise asked, "Bring Jake and Cole back from where?"

"He didn't tell you?" Colt asked.

Promise looked from Colt to Luke. "Tell me what?"

It surprised Colt that Jake hadn't spoken with Promise

before he left. He didn't know what was wrong with his brother. It wasn't like him to be so callous. "Jake and Cole are following one of the men who's still on the loose."

"Following him where?" Promise asked.

"Wherever it takes them." It was obvious to Colt by the look on her face she was devastated that Jake hadn't talked to her and explained the reason he was leaving. "Promise, this is the only man left that is not dead or in jail, and Jake wanted it finished. He knows you won't be safe with this killer running free. Luke or I would have done the same thing. And before you start blaming yourself, remember these men were responsible for ambushing and shooting Jake."

She knew Colt was right. Not only had these men killed so many on the wagon train, they had intentionally left Jake for dead. Still, she was hurt that Jake hadn't told her he was leaving. She tried to tell herself that he was in a hurry and had a lot on his mind, and he didn't owe her an explanation for his decisions. No matter the reason, it didn't lessen the hurt.

Understanding what Promise was feeling, Victoria hoped to ease her mind. "Colt said Jake would send a telegram if he traveled as far as Denver."

Promise turned her eyes on Colt. "Do you think they will have to go that far?"

"It's possible."

"Jake and Cole stopped in town to make sure Newcombe wasn't waiting for the gang there, but L. B. said he'd left town with the others," Luke offered.

After dinner was over, Promise delivered some pies to the bunkhouse. More than anything she wanted to see with her own eyes that Shorty was okay. Shorty would understand how she felt since they'd already been through so much together.

"I guess you'll be wanting your hat back, missy?" Shorty teased as soon as he opened the door.

"It's probably shot full of holes, just like your head could have been for taking such a chance! I shouldn't even be bringing you pies for doing something so addled!" she scolded.

Since ladies weren't allowed in the bunkhouse, Shorty took the pies from her and handed them off to Rodriguez. He took her by the arm and steered her toward the corral. When he had a lot on his mind, watching horses had a way of calming him down. He hoped it did the same thing for Promise. When they reached the fence, Shorty braced his arms on the top rail. "Now don't get a bee in your bonnet about this. It was a good plan, and we weren't really in any danger. Have you seen those McBride brothers shoot? Jake is one heck of a shot, but I swear that big brother of his could shoot a gnat off a horse's backside a mile away. Besides, as you can see, I don't have any extra holes in my noggin."

That didn't make her feel a lot better. "How do you think I would have felt if something happened to any of you?"

"We knew nothin' was going to happen to us, and that was why we didn't tell you. You woulda been frettin' over nothin' all day."

"Now Jake has gone off again, risking his life because of me."

Shorty saw her teary eyes. "You quit worrying about Jake. He can take care of himself. You should know that by now."

"I know he already got shot once."

"That just goes to show you that he's too dang mean to die. Those lily-livered cowards don't stand a chance against him."

Promise couldn't help but smile at Shorty's nonsense.

"There you go. Let me see that beautiful smile," Shorty urged.

Promise hugged the little man she'd grown so fond of over the months. "Just don't ever take another chance like that," she whispered in his ear.

When Promise released him, Shorty stuck his hand in his pocket and pulled out a bandanna. "I almost forgot. Jake told me to give you this."

Promise recognized it as one of Jake's. "Why?"

He thrust it at her. "Look inside."

Taking the bandanna from his hands, she felt something wrapped inside. When she unfolded the cloth she was stunned to see her matching comb, the one she thought was lost forever. She looked at Shorty. "Where did he get this?"

"He said he got it when he was playing poker at the saloon."

She started getting teary-eyed again. Maybe in some small way Jake still cared, she told herself. She wrapped the comb in the bandanna and held it close to her heart. "That was so thoughtful of him."

Thoughtful, but stupid, Shorty decided. If Jake couldn't see how this gal cared about him, he didn't deserve her.

Some of the horses ambled over to them, hoping for an ear rub or something to eat. When one of the horses sniffed Promise's hair, she laughed.

Just as Shorty figured, watching horses could cure just about anything ailing you. He scratched the ears of one mare, and said to Promise, "Jake will be okay. I know the Good Lord has big plans for Jake McBride."

Chapter Thirty-Four

Jake didn't really expect to find a trail leading to Newcombe unless the man was lying in wait for an ambush, which was his specialty. That fact alone kept them on high alert at all times.

"Why do you think he wasn't with the rest of the gang?" Cole asked.

"I can't really figure that out. Maybe he wanted the men to get the job done and get the money. He might be thinking to ambush them and keep all the money for himself, but that kind of man doesn't usually have the courage to do anything alone."

"That's what I thought. But I don't think he's the kind of man who would trust them to come back with his money," Cole added.

"Yeah, I know."

"Do you think he just told them to kill Promise, and if she happened to have the money with her, so much the better? Maybe he's given it up and is going down to the border to see his woman and hide out for a spell. He had to know Promise was well protected, so maybe he didn't like his odds."

Jake tried to put the pieces of the puzzle together.

"Promise did put most of the money in the bank in Denver. Maybe that information got back to Schott, and he mentioned it to Newcombe."

"That son-of-a-buck wouldn't think twice about taking a job and not seeing it through if he knew there was a better-than-even chance he was going to get killed."

"If he knew the money was in the bank, I can guaran-damn-tee you that he didn't tell his gang," Jake replied.

"I think that's a safe bet."

"It's possible Newcombe just wanted the gang to kill Promise and never planned on meeting up with them. He's probably hightailing it to Mexico for some señorita, thinking no one will chase him down there," Jake mused.

"So he wanted them to save his hide by killing Promise."

"Yeah, but I have a hard time believing he would give up without getting something for his trouble," Jake said.

"It's possible he realized he was running on borrowed time, and as long as Promise wasn't around to put a noose around his neck, he'd settle for that," Cole said. "It wouldn't be the first time that a man double-crossed everyone when he was itching to see his woman."

"That's the truth. We'll still go on to Denver to see if he happens to show up there."

Two weeks had passed with no word from Jake and Cole. Promise could see the worry was taking a toll on Colt. Victoria confided to her that most nights she would awaken to find him pacing the floor. Promise understood his desire to do something, but with Victoria's condition, he felt his hands were tied. Victoria rarely came downstairs for dinner because she was so uncomfortable most of the time, so Colt always ate with her in the bedroom.

Every morning before dawn, both Colt and Luke left

the house without waiting for breakfast. Promise would put together a basket of food for Charles to take to them when he rode out in the mornings. Charles had become so enamored with the ins and outs of running a large, successful cattle ranch that he would spend time daily with Colt, asking dozens of questions. His family owned two large estates, but they paled in comparison to the McBride ranch. Shorty told her Charles took to ranching like a man takes to good whiskey. She had to admit, Charles was a changed man. He'd developed an appreciation for the rugged beauty of the West, telling her he now understood why she wanted to come here.

The changes in Charles didn't end there. Probably the thing that surprised her the most was he had stopped asking her to marry him. She didn't know if he'd had a change of heart about his feelings for her, or if he was just giving her a reprieve in view of the circumstances. Either way, their relationship was less strained. She liked the changes in Charles, and had even allowed herself to think that one day she might be able to develop deeper feelings for him once they were back in Charleston.

Like Colt, the stress of worrying about Jake was getting to her. To keep from driving herself crazy imagining every dire thing that could befall Jake and Cole, she filled her days with cooking and household chores. When the boys were inside, she'd find time to play games with them. She wasn't sleeping well either, but instead of pacing, she spent the long nights painting in her room. Painting helped to take her mind off Jake, and at the same time complete the Christmas gift she had planned for Victoria and Colt.

The mood around the ranch could only be described as glum. Too many days had gone by with no word from

Jake. Even the boys had picked up on the adults' concern about Jake and Cole, and were not their usual chatty selves. That changed early one morning when they awoke to the first snowflakes of November. The boys were as excited as if they were opening presents on Christmas morning, and their excitement was contagious. Promise's enthusiasm was tempered by the stories she'd heard of the harsh winters in this part of the country, and that added to her worries. By nightfall the flurries had turned into a full-fledged snowstorm, followed by more snow and freezing temperatures for a full week. Promise and Charles learned the difficulty of ranch work in the extreme conditions.

Colt chose that weekend to go to town to see if there was a telegram from Jake. He knew it would be difficult for anyone to make it out to the ranch, but he couldn't wait for better weather. It took him twice as long to get to town and back, but the trip was worthwhile. Luke and Rodriguez were walking from the bunkhouse when Colt came riding in.

"We were just talking about going to look for you," Luke said.

"That snow is really coming down," Colt responded as he dismounted and led his horse to the stable.

"Any news, señor?" Rodriguez asked.

Colt handed his reins to one of the men in the stable. "Come on in the house so I can tell you all at once."

Promise and Charles were in the kitchen when the three men walked through the door. Colt hustled to the stove, removed his gloves, and Promise was instantly beside him with a cup of coffee.

"Thanks," Colt said, holding the cup with both hands to warm his fingers.

"Let me take your coat," she said.

Before he handed Promise his coat, he pulled the telegram

from his pocket and read it aloud. "'In Denver. No sign of him. Talked to Hollister. Headed to Mexico. Jake.'"

"Mexico?" Promise shrieked. "What does this mean?"

"He must think that is where he'll find Newcombe," Colt said.

"But won't that take a long time?"

"Yes, but Jake and Cole won't let it go," Colt said. "They will follow him to hell if necessary."

Luke walked over and put his arm around Promise's shoulders. "Don't fret, honey. They know what they're doing."

Promise's mind was going in a dozen different directions at one time. At least she knew Jake saw her aunt and uncle while he was in Denver. She was thankful she'd written a letter to her aunt over a week ago. She felt certain her aunt would write about Jake and Cole's visit.

Luke directed Promise to a chair, and Colt sat down beside her. "Luke's right. We wanted to know what was going on, and now we do. It has to be enough to know that they are alive and well. Let's not borrow trouble." He was heartbroken that Jake would be away another few months, but he was determined not to let that show.

Promise knew that was one of Colt's favorite sayings, *let's not borrow trouble*. In this instance she agreed it was sound advice. Colt did look relieved now that he'd heard from his brother. She smiled at him. "I think you're right, this is wonderful news to know they are well. Now go tell Victoria. I know she's worried too. I'm going to see to the boys, then prepare dinner."

When she left the room, Rodriguez said, "I will go to Mexico. They may need my help. They may need someone who speaks Spanish fluently."

"You don't even know where in Mexico they are headed," Luke replied.

"And I don't know if you can catch them now," Colt said.

Rodriguez laughed. "As slow as you gringos ride, I will catch them before they reach New Mexico. Don't forget, this is my part of the country. I know all the trails, and my father has many friends. Gringos often find themselves in trouble across the border." He shrugged. "If they don't need my help, I need to see my family anyway."

Colt appreciated his offer, particularly since he couldn't do anything to help his brother. He wasn't going to reject the idea if it would help Jake. "Thanks, Rodriguez. I'm indebted to you."

Rodriguez really did want to help Jake and Cole if he could, but if they didn't need his help, he would go see his family for the first time in a long time. He was feeling guilty he'd been gone so long. As his father's only son, he knew it was up to him to take over his family's ranch one day, and that day was getting closer. After spending time with the McBride brothers, he finally realized the importance of family.

Jake and Cole nearly froze to death before they reached Denver. Their provisions hadn't included clothing for colder weather. Cole had gathered their gear when they left the ranch, and the last thing he'd thought about was facing a snowstorm halfway to Denver. They didn't turn back since they were as far from Denver as they were from the ranch. What provisions they did bring lasted a few days, and then they had to eat whatever they could shoot. More than one night Jake had fallen asleep thinking about Promise's biscuits and apple pie. Hunger wasn't the only reason his mind was on Promise. Time in the saddle gave a man time to do a lot of thinking. He replayed in his mind all that had happened from the moment he'd found Promise unconscious in the driving rain. The kisses they'd shared had a way of popping into his mind at the most inconvenient times. To rid his mind of those unwanted thoughts, he kept telling himself Charles was the perfect man for her. She could return to South Carolina and resume the life she'd always known. Wyoming was too rugged for a woman like her.

When they arrived at Hollister's ranch, they didn't know what made them happier, a home-cooked meal or a dry, warm kitchen with hot coffee on the stove. They spent the night at the ranch, and learned from John that a U.S. Marshal had arrived and taken Schott into custody. Schott admitted to bringing in Newcombe to scare off the people on the wagon train, but denied any involvement in the killings. Jake had a feeling that the two men they'd captured would counter Schott's claim.

Before they left for Mexico the next morning, Nettie insisted they sit down to a good breakfast, and they didn't refuse. She placed a heaping plate of food in front of Jake. "I just received a letter from Promise before you arrived. She seems happy at your ranch."

"Everyone at the ranch enjoys having her there, but I'm afraid we are working her too hard," Jake replied.

Nettie thought Promise had never sounded better. Even though her niece didn't say outright that she was in love with Jake McBride, Nettie read between the lines. She'd mentioned Jake several times in her letter. "Nonsense. That gal has always been a worker and I think she's enjoying every minute."

Jake figured before Promise left South Carolina she probably had servants seeing to her every need. "Considering her background, I didn't think she would be accustomed to cooking and cleaning."

Listening to the conversation, Cole felt he was finally getting a handle on why Jake kept his distance from

318 Scarlett Dunn

Promise. Up until now he hadn't understood why he kept her at arm's length. No matter how much he wished Promise cared for him, every cowboy on the ranch knew she had powerful feelings for Jake. Obviously, Jake thought since she was from a privileged background, she wouldn't be happy on a ranch in the long run.

After setting a large plate of biscuits on the table, Nettie took a seat. "They had servants at the estate, but Promise wasn't one to let others wait on her. Don't go thinking she was a spoiled, wealthy young lady, because her life wasn't like that."

Jake digested that piece of information without comment. Instead, he asked, "Is everyone at the ranch okay?"

"Yes, she said Mrs. McBride wasn't coming downstairs now since she is so far along, but she seems to be doing well. Promise told me about those boys. She's really taken with them."

"They're good boys," Jake agreed.

"That's what you two need to do," she said with a pointed look at Jake and Cole. "Settle down with a wife and have some boys of your own."

Cole and Jake both laughed.

"I think we have a while before we need to do that," Cole said.

"Tell me, would you rather wake up on the cold ground for the next five years, or with a warm woman in bed beside you in the mornings?" Nettie asked. "You two are used to riding free, but ranch life can get mighty lonely without a partner."

John walked into the kitchen, saving the two men from a response. Having overheard his wife's comment, he said, "Nettie, stop trying to marry these two off."

Nettie jumped up to get him a plate. "You know I'm speaking the truth, John Hollister."

John kissed her cheek when she leaned over to pour his coffee. "I know I prefer waking up to you any day of the week."

Jake and Cole exchanged a glance. They enjoyed the couple's banter. Each of them a bit envious of the Hollisters' loving relationship.

"I got a pack horse ready for you. You can drop him off on the way back," John said.

That was an unexpected surprise. Jake had planned to buy a horse in Denver along with the provisions they needed. "I appreciate that. I'll pay you for the supplies."

"Not necessary, Jake. I'll always be indebted to you for what you did for Promise."

There it was again, Jake thought. Promise wasn't the only one who felt indebted to him. "I would have done the same thing for anyone," he replied, but Colt's words played in his mind. He reminded himself Promise had done the same thing for him.

Cole heard the change in Jake's tone and glanced at him. What was going on with his partner?

"Of course you would," John said, not noting anything amiss in Jake's manner. "Nettie packed up enough grub to last you a while, and I've pulled out a couple of coats for both of you. You may not need them the closer you get to Mexico, but I have a feeling this snow is going to last awhile."

"We were going to buy some warmer gear in Denver," Jake said.

"Now you don't have to make the stop. You be careful on the trail. I wouldn't put it past Schott to still have his hand in whatever is going on. He's a slippery one, that's for sure."

Jake and Cole stood and shook hands with John. Nettie

hurried to them and gave them a hug. "You two come back safe and sound."

"Yes, ma'am. When you write Promise . . ." What in the world made him say that? Jake had no idea what he'd been about to say, but he quickly improvised. "Tell her to quit worrying."

Chapter Thirty-Five

Promise sat down in the bedroom with Victoria and Colt to read aloud the letter from her aunt. Nettie wrote that Jake and Cole looked good considering they weren't dressed for such extreme conditions. When she reached the last line of the letter, Promise was surprised there was a message from Jake. *Jake told me to tell you to stop worrying.* He had told her many times on the way to Denver that she worried too much.

"That was nice of your aunt and uncle to fix them with provisions," Colt said. "I didn't know they took off without proper supplies. They should have known better."

"They weren't thinking," Victoria replied. She reached out and latched on to her husband's hand. "I'm so sorry he won't be here for Christmas. I know you were looking forward to having both of them here this year."

Colt squeezed her hand, appreciative that his wife knew him so well. "Well, we have Luke, and he has more than enough nonsense to make up for Jake not being here," he said lightly, but deep down he was disappointed.

Victoria knew he would not rest easy until Jake and Cole were back at the ranch. She would never say this to him, but he reminded her of a mother hen that was never satisfied unless all of her chicks were under her wings. "We will have another Christmas dinner when they come back."

Promise stopped thinking about Jake's personal message. "It makes me feel better knowing my aunt and uncle saw them before they left."

"Me too," Victoria said.

Colt figured Jake and Cole were probably in Mexico by now. He wished he could be with Jake to make sure he didn't get himself shot again. Life was short and unpredictable, and he wanted nothing more than his family with him.

In bed that night, Promise read her aunt's letter over and over, particularly the line about Jake's message to her. He hadn't bothered to even speak to her before he left, but now he wanted to give her a message. Well, too little, too late, she told herself. She tossed the letter aside and rolled over and hugged her pillow. The man was maddening, and she had to get him out of her head, and her heart, once and for all. She just wanted him to get home safe and sound. That was all she cared about.

Huddling around the fire, Jake and Cole were thankful for the warm clothing and extra blankets provided by John Hollister. And thanks to Nettie, they were eating a fine meal.

"I thought we were through with this life," Cole said, referring to sleeping out on the cold ground while they chased killers.

"Yeah, I did too." He wanted to be home for Christmas more than anything except catching Newcombe. He'd witnessed many horrible acts of violence that he knew would always remain with him, but seeing those poor, defenseless people on that wagon train, slaughtered, was a scene that would haunt him the rest of his life. Newcombe was going to hang for what he did. He also hated to think what Newcombe might have done to Promise if she hadn't pulled away from him and reached her gun in time.

"Jake, how come you got your dander up when Hollister said he was beholden to you for saving his niece?"

Of course, Cole would notice that. "I'm tired of people saying they're beholden to me."

"By people, you mean Promise?"

Jake felt that Promise had only gone to the ranch because she felt she owed him for saving her life. "Promise, Charles, John Hollister. Nobody owes me anything."

"That's not the reason she came to the ranch."

Jake turned to look at him. Cole knew him well, and at times it was unnerving. "Sure it is. That may not have been her only motive—I know she wanted to spare her aunt and uncle problems—but she's blamed herself for everything that's happened."

"She came to the ranch because she's crazy about you."

Jake was in the process of taking a drink of coffee and that comment made him miss his mouth. "What? You're crazy!" The coffee drizzled down the front of his coat, and he pulled his bandanna out to wipe it off.

"Believe me, I wish she didn't feel that way about you. I would love to have a woman like her feel that way about me. Hell, every man on the ranch wants her."

Jake knew that was true enough. "She's going to marry Charles, which is as it should be. They've lived the same kind of life, they know what's expected."

"Damn, man, are you that blind?"

"What do you mean?"

"Promise doesn't love Charles."

If she didn't love Charles, she was certainly spending every free moment with him for some reason. It seemed to Jake that she must have missed Charles. Maybe she just wanted to see if he would show his love by chasing her across country once she left South Carolina. "Promise needs to go back to South Carolina. She has a lot of responsibilities there, now that her brother is gone. Charles understands what needs to be done."

Cole didn't know what to say to that. He just shook his head, and leaned over and placed more wood on the fire. Finally, he said, "Well, you can act like you don't care about her, but I know different."

"I don't want to marry her, if that's what you're thinking."

"You keep saying that, maybe one day you will convince yourself."

"I'm not marrying anyone for a long time."

Leaning back, Cole pulled his hat over his eyes. "And here I thought you wanted to ranch and start a family. What about the widow Mavis?"

Jake was glad the conversation moved away from Promise. "As I told you, she might not be a widow."

"So, you're interested in her?"

"Hell no!"

"Then why in the hell would you go to her house for dinner?"

That was a question Jake couldn't answer. At the time he accepted the invitation, Promise had been surrounded by men at the picnic. He didn't know why he'd said yes, other than the fact that it was nice to have a woman paying attention to him. Now it seemed just plain stupid. He didn't want Mavis to get the wrong idea and think she might slip a noose around his neck.

Jake finished his coffee with his thoughts centered on Promise. The night he'd had to remove her wet clothes came to mind. *Church bells*, he had to stop going there! The mind was a funny thing, he mused; the things he didn't want to remember had a way of popping up at the most unexpected times. He didn't know why he couldn't get her out of his head. He wished he'd told her aunt to tell Promise . . . Darned if he knew what he wished he'd said. Reaching in his saddlebag, he pulled out a book that he'd noticed right after he left Wyoming. Obviously, Colt had tucked the book in there without his knowledge. *Shakespeare!* Maybe Cole was right, and quoting Shakespeare had helped Colt win Victoria. Well, Colt said Shakespeare was an insightful man, so he opened the book. That's what he needed right now, a little insight.

On the border of New Mexico, Jake and Cole stopped at an inn that was a stagecoach hub. In the past, they'd found the owner to be a good source of information because outlaws stopped here to load up on supplies. Their guess paid off; the owner of the inn had seen Newcombe two days prior, and confirmed he was headed to Mexico. They decided to spend the night at the inn to rest the horses. There were a few boarders at the inn, but Jake didn't recognize any of them as being outlaws, so they wouldn't be forced to sleep with one eye open.

When they sat down to have a bowl of stew, the owner walked to the door and looked out. "Rider coming in." He picked up his rifle by the door and turned back to the guests. "It never hurts to be too careful. Stagecoach ain't due till tomorrow."

Jake exchanged a glance with Cole and they pushed away from the table.

When the rider reined in, the owner of the inn walked to the porch.

"Amigo, it is not polite to greet your guest with a rifle in his face."

Jake heard the voice. "That sounds like Rodriguez."

"It sure does," Cole said.

"What's your business?" the inn owner asked.

"I'm looking for two gringos," Rodriguez said as he dismounted.

"Rodriguez!" Jake hurried to the door. "What are you doing here? Everything okay at the ranch?"

"Everything is fine at the ranch. I came here to keep you two out of trouble in Mexico."

Cole walked out to the porch and saw Rodriguez was traveling with three extra horses. "I see you brought some of your horses with you."

"*Sí.* You didn't take extras when you left. I knew your horses would be tired."

"I suppose that's how you caught up with us," Cole replied.

"A man should never travel without fresh horses. That is the mistake of many outlaws."

"Come on, we'll help you bed them down," Jake said. He was glad to see him. Rodriguez's fluent Spanish would help them.

"We're looking for Newcombe's honey. Her name is Juanita Torres. She's supposed to be in Mexico, not far from El Paso."

Rodriguez couldn't believe what he was hearing. He shook his head. "Juanita Torres?"

"Do you know her?" Cole asked. He didn't know why it would surprise him that Rodriguez knew the very woman they were seeking. Rodriguez was an unusual man.

Rodriguez hesitated, thinking of the woman he'd met a very long time ago. "She is very well-known in that area. Where she lives is more of a village, not even a town. The only building is the saloon where she dances, but she is also a *puta*. She is a very beautiful woman, almost as beautiful as Promise." At one time he would have said no one was as beautiful as Juanita, but after meeting Promise, he knew the meaning of true beauty.

Jake figured that was hard to believe, considering how

beautiful Promise was, but he kept that opinion to himself. It didn't surprise him to hear a pretty woman in a poor village made her money by lifting her skirts. Many women had to resort to that profession to eat. But for a woman to have to consort with a paying customer like Newcombe turned his stomach. "Newcombe is so damn ugly, he'd have to be a paying customer."

"Juanita is known for her loyal customers. It is said they always come back," Rodriguez told them.

Cole didn't hide what he was thinking. "If she's as pretty as Promise, no wonder the men keep coming back."

"This is a dangerous village where we are going, my friends. The villagers are on friendly terms with thieves and killers, but not the law. We will not get a warm reception," Rodriguez told them.

Jake smiled. "We figured if Newcombe was headed there, it wouldn't be a place we would want to take our mothers. We've been to places like this before, Rodriguez. We'll be ready." Jake asked Rodriguez about everyone at the ranch, and as much as he wanted to ask about Promise specifically, he didn't.

"How's the lovelorn Charles doing?" Cole asked.

"He is a willing student, wants to learn about ranching and becoming a vaquero, but something has changed about him. He is not spending as much time with Promise in the evenings. He is at the bunkhouse discussing cattle with the men."

"Do you think he's given up on the idea of marrying Promise?" Cole questioned as Jake listened quietly. Every man on the ranch knew Charles expected Promise to marry him.

"It would be difficult to give up on her if a man thought he stood a chance," Rodriguez answered.

Cole agreed, and they moved on to discussing horses.

"We'll leave at dawn. Best get some shut-eye," Jake said.

Due to the limited space at the inn, they were all bunking down in one room. Fortunately there were three beds in the room, but it didn't appear to be much cleaner than sleeping on the ground, so they threw their bedrolls on top of the bedding.

"Let's get this done and then we can make it back in time to spend Christmas at my family's ranch. I have two very lovely sisters, and my father insists they are in need of husbands," Rodriguez teased.

"I'm for getting this over in a hurry, and Christmas at your house sure beats the heck out of spending it on the cold, hard ground. But don't go thinking I want to marry up with some hot-tempered Spanish woman," Cole joked.

"So you have met my sisters, eh?" Rodriguez countered. "Actually, they are my stepsisters, and they are only half Spanish." He couldn't deny both of his sisters had a temper, and they liked to have their way.

"I can't handle a half-Spanish temper," Cole said.

"Look at it this way, my friend. Their dowries more than make up for their tempers."

"Well, on second thought, I've always been partial to a bit of a temper," Cole teased.

Jake chuckled at their banter. "'Night, boys." He wanted some peace and quiet to think over what Rodriguez had said about Charles. It didn't seem likely that a man would come across the country for the woman he planned to marry, and change his mind once he got there. Maybe Charles was just forming a new strategy. Sometimes it seemed that if a man showed too much interest in a woman, the woman lost interest. That's what he would do if he were in Charles's shoes: just come at it from a different angle.

Chapter Thirty-Six

"We are about a mile from the village," Rodriguez said. "Since I know the place, it might be wise if I ride in first to see what I can find out. If Newcombe is around, he is sure to recognize you. There is a Franciscan friar in the area that I knew at one time, and he will help us."

"That might be a good plan." Jake looked around for a good hiding place and pointed to an area that was somewhat hidden from the trail. "We'll wait for you there, but if we don't see you before dark, we're riding in."

Rodriguez nodded. "I'll be back before dark."

"Hang on, Rodriguez," Jake said. He dismounted and put his saddle on one of the extra horses. "Ride this horse. Your saddle and horse stand out." The silver embellishments on Rodriguez's saddle would tell anyone watching that he was no drifter, but a man who had some coin.

"And don't speak so proper. Say *ain't* once in a while," Cole offered.

"I'll be speaking Spanish."

"Just don't put yourself in danger," Jake told him.

Jake and Cole took the extra horses and rode to the specified area. Once the gear was removed from the animals, they staked them to graze. After making a small fire that couldn't be seen from the trail, they settled in with some coffee to wait for Rodriguez.

It had been seven years since Rodriguez had been in this godforsaken village. It was his sixteenth birthday, and some men who worked for his father insisted they take him out to celebrate. The men spent days discussing the saloon where they planned to take him. He'd never forget how shocked he was when they rode up to this dilapidated saloon with its dirt floor in this no-name place. The way the men talked, he'd expected the saloon was going to be the next best thing to paradise. The poorly constructed building looked as though a good wind would knock it over. The few people living in the village had small, one-room adobe shacks. He remembered his surprise to hear that a Franciscan friar lived in one of them. The men talked about the beautiful woman who danced at the saloon, but he didn't believe a beautiful woman would live in such squalid conditions.

When he walked into the saloon that night seven years ago and his eyes landed on Juanita, he didn't give another thought to the impoverished village. In his inexperienced mind, she was the most beautiful woman he'd ever seen.

In her room that night, Juanita told him that she worked in the saloon because her father left her family, and she had to support her brothers and sisters. After hearing her sad story, Rodriguez gave her all the money he had with him at the time. Over the next several months, when he could get away from the ranch, he'd make trips to the border, and always took as much money as he could spare.

It troubled the men to see the amount of money Rodriguez was giving Juanita, knowing full well that she was using him, so they told his father. He explained to his father that Juanita sold her body simply to put food on the table for her family. Instead of offering his support, which was what Rodriguez had expected, his father laughed at him. He said Juanita told that same story to every vaquero in the territory, just to deceive them for more money. His father told him Juanita had no family. Rodriguez refused to believe him, even though the men on the ranch confirmed his words. That very night after the confrontation with his father, he rode to the village and spoke to the friar. He was crushed to hear the truth. Juanita had been lying to him from that first night. He felt like a fool for giving her so much money, and for believing that she didn't want to be with other men. Before he'd learned the truth, he'd even planned on asking her to marry him.

Riding up to that same dilapidated saloon was a different man. Seven years ago he'd been a boy. Today, he was a man who had seen a lot of places, done a lot of things, and was much wiser to the guiles of some women. When he rode by the friar's hut, he saw that it was now a part of the earth, so he didn't stop.

As he dismounted in front of the saloon, he heard someone playing a guitar, and raucous shouts filtered to the street. He walked through the door and saw Juanita dancing around the tables, creating the frenzy. Without missing a stride, he went straight to the bar and ordered a whiskey. Leaning against the bar, he sipped his drink and observed the patrons around the room. There were ten men total in the bar, mostly Mexican, and from the looks of them, they were probably running from the law. But none of them fit Jake's description of Newcombe.

Only after checking out all of the men did he allow his gaze to fall on Juanita. Her hips swayed to the music as she ran her hands over her body in a seductive move designed to entice every man in the room. She had the same voluptuous body, and her face was still beautiful, though hardened from years of alcohol and her chosen lifestyle.

Juanita danced her way to him, holding her red skirt high in the air as she twirled in front of him. Just like the first time he saw her, she was wearing a red skirt and a white top that fell from her shoulders. It could have been the same clothing; the material was so thin from wear, he could see she wore nothing underneath. She swayed into his body, removed his hat, and ran her fingers through his hair. The very same move she'd made those many years ago.

"I've seen you before. I know you," she purred.

Rodriguez stared into her glazed eyes. He figured the money she had earned over the years went to alcohol. He almost allowed himself to feel sorry for her. Almost. "You don't know me," Rodriguez responded, his voice hard. He wasn't being dishonest; she didn't know the man he was today.

She stretched up and brushed her lips against his neck. "I do not forget a handsome man," she murmured in his ear. When he didn't respond, she whispered a question.

"I'm just having one drink and then I am leaving," Rodriguez replied.

She pouted. "Surely you have time for me, señor, like before."

He wasn't sure she really remembered him, considering all the men she had been with, or if she was guessing she'd been with him before. Probably the latter. As much as he hated to admit it to himself, she was still tempting. Luckily, his attention was drawn to the swinging door slamming against the wall. Every man in the place turned to see a big man barge in. Rodriguez knew this had to be Newcombe. Jake's description had been accurate. Newcombe's eyes landed on Juanita snuggled up to Rodriguez. He stalked directly to the bar and grabbed her by the arm, jerking her away from him.

"I told you what would happen if I caught you with another man," he warned.

Juanita didn't look cowed by the big man. "I wasn't with another man, I was dancing," she snapped back.

Newcombe looked at Rodriguez with undisguised venom. "Why are you dancing around this Mexican?"

Juanita smiled at Rodriguez as she studied his face. He was handsome, and he did look vaguely familiar. She'd noticed he didn't smell like every other man in the room, including Newcombe. "He's a paying customer, isn't he?"

Newcombe saw her reaction to Rodriguez and he slapped her hard across the cheek.

Rodriguez momentarily contemplated saving Jake a trip. He straightened and faced Newcombe, but before a word left his mouth, he felt a poke in the back. The bartender had a shotgun pressed against his spine.

"No trouble in here. If you two want to fight, take it outside," the bartender ordered.

Eyeing Rodriguez, Newcombe laughed. He didn't think the Mexican was worth his trouble, and there was also the possibility he was riding with some of the other Mexicans in the room. "Give me a bottle. I got other plans today."

The bartender placed a bottle of whiskey on the bar, and Newcombe grabbed it before taking a handful of Juanita's hair, pulling her behind him as he made his way to the staircase.

Rodriguez heard Newcombe threaten her. "No other man will look at you after today."

"Señor, I have to eat, I have mouths to feed," Juanita shot back at him.

Rodriguez heard another slap as the door slammed closed. He wondered if Newcombe was wise to her lies, or if he was just too obsessed with her to care one way or the other. If it hadn't been for his father, Rodriguez might still be obsessed with her too.

The bartender put the shotgun back on the shelf behind the bar. "You ain't going to start trouble, are you?" he asked, holding up the bottle to pour him another drink.

"Not planning on it, but I won't run from it." As the gringo bartender filled his glass, Rodriguez said, "He don't seem too friendly." He remembered Cole's warning not to use proper English.

"He's not, and he hates Mexicans."

"He seemed to like that Mexican well enough."

"Yeah, that's one señorita he likes too much, but he's so jealous he's going to kill her one of these days when he catches her with another man."

"Isn't that her business?"

"Yeah, but when he's around, she'd better not be with anyone else."

Rodriguez looked at the men at the tables; no one seemed to be too interested in what just took place. "I guess these men aren't riding with him."

The bartender gave him a long look, trying to figure out if he was a bounty hunter or just plain nosy. Figuring he was probably running from the law like the rest of the men in the saloon, or maybe he'd taken a liking to Juanita, he said, "Nope, he rode in alone, and as long as you're here, you'd best stay clear of Juanita."

On that score, the bartender had nothing to worry about. He intended to steer very clear of Juanita.

When they heard a rider coming their way, Jake kicked dirt to the fire and pulled his pistol. Hearing Rodriguez's whistle, Jake whistled back.

"We didn't expect you back so soon," Cole said.

"I think we're in luck. Newcombe is at the saloon in an upstairs room with Juanita and a fresh bottle. I have a feeling he might be there awhile."

Rodriguez gave them the layout of the saloon and they took off for the village. When they reached the saloon, Jake and Cole walked inside, and Rodriguez rode to the back. Cole stood at the door with his pistol drawn as Jake made his way to the bar. "What room?" he asked, leaning over the bar and removing the shotgun.

The bartender didn't have to ask who Jake was looking for. "Last door on the left."

Taking the steps quietly, Jake moved soundlessly down the hallway. When he reached the door, he kicked it open with such force that it splintered against the wall.

Newcombe was passed out, lying across the bed wearing nothing but long underwear. Juanita was on the settee across the room, rummaging through Newcombe's pants pockets.

"¿Que quieres?" Juanita asked.

Jake glanced at the woman. Large dark eyes were glaring at him, not the least bit concerned that he was holding a gun. Rodriguez wasn't exaggerating; she was a beautiful woman. Her long, black hair reached her waist, and she had a body most men dreamed about. "I'm taking your boyfriend here to jail. Wake him up."

"Not my *novio*," Juanita replied in broken English before sauntering to the bed. She dropped Newcombe's pants on the floor, stuffed the money in her skirt pocket, then picked up the pitcher of water off the bedside table and threw it in his face.

The big man started coughing and sputtering, and when he opened his eyes he saw Jake standing there with his gun trained on him. He scrambled to a sitting position, his gaze going to his gun belt hanging on the bedpost.

"Don't," Jake said calmly. "I suggest you get your pants on instead, unless you want to freeze your ass off on the way back to Denver."

"That blond woman shot my brother and he died. I wish I'd killed her," Newcombe said.

At least he didn't pretend he didn't know why Jake was there. "I think your brother got what he had coming, considering you and your gang killed nine people on that wagon train. Now put on your damn pants and be quick about it. My trigger finger is getting mighty itchy."

"You a U.S. Marshal?" Newcombe asked as he leaned over to grab his pants from the floor.

"Not anymore, so don't tempt me."

Once Newcombe fastened his pants he reached for Juanita and yanked her by the hair, holding her in front of his chest. Juanita tried to pull away, but he snaked his forearm around her throat so she couldn't move. Slowly, he inched his way to his holster.

"Far enough," Jake warned.

Only a few feet separated him and Jake, and Newcombe used that to his advantage. He shoved Juanita hard into Jake's body at the same time he reached for his gun.

With the force of Juanita's weight slamming into him, Jake staggered backward. He tried to keep his balance while he held on to Juanita with one arm so they wouldn't fall to the floor, but his gun hand waivered.

"Drop your gun!" Newcombe ordered.

Jake tried to push Juanita out of danger, but she held on to his arm. He heard a shot ring out, and Juanita slumped in his arms. He dropped to one knee to support her weight and managed to get a shot off before Newcombe fired again. The force of the impact had Newcombe stumbling backward toward the window. With arms flailing, he couldn't stop his momentum and crashed through the glass. He hit the ground below with a loud thud.

Jake checked Juanita and saw that she was still breathing, but he knew the wound was lethal. Cole ran into the room to make sure Jake was the one still standing.

"Ask the barkeep if there is a doctor in this town," Jake said.

Cole didn't have to go downstairs because the bartender was right behind him.

"We don't have no doctor," he answered.

Jake and Cole exchanged a knowing glance. It wouldn't make a difference one way or the other.

Rodriguez walked into the room and saw Juanita on the floor. "Newcombe's dead," he said as he kneeled down. Juanita was on her side, so Rodriguez could see the lethal wound in her back. Jake and Cole backed away. They could do nothing for her now. Seeing the hopelessness of Juanita's situation, Rodriguez crossed himself before saying a quick prayer. Taking her hand in his, he asked, "Are you in pain?"

Her eyes were filled with tears, but she said in Spanish, "No. I'm afraid of . . . Hades."

Hardly able to form a reply for the lump in his throat, Rodriguez took a deep breath and whispered, "Ask for forgiveness now, and you will see God today."

Juanita mumbled words that only Rodriguez could hear. When she finished she opened her eyes and stared at him. "I do remember you," she whispered in a fading voice.

"I remembered you all these years," Rodriguez answered softly.

She closed her eyes and smiled. "I see Him," were her last words.

* * *

Selecting the site where the friar's hut once stood, Jake and Cole dug the grave while Rodriguez prepared Juanita for burial. Even the bartender had helped by hammering together some planks for a coffin. When the grave was covered, Rodriguez said a prayer.

Jake and Cole walked away to gather the horses and to give Rodriguez a few minutes alone with her. They knew Rodriguez had some unresolved feelings about Juanita, but they didn't push. He would tell them when he was ready.

Jake rode beside Rodriguez as they left the village. "If you ever want to talk about it, I'll listen."

"Thank you, my friend," Rodriguez said.

The trip to Rodriguez's family ranch was a quiet affair. Jake and Cole both knew they hadn't heard the complete story about Rodriguez's relationship with Juanita, and they gave him time to grieve. Jake had his own thinking to do. He still hadn't come to terms with what he planned to do about Promise. He couldn't seem to get her off his mind, no matter how long he was gone. *Hell's . . . church bells!* He smiled to himself, thinking the twins would give him heck if they heard he'd almost messed up. He missed his nephews and couldn't wait to get home to see them. They were corkers, that's for sure, and Victoria and Colt would have their hands full if they had another boy. It was disappointing he wouldn't be there to see the boys Christmas morning, but he'd find some presents for them in Santa Fe. Thinking about his family, it dawned on him that he thought of Victoria as his sister-in-law now, and he was no longer obsessing about her.

As soon as they reached Santa Fe they sent a telegram to Colt.

NEWCOMBE'S DEAD. SPENDING CHRISTMAS WITH
RODRIGUEZ. SEE YOU WHEN WEATHER BREAKS.
MERRY CHRISTMAS, JAKE.

Jake also stopped at the general store and picked out
presents for everyone. He wasn't going to come home
empty-handed and disappoint the boys.

Chapter Thirty-Seven

Jake's telegram arrived on Christmas morning, right after Colt presented the boys with their new saddles. Though disappointed Jake would be away for another Christmas, Colt reminded himself his brother was safe and there was always next Christmas. He had so many blessings when he thought of his family and the new baby that was soon to be added, that nothing could ruin his day. He had more than enough to thank the Good Lord for at the dinner prayer.

Colt helped Victoria unwrap their gift from Promise, and their smiles told Promise she had pleased the couple with the family portrait that included their beloved dog, Bandit.

Victoria was moved to tears by the painting. If she didn't know better, she would have thought the family had posed together for Promise. "How did you do this? Colt certainly didn't sit still long enough for you to draw him!"

"It wasn't easy, but whenever I saw him sitting still for a minute, I tried to sketch him. The boys were almost as difficult. Bandit was the easiest," Promise teased.

Victoria dried her tears on her handkerchief. "It's a lovely gift. I will treasure it always."

Promise handed another large package to Colt. "This is for the three brothers. I'm sorry Jake isn't here to see it."

"Would you like to wait until he returns?" Colt asked.

Finally, the opportunity presented itself to ask what she'd wanted to ask all day. "When do you think he might return?"

"It depends on the snow. It could be a few months."

"He can see it when he comes back, but I want to see it now," Luke cut in.

Promise smiled at his eagerness. "Okay, go ahead. It is Christmas after all!"

Colt handed the large present to Lucas. "You can open this one."

Luke ripped into the package. His and Colt's mouths dropped open when they saw the painting. Promise had painted the three brothers outdoors with the mountains in the background. Colt was in the center, one arm looped over Jake's shoulders, his other arm over Lucas's. Somehow Promise had captured their personalities. Lucas's dazzling blue eyes and mischievous nature nearly jumped off the canvas. Jake's intense black eyes revealed his serious nature, and Colt's physical stature expressed his authority, but his eyes were full of love for his brothers. Colt knew without walking outside that the painting was an exact replica of the mountains behind the house. It was the scene he saw every day of his life. But he could hardly believe that Promise had captured the sun shining at just the right angle to see the cross reflecting on the mountains.

"Oh my," Victoria said and started weeping again.

Colt pointed to the cross. "You saw that?"

"Yes, a few times."

"A lot of people never see it."

Lucas said, "Promise, I swear I'm stealing you from Charles! You are beautiful and talented."

Charles was sitting across the room, absorbed in a book that Colt had given him about breeding cattle. Hearing his name, he glanced up and said, "Pardon?"

"I'm stealing Promise," Lucas repeated.

"Okay," Charles replied, then promptly stuck his nose back in the book.

Everyone laughed, but secretly Promise was relieved that Charles seemed to be over his obsession to make her his wife. She had worried that he might try to give her an engagement ring again for Christmas, but he'd given her a lovely cameo brooch. She'd had Colt pick out a Western saddle as her gift to him.

Christmas Day was almost perfect, with one exception. Jake was not there for the festivities, and no one felt his absence more than Promise. Her present to him would have to wait. It was a painting of him by the campfire. She'd painted it from the sketch she did that night on the trail. She was thrilled she'd completed all of the paintings because she had a feeling that once she returned to Charleston, she would no longer have the heart for painting. She'd been inspired by her surroundings, and by Jake. She'd take her memories with her in the form of the many sketches she had of Jake and his family.

"This woman you found is still at your ranch, señor?" Margaretta, one of Rodriguez's sisters, asked while they were having dinner. Rodriguez had told his family about the cattle drive and the events that had taken place.

"Yes, she is looking after my sister-in-law until she has her baby," Jake replied.

"Which could be any day now," Cole added.

Jake remembered Colt saying they could have a Christmas baby. Wouldn't that be something, to have a new baby when he got back home! He hadn't purchased a present for a baby, something he needed to do before he got home. But what did you get a baby, particularly if you didn't know if it was going to be a boy or a girl? He asked the women that question, and they were still discussing it an hour later. Jake decided he would pick something up in Denver for the baby since he had to stop there to pick up a present for Promise.

Colt snuffed out the last candle on the Christmas tree in the front room, and was ready to join Victoria in bed when Promise ran into the room. "Colt, I think Victoria is ready."

"I'm coming up now," he answered, thinking she meant Victoria was ready for bed.

"I mean the baby is coming now," Promise stated impatiently. "I've already told Mrs. Wellington."

Colt whipped around to face her. "Now?"

"Now. Mrs. Wellington said there wasn't time to send someone for the doctor because that would take hours in this snow. I'm going to boil some water and get everything ready."

Colt hurried for the stairs. "Luke!" he yelled.

"Something on fire?" Luke shouted, running from his bedroom.

"No, the baby's coming!" So many thoughts were racing around in Colt's head. The doctor expected the baby to be large, and he wondered if Mrs. Wellington could handle it if anything went wrong. Should he send someone to town for the doctor?

"You want me to help deliver the baby?" Luke asked,

thoroughly confused. He'd helped deliver his share of colts, but never a baby.

"No, go help Promise with whatever she needs," Colt said.

Promise heard the exchange and laughed. She could hear the excitement and trepidation in Colt's voice.

The boys ran into the hallway. "The baby's coming?" they exclaimed together.

"Yes, so you two can stay up, but go see if Promise needs help," Colt told them before he went into his bedroom. He didn't think they needed to see Victoria right now.

"Yippee!" they chorused and scrambled down the steps.

Colt took a moment to calm himself before he stepped into the room. No matter what happened, he told himself, he'd seen many animals born, so he could handle this. He was determined to stay calm for Victoria. He opened the door and stepped inside. When he saw the pain etched on his wife's face, it was all he could do not to scream in frustration.

Mrs. Wellington handed him a damp cloth. "Wipe her forehead and try to keep her calm."

Colt sat on the bed beside Victoria and put the cloth on her forehead, thankful he had a task. "Can I do anything else for you, honey?"

"No, I . . . just . . . need . . . to . . . have . . . this . . . baby," she said calmly between contractions.

Colt smiled at her control. He'd never seen a woman have a baby, and the longer he sat there, he wasn't sure he wanted to see his wife endure this much pain. It was breaking his heart to see her like this, and there wasn't a thing he could do to help her.

Mrs. Wellington told her to scream if she wanted, but Victoria knew the boys were up and didn't want to worry them. Promise and Luke carried water into the room, but

Luke didn't stay. He decided to go find some cigars and whiskey in preparation for the big event.

They waited and waited, each of them wincing whenever Victoria had a contraction. For such a tiny woman, Colt was surprised at her strength each time she gripped his fingers.

Three hours later, just before midnight, a new McBride came into the world.

Chapter Thirty-Eight

"I thought you might stay with Rodriguez. It looked like you were getting mighty friendly with Margaretta," Jake teased.

"I couldn't let you ride all this way alone. No telling what kind of trouble you might get into," Cole responded.

Just one week after Christmas, Jake had been itching to leave New Mexico. Cole thought he was crazy to travel in such inclement weather, but he didn't try to dissuade him. On their way back to Wyoming they'd stopped in Denver, and also paid a visit to John and Nettie Hollister. They were invited to spend the night, and as usual, Nettie prepared a fine dinner, and then breakfast to send them off to face their cold journey home. It was still snowing when they left Denver, but Jake was determined to go.

"Why do you think Rodriguez didn't come with us?" Cole asked.

Jake had given that question some consideration. "I think he had some things to work out, and I think he missed his family."

"Yeah, I think he did. He has a fine family."

"The sisters are especially fine," Jake teased. "I expect we'll see Rodriguez in the spring. He'll come for his horses." Rodriguez had loaned them two extra horses for their trip home. He'd left some horses at the ranch, so he told them he would come to Wyoming in the spring for them.

Cole smiled. "Yeah. If he doesn't come back in the spring, I might have to take them to him. Then I can see those pretty gals again."

"What about Promise?" Jake asked.

Cole expelled a loud breath. "What about her?"

"Well, it looked like you two were getting pretty close."

"I don't know how many ways to say this to you, partner, but Promise has her sights set on someone else, and here's one guess—he's one dumb son-of-a-buck!" That said, he rode off at a faster pace before he got the urge to land his fist on his friend's jaw.

Jake grinned. He just wanted to see where Cole's head was as it related to Promise. He had his answer.

The two of them were nearly frozen when they rode up to the ranch in mid-February. They were met at the stable by some of the ranch hands, who helped them remove their gear from the horses. Suddenly, a loud cry came from the house. Cole and Jake looked at each other and smiled.

"I guess that is your new niece or nephew," Cole said.

The little cry warmed Jake's heart, and he was grinning from ear to ear. "Sounds like."

Cole knew Jake was itching to see the new baby and Promise. "Go ahead and see that new baby. I'll finish here."

"Don't take too long. It's time for dinner, and I know everyone will want to see you." Jake grabbed the packages and headed toward the house. It was Sunday, so he expected everyone to be at home.

The boys ran from the side of the house, shouting, "Uncle Jake, Uncle Jake!"

Jake dropped his packages as the boys hurled themselves at him. "My favorite nephews!" Jake said, hugging them to him.

The twins laughed. "We're your only nephews." Seeing the packages, they said, "We missed you at Christmas. We got presents for you too."

"What makes you think these are for you?"

"Aw, we know they are," Cade said.

"Yeah," Cody agreed. They helped Jake with the packages. "Come on, we got something to show you. Boy, are you gonna be surprised."

"I bet I am." Wanting to surprise everyone, he headed for the front door instead of going through the kitchen.

"Promise is still here too. We don't want her to go home," Cody said.

"And wait till you see the painting she did of us and Ma and Pa and Bandit," Cade told him.

"It made Ma cry," Cody said, making a face.

"That was nice of Promise," Jake said.

Cade looked at him like he had grown two heads. "To make Ma cry?"

Jake chuckled. "No, to give her a painting of you handsome boys."

"Yeah, Promise is real nice," Cody said. "She's putting supper on the table."

"Good, I'm hungry enough to eat two growing boys."

"Aw, Uncle Jake, you wouldn't eat us," Cade said.

"Not if dinner is good. What are we having?"

"Fried chicken, taters, and gravy," Cody told him.

"You like that," Cade added, remembering how much fried chicken his uncle could eat.

"Yep, I do. Are we having apple pie?" Jake asked hopefully.

"I dunno," Cade said. "Do you know, Cody?"

"Nope. Maybe it'll be apple pie."

"I sure hope so. I'm partial to Promise's apple pie," Jake told them as he opened the front door.

Walking from his office, Colt was the first to see his brother. "Jake, what in the world are you doing here?"

"I missed home," Jake replied, stacking his packages on the floor.

Colt thought his brother looked tired, which was understandable riding home in this frigid weather. He pulled Jake into his embrace. "Thank God you're back. We missed you too."

"Look, Uncle Jake," the boys said, taking his hand and turning him around so he could see Promise's painting of the three brothers on the wall.

"Wow! How did she manage that?" Jake stared at the impressive painting. "She even saw that cross that you showed me on the mountains."

"She's something, isn't she?" Colt put his arm over his brother's shoulder and led him to the dining room. "We have another surprise for you," he said, beaming.

"I've already heard it, but is it a niece or nephew?"

As they entered the dining room, Jake's eyes landed on Victoria holding the little bundle in her arms.

"Jake! How wonderful to have you home. Come see little Tate."

Jake shook his brother's hand. "Congratulations, brother. Tate, that's perfect." He hurried across the room to see his new nephew, and took him from Victoria's arms as comfortably as if he held babies every day. "Now this is a big boy," he said, feeling the baby's weight. "He's going to be just like his pa. And look at all that black hair!"

"The doc said he thought he was bigger than me." Colt beamed proudly like a new father should.

Jake gave Victoria a concerned look. "Are you okay?"

"I'm fine," Victoria responded.

"Don't let her fool you. It was a long Christmas night, and she was in bed for three weeks afterward," Colt added.

"He was born on Christmas Day?"

"Right before midnight," Colt said.

"Ma says he's gonna be tall," Cody said.

"Yeah, and Pa said the way he eats, he'll be as big as us in no time," Cade added.

Colt pulled the twins into his arms. "I'm counting on you to watch after him and make sure he's a good boy, just like you two."

Their faces lit up at his words. "We will," they said in unison.

"Jake, why did you come home in this weather?" Victoria asked.

"I found something awhile back, and I had to see if I lost it."

Colt exchanged a look with his brother, his meaning not lost on him. "I don't think you did."

"What?" Victoria said.

Jake barely heard her question because the baby was looking at him and cooing, and Jake was making baby talk back to him. Colt couldn't stop grinning as he watched his brother hold his new son.

No one saw Promise and Charles walk into the room.

"What did you find and lose, Uncle Jake?" Cody asked.

"Jake! What are you doing here?" Promise hadn't expected him to be back for months, and she couldn't believe he was standing in front of her.

Jake turned to her. She was wearing his favorite blue dress, and she looked so beautiful he feared his heart would burst at the sheer joy of seeing her.

"Everyone keeps asking me that. Isn't anyone glad to see me?" he teased.

"We are!" the boys exclaimed.

"Of course," Promise said, more thrilled than she could say. Silently, she thanked God for bringing him home. Watching him hold little Tate brought a lump to her throat. It was tempting to imagine him holding their baby, but she wouldn't allow herself to dream of something that would never happen.

"But what did you find and lose, Uncle Jake?" Cade repeated his brother's question.

"Promise."

Everyone but Colt looked confused.

"What?" Promise asked, thinking he wanted to ask her something.

"But Promise is not lost, she's right here," Cade said, and Cody agreed. "Yeah, you already found her."

"Did I?" he asked.

Promise's eyes widened. What was he asking her? "Jake?" she whispered.

He planted a kiss on little Tate's forehead and passed him to his brother, then walked across the room and took the platter of chicken Promise was holding and handed it to Charles. "Sorry, Charles, but you will have to excuse us." With that said, he took her by the elbow and headed for the door. Once they were on the porch, he removed his coat and wrapped it around her shoulders. When he felt her shiver, he asked, "Are you cold?"

"No." She wasn't cold, she was nervous. She'd planned what she would say to him when he returned, but right now she couldn't think of a single word. All she could think about was how handsome he was, and how she loved the way he smelled of outdoors and leather, and how grateful she was that he was home in one piece.

Jake stared at her, trying to gather his courage. All the way home he'd memorized the words he wanted to say, but now that he was in front of her, he questioned why a woman like her would want him. She was beautiful, talented, smart, and brave, and she could have her choice of any man in the world. Charles might be a better man for her. He hesitated. Nope . . . there wasn't a better man for her. He was the one. He gave her a brilliant smile. "Did you miss me?"

For months, she'd waited and waited for the Jake she knew when he first found her to surface, but he'd made it clear he wanted nothing to do with her. She'd lost hours of sleep wondering why he hadn't even said good-bye, and she hadn't forgotten how devastated she'd been. "I've been pretty busy," she said hesitantly.

Oh, she'd missed him, he could see it on her face, but he'd hurt her, too. He needed to make up for that. "Too busy to miss me?"

"Well . . ." She faltered. She wanted to say no, but the lie would not leave her lips. If only he knew how much she'd missed him.

He moved toward her and she stepped backward into a column on the porch. Jake braced his hands against the column, fencing her in. "I missed you," he said, lowering his face to hers.

She stared into his black eyes. "Really. Since you didn't say good-bye, I didn't think you gave me much thought." Her words didn't contain rancor, just honesty.

"I was wrong," he admitted. "I'm sorry." He inched his face closer. "I gave you a lot of thought."

He was so close she could see the playful glint in his eyes, feel the heat of his skin, and she wanted so badly to pull him even closer. What did he want from her? She'd vowed she wouldn't throw herself at him if she ever saw him again. "I'm glad you are safe." And she was. She'd prayed and prayed that he would return home safely, and her prayers had been answered.

He took a deep breath and decided to jump in. He wasn't a man who equivocated about anything, other than his feelings for Promise. He intended to put an end to that today. He loved her, and he knew he would never be happy without her. The way he saw it, the rest of his life was riding on her response. "I found you, Promise, and I don't want to lose you. You might think Charles is the best man for you, but he isn't. I am." Looking into her eyes, he couldn't tell what she was thinking. "I'm not letting you go."

Promise could hardly breathe. He was saying the words she'd been longing to hear. Jake was the most wonderful man she'd ever known. He was the very kind of man she'd expected to find in the West. But she had convinced herself that he didn't want her. Tears started welling in her eyes.

Her silence made him anxious. "Do you plan on marrying Charles?"

She shook her head.

"Good. I wouldn't want to shoot him, but I would," he teased. At least, he told himself he was teasing.

She had to ask the question that had been on her mind for months. "What about Victoria? I know you care for her."

He didn't hesitate. "She's not the woman I've been thinking of day and night. Colt was right, I was envious of what he'd found. I wanted the happiness he had, not his wife, or his life. Promise, I've made a mess of things, but now my head is on straight. A smart man once said 'the course of true love never did run smooth.' I'd say that pretty much sums it up, since you are my true love." His big brother wasn't the only one who could quote Shakespeare. He reached in his coat and pulled something out. Promise couldn't see what it was, but when he lowered himself to one knee, she started shaking. "I won't lose you. You are going to marry me," he stated, his voice deep and clear.

"Is that a proposal?" she asked, breathless. To her, it was the most beautiful proposal in the world. He'd said she was his *true love*, and that was all she needed to hear him say.

"Sort of." He stood and leaned over. His face was so close to hers, if he leaned down just an inch more his lips would be on hers and he could kiss her senseless. His eyes lowered to her lips, and he was just about to give in to his urge, but he was determined to make a proper proposal. She deserved that. He also wanted her to know he could be a cowboy and a gentleman of the first order, just like she'd expected to find out West. He took her hand and held the ring to her finger. "Promise, I love you and have from the moment I found you. Will you marry me?"

The tears finally flowed over her pink cheeks. She didn't know how he'd come to this decision, but she thanked God that he had. "Yes, Jake, I will marry you."

"Do you love me?" he asked, thinking it was high time she said the words.

"Yes, very much."

"Tell me."

"Jake McBride, I've loved you since I awoke to the sound of your voice," she said tearfully.

"Really?" He hadn't realized that. He remembered all the times he'd tried and failed to keep his distance from her. He was a darn fool for wasting so much time.

She nodded.

"Good." He felt his chest swell at the very thought of this beautiful woman loving him. He slipped the ring on her finger and was pleased that he'd guessed the right size. He wrapped his arms around her and pulled her to his chest.

Promise held her hand in the air to admire the diamond sparkling on her finger. "Oh my, it is so lovely. Where did you find something so beautiful?"

In his estimation, it paled in comparison to her beauty.

"Denver. It was a long ride back, and I had time to do a lot of thinking." His brother was right when he'd called him a dumb son-of-a-buck. For the life of him, he couldn't figure out what had taken him so long to figure out how much he loved this woman.

"Were you sure I would say yes?"

"I wasn't going to let you leave if you didn't, and I sure as heck wasn't going to let you marry anyone else."

She smiled at his high-handed manner. His supreme confidence was one of the many reasons she fell in love with him in the first place.

He looked into her eyes, and his tone turned serious. "I prayed I wasn't too late."

She was so happy she could barely speak, but she managed to whisper through her tears, "You weren't too late."

"You're beautiful. The most beautiful thing I ever found on the Plains." He lowered his lips to hers and finally kissed her senseless. When he came up for air, he asked, "Are we having apple pie for dessert?"

The heart always finds a home . . .

For British heiress Mary Ann Hardwicke, the Wild West is the perfect place to make her own life and escape the stifling privilege of an arranged marriage. Hard at work proving her independence, it's little wonder she has no time for handsome cowboy Luke McBride. No matter that he somehow understands the freedom she so badly needs— how could she trust such a wild spirit, much less find a way to love him?

Like the broncs he busts, Luke doesn't see himself settling down in one place, let alone with one woman. So at first, Mary Ann is just an intriguing challenge. But her determination and bravery are sparking a longing to prove he can be the truly good man she deserves. Now, as their enemies work to separate them, they will take a dangerous gamble on faith to claim an enduring love . . .

Please turn the page for an exciting sneak peek of Scarlett Dunn's

LAST PROMISE,

coming in May 2016 wherever print and eBooks are sold!

Prologue

London, England

Dearest Mother,

I simply cannot allow Father to force me to marry Edmund Stafford. Contrary to Father's belief, I was not compromised by the rake, but he would not even allow me to explain. While Father professes to be a man of God, he displays no hesitation in judging his own daughter. Are we not taught "Judge not, that ye be not judged?"

Edmund was forcing his attentions on me, and in my struggle to get away from him, my dress was ripped. If anyone should be called to account, it should be Edmund! It does not matter one whit to me if he is as rich as Croesus himself; I cannot abide the man, and I am baffled why he wants to marry a woman who finds him totally insufferable.

I am sorry, Mother, but I must leave.

Mary Ann

Chapter One

What a piece of work is a man!
SHAKESPEARE

Promise, Wyoming

The soiled doves were hanging over the second-floor balcony of L. B. Ditty's Saloon, wearing nothing but their chemises and bloomers when Luke McBride exited the bank across the street. One gal gave a shrill whistle, louder than any man could make, causing all of the gals to burst into laughter.

"Hi, Luke, honey, you sure look handsome this morning," one gal hollered. The other women chorused their agreement.

"Where you going, darling? It's noon, ya know, not too early to come in," another gal offered.

Luke glanced up to see the bevy of beauties displaying their wares to anyone who happened to be passing by. He had to hand it to L. B. Ditty; she hired the most attractive girls she could find, and he knew each one by name. He stopped and tipped his hat to the women. "Hello, ladies. I can't join you today. I'm picking up some supplies." There wasn't a man on earth who appreciated God's design of the female form more than Luke McBride. And he took time to show his appreciation whenever possible. Looking at them from his vantage point, he couldn't decide if he preferred the more voluptuous figure or the tall, lanky gal with less cleavage to display. The way he saw it, they each had their advantages.

"Are you sure, honey? We was just getting dressed to go downstairs."

Before he told them they shouldn't bother to change because they sure looked lovely in what they were wearing, he heard the voice of L. B. filtering down to the street.

"Girls, what in heaven's name are you doing out here on the balcony when you should be getting dressed?" L. B. Ditty didn't abide the girls making a spectacle of themselves outside the saloon. It wasn't good for business, at least not with the ladies in town on a Saturday morning. L. B. was adamant her girls maintain decorum so the local ladies wouldn't complain to their husbands. Inside the saloon, they could walk around half-dressed if they chose, since she figured that was good for business.

"We was just saying hello to Luke," one gal answered.

"Come look, L. B. Luke looks so handsome today," another gal said.

"The way you're carrying on, I'd expect him to be walking down the street buck naked." Even as the words left her mouth, she couldn't resist walking to the rail and leaning over to see if Luke happened to be in his birthday suit. That sure would give the ladies in town something to talk about instead of her girls.

Hearing the exchange between L. B. and the girls, Luke saw L. B.'s bright red curls appear over the railing. He tipped his hat, smiled, and spread his arms wide. "Sorry to disappoint, L. B., but as you can see, I'm fully clothed."

Grinning, L. B. shook her head at him. "And that's a good thing, Luke McBride, or you'd have all the ladies in town in a dither. But the gals are right; you surely are a sight to behold."

The gals flocked over the railing again, each exposing more bosom than the next.

Luke couldn't help but chuckle at the lineup of well-endowed females. "Thank you, ma'am. And might I say, you ladies look mighty fetching today."

"You are full of nonsense, but it's a pleasure to see you this fine morning," L. B. retorted. To her way of thinking, Luke McBride had the world by the tail, and he often liked to twirl it on a whim. She figured he would take exception if anyone ever said he strutted down the sidewalk, but there wasn't a man or woman who didn't take notice when he passed. Of course, that was partly due to his size. Like his brothers, Colt and Jake, Luke was well over six feet, had a rock-hard muscled body, and broad shoulders that naturally demanded a wide berth. His handsome face sported the same signature McBride square jaw, but where his brothers had black eyes, Luke's eyes were a vivid turquoise blue. She imagined that blue shirt he was wearing really made those blue eyes sparkle. He was definitely spit-shined, his shirt starched and pressed to perfection, not a speck of dirt on his pants, boots polished to a high shine, his black Stetson brushed, and even his holster was gleaming. Luke always looked attractive, yet there was something special about him today. Maybe it was his cocksure attitude that made him look exceptionally handsome.

No one could deny Luke McBride was a charmer, and he had a full calendar of Friday-night dinner dates to prove it. Women loved him, and there wasn't a man who didn't envy his carefree approach to life. Luke's motto was simple: He loved to laugh, loved horses, and loved women. Depending on the availability of the latter, he often re-arranged the order.

Sally Detrick was shopping in the mercantile when she spotted Luke through the window talking to someone across the street. Hurrying to the door, she saw what was drawing his attention. Seeing those saloon women in their undergarments hanging over the railing, oohing and aahing over Luke, made her see red. Marching over to him, she hooked her arm through his and pulled him toward her. "Why, Luke McBride, you sure do look handsome today, even if you are just full of the devil!"

L. B. saw the look on Sally's face when she'd looked at the girls. That did it; Sally was sure to run to her daddy and tell him about the evil ways of her girls. Knowing Detrick would raise all kinds of hell, L. B. quickly ushered the girls away from the balcony.

"Hello, Sally," Luke replied, glancing at the balcony one last time to see the girls' backsides as they were being herded inside. With some regret he turned his attention on Sally.

"Why did you turn down my dinner invitation?"

Luke knew that question would be coming. The main reason he'd declined her invitation was because of her daddy. Every time he went to dinner at their ranch, old man Detrick stuck to him like glue once his feet were over the threshold. Detrick wanted a husband for his girl, and no cowboy was going to do anything untoward until he had that ring through his nose. He couldn't actually blame Detrick for keeping a tight rein on Sally. But if the old man was aware of all of Sally's shenanigans, no cowboy would be allowed within one hundred feet of his girl. As proven by Luke's last date with Sally, she certainly wasn't the prim and proper young woman she presented to the world. She'd invited him to go for a ride and picnic by the lake, telling him that her daddy would not be joining them. Within minutes after they reached the lake, and without any coaxing from him, Sally surprised him by stripping down to her bloomers and chemise and jumping into the water. Luke was the one who always pushed the boundaries of propriety in good fun, but she'd turned the tables on him. That day, she was the devil on his shoulder encouraging him to remove his pants and jump in. He jumped in, but he'd wisely kept his pants on. He wondered how many men she'd *picnicked* with in the past, because she seemed way too comfortable being nearly naked with him. He'd seen uninhibited women, but not even the gals hanging over the balcony could hold a candle to Sally in that department. All afternoon she'd tried every move in her vast repertoire to get him in a compromising position. As much as he was tempted, and he was sorely tempted, he didn't want old man Detrick to take a horsewhip to him if he found them. He could always shoot the old buzzard, but if he did something as stupid as compromise his only daughter, he figured Detrick would have every right to demand a shotgun wedding. Luke leaned over and whispered in her ear. "You want to go for a ride?"

Sally pressed closer and seductively batted her eyelashes at him. "Yes, I want to! I didn't want to leave the lake the last time. You know what I want, but I can't go. I'm shopping with Lucinda Sawyer. We came to town together."

It was probably for the best, Luke thought, because he did know what she wanted. It was a puzzle to him why he was still playing with fire, as his big brother Colt warned him. One of Colt's favorite sayings played in his mind. *If you play with fire you are going to get burned.* He wondered if this was a Shakespeare quote. Colt was fond of quoting Shakespeare. Playing with fire seemed to be a recurring theme for him lately. And Luke knew if Sally used the same tactics as last time, he wouldn't have the will-power to stop her even if he wanted to. Hell, he wouldn't be playing with fire, he'd be in flames. While he wouldn't mind knowing her in the biblical sense, he thought it would be wise to listen to that little voice in his head. Or was that his brother talking? It was pure hell trying to clean up his act, as his brothers had been haranguing him to do. Just because God had blessed them with beautiful wives and they'd settled down didn't mean he wanted to follow their lead. He didn't want to be hog-tied into marriage either, so he altered course with Sally. "Since you can't go for a ride, I'll take you two lovely ladies to lunch instead."

Glancing through the window of the mercantile, Sally saw Lucinda walking to the door. She leaned closer to Luke and whispered, "Meet me at noon tomorrow at the river. I have something special I ordered from Paris, France, that I want to show you."

Luke almost groaned aloud at his imaginings. He fig-ured something from Paris, France, meant silky and see-through. Sally might not be as beautiful as his two sisters-in-law, but she did have a nice full figure, and judg-ing by her display at the lake, she liked to show it off. And he didn't mind looking. He still couldn't get the image of her in a wet chemise out of his mind. Before he had time to respond, he felt a warm body press against his other side.

"Hello, handsome. What are you doing in town on a Saturday afternoon?" Lucinda inquired. Lucinda had been trying to wrangle a date with Luke since she met him at Sally's house last winter. She was aware of Sally's plans to marry the very handsome and available McBride brother, but to her way of thinking, if a proposal hadn't been made, he was fair game.

"I'm here to take two lovely ladies to lunch," he replied smoothly. Neither woman was what he would call beautiful, but in his opinion all women were lovely in some way. In his experience, a little gallantry went a long way with the ladies. What did it hurt to do a little harmless flirting?

"How wonderful!" Lucinda leaned around him to look at Sally, managing to keep in close contact with his chest. "You're a dear to share your handsome man."

Sally didn't want to share Luke, but she had no control over him. Yet. That wouldn't be the case much longer; she planned to have him standing at the altar before he knew what hit him. She'd set her sights on him when he'd returned to Wyoming a year earlier. Everyone knew he was the most eligible bachelor in the state since his brothers had finally married. Her father told her Luke had made a small fortune while he was traveling around the country busting broncs. She couldn't remember exactly how he'd made so much money—seemed like her father mentioned it had something to do with silver mining. The details weren't important. He was handsome and he was well-off. Her father wasn't a pauper by any means, but even their ranch paled in comparison to the McBride Cattle Company. Sally gave Lucinda a knowing smile. "Isn't it wonderful of him to surprise *me* this way?"

Luke picked up on the feminine undercurrents, but he didn't know what it was about, and he was smart enough not to ask. "Would you two ladies like to go to the boardinghouse or the hotel?" Since he was in town, he might as well eat and enjoy some female companionship. His favorite pastime.

They started to cross the street when the stagecoach came barreling down the road. At the same time, Mrs. Rogers came out of the mercantile trying to hail them by waving a package in the air. Sally realized she'd left her package in her haste to join Luke and hurried back to Mrs. Rogers. Lucinda took advantage of that moment to tell Luke she wanted him to call on her, but Luke wasn't really listening. His attention was on the stagecoach that pulled to a halt a few feet in front of them. The driver scampered down from his perch to open the door for the passengers. A man stepped from the coach and helped the driver assist an elderly woman to the ground. Both men quickly redirected their attention to the interior of the coach. Their faces were beaming when a young woman placed her hands in theirs, allowing them to assist her from the coach. She was looking down and the wide brim of the pink hat she wore hid her face. Luke stared at her pink hat. He liked the color; it was vibrant and the brim was decorated with an array of feathers and lace. His sisters-in-law would love that hat, he thought. Victoria and Promise were lovely women and they enjoyed keeping up with the latest fashions. He just knew a woman who wore a hat like that would be beautiful.

Sally rejoined them and curled her arm through his again. "Mrs. Rogers saved me a trip. I can't believe I forgot this package." When Luke didn't look at her, she flapped the package in his face. "This is the one from France," she reminded him playfully.

Luke couldn't help but glance at the package since it was blocking his view of that pink hat. It was small, real small. That meant whatever was inside of that package was really small. His mind started imagining again. His thoughts were disrupted when he heard a feminine voice speaking with a British accent. It was the woman in the pink hat conversing with the stagecoach driver. She was facing the driver and he still couldn't see her face.

The next moment changed Luke's perfect day. A man came flying through the batwing doors of the saloon behind him. He slammed into Sally's back, causing her to stumble forward. Thankfully, she was still holding on to Luke's arm and he managed to keep her from hitting the ground. Luke turned around to see what was going on and he saw Tubby Jenkins on the ground. It didn't take long for Luke to see how he got there. Clyde Slater, the town troublemaker, came charging out of the saloon after Tubby.

"You need to mind your manners, Clyde," Luke said in a no-nonsense tone. It wasn't the first time he'd exchanged words with Clyde.

"Why don't you mind your own business, McBride?"

Clyde was a big man, but he spent too much of his time drinking to stay in top form, unlike Luke, who kept his body in tip-top shape working on the ranch. Still, when Clyde was drinking, he thought he was invincible, and most times, he was.

"Tubby almost knocked me down!" Sally yelled her indignation to Clyde.

Clyde smirked. "Honey, from what I hear, you like to do a little rolling around."

Oh hell, Luke thought.

"How dare you!" Sally rushed forward with the intention of giving Clyde a good slap.

Luke wasn't going to allow a woman to defend herself as long as he was drawing breath. It was one thing if Clyde thought his comments about Sally were true, but it was another thing to express them in the middle of the street with everyone gawking. Luke grabbed Sally by the waist and pulled her back. He took a step forward. "You might be drunk, Clyde, but that doesn't give you the right to be rude to a lady. Apologize."

"I'm sure you know firsthand how she likes her skirts tossed up." Clyde was grinning like a half-wit.

And that was when the first fist slammed into Clyde's nose. Luke landed three good punches to Clyde's jaw, sending him reeling backward. Tubby, still on the ground, managed to get to his knees in an effort to gain his feet and

stumbled into Luke's back, knocking him off balance.
Clyde took that opportunity to land a right hook to Luke's
jaw. Staggering backward, Luke fell over Tubby and hit the
dirt. He jumped up and plowed headfirst into Clyde's
stomach, both of them going to the earth in a heap. They
rolled around in the dirt, each landing punches, neither
able to get to their feet because Tubby was groveling in the
dirt trying to stand and getting in their way. The women
were yelling for Tubby to get out of the way so Luke could
finish off Clyde. Tubby wasn't really trying to help Clyde,
but you couldn't prove it by Luke. The man made a habit
of teetering into Luke when he was about to land another
blow. Luke tried to stand to put some leverage into his
punches, but Tubby bounced into him again. Frustrated
with this unintentional interference, Luke turned around
and rammed his fist into Tubby's jaw, hitting him so hard
he reeled back several feet and landed in the water trough.
With Tubby out of the way, Luke traded a few more
punches with Clyde before he finally landed the giant-
slaying blow. Clyde hit the ground and stayed there like a
dead jackass carcass. Luke grabbed him by the shirt and
dragged his heavy ass to the water trough and dunked his
head in the murky water a few times. Water sloshed over
the sides and landed on Luke's perfectly polished boots.
"Dammit to hell," he muttered.

"What'd ya hit me for? I didn't do nothin'." Tubby
struggled in vain to get out of the trough.

"Shut the hell up and stay down," Luke warned.

Tubby flopped back down in the water and glared at
Luke with bloodshot eyes. Luke released Clyde's shirt, and
watched as he slid down beside the water trough in a filthy
heap.

Running his fingers through his black, wavy hair to get
it out of his eyes, Luke spotted his Stetson a few feet away.
Snatching if off the ground, he had to smack it against his

thigh a few times to remove a fraction of the dust before
he slammed it on his head. He glanced down to see his
favorite blue shirt was torn and had blood on it. He was
dusty from head to toe and his boots were filthy. *Dammit
to hell!* And the day had started out so perfect.

Sally and Lucinda ran to him.

"Oh, Luke, are you hurt?" Sally ran her hands all over
him, half pretending to dust off his shirt.

"You are so brave," Lucinda said. "You certainly taught
Clyde a thing or two!" She pulled a handkerchief out of her
sleeve and dabbed at Luke's split lip.

They were giving him so much attention, he quickly
forgot about his appearance and thought maybe he should
get into a fight every time he came to town. "Ladies, unless
you are too embarrassed to be seen with me, I'd still like to
take you to lunch. I promise to show you two a good time."
Maybe he should take them both to the lake and salvage
his day in a more delightful way.

"We're proud to be seen with you, Luke McBride," Sally
said. She meant every word. She'd rather be with Luke than
any man she knew.

"We certainly are. It was high time someone put that
bully in his place," Lucinda agreed.

Once they finished dusting him off they started toward
the hotel, but were brought up short when they encountered
the people from the stagecoach standing there staring at
them. From the looks on their faces they'd obviously wit
nessed the encounter with Clyde. The lady with the pink
hat was staring directly at Luke, and she didn't look nearly
as impressed as Sally and Lucinda.

Luke couldn't tell what she was thinking, but whatever
it was, it wasn't good. He stood there as if he'd grown
roots. All he could do was stare at her large eyes, the color
of quicksilver, he thought. His eyes skittered over the rest
of her face, noting her delicate features. Her complexion

was so fair he figured she'd never spent one day in the sun. He was right about a woman wearing a hat like that: She was one beautiful woman. Remembering his manners, he reached up to tip the brim of his black Stetson, dragging Sally's arm up with his. He'd forgotten she was hanging on to him like a leech.

The woman's eyes widened when he acknowledged her, and her gaze did a slow traverse down his body, stopping at the Colt .45 on his hip. She didn't respond to his greeting, she simply turned to the stagecoach driver. "My trunk and portmanteaus."

"I'll bring them right along," the stagecoach driver promised.

"Thank you."

The gentleman who was on the stagecoach stepped to her side. "I'll escort you to the hotel, ma'am."

For the first time in his life Luke had been snubbed by a female. That in itself was an unusual circumstance because the McBride brothers were legendary for their appeal to the ladies. Before his brothers married, women had flocked to them like they had magnetic poles in their holsters instead of six-guns. Unlike his brothers, Luke didn't run from the ladies, he ran *to* them. While he wasn't one to kiss and tell, he was one to love 'em and leave 'em, as he often reminded his brothers. And he'd left plenty in his wake. But he couldn't remember a time when a woman had rebuffed him.

Luke couldn't figure out why the woman looked at him like she couldn't decide if he was Satan himself or a bug to be squashed. Admittedly he looked pretty grubby after the fight, but if she'd seen the whole thing, she had to realize he was defending a lady's honor.

Luke and the ladies had no choice but to follow the woman being escorted to the hotel. Luke had ample time to take in the woman's shapely backside.

"That dress is lovely," Lucinda said.

"Fine quality too," Sally added.

"And that hat is surely a Parisian design."

"No doubt, and the color is delightful," Sally agreed.

Luke wondered what it was about Paris that seemed to get women all lathered up like a racehorse. He'd heard more than he cared to know about fashion from his sisters-in-law, who were forever expounding on the virtues of clothing from Paris. His appreciation of women's garments was generally based on how easily they could be removed. Although he did notice the woman was wearing a silky-looking silver dress that matched her eyes. And of course he couldn't help but notice how it complemented her petite trim figure. She certainly didn't have Sally's more than ample curves, but he liked the way her little backside swayed to and fro.

"British," Lucinda said.

"Rather rude, if you ask me," Sally said.

"I can't believe she didn't even acknowledge us."

On that point, Luke silently agreed with them. If he were as intimidating as his brother Colt, with that black stare of his, he might have understood the woman's slight. But Luke knew he was considered the charming brother, and not bragging, he was—as even his sisters-in-law would acknowledge.

Once inside the hotel, Luke and the ladies veered toward the dining room, as the British woman walked to the desk. Luke noted it was the clerk, Eb, behind the desk and not the owner of the hotel. When they entered the dining room, he was too far away to hear the conversation between the woman and Eb, particularly with Sally and Lucinda chatting away. He held the chairs for the women and positioned himself so he had a clear view of the front desk. Straightaway the stagecoach driver and another man walked into the hotel sharing the weight of a large trunk with several pieces of luggage on top. The woman turned and smiled at the driver, and Luke was held spellbound. He couldn't think of a word for her, but *beautiful* didn't even come close. She was much more than beautiful. He felt like he was looking at a magnificent work of art. He watched as she pointed out the four pieces of luggage that belonged to her. After thanking the men, she accepted the key from the clerk and walked to the staircase.

Lunch ended and Luke was eager to escort the two women to their buggy. Generally, he might have stretched out the lunch, taking pleasure in the subtle way the women flirted with him, but today he had another matter on his mind, and it was wearing a pink hat. Besides that, Sally was making it obvious she had big plans for him. During lunch she'd made several remarks to Lucinda that led him to believe she was gearing up for marriage. And it sure as Hades wasn't going to be him in the church wearing a string tie that was sure to feel like a noose.

"Tomorrow, then?" Sally asked, squeezing his hand as he assisted her into the buggy, her silent message promising another intimate encounter.

"Sorry, tomorrow is Sunday. Church with the family, then dinner. And I promised the twins I would take them riding afterward." He knew his refusal didn't please her, but he thought his brothers were right when they told him to limit his womanizing to the gals at the saloon. Good advice he intended to follow from now on.

That promise to himself lasted about a second, then Sally waggled the itty-bitty package in his face again. He was spared from his weakening resolve when Lucinda thanked him for lunch, and he said his good-byes and quickly took his leave before he changed his mind about Sunday.

Luke made his way back to the hotel, but Eb wasn't behind the desk, so he spun the register around so he could read the names of the guests who had just arrived. He figured the elderly woman on the stage registered before the British woman, so he looked at the next signature. Miss Mary Ann Hardwicke. He glanced to see if the gentleman who escorted Miss Hardwicke to the hotel had the same last name. He didn't. Just then, Eb returned to the desk, and Luke asked him about the woman. Always ready to deliver some gossip, Eb told him Miss Hardwicke asked to speak with the owner, Mr. Granville, but she didn't state her business. He also indicated Mr. Granville wouldn't be back until later that evening.

Spying her trunk and valises still piled by the front door, Luke figured Eb couldn't lift them alone. He also saw another golden opportunity for a little more harmless flirting, already forgetting his vow to mend his ways. One of his favorite sayings was *don't look a gift horse in the mouth*. "Want me to get that luggage for you, Eb?"

"I would appreciate it, Luke. My back can't handle anything so heavy."

"Is she traveling alone?"

"Yessir, that's what she said."

Perfect. Luke hoisted the large trunk on his shoulder, leaving a free hand to carry the three valises. "Which room?"

"Number six at the top of the stairs to the right."

His lucky number.